# *Henry's* BATTLE

First published in Australia 2014
by JACOKAT Publications.
www.gloriaeswan.com



National Library of Australia Cataloguing-in-Publication entry:
Author: Gloria E Swan
Title: Henry's Battle

ISBN:    978 0 9875735 0 6 (Print book edition)
         978-0-9875735-1-3 (PDF ebook edition)
         978-0-9875735-2-0 (EPUB ebook edition)
         Dewey Number: A823.4

Edited by Marian Edmunds:  www.thewritingbusiness.com
Cartography by Ian Faulkner:  www.ianfaulknerillustrator.com
Cover Design by Nanette Backhouse: www.bookdesignbysaso.com.au
Typeset in Birka 12/16 by Charlie M Typesetting Services

# *Henry's* BATTLE

## *Love and lives in conflict in World War Two*

Gloria E. Swan

To the many men and women who put their lives and relationships on hold to fight for their country during wartime. In particular to my own parents who met and fell in love during WW2, but because of it, endured hardship through a long and happy marriage.

CHAPTER 1

# RESTLESS HENRY

*What General Weygand called the Battle of France is over. I expect that the Battle of Britain is about to begin. Upon this battle depends the survival of Christian civilization. Upon it depends our own British life, and the long continuity of our institutions and our Empire. The whole fury and might of the enemy must very soon be turned on us. Hitler knows that he will have to break us in this Island or lose the war. If we can stand up to him, all Europe may be free and the life of the world may move forward into broad, sunlit uplands. Let us therefore brace ourselves to our duties, and so bear ourselves that, if the British Empire and its Commonwealth last for a thousand years, men will say, "This was their finest hour."*

EXTRACT FROM SPEECH BY WINSTON CHURCHILL,
PRIME MINISTER OF THE UNITED KINGDOM, ON JUNE *18, 1940.*

Henry stuck out his chest and strode off the pitch with his head held high. The crowd at Lord's rose as one to applaud him. He had just saved Australia in the deciding Ashes test. Oh, how he had dreamed of this day.

"Oh Henry – you were just magnificent today".

Henry had not seen Ginny approach and was quite annoyed to find he wasn't at Lords but at his local club. He had hoped to slip away with the boys for a few after-game drinks. Nothing alcoholic for him though – his mother forbade it. Now he would be stuck with walking Ginny home! Still he'd had a good game. He had top scored with the bat and taken four wickets including the opposition's hot-shot batsman. He looked across at the bumpy pitch, unmowed grass and soccer goal posts still in place for the winter season finals. It was a beautiful setting – the grass was always so green here. The gums bordering the ground swayed in the gentle afternoon breeze and Mount Warning stood like a preacher in his pulpit, looking out over his flock with all-seeing eyes.

"Why, thanks Ginny. It was good of you to give up your afternoon to come and watch me play."

"Henry, I can't think of a better way to spend Saturday afternoon than watching my favourite man play his favourite game." Something in the way she said this made Henry cringe. *Shame she isn't a bit easier on the eye.*

"Well Ginny, we best be on our way home, Mum will be watching the clock by now and you know what she's like if I am late."

"You know Henry, there comes a time in a man's life when he has to start looking past his mother's plans for him and look to establishing a family of his own. There are a few girls around here who would be flattered with such attentions from you."

Henry stepped backwards quickly as she edged closer and gave him a lingering, coy glance. *My God that perfume she is wearing is strong. I wonder how she managed to get away with it in her father's presence; good Methodist girls do not disgrace themselves with such immoral indulgences.*

"I am not in any position to even start thinking about that. The world is in such a state of turmoil with this damn war starting to spread, I feel that all men should consider giving some of their time to the cause. I read somewhere that 'bad men only prosper when good men do nothing'. I want to do something. I want to make a name for myself helping to rectify this wretched situation. It would not be fair to have a family left behind while I do what I feel I have to."

Henry tried to ignore the stiffening of Ginny's back and the pouting of her lips as he uttered these words. *Perhaps our little preacher's daughter is not the inexperienced little innocent she makes out.* It was not something Henry found endearing. When they reached his front gate a familiar demanding voice spared him the need to make up an excuse to escape from Ginny.

"Henry, have you collected those eggs and locked the chooks up for the night? I think there is a storm coming."

Henry walked up Hospital Hill on his way home from work. The first day of the week was always a drag. *At least I have cricket training tomorrow, helps me to forget about my troubles.* A push bike squeaked to a halt beside him. Without even looking around Henry knew who it was – he knew that pathetic sound and the laboured breathing of its rider.

"You're on your way home late today son. Are things that busy at the quarry?"

"Gee, Dad I wish you would do as Mum has asked you many times and get that bike oiled – it would make the push up the hill easier for you."

"Come on, you know she would expect me to pay for it out of my beer money. Now that she won't let me make my own it takes all I get to quench my thirst."

"Well, she takes all my pay and only gives me a few shillings now and then. Besides I thought you had learnt your lesson with that vile "magic elixir" you used to make down in the shed on the farm."

"With you and Stewart now earning she should be able to spare us some money for our recreation, hey son?"

"I might not be around much longer. Not with this war."

"This war is no concern of ours Henry. Besides our allies will come to our defence if we are attacked."

"I heard on the radio the other day that Hitler is preparing to invade England. What if they get control of the British Empire?"

"That's not going to worry us. I'm sure the United States will come to our rescue."

"But Dad, we will have to go to the aid of our mother country."

"That radio your mother won causes more trouble than it is worth. Who needs to know what is happening over there? I try not to listen too often."

"Don't you think all able bodied men should do their bit? They are starting to say it will spread further afield than World War 1."

"Try not to think about it son. It's not going to get anywhere near us. Besides, your mother will never consent to your leaving home."

"I have to start thinking about my future. I am not going to spend my whole life in Murwillumbah. Mum is just going to have to get used to the idea."

They reached the crest of the hill and Arthur stopped to regain his breath before they began the short descent down Peter Street to their home.

"Hang on there Henry."

"Hurry up then. You know what she's like if we are both late home."

"She wasn't always like this Henry. When we married I admired her spirit of independence but now she wants to control everything."

"Well, you should have stood up to her. A man needs to let a woman know where she stands with him. I will never let my wife dictate to me like that."

"No, only your mother."

"I know how hard she has to work at getting the money to go round."

"I have found out over the years son, that it is better to go along with what she wants. Things stay much more peaceful that way."

"You know what I would really like to do? Join the Army. I would like to do my bit."

"I am sure you could son, but I don't want to be around when you tell your mother. You know she has your life all worked out for you here."

⋯ ⊰❈⊱ ⋯

Henry bounded up the back steps. He had just finished two hours of cricket practice. He could hardly believe that Coach Brown wanted to take him to Grafton next weekend to try out for the regional team. *Could be just the break I need to move to a higher level of the sport.* His mother was seated at the kitchen table filling out cards for the church fete. *Oh no, forgot about the damn fete this Saturday, she'll never let me go but I'm still going to try.*

"Mum, Coach Brown thinks I have a good chance of being selected in the regional team this year. Do you think I could attend the trial game next weekend?"

"Henry Thompson, I can't believe that you would even ask. You know it is the most important weekend of the year in our little parish. It's all hands on deck."

"But Mum, this is a chance of a lifetime for me. What if I can round up some of the boys to do the setting up on Friday afternoon, then you won't need me on Saturday and I can be back on Sunday in time to do the clearing up? "

"You know how Reverend Taylor feels about playing games on Sunday. I thought playing the wretched game every Saturday would be enough for you. "

"Mum, I am twenty-four years old you know. Perhaps it is time I started to think about making my own way in the world."

"Enough of that! You have very good prospects right here in town. Mr Marshall, I know, thinks very highly of the work you do for him."

"But I could even end up playing for Australia one day."

"Fiddle, faddle Henry. I suggest you get such notions right out of your head and concentrate on what you know you can achieve."

*Oh well, I wonder what she will think about my Army plans. I don't think today is the right time to bring that up.*

# CHAPTER 2

# THE FETE

Henry struggled to get out of bed on the morning of the fete. Rain pounded the tin roof. It made him want to pull the covers up over his head and stay there all day. His mother was banging things around in the kitchen. It was a sign that she was in a foul mood. He gingerly poked his head around the kitchen door.

"It's about time you were up and about, Henry Thompson. This rain has ruined all our plans."

"Really Mum, wouldn't it be better just to cancel the whole thing?"

"We need to round up a large tent to house the knock-em-over and dunk-em. Reverend Taylor has several town dignitaries who have agreed to participate. He's hoping for a sizeable donation."

"Please Mum, can't you listen to reason for once?"

"Henry you know how important the money raised is for our parish. It must proceed regardless. So get cracking. You'll have to do without breakfast seeing you slept in." Myrtle slammed a baking tray full of scones onto the table with such force that Henry had to dive forward and grab it before everything ended up on the floor.

"You'd think that with all the influence you have up there, you would have been able to get HIM to fix the weather for you."

"Henry, I won't have you talking such blasphemy. I don't know who is influencing you these days, but you seem to be becoming more un-righteous every day."

"If you didn't keep ramming it down my throat all the time I might be more agreeable. HE has a lot to answer for in this mixed up world."

"I would appreciate it if you would keep such thoughts to yourself in front of Reverend Taylor. You and Ginny are getting on so well these days."

*Will she never give up on this "Ginny and I" thing?* Henry took a deep breath and positioned himself by the kitchen table where she was assembling her goods for sale. She shouldered him aside, still clutching another batch of her popular delicacies.

"Look Mum, I'm here to help you today aren't I? Isn't that enough? I wish you would stop trying to make me feel guilty just because I have plans for the future that you may not agree with."

"You know we are the only ones who can get this family of ours back on track. Heaven knows your father is no help."

"If you left Dad alone for once he might not have his "little problem"."

"Henry!! Enough of that sort of talk. We have work to do. Now I want you to go round to Mr Marshall's place and see what he can do for us about a tent."

Henry slowly turned away from his mother so she couldn't see his despair. *What's happening to me? I'm not usually so disrespectful to my mother.* He walked slowly down the back stairs.

Henry was light-headed when he finished the chores set for him by his mother. The rain was like a full symphony orchestra as it drummed on the church hall roof. People bustled about here and there putting the final touches to their stalls. Mrs Phillips from the local nursery was assembling what looked like an English country garden on her table and the local Junior Farmers' group had a wonderful array of hand-crafted goods. *What a shame they have gone to so much trouble — no-one is even going to come to their fete in this weather."*

"Henry, over here please. Ginny needs some help with this display." His mother's piercing voice rang in his ears for the umpteenth time.

*God damn it; haven't I done enough for one day? The last person I need now is sweet Ginny.*

"Oh Henry, you are such a help. There are certain things a girl needs a man around for and there is no better man for the job than you." Her table was stacked with toilet roll dollies of pink and mauve. Looking at her all tarted up in her Sunday best finery it was hard for Henry to tell them apart. He shuddered as a fleeting image of life with her at his side flashed before him.

"Only too pleased to help Ginny." His mother hovered close by.

The day dragged on for Henry. Every time he looked at his watch only a few more minutes had passed. He tried to talk to the older ladies but every time he turned around Ginny seemed to be at his elbow. He wished some people would turn up to keep her busy. There was an air of gloom over the proceedings and Henry resisted the urge to say "I told you so." As the rain fell unabated only a handful of paying customers braved the conditions. Merchandise lay untouched on the stalls. The tent Henry had worked so hard to procure was not required. Not even the star attraction, the Town Mayor, had shown up. The grounds were so soft and saturated under the mechanised "dunker" that not even Barry Martin, the town's premier mechanic, could get it to operate safely enough for them to open for business.

***

Henry settled down on the lounge on the veranda to enjoy his favourite view. The rain had eased and the valley looked magnificent in the fading light of the late afternoon. He had slipped away from the fete without a word to his mother or Ginny. He relaxed at last but his peace was soon shattered. A car screeched to a halt. The stairs shook as his mother stormed up towards him. Her face was fiercer than when she had greeted him first thing this morning.

"Henry Thompson, I can't believe you just walked out like that — poor Ginny was beside herself when she couldn't find you to help her pack up. Then that nosey Mrs Parker had great delight in informing me that your father has been holding court in Bryant's Hotel all day, making a fool of himself as usual. What an embarrassment this whole day has been!"

"I think Dad probably has had quite an enjoyable day."

"You just get yourself down there and order him home immediately."

"Mum, don't you think Dad can decide for himself when he wants to come home."

*If he has any sense he won't come home at all, ever.*

"Now don't you start defying me again, I am just about at the end of my tether."

By this time Bob Marshall and his flash car had turned around and headed back to town. *Could have at least waited for me.* Henry started slowly up the hill.

Henry didn't have to look around to find his father as he peered over the swinging doors of the saloon bar. The motley crowd of local men gathered at the long bar were shouting encouragement.

"Go for it Arthur."

"Bet Myrtle hasn't got a pair like that, Arthur."

*Call yourselves gentlemen when you're in this state?* He barged through the doors with such force that he momentarily silenced the crude guffawing. Everyone swung around to look at the intruder. The crowd parted as Henry strode across to where his father was sitting on top of the counter, a glass of dark ale in one hand and the other affectionately on the shoulder of a rather comely, though somewhat weathered, barmaid.

"It's Charlotte the harlot, the girl we adore. The pride of the prairie, the cowpuncher's whore."

Arthur was singing at the top of his voice. It was a bawdy ballad that Henry knew didn't come from Clark's 5th Series Hymns of Glory, the only musical fare he had ever heard his father indulge in before. He was looking lewdly down the front of the barmaid's low-cut top. The whole scene made Henry cringe. He recognised a number of husbands of women who had slaved at the fete all day and for months before. Nev Phillips leaned over the bar looking lustfully at the barmaid. *His wife had manned a plant stall all day!* Henry elbowed Nev out of the way and turned to his father. "Dad, I think it might be time to call it a day."

"Come on mate; let your old man have some fun. He's not hurting anyone. He'll have a sore head tomorrow though, I'll bet." Nev laughed as he shoved Henry aside, stumbling into the bar stool as he lost his balance.

"Yeh, a man needs to get away from the old woman for a while." Another of the inebriated "gentlemen" joined in.

"Especially when she's doing her good deeds." More loud laughter rang out and for a fleeting moment Henry felt sorry for his mother and her band of helpers. He gently pulled his father from the bar counter and turned to the barmaid.

"I have heard that women who work in these sorts of establishments are of poor moral fibre. How dare you lead my father on in his drunken state, exposing yourself like that? I will certainly be reporting you to your employer the first chance I get. I would hope that he will see fit to terminate your employment!"

# CHAPTER 3

# DECISIONS

The rain was teeming down as Henry trudged home from work. He detoured down the main street to get some protection from the overhang on the shops. The evening lights were already flickering from the living quarters above. He should call in to see Shirley – he owed her an apology. He replayed his conversation with Tom as he walked along. Tom strode up to him the minute he arrived at work.

"I heard you had a bit of a to-do in the pub on Saturday night. My Aunty Shirley was very upset about the way you spoke to her."

"Your Aunty Shirley? I didn't realise she was related to you."

"She is my favourite aunty and she has had a very hard life. Aunty Shirley only works in the hotel because the hours suit her. She was widowed at a young age and has brought up three children on her own. She also looks after her elderly parents. A more moral lady you would not find. She only dresses as she does because that is what her boss wants".

As Henry approached the hotel door, he glanced through the window. Shirley was quietly wiping down the bar. He took a few deep breaths and pushed open the swing doors.

"Excuse me, Mrs Walsh. Could I please have a word with you in private?"

"Anything you have to say to me can be said in public young man. The more public the better."

"Look, I really must apologise for the other night. I had a very stressful day and was ready to jump to conclusions to justify my father's appalling behaviour."

"Your father is a very nice man and a regular customer of ours. He has often poured his heart out to me and I have been willing to listen as I know what it is like to have a difficult home life."

"I am very sorry. I love my father dearly and I wish things could be better for him at home."

"He has never acted improperly to me even when he is very drunk which you must know is quite often these days."

Henry let out a big sigh. "I think I could do with a stiff drink myself."

"I think you should have a good look at the way your life is unfolding. Drink is not the answer."

Henry was still seated on the bar stool staring at the wall when Bob Marshall walked in. "Down in the dumps are we?" Henry almost fell off his stool.

"It's all right Mr Marshall; I am not usually in this place. My mother would skin me alive if she knew I was drinking in a public bar."

"How old are you again, Henry Thompson? If a man wants to have a quiet drink in a public bar, I don't think he should have to ask his mother. The pub is one of the few sanctuaries a man has from the demands of the female of the species."

"But you know what she is like. It is better to fall in with her wishes than suffer the consequences."

"You are starting to sound more like your father every day."

"I really would like to break away from it all, but I just can't seem to get Mum to listen when I bring up the subject. She keeps on about my forging a career here in this God-fearing little town and keeps pushing me in the direction of Ginny Taylor. "

"Yes, she has spoken to me a few times about your prospects and led me to believe that Ginny would be the reason you would never leave this town."

"Well, she is very much mistaken. The more I get to know that conniving girl, the less she appeals to me."

"I think it is time you made it clear to her what your wishes are. As much as I would like you to continue working for me, I think you have too much potential to rot away in this town."

"You know Mr Marshall, I think I will do just that."

"Good for you, Henry."

It was almost closing time. The longer he put off going home to face his mother, the worse he knew it was going to be. He was starting to feel very relaxed and understood why his father and Bob Marshall spent so much time here. The doors of the saloon bar swung open and his brother Stewart charged through.

"Henry, thank goodness I have found you. I have been looking all over. Mum's in a real tizz over you not being home from work yet. Please come now."

"Why should I? I am done with what Mum dictates. I'm a grown man and I am going to make my own decisions."

"Just come home anyway – we can talk about it on the way. You know how Mum feels about us making a spectacle of ourselves in public."

Henry reluctantly followed his brother out of the hotel but not before going over to Shirley and giving her an affectionate hug. The wistful look in her eye told him all he needed to know.

Henry and Stewart began the slow walk up the hill. "Are you really going to start standing up to Mum, Henry?"

"Don't you think it is about time someone did?"

"I sure do, but I didn't think you would be the one to do it."

"I am only just starting to realise how miserable she has made Dad's life over the years. She hasn't given him a fair go."

"Well, he does seem to lack a bit when it comes to shouldering family responsibility."

"He told me it wasn't always like that. I think she has driven him to drink!"

"What are you going to do?"

"Firstly I am going to the postponed cricket trials next weekend."

Henry and Stewart arrived home and slipped wordlessly through under the house with the intention of sneaking up the back stairs. They made it to the first landing when the backdoor was flung open and there silhouetted against the light, Myrtle loomed menacingly. Stewart let out a gasp and Henry had to lunge to stop him from tumbling backwards down the stairs. Henry, for the first time in his life, felt no fear of her at all.

"Evening Mum. You didn't really have to wait up for us you know. We can find our own way to bed."

"You insolent young pup! I feared one day you would turn out like your father but I think you are heading to be a whole lot worse. The devil has obviously taken hold of your senses."

As if buoyed by Henry's boldness Stewart pushed ahead of him on the stairs and pulled himself up to his full height as he drew level with his mother.

"Mum, I really think you should listen to what Henry has to say."

"As for you Stewart, I thought better of you. I think you should just go to your room and leave this to Henry and me to thrash out."

"There's not really anything to "thrash out". Henry's hands were shaking so hard behind his back he had to hold them tightly together. "First I am going to Grafton for the postponed cricket trials next weekend. Then, when that is out of the way I am going to look into joining the Army."

# CHAPTER 4

# THE CRICKET TRIALS

The journey on the train to Grafton for the cricket trials was one Henry would long remember. It was a beautiful day. There was a cloudless blue sky and for the first time he felt completely free. The hills were crystal clear following the spring rains.

Henry walked out onto the field to bat, his head held high and his chest puffed out. He looked around at the small crowd. He had hoped there would be more people here. His team was two wickets down already for only 10 runs so he needed to play at his best. His cricket whites shone so brilliantly he had to screw up his face to focus on the opposing fieldsmen. *It was decent of Mum to do such a good job cleaning and pressing my clothes.* As he approached the bowler's end a giant of a man stepped into his path and glared at Henry from his full height. *He must be the demon fast bowler they are all talking about. He doesn't worry me.* Henry reached the crease and after drawing the toe of his boot across the pitch, he leant on his favourite old bat and took guard. He looked around the field to check the placement of the opposition team. The pitch was still wet, slow but not menacing.

The wicket-keeper stepped up close behind him. "I hope you have your nuts covered. Joe likes to see how many he can knock off in an innings." Henry didn't turn around. He steeled himself and lifted his head to face the menacing bowler. The enormity of this moment flashed through his mind and his stomach did a cart-wheel in anticipation. As he focussed on the ball hurtling towards him his mind went blank. All the carefully drilled procedures drummed into him by his coach were gone in an instant. The ball had shattered his stumps before he even moved his bat off its carefully positioned mark.

*How humiliating, a "golden duck".* The sheer joy on the faces of the opposition fielders was not something Henry was going to acknowledge. He kept his head down until he was well outside the playing field. *Glad there aren't more people here.* As he entered the dressing room he flung his bat. It catapulted into the far wall and almost hit his coach in the head. Henry slumped onto the bench.

"Henry, that is not the attitude I like to see in my players. What happened out there? You usually rise to a big occasion."

"Sorry coach. I just froze. Maybe I'm not going to be any good in the big-time if I can't handle a situation like this."

"Henry, don't be so hard on yourself. Everyone has a bad day. I'll put in a good word for you for future trials and we'll put in some extra work before then."

"Don't bother. I think I'll just be content with playing at a local level from now on."

"You have as much potential as I've seen for some years. I know you, and you don't usually give up."

"I could risk everything and then have nothing to show for it. If I gave up my job to concentrate more on cricket it would be devastating for Mum and my family."

"Henry, you know the day is not far away when you'll have to put yourself first if you want to achieve any of the things you have planned."

"I know, but I don't think that day is here yet."

⋅⋅⋅✦⋅⋅⋅

Henry stopped mid-way across the bridge. The sun was going down behind Mt Warning. The long shadows cast by the large fig trees on the river bank were interspersed with reflected light on the surface of the river. *This wasn't such a bad place to live.*

As he approached Main Street he saw Shirley walking with her dog on the other side of the street. He crossed over to talk to her. *She will understand.*

"Why, hello Henry. I didn't expect to see you. Weren't you supposed to be in Grafton for your cricket trials?"

"Just back. Didn't feel like going home yet."

"The news isn't good, I take it." As usual she gauged his mood before he even started talking.

"I stuffed it up well and truly. Nerves got to me or something."

Shirley patted his hand in a motherly way. "Don't worry. You'll get another chance."

"Not sure I want one. Decided that maybe I am not cut out to be a first class cricketer. Besides Mum would never consent to my going again."

"Look here Henry Thompson, your mother has just got to accept that you are bigger than this small town. You'll have your father's support."

Henry started to walk home, relaxed now and feeling able to face his mother, but by the time he got there his new found confidence had already started to wane. As he started slowly up the back stairs, his young sister Anne threw open the back door and greeted him with enthusiasm.

"We wondered where you were. We heard the train ages ago."

"Is Mum on the war-path?"

"Well, no. Dad has actually been home all day and she's in quite a good mood. We've all been wondering how you went."

Henry was apprehensive as he walked through the kitchen door. His father and mother were seated at the table.

"Come in Henry. Your father and I had a long chat about you today."

"Well how did it go? Coach Brown said you were almost a certainty." His father butted in.

"Things didn't go well at all. Don't know if I'll try-out again."

Henry hung his head and could feel tears welling up. Wouldn't do to show that sort of emotion around his mother. He held his head up high, stuck out his chin and continued.

"I have decided that maybe life in the Army would be the best way to fulfil my ambitions. I believe they have a quite strong inter-battalion cricket competition. That would let me have the best of both worlds. After this wretched war is over I would have a career to fall back on, and I could still keep my hand in at cricket."

His mother put her arm around him but he didn't feel the same genuine warmth he had felt from Shirley's touch just a little while before.

"Henry, you have been such a good support for your family for so long, I am sure any decision you make will be in its best interest. Ginny will wait for you."

Henry stole a sideways glance at his father. The years of pain inflicted on him by his wife were clearly etched on his face; his jaw was set and there were deep creases on his forehead. Arthur put his hands up to his face, closed his eyes and shook his head.

# CHAPTER 5

# PLANS COME UNSTUCK

*Directive No. 16. On preparations for a landing operation against England.*

*Since England, in spite of her hopeless military situation, shows no signs of being ready to come to an understanding, I have decided to prepare a landing operation against England and, if necessary, to carry it out.*

*The aim of this operation will be to eliminate the English homeland as a base for the prosecution of the war against Germany and, if necessary, to occupy it completely.*

*Preparations for the entire operation must be completed by the middle of August.*

THE FUHRER AND SUPREME COMMANDER
FUHRER HEADQUARTERS OF THE ARMED FORCES
16TH JULY, 1940.

Henry had never felt more confident. He had stood up to his mother and would never be a push over again he thought, as he walked home from work with Tom.

"You know Tom, young blokes like us should really be trying to do our bit in this war."

Tom turned his head and looked at Henry closely. "Yes, I have thought about joining the Army but war is a pretty dangerous place."

"Agreed, but if we don't do something, who will? Hitler is about to invade England. That sure will have repercussions for us."

"How do you know all this Henry?"

"I have been listening to the BBC on the radio Mum won at last year's fete. You know what I would like to do?"

"What's that? What are you planning now Henry?"

"Well, I would like to join the Army and see if I can rise through the ranks to be in a position to make them see that killing each other is not the answer."

"That's going to be a bit hard if you are being shot at." Tom grinned at Henry.

"Look Tom, I bet the ones shooting at us don't want to do it any more than we do. It seems to me that those making the decisions are not the ones risking their lives."

"I don't think I want to be the one sending other men to die."

"Nor do I. That's why I would like to be one of them. Make them see reason."

"Hey Henry, why don't we both give it a go?"

"If I could just sort out my family's problems I would do it tomorrow."

"My Mum would worry about me I know, but I think she would be very proud of me too. I'm sure Aunty Shirley would support me."

"I've told Mum it's what I want to do Tom. She seems to be more supportive of it now but your aunt warns me not to trust her."

"Aunty Shirley is a very wise woman for someone with little education."

"I know that. I think I am finally going to test Mum's resolve on this matter and tell her tonight I'm going to join the Army as soon as possible." Henry felt good to be making this decision.

As they turned the corner of Main St, they could hear a commotion outside Bryant's Hotel. Even at this distance Henry recognised his father's angry voice. *Oh no, what has he done this time?* For a moment he was tempted to carry on up the hill and simply leave him to it. He was sick and tired of coming to his rescue. But Henry still felt responsible for any member of his family.

The first person Henry saw was his father's employer, Bert Mitchell. His father was holding tightly to Bert's coat sleeve as he tried to pull away.

"I have turned a blind eye to your doings in the past Arthur but this time you have gone too far. I can't have an employee of mine acting like this in public."

"But yoush don't undershand Bert," stammered Arthur in his drunken state. "Yoush jush don't know whash ish like living wish sush an evil woman."

"I am sorry Arthur, but I just can't employ you anymore. My business is suffering because of your behaviour."

"Please, Mr Mitchell," Henry intervened. "I will look after him. I'm sure we can work things out in the family. Just give him another chance."

"I'm sorry Henry. This has been going on for too long. Tonight he picked a fight with one of my best customers. This is costing me too much."

It was dark when Henry finally arrived home with his father. Henry had held him back from returning to the hotel. He had to keep pulling him to his feet so they could continue the slow trip up the hill. After he struggled up the stairs with him and reached the top landing, Henry slumped exhaustedly onto an old chair. The door was flung open.

"So, you have started to lead our son into your immoral ways have you, Arthur Thompson. I thought we had agreed yesterday that you were going to mend your ways."

"Gesh out of my way, yoush old bag. Yoush are nosh going to ruin my shon's life the way yoush have mine."

"Please Mum, give him a break. He has just been fired from the mill."

"What?" screeched Myrtle hysterically. "What on earth am I going to do now?"

"Yoush are the one ruining thish family, yoush witsh."

Henry positioned himself protectively between his parents. He was worried that his father, in spite of his lack of control, might harm his mother. His mother dissolved into a sobbing heap. He ushered his father inside and down the hall to his bedroom, and without bothering to undress him, tucked him into bed.

Henry returned to the kitchen where his mother was sobbing quietly. Henry gently put his arm around her shoulders.

"Please Henry you just couldn't leave home now. Could you?"

"It's ok Mum, we'll work something out."

"No, please tell me you are not going to put yourself in danger by going through with this Army thing of yours."

She looked at Henry with a pitiful look in her eyes, tears still streaming down her weathered face. Henry felt his stomach tighten into a knot as he took out his handkerchief and gently wiped his mother's tears.

"Don't worry Mum, I won't leave you alone to deal with Dad's problem."

"Henry, I always knew you would come to the rescue. It's not something I can deal with without you."

Henry's chest suddenly became taut as he saw the look of triumph in her eyes and how quickly her tears had dried up.

It was quiet in the saloon bar of Bryant's late on Saturday afternoon. The weather had been good for outdoor pursuits. Henry's cricket team had not had a game this weekend but he had needed to get away from the house for a while. He felt a bit sheepish as he entered. He was glad that the bar was almost empty. He didn't want too many eavesdroppers as he explained things to Shirley.

"Hello Henry, I had been wondering how you and your father got on the other night."

"It wasn't something I would like to happen again. I really thought Dad was going to hurt Mum in some way."

"A gentle man like Arthur would have to be pushed to the limit before he harmed a woman."

"That is what it has come to, I am afraid. I have decided that I can't leave home with my family in such a crisis."

"So, she has managed to get her own way again, has she?"

# CHAPTER 6

# A REPRIEVE?

*"At the end of July Hitler ordered Goring to prepare "immediately and with great haste ... the great battle of the German air force against England." On August 2 Goring issued the final order for Adlertag (Eagle Day)on which the destruction of Fighter Command was to be accomplished. This was set for August 10, but bad weather caused its postponement for 3 days while the air fighting intensified. On August 12 Luftflotte 2 struck at England's central south coast. Targets included the docks and war industries in Plymouth and Southampton, and the radio station at Ventnor on the Isle of Wight. Hitler had set September 15 for "Operation Sea Lion", the land invasion of Britain."*

CHAPTER 2. *"BRITAIN IN PERIL"* WORLD WAR 11.
H.P. WILLMOTT, ROBIN CROSS, CHARLES MESSENGER.

The warm sun beat down on Henry and Tom as they sat on the logs outside Bob Marshall's shed waiting to be assigned their runs for the day. They were relaxed as they looked out over the river wending its way down the valley.

"Summer is going to come early this year, don't you think Tom?" Henry pushed back his canvas hat and wiped his brow with the back of his hand.

"Yes, I hope it's cooler than this where I'm going."

"What do you mean? Where are you going?" Henry felt his chest tighten.

"I gave in my notice yesterday. I'll only be here another week. I am going to join the Army."

"Tom, you don't know how much I long to do just that."

"Why don't you?"

Henry turned abruptly so the pain on his face didn't show. "It's just not possible, that's all."

"I think it is the duty of every able-bodied man to fight for what this country stands for. I've started listening to the BBC too after you mentioned it. Those bastard Germans are already bombing the daylights out of England."

"Yes, I know. Ed Murrow thinks a land invasion is imminent."

"Yes, I've been listening to him too. I like his attitude. Freedom and equality. That's what it's all about."

"But it's Mum I'm worried about. Now that Dad's lost his job, she needs my income more than ever."

"You can make allotments to your family from your army pay, you know."

"They feed and clothe you don't they? I shouldn't need much for myself so that should help," mused Henry.

"It may not be as hard to do as you think. You're not going to be able to live at home forever you know."

"Mum says she's more than a bit afraid of Dad when he's been drinking. I couldn't leave her to deal with that on her own. "

"Has he ever hit her?"

"No, but she has sure given him every reason to." Henry let out a big sigh. "You know, I have often thought how different my life would have been if I had a mother like your Aunty Shirley."

"She thinks your mother will stop at nothing to get her own way."

"Mum's had a tough job bringing up us kids. I'm sure she's only doing what she thinks is best for us."

Henry was about to jump up into the cabin of his truck when Bob Marshall called to him from his office door.

"Word with you Henry?" Henry was used to his boss's abrupt manner.

"You know Tom is leaving on Friday?"

"Yes, he told me about it this morning. We are going to miss him."

"It may mean you will have to do some overtime while we try to fill his job."

"You wouldn't consider my Dad for the job, would you? I am sure he would be able to handle it. He has the proper licence and he used to drive bigger equipment when he worked at the sawmill."

"I'm not sure if that is a good idea Henry. It would be a risk to our vehicles and the public putting someone with his problem behind the wheel."

"He has never let his drinking habits interfere with his work, you know. It's just that Mum has been giving him such a hard time lately."

Henry's mind was racing. He had to convince Mr Marshall to give his father a try. Then his mother wouldn't be able to use it as an excuse to keep him at home.

"What about putting him on for a trial period? It would give him a chance to prove himself."

"Whoa there Henry, don't get yourself all worked up about it. I know what your mother is like. I have known her for a long time."

"Then you will know how tough she is on Dad."

"Ok, I will give him a chance. Myrtle needs to realise that she can't run everyone's life," said Bob with a broad smile on his face. *Mum talks about Bob quite often. Maybe they were more than just friends.*

Henry felt like giving his boss a hug but just grabbed his hand and shook it so hard that the poor man's arm nearly popped out of its socket.

"Thank you, thank you, and thank you."

Henry bounded up the back stairs when he arrived home. He couldn't wait to tell his mother about the job offer. His mother was in her usual spot, languidly shuffling through a pile of bills.

"You look down in the dumps, Mum."

"I just don't know how we are going to pay all these bills Henry."

"I have good news for you. Mr Marshall has agreed to give Dad a trial at the quarry. Tom is leaving this week to join the Army."

"Bob Marshall gave him a job. Well I never," she said with a smile. Henry smiled too but not for long. "If he could stay off the drink long enough to hold a job, it might help," she snapped.

"I am sure it will be an incentive to him to show that he can be a good employee. It really hit him for six when he lost his job."

Henry took a deep breath. "Mum, you know how I said Tom is enlisting? That's what I would really like to do."

"You are needed here more. I won't have you going off shooting at people and maybe getting shot yourself. What would I do then?"

"But Mum, there are so many things happening in the world that I think I can make a difference about. I really want to go and try."

Myrtle jumped to her feet and scattered the papers in front of her all over the kitchen floor. "This is what you need to make a difference about. These bills. I don't want any son of mine turning into some sort of crusader. God takes care of those who help themselves, you know."

"But sometimes they need a helping hand from those better off than themselves."

"Where would you find anyone worse off than us?"

"I can send you back some of my Army pay and Dad being back in a job should help. Where is Dad anyway? I would like to give him the good news."

"Where do you think he is – where he always is – down there fraternizing with that brazen woman? If he gets money in his pocket again that's where it will go – more drink."

Henry squared up his shoulders and gritted his teeth. "Do you think that perhaps it is your nagging him all the time that makes him turn away from you and he uses drink to cope?" He turned on his heel and headed down-town to find his father.

He was quite out of breath when he reached the hotel. He was so excited about the news he had for his father that he had run most of the way. At the same time he was a bit apprehensive about the way he spoke to his mother. He knew he would cop it when he got home.

"Hi Shirley. Has Dad been in?"

"Yes he was here a while ago but he left after a few minutes. He's not drinking as much these days."

"I have some good news for him. Bob Marshall has agreed to give him a trial at the quarry; in your nephew Tom's job."

"That is good news. I think losing his job made him have a good look at himself and he didn't like what he saw."

"What do you think about Tom joining the Army?"

"I'll worry about him of course but I think when you feel as strongly about something as he does, you need to give it a try. It's better than spending your whole life regretting."

"Like me, you mean?"

"Like both of us, Henry. I wanted to be a school teacher, you know."

"Why didn't you?"

"Like you, I had a mother who had it all mapped out for me. I married the first man who showed any interest in me to please her. Then it all fell apart when he died and left me with young children to rear on my own. It was too late then. That's why I am here doing this now."

"Yes, I know how that feels. Mum is still trying to push Ginny and I together you know."

"She's not right for you, Henry. You need someone with a gentler nature than her."

"I admire her sense of duty and her loyalty to her father but she just doesn't do anything for my heart- strings, if you know what I mean."

"Keep a close eye on that one Henry. She can be as devious as your mother. She will stop at nothing to get what she wants. She has the poor Reverend wrapped around her little finger."

Henry didn't bound up the stairs when he arrived home for a second time that day. He was rather sheepish about facing his mother after the way he had spoken to her earlier. She was still seated at the kitchen table when he entered the room but his father was there too. He had a broad smile on his face.

"I believe I owe you some thanks son. I can assure you I will do everything I can to hold this job. It's a second chance for me." Henry glanced at his mother but her face was set like stone.

"Henry, I have some good news for you too. Reverend Taylor finally has a place for you in the church choir. I know you have wanted this for a long time but there just wasn't a vacancy."

"But Mum, I thought you were of the opinion that being an entertainer was not for people of good moral fibre."

"I'm sure if you confine your singing to praising the Lord, He will look kindly on you. The Reverend says you may be up to solo parts."

Henry couldn't believe what he was hearing. He had always loved singing and his teachers at school told him he had the makings of a fine voice. His mother always opposed it so he did not pursue the matter. *Was this just another of her ploys to keep me at home?*

"I am serious about this Army thing you know," Henry said in a forceful voice as he looked his mother straight in the eye.

Henry saw the look of admiration on his father's face. "Good for you my boy. Your mother and I will be very proud of you if you serve your King and Country in this way. Won't we Myrtle?"

Henry saw for the first time a hint of rebellion in his father's eyes and started to feel that his dream might come true after all. His mother pushed her chair abruptly away from the table and flounced out of the room without uttering a word.

# CHAPTER 7

# PLOTTING

Henry walked down the hill in a contemplative mood, kicking stones as hard as he could. His toes hurt but he didn't care. Nor did he care about his mother's warning that kicking stones took years from the life of shoes. Today was Tom's last day at work. Henry wanted to follow him into the Army so badly it welled up inside him like an over-inflated balloon.

He went through underneath the house and started up the back steps. Near the landing he bent down to scratch Fluffy, the family cat. As he straightened up, voices filtered out the kitchen window. He sat on the top step and listened. All he could see was a cracked vase of wilting daisies sitting forlornly on the window sill.

"You know Ginny, I really think you would make the perfect wife for my Henry". *It would be nice if she asked me about that!*

"Oh, Mrs Thompson, you know that nothing would make me happier but I don't think Henry really thinks of me in that way."

"Men are weak creatures Ginny. Look at my Arthur; we had to leave our dairy farm and come to Murwillumbah to live because he couldn't stay off his home-made grog long enough to get any work done. Now he has gone and lost his job."

"But he is going to work at the quarry now that Tom is leaving, isn't he?"

"Yes, but who knows how long he will last there? If it hadn't been for Henry leaving school early and getting a job I don't know what we would have done."

"He is a lovely young man Mrs Thompson, you must be proud of him."

"Lovely or not, you still have to know how to get them where you want them. Clever women will lead them on only just so far and then withhold the final trophy, if you know what I mean, until they make that commitment."

"I would have thought that giving them a little taste of what was to come would be more effective. One could then pretend to be guilty and pull-back. My mum was pregnant with me when she married Dad, I know that from the dates, even though she never admitted it." Henry spluttered, trying to hold back from shouting his indignation.

"Maybe that's the answer. If you worked things out right, I'm sure Henry would never leave a girl he had put in that condition."

They were startled by a choking sound from the back stairs. Myrtle flung back her chair and charged through the kitchen door to find a very sheepish Henry.

"Eavesdropping, hey? You know no-one hears well of themselves when they do that."

"Gee Mum, just stopped to scratch the cat and then sat here to soak up the peacefulness – didn't hear a thing." Henry resisted the urge to lash out at the two women, to put into words the anger that was boiling away inside him.

Henry walked to the kitchen door but couldn't bring himself to go inside. The old wooden table was strewn with empty cups; a dinted metal washing–up dish was on the bench beside the open window, filled with dirty dishes waiting to be washed by Henry's sisters when they arrived home. Ginny brushed past Henry and down the steps without a word. She looked sheepish. Henry flopped down on the old chair on the landing. He still couldn't bring himself to go in and face his mother. He might do or say something he would regret.

The silence of twilight was settling over the valley and Henry was still seated outside, clinging to Fluffy. *At least her love is unconditional.* He gave a start when he felt a hand on his shoulder.

"You are looking very troubled, son. Anything I can help with?"

"How about we go for a bit of a walk? There is something I'd like to talk to you about."

Henry and his father walked along in companionable silence until they were some distance from the house. Henry thought how relaxed he was in the company of his father.

"Dad, you know how I've been thinking about joining the Army, well I think the time has come. I want to do it now."

"You know I will be behind you all the way."

"It's Mum who has me worried. She is doing all she can to keep me at home."

"Leave her to me. I fell victim to her conniving ways but I didn't find out about it until it was too late. I don't want you to go the same way."

"She tried to get Ginny to lead me on and get herself pregnant to tie me down here."

"Up to her old tricks. You know son, if I hadn't been so naive at your age I would have seen through her and my life could have been very different."

"What did she do?"

"I was very fond of another young lady in those days. Then your mother came on the scene and told me a whole lot of unsavoury stories about Lizzie. By the time I found out they were not true she had married someone else."

"Why did you end up with Mum if you found out she lied to you?"

"Oh, she was very clever. She managed to turn it around and blamed her sister. She was very sympathetic towards me and I was too stupid to see through her."

"When did you find out the truth?"

"Actually it wasn't until after you and Stewart were born. There was no way I was going to leave you two kids with her. You were my reason for living. "

"You know, I have often wondered what life would have been like with a less demanding mother. Someone like Shirley."

"Lizzie was very like Shirley. That's why we get on so well. You know there is nothing untoward going on between Shirley and me. We just understand each other very well. The sanctity of marriage is something I would never betray."

"That's how I feel too but I don't know if I could ever trust a woman completely enough to make that commitment after the way Mum and Ginny have behaved."

"I think the Army will change the way you look at things. Just get on with that and see what happens. All women are not like those two, you know."

Henry felt the tightness in his stomach relax. He had made his decision. Tomorrow he was going to enlist!

When Henry and his father returned from their walk Myrtle was nowhere to be found. It was not like her to be out and about after dark. Henry felt a momentary pang of guilt. *I hope she is ok.*

"I wonder what she is hatching now." Henry was jolted back to reality by his father's assessment of the situation.

"Perhaps you are being a bit harsh on her Dad. She might have been worried about us."

Before Arthur could reply, the back door slammed and in marched Myrtle. She reminded Henry of the cocky little bantam rooster that ruled over their chook pen and strutted around with his chest stuck out daring any of the other fowls to defy him.

"Where in the name of heavens have you two been? I suppose you've been to the pub again. Your dinner is cold now. Don't expect me to fix anything else for you. You can eat it as it is."

"Hold on there Myrtle. Our son has something very important to tell you, so can you just shut up and listen for once."

"Arthur Thompson, I never thought I would see the day when you would speak to me like that. No doubt those types you are mixing with at the pub are egging you on in this."

"Myrtle you could just forget yourself for once and listen to what Henry has to tell you."

Henry watched this altercation between his parents with a heavy heart. This was one of the things he feared would happen when his mother saw that she was losing control of the family unit she had ruled with an iron fist for so long. He took a deep breath.

"W...w...well, Mum, "he stuttered. "I am going to enlist tomorrow."

"You are what? I thought we had settled that once and for all. I have just been talking to Reverend Taylor about when you could start choir practice. He wants you there this Sunday evening."

Henry's new found confidence and determination came to his rescue. He was going to put up a fight this time. "Well I am sorry Mum, but I don't think there is any point starting that. I expect to begin my basic training within two weeks. Tom got his notice to be in Cowra at the end of this month. They are putting a special train on to get us there. I intend to be on that train too."

Henry glanced at his father and saw the look of satisfaction on his face. His mother slumped into a chair and started sobbing. "I don't know what I am going to do without you Henry. This family will be fall apart without you here to support me. No-one else cares but you and me."

Henry started to move towards his mother to comfort her but his father pushed him away. Henry's confidence was starting to waver.

"It's no use, Myrtle. The tears are not going to work this time. It's time for the boy to make his own way in the world." Henry's father came over and put a firm arm around his shoulder. "You go get yourself something to eat son and then go to bed. You have a big day tomorrow. I'll deal with your mother."

⊷ ━◆━ ⊷

Henry slept surprisingly well. He went out onto the back porch to savour the early morning. It was his big day. Today he was going to the recruitment office as soon as it opened to fill out his papers. As he inhaled the crisp morning air, a movement in the backyard next door caught his eye.

Ginny was already hanging out some washing. *She must get an early start. Guess she is kept pretty busy now that her mother has passed away, with her father having all that parish business to attend to.* Henry walked down the back stairs and over to the fence. He was too much of a gentleman not to face her with his news.

"Good morning Ginny. You've made an early start."

Henry noticed her eyes light up when she saw him hanging over the fence and his heart gave a bit of a flutter but he quickly pulled himself back together.

"I wanted to tell you something before you got the news from someone else." He saw the look of pleasure on her face quickly change to one of alarm.

"Don't tell me you have lost your job too."

"No, it is much more exciting than that. Today I am going to enlist in the Army."

The silence of the morning seemed to take over. Ginny just stood there looking straight at Henry. It was as if she was trying to plan how to combat this startling news.

"I always knew you would break away sooner or later. I am sorry that you and I haven't been able to get to know each other better before this happened."

"What do you mean Ginny? I have always regarded you as a friend."

"I meant in a different kind of way Henry. More intimate, if you know what I mean."

Henry felt a flush of red come over his face and spread down his body. He wasn't quite ready for this reaction.

"It may not be too late Henry. I wouldn't want you going away to war not knowing what you were leaving behind. Maybe we could meet somewhere later, in private, where we would not be disturbed."

*What a contrast to Mum's reaction.* He half expected Ginny to turn on the water-works too. *Is she just being a bit too clever?* Henry was still a virgin at 24 and for a fleeting moment he wondered what it would be like to go all the way with a preacher's daughter. The overheard conversation from the previous day sprang back into his mind. As much as he was tempted, he was not going to be out-manoeuvred at this point.

"I'm going to be very busy over the next few weeks Ginny and when you think it over I believe you will find that is not such a good idea. Maybe when the war is over and I have achieved some of the things I have planned, we can think about it."

"I would wait for you if you asked me Henry."

"No Ginny, I don't think it is fair to ask any woman to do that for a man when the future is so uncertain." He turned and fled back up the stairs.

Henry stood at the top of the stairs and watched as Ginny finished hanging out her washing. The weather had finally cleared. A gentle breeze flapped the sheets as Ginny tried to peg them on the heavy wire. Henry let out deep sigh.

"Well Henry, have you finally come to your senses?" That familiar whining voice interrupted his peaceful contemplation.

"What do you mean?"

His mother nodded towards the backyard next door. "She'll make some lucky man a fine wife."

"But it won't be me!"

"I thought when I saw you talking to her just now that you two must have made up."

"Mum, there was never anything to make up and you know it! There was never any commitment."

"Don't try to tell me that, I've seen you looking at her with that indecent glint in your eye."

"For heaven's sake Mum, give up. I am going to enlist. Today!"

"She will wait for you, I know."

"For the last time Mum, apart from the fact that I will be going off overseas before long and would never ask any woman to wait, I just don't feel that way about her!"

Henry turned and strode purposefully towards the front gate on his way to the recruitment office.

CHAPTER 8

# LEAVING HOME

Henry knew his mother would have something to say about the serving of eggs, bacon and toast on his plate but after a long night on the train, he attacked the meal as if it was his last. And in a sense it was – the last stop before they arrived in Cowra.

"Well Tom, we're almost there. Isn't this just the most exciting thing you have ever done?"

"I'm excited but I'm also worried about the danger we may be headed into," said Tom.

"All I can think of is that I want to make a difference in this screwed up world of ours," said Henry.

"I just want to make sure our way of life is preserved. My Dad says we could all be working in rice paddies if we don't win this one." Tom packed a mouthful of runny eggs and bacon onto a piece of toast and crammed it into his mouth.

"But wouldn't you like it if we could all live together peacefully and respect everyone's way of life."

"The only thing I know is that I don't want to be overrun by the bastards. I could never respect them after what they are doing to our soldiers."

Henry put down his knife and fork and looked squarely at Tom. "I think that if I can rise to a high enough rank I will be able to influence the policy-makers to realise that war is not going to solve anything."

"How are you going to be able to fight them if you think they're our equal?" said Tom, gesturing with his fork.

"It's not going to be easy and I don't know how I am going to be able to kill another human being."

"Maybe you shouldn't be doing this Henry. Maybe you should be running for politics or something."

"No Tom, I want to be where it is happening. I don't think you can change things from behind an office desk."

"I just hope we survive to come back to see our families again."

"Yes and I hope that my family survives until I get back!"

Henry was deep in thought when he felt a tap on his shoulder from the table behind him. He gave a little start and turned around and looked straight into a weathered face.

"Sergeant John Cooper." Henry shook the proffered hand and winced at the force of the grip.

"Pleased to meet you, Henry Thompson's my name. Haven't got any rank to go with it yet."

"I couldn't help overhear you young'uns talk. Would you like a bit of advice from an old hand?"

"Sure. We're going into the unknown."

"Well firstly, I wouldn't go around sprouting about how you are going to rise through the ranks and show 'em how to do things. Those thoughts are best kept to yourself."

"I didn't mean it like that. But I do think I have what it takes to lead. Have always been up to the task."

"Well, just watch yourself. Lead by example rather than by words. You will have to get on the right side of Coulthard or you won't get anywhere in this Battalion."

"Coulthard?"

"Yes, Captain Edwin Charles Horatio Coulthard. He'll be the one who calls the tune where you are concerned. Old army family. Born and bred to command – that's the way it is with the brass. You will have your work cut out to break into that circle."

Henry was left with much to ponder for the remainder of the journey. *I'll have to keep my wits about me when I meet this Captain Coulthard.*

The hissing of the engine echoed in the crisp morning air as the train got up to its full head of steam. Patches of fog hung around the low reaches of the distant hills and the sun's rays peeped over the eastern skyline. It was the dawn of a new phase of their young lives and Henry's heart was pounding.

***

Henry was half asleep when the train pulled into Cowra station. He had spent the final hours of their journey thinking about Sergeant Cooper's advice. The squealing of the brakes jolted him awake and he sat bolt upright in his seat. He pressed his nose to the glass to get his first glimpse of his new home town.

The platform and station were dilapidated, with dust, leaves and rubbish swirling in the air currents made by the train. It was yet another sign of how many men were away attending to matters on distant fronts. The rickety seats with their peeling paint and rusty armrests made the whole vista look like something out of a western movie. A small crowd had gathered and amongst it a flash of blue caught his eye. *Was that an apparition?* Standing there only a few feet away, right where the train pulled up, and separated from him only by the sooty glass of the window, was the most beautiful woman he had ever seen. In her gossamer blue dress she appeared like a floating angel. His doziness was gone. He was on full alert and jumped to his feet and almost lost his balance before he landed half in Tom's lap.

"Did you see that Tom?"

"What on earth do you mean Henry? Calm down. It all looks pretty dismal to me."

"That woman. Look over there." Henry's apparition was indeed a live being. They saw her rear view disappearing into the ladies' waiting room.

"Get a grip on yourself Henry. We are here to train to be soldiers, not to check out the local sheilas."

"There might be some unforeseen bonuses if that is an example." Henry felt a shiver of excitement. *I just know I am going to see more of that young lady.* A languid smile crept across his unshaven face.

⚹

Henry and Tom stood with their luggage at the end of the platform waiting for their transport. The shabby seats on the platform were all occupied so Henry leant against the station-house wall keeping his eyes open for the vision in the blue dress.

"She's long gone by now Henry. It took us a while to get our luggage."

"I'll meet her someday Tom, I know I will. I have never felt this way before about a woman I don't even know."

"I thought you were trying to get away from committing to a relationship with a woman while we were heading into such uncertain times."

"Yes, well I didn't know a blue angel was going to cross my path."

"Anyway, this looks like our lift."

An Army truck was backing into the space next to the station house. Henry gathered his belongings and turned and took one last glance down the platform. His heart started to race. He could see the floating blue dress milling amongst the now, quite large crowd.

"There she is Tom. Load my things for me please. I won't be long."

Tom lunged out and grabbed Henry's forearm. "You can't just go up and introduce yourself. Besides it looks as though she is going to board the train. She probably doesn't even live here."

"Come on you stragglers. We're leaving now. If you don't want to walk the five miles to the camp you had better get on board now". Henry recognised the booming voice of Sergeant Cooper. Reluctantly he took one last look as his blue angel disappeared through the door of the train, helping an elderly lady mount the unstable steps. He turned, picked up his two shabby suitcases, threw them onto the back of the truck and reached to take Tom's outstretched hand.

"It will work out my friend. If you are meant to meet I am sure it will happen. But for now you would be best to stick to the job at hand. We have to get this Army thing rolling."

"Yeh, sure Tom. Sometimes you only get one chance in this life. I hope I haven't missed mine."

# CHAPTER 9

# MATES

The newly painted huts stretched in orderly rows as far as the eye could see. Henry and Tom waited to reach the top of the line to the supply hut. The countryside was lush and green just like his beloved Tweed Valley. He felt an ache in his heart so strong that it almost took his breath away. They had been assigned to the 2/3rd Pioneer Battalion, where their main tasks would be in engineering and construction. This would also include field training, basic weapons skills, and the handling and use of explosives.

"No turning back now, Tom. I'm a bit nervous, aren't you?"

"Sure am Henry. Didn't know we were going to have to learn all this extra stuff. I just thought we would be learning how to shoot and throw grenades and things."

Henry chuckled at his friend's simple view of the art of war. "And the marching of course. Always knew we would be doing a lot of marching!"

"All right, you two get a wriggle on. Country boys I bet. Always day-dreaming you farm boys."

Henry turned in the direction of this shrill voice. *Sounds like someone trying to impress us.* He was confronted by a fresh faced, skinny runt of a man dressed in his brand new uniform, creases still crisp and defined, boots gleaming, and hands that looked as though they had never seen dirt. His hair sat neatly in place. *Brylcream, no way – I couldn't afford that!* Henry pulled himself up to his full height which wasn't much taller than the newcomer but he probably weighed half as much again as him. *Wouldn't be much of a match for me physically.*

"Whom do I have the pleasure of meeting?" Henry used his best dramatic voice, thankful for  the elocution lessons he took at school.

"Smart alec, hey? There's one in every batch. We'll soon have that out of you."

"You and who else, you young pup?" Henry was quite indignant.

Tom pulled him back into line. "Come on Henry; remember what the Sergeant told us on the train. Let's not get off to the wrong start."

"Your friend is a lot smarter than you Henry; that's your name is it? Ok Henry, I think you and I will have more to say to each other before we leave this place."

"Hey, Serg. Over here." Henry spotted Sergeant Cooper passing by.

"Hello Henry. How's it going?"

"Fine. Say, who is that young bantam rooster over there? The one who looks as though he just stepped out of the beauty parlour."

"Reg Wentworth. Steer clear of him. Old money, military family. He's Coulthard's curly-haired little boy. Don't get on the wrong side of him."

Henry felt sick. *My first big mistake; I am going to have to curb my impulsiveness; hope there are not too many like him around or this whole deal will be harder than I thought.*

Henry and his blue angel were resting on the green bank, their feet playing in the sparkling water that trickled down over a little waterfall. Henry awoke with a start, for a moment forgetting where he was. The bugle was sounding loud and clear. He had slept poorly on the hard camp stretcher, only dozing off in the early hours of the morning. It was still dark in the cold hut. Before he had time to get his bearings the unmistakeable voice of Reg Wentworth shrieked in their ears.

"Come on country boys. Thought you were all used to being up with the sparrows. Five minutes to roll-call. Full battle gear. Captain's orders."

*And don't you love it, pretty boy. Why are you in your full dress uniform?*

Henry and Tom were the first to line up in front of an impressive figure in a Captain's uniform; well-built and straight-backed, with a stern yet likeable face.

"Has to be Captain Coulthard," whispered Henry.

Reg was at the Captain's side with a sadistic grin on his face, as if there was something he knew that the bedraggled lot lined up in front him didn't.

"Welcome to Cowra gentlemen. I hope you all realise what we have in store for you over the next few months. This is no place for the faint of heart. We are going to turn you into a fighting unit that will have old Adolf quaking in his boots." *Not such an intimidating bloke. Could get to like him.*

"Today we are going to introduce you to what we call the route march. Private Wentworth and I will go ahead in the jeep and leave markers for you to follow. Please keep moving and don't wait for anyone else. It's every man for himself. We need to sort out the men from the boys. Just a short one today seeing as it is your first – only 10 miles or so."

A groan reverberated around the group. A few stragglers were still shuffling into their places, half-dressed with backpacks and rifles all over the place. Henry was feeling the weight of his heavy kit but stood up straight, with everything in its right place, determined not to show any sign of weakness.

Sergeant Cooper came up next to the men and bellowed: "BY THE RIGHT, QUICK MARCH!"

The new recruits trudged off in the direction indicated. They were out the gate and heading up a slow incline. The formed roadway soon gave way to open country. The bushy shrubs were high enough to obscure the men from each other as they spread out along the track. An occasional majestic gum was silhouetted against the distant glow of the sun as it started to appear over the eastern hills. Partly formed tracks, made by the wheels of army vehicles meandered all over the place. Every now and then they came to a fork in the track where small red and green flags indicated which way to proceed. Thick wooded trees started to close in around them and some men were already starting to falter. Henry and Tom had forged their way out in front and were soon well ahead. Henry was fit from his cricket training but Tom was not used to such exercise.

"It's all right Tom, I'll slow down a bit. You tell me if you can't keep up."

"You heard what the Captain said Henry. Don't wait for me, I'll be ok."

"I don't care what the Captain said, I'm not going on without you."

Henry and Tom were soon overtaken by the other recruits who were now striding out. They came up a steep incline and were confronted by a fork in the rough track. There were no flag markers in sight and they couldn't see which way the other men went. Henry pulled out his compass to see if he could get some indication of the direction they should be going but he had no idea where they were.

"It's not going to look good for us if we get lost on our first route march."

"I told you to keep going without me, Henry. I'll get my breath soon and try to catch up."

"Why don't you sit down and have a bit of a rest while I have a look around and try to figure out which way to go."

"I think there must be some flags missing. I wonder if our friend Wentworth had anything to do with it."

"Yes Tom, the thought had passed my mind but we shouldn't be so quick to judge the bloke. We hardly know him."

Henry started to help Tom take his kit off when a vehicle approached. Over the rise came a jeep carrying the Captain. Reg Wentworth was in the driver's seat with not a hair out of place. The smug look on his face made Henry's neck bristle.

*Why does this guy affect me like this? What does he have against me? I must look like a kid caught with his hand in the cookie jar".*

He dropped Tom's kit to the ground, narrowly avoiding his own foot. The Captain was taking in their every move. "Not very fit for country boys are you? Are you both struggling or are you sticking together?"

Tom pushed in front of Henry. "Please Captain, it is me who is holding Henry back, he's the fittest one in the whole group."

"Is that right Thompson? I thought your orders were not to prop up the laggards."

"I will never let my mates down, no matter how bad it looks for me."

"That may be ok in civilian life but in the Army orders are to be followed above all else."

Henry glanced behind the Captain at Reg. The look on his face told him that he was enjoying every minute of this. *This guy is going to be a real thorn in my side; wonder if he did have anything to do with the missing marker.*

"Ok Williams. Get in the jeep. Thompson, off you go. See if you can get back to camp before dark."

It was three hours later when Henry dragged himself back through the camp gate. The other recruits were standing around in little groups, no doubt sharing their thoughts on Army life after this baptism of fire. Many of them turned to look at Henry.

"Where've you been mate?"

"We were going to send a search party out for you."

"Gunna have to do better than that Thompson."

Tom came over and pulled Henry away. "Come on mate; let's find somewhere we can talk."

They settled down on log in a quiet corner of the parade ground. Henry put his head in his hands. "Thanks Tom, for getting me away from that."

"The least I could do seeing it was my fault. I'm sorry Henry."

"Hey, don't blame yourself. I didn't want to leave you to face the music alone."

"Anyway I've copped extra drill next week to make up for being so slow," said Tom with a shrug of his shoulders.

"Well Tom, If I ever get to lead some men in this messy business, they will always come first."

"That's a noble principle Henry, but it may not always be possible. What if the good of your country is in conflict with it?"

"Well I'll deal with that when the time comes. I suspect we will both have some tough decisions to make in the months ahead."

⚊ ⚌ ⚊

Henry sat in a quiet corner of the camp library. He needed to get away from the hustle and bustle of camp life and have some time to himself. He was quite happy with his own progress after three weeks in training but he was worried about how things were back home. The scraping of a chair nearby made him look around to see Captain Coulthard leaning back, puffing on his pipe. Boldly Henry approached his commanding officer. *Not sure if this is the right protocol but now is as good a time as any to find out.*

"Good morning Captain. I see you like a bit of peace and quiet too." As an after-thought he managed a half-hearted sort of salute.

"Easy Thompson. No need for that in here. Feeling a bit homesick are you?"

"Just a little, sir. Things weren't that good at home when I left."

"Want to tell me about it? I like to get to know my men better. A little insight into their home-life can tell me a lot about the sort of person I am dealing with."

"Well I certainly don't come from a wealthy background like you, sir."

"That's none of your business. It's you we are talking about."

"Sorry Captain, but I was told you put a lot of store in a person's heritage."

"Yes, I do feel that it is important Thompson, but that doesn't mean I can't admire a man who can rise above his upbringing."

"I come from a very poor family. I was a major contributor to the family income and my mother really didn't want me to enlist. It is very important for me to succeed in the Army to show them that I made the right decision."

"That's very admirable but it takes a bit more than that to advance in the ranks."

"I know. I did very well at school and always thought I would go on to university or something. I am a very quick learner."

"Well, we will soon find out if you are up to the task young man. There are opportunities in the Army for those with the right attitude and discipline. Just don't expect it to happen all at once." He rose from the table and walked briskly out of the room. Henry was a little taken back by this abrupt exit but felt that he had made some progress. Beneath the gruff formality there seemed to be a very decent man.

# CHAPTER 10

# CONNECTIONS AND CRICKET

Henry stood looking at the camp notice board. *There's so much on if a fellow had any time or energy left. A cricket game this Saturday, must look in on that – check out the talent before sticking my neck out. Camp choir, that would please Mum – maybe not – unless praising the Lord was involved. A bible study group, –"thou shalt not kill" – here we are being trained how best to kill our enemy.*

"Hello Henry. Looking for something to do in your spare time?" Sergeant Cooper came up behind him. "We can't be working you hard enough."

"You always need some relaxation no matter how tired you are – helps keep your mind alert."

"Never felt the need to stimulate the old brain cells too much. Thinking too long about something before acting can be the difference between life and death in the Army."

"Perhaps if some of our leaders thought a bit more before acting the world wouldn't be in the mess it is today." *Better not dwell on that too much. Need to get through this basic training stuff first.* "Actually it is the cricket I am interested in. Played a bit back home."

"Always thought it was a bit of a toffy game myself. Too slow for me."

"Great game – physical skills are important but it's really a game of tactics. You have to use your brains as well as your brawn."

"Well you should get brownie points from Captain Coulthard if you get involved. Cricket is his great passion after the Army." A smile crept across Henry's face. *That could be my entry into the club. Bet that stuck up Reg wouldn't be any use in a cricket team.*

Henry strolled down to the oval and sat on a wooden bench near the gate onto the field. He didn't want to miss the start of the match. A low wooden fence with peeling white paint ran all the way around the oval. There were a few spindly gum trees towering over a nearby dressing shed, as dilapidated as the fence. It had an open stand on top, three rows only, reached by a steep flight of old wooden stairs. Several players were already out in the middle warming up. *That dry pitch looks a bit rough but shouldn't be too bad to bat on.*

"Good morning, Thompson." Captain Coulthard had come up on him quietly. He looked almost human in his cricket clothes.

"Interested in cricket?" *Straight to the point as usual.*

"Sure am Captain. I have played quite a bit."

"No vacancies in the team at the moment I'm afraid. Can use some help with the gear if you are interested." *Not quite what I had in mind but a start. If I stick around enough I am sure to get a chance to show them what I am capable of. Actions speak louder than words.*

"I'll be happy to help in any way I can, sir."

The Captain turned to greet an approaching player. "You know Private Wentworth, don't you Thompson. He comes from a long line of great cricketers. His great grandfather played for Australia, you know." *Thanks Captain, just what I wanted to hear. Is this clown going to haunt me wherever I turn?*

"We make a pretty good opening pair at times, don't we Reg." Tilting his chin upwards Reg turned to Henry with a look of sheer contempt.

"Yes, we do seem to know each other's game quite well, sir."

Reg and the Captain strode out to bat. He didn't normally pray to the Lord about such trivial matters but this time Henry felt HE would understand. *Please don't let him get too many runs.*

"Good luck you two. Let me know if you need anything," said Henry, trying to sound enthusiastic.

A despondent Henry turned to find somewhere to sit when a flash of colour caught his eye. There, seated in the front row of the stand, looking every bit as beautiful as she did at the station was his blue angel. She was dressed in a floral print dress with a dainty matching parasol. Henry blinked twice to make sure that she was real. She was still there. *I knew she would show up again, I just knew it.* She turned in his direction and a flush of colour crept up his face and he didn't know whether to turn and run or pretend he didn't see her. *If only I was out there now batting with the Captain.* He need not have worried about her seeing his confusion as she was too busy waving a dainty lace handkerchief in the direction of the players on the field. Reg raised his bat in her direction in a kind of salute. *Damn that Reg. What chance have I got in anything with him always butting in.* Henry slumped back onto the bench and tried to concentrate on the game.

The first ball from the opposing team thundered through to the keeper's gloves at such a speed that the Captain didn't even appear to see it. The wicket-keeper fumbled the ball and it flew past him.

"Run," cried Reg. Before the Captain could answer Reg was charging down the pitch and the Captain had no choice but try to reach the other end but to no avail. *Run out, first ball by a nincompoop who couldn't wait for his partner's call. Should drop him from the team for that. Thank you Lord.*

The Captain stormed from the field with a look that could have sunk a battleship. He slumped down beside Henry and spluttered. "If only his grandfather hadn't paid for all of our equipment, I'd be able to give you a go in his place. You'd have to be able to do better than that." Henry hardly knew what to say.

The Captain looked at him with a glint in his eye. "Why not? Get yourself ready to get out there Thompson. Should be interesting."

The Captain gestured to the men on the field to hold things until Henry was ready. Henry flew into the dressing room to grab some suitable shoes. He didn't have any whites but this was only a trial game. He tried hard not to look up at the stand as he ran out onto the field. *This could be my big chance. Please Lord, stay with me for a bit longer.* He didn't look in Reg's direction as he walked past on his way to the crease. His hands were shaking as he took up his stance to face the first ball. *Why do I get so nervous on these important occasions? This one is a whole lot more important to me than that district trial. My whole future could be at stake. Am I being melodramatic? Maybe she won't even notice. She'll be too busy looking at him.* These thoughts were still rushing through his mind as the first ball whizzed past his ear and thudded into the keeper's glove.

"Good ball Wazza."

"Let the farm boy know who he's up against."

"Hit him where it hurts."

*Farm boy? Who are these blokes? They sound like they are friends of Reg. Maybe that's why he is so cocky.* Henry was very resolute as he took his stance again. *Not going to let them know how important it is to me.*

The bowler turned for his approach as Henry gritted his teeth and stared down the pitch at the approaching speedster but his off stump cart-wheeled out of the ground as the ball slammed into it. Henry nodded his head in tribute to the bowler on his way back to the dressing-room. As he passed Reg at the other end of the pitch he heard a low taunt: "Should have stuck to milking the cows, farm boy."

Henry kept his head hung as he made the slow trek back to the bench. Captain Coulthard reached out and gave him an affectionate pat on the leg as he passed. "I probably should have warned you about our demon fast bowler. He's the best we've ever had in the Battalion team. You'll get another chance."

Henry managed a furtive glance up to the stand as he came out of the dressing room. *Yes, she was still there, eyes glued to the field.* "Say Captain, who is that young lady in the stand? I think I have seen her before." He tried to sound nonchalant but his heart was beating so fast he thought the Captain would be able to see and hear it! Before the Captain could answer there was a big shout from the field and Henry's spirits rose as he saw a not-so-cocky Reg be given out to the demon bowler.

"Her name is Connie Foster, a local lass, I believe. I think she and Reg are an item. His money and his breeding draw the ladies to him like flies."

Henry watched as Reg walked straight over to Connie who was down at the gate. Henry saw what he thought was a look of adoration on her face as she gazed at him. Henry felt like he had been hit amid-ship by a German torpedo. He turned on his heel and left the ground as quickly as he could.

⚌◆⚌

Henry and Tom were seated at the long wooden tables that were the recruits' dining facilities. It was early morning on their first weekend off since they started their training. The bacon and eggs served on Sundays was the best meal of the week. *Must be trying to make up for that tough meat with lumpy potatoes and watery peas they were served for the rest of the week.*

"Henry, how did the cricket game go?"

"There was some good came out of it and some not so good."

"Tell me the good bits first."

"Well I did manage to get Captain Coulthard's attention and I am now a member of the support group. Got a chance to bat but messed it up. Was too nervous."

"You've made a start anyway. Maybe a chance will come sooner than you think. What's the bad news? "

Henry gave a big sigh. "It looks as though skill hasn't a lot to do with getting into the team. The old school tie rules, it seems."

"What do you mean? Surely someone as good as you would be able to force their way in."

"That bastard Wentworth seems to have got a permanent place by virtue of his grandfather's generosity in supplying the team with gear."

"A bit like back home when Billy Smith got to carry the flag on Anzac Day because his dad was the Town Mayor."

"Yes, a bit like that. Captain Coulthard said that he would like to give me another go so I guess I will have to be patient. He seems like he will be a man of his word. "

"Don't know if you can put too much store in his word if what you tell me about being 'connected' is needed."

"There's something else though."

"What else could influence things?'

"No, not that. More exciting. She was there!"

"Who, his mother or someone? What more help does he need?"

"No stupid. Connie. That's her name you know."

"Who the hell is Connie?"

"The girl at the station. Her name's Connie and she is a local. Found out from Captain Coulthard."

"Your blue angel? What the heck has she got to do with the cricket?"

"Well that's not all good news either."

"For heaven's sake Henry stop talking in riddles and tell me what happened."

"It seems she is a regular at cricket games. Would you believe that she and that bastard Reg are in some sort of relationship?"

"Geez Henry, is this bloke going to be a thorn in our sides forever?"

Tom nodded towards the door. "Don't look now but he has just walked in and he is headed this way." *Damn, what a perfect way to spoil a peaceful morning.*

"Well, how are our little country boys this morning?" *We were much better before you happened on the scene.*

"Say Thompson, how about you come a bit earlier for each game and get my gear cleaned up and laid out for me? It'll give me more time to warm up. That's important when you're the opening bat, in case you don't know."

*That's it; I've had enough of this upstart.* Just as Henry took his arm back to make a huge lunge in Reg's direction, Tom grabbed it and pulled him back. Reg turned and strutted towards his usual mob over in the corner.

"Hey boys did you hear about the cricket? We've got a new member of the back-up team. Hope he can hold his own with the kit-bags. Not much use with the bat." Henry was seething.

"Don't let him get you riled up like this. He's not worth it."

"Bloody stuck up little pansy. Don't know how long I am going to be able to hold off before giving him one between the eyes."

"Settle down Henry, his kind always get their come-uppance before long. Not worth getting a black mark on your record over him."

"Well let's get out of here Tom. I may not be able to control myself much longer."

# CHAPTER 11

# HENRY MEETS HIS ANGEL

It was unusually quiet in the Rec hut. When the recruits got together in the small amount of spare time allotted to them it could be rowdy. The long hut was set out with little else but table tennis, dart boards and quoits. Henry wondered about the competitive nature of all these leisure-time activities. *Wasn't there enough of that in their training?* A loud conversation interrupted his thoughts. It was that voice. *Should have guessed, that damned Reg again.*

"Look mate, I tell you most women like the man to be the boss. They even enjoy being pushed around a bit. It is man's God-given right to keep women in their place."

"Hang on Reg," another of the group chimed in," I would rather think of it as a man wanting to protect and support his woman. They are the weaker sex after all."

"That's why we have to keep them subservient to us. God put them on earth to serve man."

"They do come with some other benefits." A tall, ruddy-faced man chuckled lewdly.

"That's one of the ways they are meant to serve us," said Reg, arrogantly.

Henry got abruptly to his feet, turned to Tom with a loud voice; "Let's get out of here Tom. We don't have to sit here and listen to this private school boy rubbish." He strode purposefully out the door. He didn't trust himself in the same space as this disgusting man.

Henry sat staring at the letter in his hand. *Things don't seem to be going too bad at home but I just wish Mum could accept what I am doing with a bit more encouragement.*

"Hey Henry, it can't be that bad. Get that frown off your face." Tom had come up behind him.

"It's hard to Tom. Mum is not happy about my not going to church down here."

"Gee we hardly have time for that. They keep us flat out."

"You know how much store Mum puts in pleasing God.

"Well, you know what I think about this religion thing. It won't be much help to us where we are going."

"I've been having such un-Christian thoughts about that damn Reg Wentworth, maybe it is time I went to a service."

"If it's going to stop me having to pull you back from him all the time, maybe it is time you went".

"We have Sunday free this week, don't we? Maybe I will see if I can find a service that will suit me."

"Just don't expect me to come with you, that's all."

"It's ok Tom – it's something I have to deal with on my own. Religion is a personal thing."

Henry took the morning bus into town and walked briskly down the street to the small Methodist church that he had passed a number of times. Summer was starting to give way to autumn and vivid coloured leaves were beginning to fall off the large oak trees. They fluttered to the ground around Henry but he hardly noticed them as he was deep in thought. He was normally very tolerant of his fellow human beings and thought that every man was his own judge and jury in the sight of God and was thus responsible for his own actions and beliefs. *Pity the Lord couldn't do something to stop that Reg Wentworth from annoying me so much. He probably has some good in him. I just can't seem to find it at the moment! Is it this Army training that is making me so unforgiving?*

He paused before entering the ornate little church. The stained glass windows were some of the most beautiful he had ever seen. He was early for the service so there were few people around. A feeling of absolute calm came over him as he walked slowly and reverently down the short aisle and sat in the second row. He was admiring the lovely old organ in the corner in front of him when the vestibule door opened and in walked Connie. In the soft light of the church her beautiful auburn hair glinted red and made her skin look almost translucent. She floated, rather than walked, as the soft folds of her full-skirted, pastel-coloured dress swayed from side to side. *Am I starting to see her everywhere?* His apparition seated herself before the organ and started to tinkle with the ivory keys. He realised that she was indeed real. Before he could get up the courage to throw caution to the wind and introduce himself, the little church started to fill with people for the morning service.

Soon Henry was surrounded by people of various ages, all with that friendly country town look about them. *Just like home.* He shuffled down to the end of the row. Seated next to him was an elderly lady dressed in a voluminous skirt with a cropped-waisted jacket that Henry recognised as the latest fashion trend. *Obviously a quite well-off member of the local community – landed gentry most likely.* Next to her were two rather pretty young girls in their early teens chattering away to each other as they eagerly glanced around the congregation. *Checking out the local boys no doubt.*

"Come on now girls, settle down. The service is about to start." *Their grandmother for sure.*

A ruddy faced minister took his place in the pulpit. His hair was thinning on top and he had a distinctly rounded tummy – an attribute Henry had observed in many of the clergymen of his acquaintance. *Not much self-sacrificing going on there.* He admonished himself silently for such thoughts and settled down to concentrate on the welcoming words of the minister. Although at the end of the pew furthest from the organ, Henry spent the whole service gazing doe-eyed in Connie's direction as she produced some of the most perfect music he had ever heard. He paid no attention to the sermon but he sang the hymns with great enthusiasm. It was the one thing he missed about going to church. He enjoyed being able to sing as loud as he liked without being told to "turn down the volume" as he was at home.

After the service Henry lingered outside the front of the church hoping to get another glimpse of Connie but she was nowhere to be seen. The elderly lady who had been seated next to him made a bee-line in his direction.

"Hello, young man. Welcome to our little church. It is nice to see one of your kind here. I think that some of you soldiers forget your Christian values when you start training to kill people. Mabel Thurston is my name." His hand shook a little as he took the white, lined hand that was proffered in his direction, not quite sure what to make of this dowager lady. She gripped his hand firmly. *No shrinking violet here.*

"W...w...well, I was a regular church goer back home. My Mum likes to think I am still being spiritually nourished."

"Good for you. We do appreciate the sacrifices you young men are making for our country. I just wish there was another way of settling these things other than shooting each other."

He instantly warmed to this forthright lady. "My thoughts exactly madam. One of the reasons I joined the Army was to try to change a few of these things."

"Wonderful, wonderful thoughts. The good Lord will look on you kindly I am sure. Now where have those errant young granddaughters of mine gone? I must go find them." She moved away as quickly as she came. *Reminds me of Mum. Best not to mess with her.*

Henry took another look around for Connie but there was still no sign of her. *Oh well, looks as though I have missed my chance. At least I know where to find her.* He turned slowly in the direction of camp feeling uplifted, knowing he would certainly be a regular attendee at church from now on. He hadn't reached the edge of the road in front of the church when he heard footsteps on the gravel driveway behind him. He turned quickly around and there she was pounding after him.

"Please wait." She was out of breath by the time she caught up with him. "Rev McGraw wants to talk to you. He was very impressed with your voice. Couldn't help but hear it – you certainly have a strong pitch to it." She had a glint in her beautiful blue-green eyes as she said this. Henry felt his heart miss a beat as he was lost in their depth.

"W…w…what does he want from me?" stammered Henry.

"He would like you to consider singing some solos for the service sometime."

"Would that mean you would accompany me?"

"Well yes, if that would suit you?"

"We'll have to get a bit of practice in then." This would be a chance to spend time with her. He wasn't going to mess it up. "I won't always be available on a set day but we should be able to work something out. I really would like to get more practice in with my singing. Music has always been one of the true joys in my life."

"I feel the same way myself. I think you and I are going to be friends. You do have a name I presume?"

"I am sorry. How rude of me. You took me by surprise. Henry Thompson is my name and as you can see from my clothes I am in basic training at the Army camp."

"Pleased to meet you Henry. I'm Connie Foster – part-time musician, book shop assistant and procurer of singers for the Rev McGraw."

Henry didn't let on that he already knew her name. She obviously had not been aware of his existence till now. She was lovely and she had a sense of humour. That only served to make her more engaging to him. Henry turned around and followed Connie back inside. The Rev McGraw was waiting for them by the altar.

"Glad you could spare the time young man. They keep you soldiers busy up there at camp, I know."

"My pleasure, sir. I have been a bit remiss not having come to a service before this."

"No problem. The Lord always welcomes lost souls back into his fold."

"I will certainly be a regular attendee from now on. Didn't realise how much I missed Sunday worship. And the singing. As you have obviously noticed I love to sing."

"I sure did. It is a long time since I have heard a tenor voice of the calibre of yours."

Henry blushed at this effusive praise but he also felt a warm glow over his whole body. He glanced in Connie's direction and saw the gentle relaxed look on her face. *This is more like what I have been dreaming about.*

"I have to be back at camp for lunch."

"Just wanted to see how you felt about singing a few solos for us when you have the time."

*No way am I going to leave until I arrange another meeting.* He turned to Connie. "Would next Thursday night be ok for us to have a bit of a practice?"

"It should be as long as Grandma Star hasn't made other plans for me. There is a dance at the church hall on Saturday night. Why don't you come along? We usually get around to a sing-a-long around the piano before the end of the evening."

Henry walked back to the camp feeling as though he had wings on his Army boots. His un-Christian thoughts about that pompous fool Reg couldn't have been pushed further from his mind.

# Chapter 12

# The Dance

Henry walked into the church hall, eyes alert for a glimpse of her. Streamers flapped gaily under the slowly rotating fans and patriotic flags of all the different services draped the stage like silent sentinels. He admired the enterprise of the Cowra Methodist Ladies Guild. In the corner was a dilapidated piano that had probably been there since World War 1. Along the side wall were tables laden with delicious looking concoctions for the evening supper.

He spotted Connie already on the dance floor with a fresh-faced young soldier perfectly dressed in his new uniform. *Must be a new recruit – won't look as unwrinkled as that in a few weeks time*! He waited for the dance to end then strolled over in her direction, trying to look suave and sophisticated, in order to secure the next dance. Before he could cover the short distance, who should charge up to her but that damn pest, Reg. *I should invite him outside to settle this once and for all – like men! Fat chance of that – he wouldn't want to get his hands dirty or his slimy, smooth-skinned face marked in any way!*

The band started up again and Reg led Connie onto the dance floor and she slipped into his arms as if she had been there many times before. Henry looked broodingly around and saw a plain girl seated shyly in the corner by the piano. She was dressed in a faded green satin gown and her hair was pulled sharply back from her angled face, pinned at the sides with cheap diamante clips. Normally Henry would have been sympathetic to such a forlorn looking girl but at this moment all he could think of was that she was going to serve his purposes quite nicely. He gallantly bowed to her and asked: "Please would you do me the honour of this dance?"

She almost fell over in her eagerness to stand and get out on the dance floor. Henry didn't even bother to ask her name. He kept one eye on Connie and Reg and manoeuvred his partner in their direction. Several times he bumped right into them trying to upset their private little world. Connie glared at him.

Finally, several dances later, Henry got close enough to ask Connie for the next dance.

"Only if you try not to knock the other couples over!" she said. *There's that twinkle again.*

Henry was in a state of heavenly bliss as he and Connie floated around the dance floor not noticing the number of times he trod on her clean white shoes. He stayed close to her for the rest of the evening and claimed her every time he got the chance.

As the dancing slowed down most of the men drifted outside for a cigarette or left to head to a part of town where they could get something stronger to drink than lemonade. *No alcohol in a Methodist Church Hall, thank you!* Henry grabbed Connie's hand and pulled her over to the piano. He knew she needed no sheet music as she had done this many times before. They broke into a rendition of "When Irish Eyes Are Smiling" that brought rapturous applause from the ladies of the Guild and the remaining young girls who hadn't been snapped up.

Henry did not want the evening to end. He and Connie were so obviously meant for each other, no other man could be considered a threat. Reg was nowhere to be seen. Henry suspected that he would have been part of the exodus to town. After running through their whole repertoire of songs Connie seemed to tire.

"You look tired," said Henry as he gazed into her eyes.

"Yes, I've had a long day."

"W...w...would you like me to walk you home." His heart was in his mouth as he uttered these words. She turned her face towards him with a look that made his heart quicken.

"Yes, I think I would like that."

The air was cool as Connie and Henry walked the short distance from the church hall to her grandmother's house. The full moon bathed them in a soft light that was almost like some higher power anointing their union. Henry kept himself as close as he dared without touching her. He sensed, rather than felt, a shiver go through her body. He took off his jacket and placed it around her shoulders. He was sure the warmth that he felt from her could not only be attributed to the jacket and her sigh of contentment was not missed by Henry.

"Henry, I think we should go around the back way so as not to disturb Ma," Connie said as they approached her grandmother's house. This sounded like a fairly practical suggestion to Henry until they rounded the corner and he saw the love-seat on the back landing. He wondered if this was what she had in mind by bringing him this way. *What a perfect place to end the evening.* He pulled her towards the seat and she put up no resistance. He felt that this night could be the one that shaped his future. As they sat looking out over the backyard with the trees slowly waving in the moonlight, the seat swayed in time with them. With his arm around her shoulders he gently drew her closer.

"So tell me Connie, what are you going to do with your time until this war is over."

"What do you mean?"

"Well, I'll be going into battle soon. I could be away for some time."

He felt her stiffen as he uttered these words. Just when he was going to declare himself, a feeling of foreboding came over him and his heart felt like it had been torn in two.

"What makes you think I should put my life on hold for you? For anyone for that matter!"

"Connie, we can't really plan our futures until this war is over, can we?"

She sat upright so quickly his arm fell off her shoulder. "Henry Thompson, those of you who chose to go off playing these dangerous games will just have to accept that things won't be the same when you return."

"I think that any girl would be wise to think very carefully before she became involved with a soldier in these uncertain times but think of those who are going to be away. They need some hope to come home to, something to fight for," Henry replied cautiously.

"Well, I have an understanding with Reg." Henry felt his spirits drop even further but he managed to keep his alarm to himself.

"I am sorry, I didn't realise you two were that close. I would never encroach on another man's territory – especially another soldier."

"Well, actually it is more to do with my career aspirations. I want to be a concert pianist one day and his grandfather has all the connections to make that happen for me, so he tells me." He noticed she had that glint in her eye again as she spoke.

*Well, I can't compete with that. My career is important to me too but I wouldn't allow it to get in the way of true love.*

# CHAPTER 13

# CONSEQUENCES

The Pioneers had just returned from a gruelling three-day tactical exercise. The route had been triangular with two companies setting out along the western route and another two taking the eastern route in the direction of Holmwood, the two forces passing each other on the second day. The first day for Henry's company had consisted of a withdrawal, harassed by enemy A.F.V.'s (tanks), gas attacks and enemy aircraft. The second day was supposed to be a route march but they spent a great deal of time in respirators taking cover from enemy aircraft. The heat was oppressive and the exercises were very strenuous. On the third day they staged a mock attack towards Cowra where the value of discipline and good training came to the fore.

"Got any matches?" said Henry to Tom across the table in the mess hut. "I need them for my eyes. These mock war games sure take it out of you."

"That and all of this drama with Reg over Connie, along with your cricket practice. I don't know how you keep up with it."

"It is all starting to wear me down a bit."

"How did the big dance go? Did you get plenty of dances with Connie?"

"It was a real battle. That damn Reg monopolised her for most of the evening."

"Didn't you even get to dance with her?"

"Yes I did but the evening was almost over by then. But I think I may have won the night."

"How was that if you could hardly get a dance with her?"

"Oh well, Reg tired of the game and went outside with his mates. Maybe for a smoke and something stronger than the orange juice the ladies were serving, I would guess."

"So that's when you moved in?"

"Yes, but I also got her to play and we had a bit of a sing-song. Seemed to go over well with the crowd."

"What did Reg think of that?"

"He hadn't come back when I asked her to let me walk her home. She was looking very tired by then."

"And you snuck her out the back door, no doubt?"

"Well not quite, but she quickly agreed to let me walk her home."

"Would she have gone if Reg had come back?"

"I'm not sure. He seems to think she is his girl and has promised her that his grandfather will help her with her career. Not sure I can fight that. You know Tom, I will be glad when we finish all this mock stuff. I want to get onto the real thing."

"You realise that when we leave here we are not going to be back for a long time."

"Yes but I am not really going to miss the place."

"What about Connie?"

"That is a big problem. If I thought I had a chance with her I would ask her to wait for me but I can't seem to fathom her out. She seems to run hot and cold with me."

"Reg seems to think she is his. Don't look now but he and his cronies have just walked in."

"I just can't seem to escape that blasted nincompoop."

As the raucous group passed close to Henry and Tom, loud laughter erupted from their midst. "So you really are getting some from this little church organist of yours, are you Reg?" The tall red-faced man chortled. Henry had noticed that he always seemed to be mouthing off some lewd thing or other.

"Yeh," chimed in one of the others, "what's it like with a God-fearing little wench like that. Was she a virgin before you got her in your clutches?"

"Look boys, she is like putty in my hands. She amuses me for the time being but you don't think my family would want me to make a match with a low-bred working girl like her, no matter how pretty and talented she is?"

Henry jumped up from the table, his head almost exploding with rage. Tom reached out to grab hold of his arm but Henry had seized Reg by the collar of his uniform, spun him around to face him and landed a perfect punch right on the side of his face. Blood rushed from Reg's nose as Tom pulled the struggling Henry away.

"If I ever hear you talk like that again about that wonderful girl, I will kill you with my bare hands. You stuck up son-of-a-bitch."

"Come on Henry, he's not worth jeopardising your career over." Tom grabbed Henry by the arm and dragged him out the door.

"Let's get out of here before you do some real damage."

"Let me have one more go at him. I'll make him eat his words. How can he talk like that about such a lovely lady?"

"We'll talk about it back in our hut. You need to calm down."

Henry allowed himself to be steered in the direction of their quarters just as several of Reg's mates appeared at the door of the mess hall.

"There they go, after them. Don't let them get away with this."

"Let's teach these country boys a lesson."

Henry and Tom ducked down between the first row of huts and then back up past the officers' quarters. They were almost out of breath and as they slowed down a figure appeared at the top of the stairs. "Hang on there you two, is something on fire? I would have thought by now you would have learnt that you need to think about your actions before you charge off at that sort of speed."

"It's ok Captain, we are just having a bit of a race. No harm intended." Tom got between Henry and their commanding officer, managing to cover the shaking figure behind him.

"Off you go then, have your bit of fun but try to keep your energy for the task at hand. You are going to need all of it soon." He turned on his heel and moved off in the opposite direction.

"Geez, Tom. What are we going to do? He's heading straight for the mess hut. We are done for now."

"Get a grip on yourself, mate. I don't think Wentworth is going to want the Captain to know what made you react this way. The Captain is a true gentleman when it comes to dealing with the ladies."

"I'm not so sure Tom; Reg never misses a chance to get me into trouble."

"Well let's wait and see. Let's stay out of those toffs' way for the time being. We'll be leaving this place pretty soon anyway if the rumours are correct."

⁘

The recruits had been given an unexpected day off their gruelling schedule. The only thing Henry could think about was Connie and how she was going to react when she found out about the incident. He had sought refuge in the camp library. It was the place he felt the least threatened by Reg and where he was most at peace with himself. Of course he knew it was also frequented quite often by Captain Coulthard and it would not hurt his standing to be seen there. Henry had just finished a letter to his mother and was about to stroll down to the Rec hut to find Tom when the Captain walked in. He strode straight over to Henry.

"Well lad, we have a good chance of making the final next weekend against the 5th Battalion."

"Will I be playing sir? I would certainly like the chance."

"Yes I think you will be getting your chance. Billy Barnes has suffered an injury negotiating the obstacle course and looks like being out for some time." Henry's heart missed a beat. Could this be his big break?

"We need more players like you. Don't know what I am going to do with Wentworth though."

"Perhaps you could just drop him down the batting order a bit and then we may not even need him to bat if the rest of us get enough runs." *How degrading that would be for Reg and how good would it be for me?*

"He really shouldn't be in the team but his grandfather is not well so it would not look good for us to drop him at this time."

"I wouldn't want to be the one to replace a man in those circumstances."

"I am glad you feel like that Henry. I have heard that you and Reg have not been seeing eye to eye over things lately."

"I am afraid I lost my temper the other day. I am sorry. I don't like to hear any man talk about women the way he does. It really makes my blood boil. I think women deserve to be respected."

"I agree with you that sometimes he does get under your skin but it doesn't help to fly off the handle like that if you want to get somewhere in the service."

"I certainly want to do that."

"Well, it might be an idea if you control your feelings a bit better in future. Otherwise I may have to take disciplinary action against you."

"Don't worry sir, if I get a chance to play in the cricket team I will be on my best behaviour."

"It may be your last chance. Be at practice on Friday." He turned and strode away.

⊷━◆▤━⊶

Henry was supposed to be practising with Connie on Friday for the Sunday service but he knew she understood how important cricket was to him. Since the dance they'd had several long sessions sharing each other's aspirations for the future. She'd encouraged him to make the most of his talents. With an hour or so to spare before dinner he decided to see if she was at work in the town bookstore. He barged through the door, out of breath after almost running all the way from camp. He stopped dead in his tracks. She was engrossed in conversation with Mabel Thurston.

"Look Connie, here's that lovely young soldier I was telling you about."

"Hello Henry, what brings you here at this time of day?"

"W...w...well, Connie I was hoping to have a word with you about our practice on Friday."

"You two know each other, do you? I was telling Connie what a lovely young man you seemed to be."

Henry didn't know what to do. He hoped to get a word in private with Connie about their practice session. "Yes, Mrs Thurston, Henry and I have been rehearsing some numbers for the service on Sunday," said Connie.

"How wonderful. I will really look forward to that. I must bring the girls along. It will be a real treat for them."

"I need to talk to you about that Connie. I won't be able to make it to practice on Friday."

"Going to be busy roughing up your fellow soldiers, are you?" Henry felt the colour rising in his cheeks but he was very aware that Mrs Thurston had stayed well within hearing range so he didn't want to get into an altercation with her over the incident with Reg.

"Well, I have cricket practice – I have been offered a place in the team for the big match on Saturday. "

"That will be more important then." There was an edge on her voice that Henry hadn't heard before.

"I was hoping you would be my guest at the game."

"Of course I will be there. It's an important match for Reg too, you know." Henry felt deflated. He would just have to try hard to impress her with his cricket.

"I'll see you there then." He turned on his heel to leave the shop, turned back to try and make some conciliatory comment but Mrs Thurston was too quick for him.

"Well now Connie, about that book I was asking you about. Do you think you could let me know if it comes in?" Henry left the shop and began the long walk back to camp.

# CHAPTER 14

# SUCCESS

Henry strolled onto the cricket ground, savouring the moment. There was a crowd here today. The ground looked colourful with the ladies' parasols fluttering in the light breeze. It hadn't rained for weeks and the grass on the field was starting to brown off. The pitch would be hard and fast. Henry liked it that way. They needed a good win to finish on the top of the table and make the final the following week. Henry was full of confidence.

"Come on Henry. We are nearly ready to start. I want you and Reg to open together today." Captain Coulthard beckoned him from the dressing room door.

"Of course, sir. I wasn't expecting to be in so early."

"You two young'uns should be able to give us a good start."

Henry turned to Reg to make a friendly remark. *I have to make it look good in front of the Captain.* Reg was standing with his head bowed and, as he slowly raised it, Henry almost laughed out loud. Reg's nose was swollen and his right eye was black and almost closed. *Boy, does he look a sight. I sure got him a good one. Better not comment.*

"Come on Reg let's see if we can hit this mob out of the ground." Reg just stared at him with a look of pure venom, picked up his bat and marched onto to the field ahead of Henry. *It's my big chance to show Connie how much better I am than this fool.*

Reg took strike and the first couple of balls went whizzing through to the keeper head-high. *He's not comfortable. Maybe I should call him through for a quick run and get him run out. No, that would be too obvious. Think I'll just let him make his own mistake - it will make me look better.* Henry didn't have to wait long. On the fourth ball of the over Reg called Henry for a run, took a couple of steps and then yelled "no", sending Henry back. He made it back into his crease just in time. *Geez, there was no run in that.*

The next ball thundered in at Reg, again he called Henry for a run. "No," screamed Henry and stood his ground. Reg was forced to dive back into his crease. Not quick enough this time, the umpire's finger was raised to signal the run out.

Reg stormed past Henry on his way back to the dressing room. "There was a run in that, you fool."

"Not for me."

"You'll pay for this."

As the Captain came to the crease his calm voice put Henry at ease. "Just play your natural game, boy. Listen to my calls and we should make a good show of it."

"I'm ready for anything they can throw at me." *Wish I was as confident as I sound. Better not stuff this up. Need to make a show if I am not going to get the blame for running Reg out.*

They settled down very quickly into a run scoring blitz that left the opposing team rattled. It was as if they had batted together many times before. When they left the field for lunch two hours later the Captain and Henry were both not out and there were 150 runs on the board. They got a rousing reception. Henry looked around for Connie and gave her a wave as he entered the dressing room. She waved back gaily. He was elated.

Henry and the Captain batted through the post-lunch session and the Captain declared their innings closed at 1- 275.

"Well done lad. We have made the final."

"Pity Reg had to get out so early." *Better not let the Captain see how smug he felt.* He looked around for Connie. She was nowhere to be seen. Nor was Reg for that matter. Then Henry spotted them, in a part of the grandstand away from the rest of the crowd, quite oblivious to the accolades that were being bestowed on the Captain and Henry. He stood there staring up at them. *Damn the man, trust him to spoil my moment of triumph.*

"Do you have a problem with those two being together?" The Captain had come to stand beside him.

"Well, yes sir I do. I have been spending quite a bit of time with her."

"I don't think that you have a realistic chance with her if you are up against Reg. He has it all going for him when it comes to impressing the ladies."

"Yes, I know. His grandfather is going to help her with her career. I can't match that."

"You would do well to put any thoughts of her behind you and concentrate on your Army career." Before Henry could answer the Captain turned on his heel and strode away. *I really thought he would be on my side.* He took one last look at Connie and Reg and set his jaw.

"Get that look of stone off your face Henry Thompson; you won't change a thing by being so stubborn." His mother's words flashed through his mind. *Well, I'm not going to give up yet. Once I leave this town I may not get to see her again so I am going to tell her how I feel before I leave.*

# CHAPTER 15

# A Big Decision

The sun was sinking below distant hills. They looked surreal; like paper cut-outs on the relief maps of battlegrounds used for training. But Henry did not register this. He pushed open the door of the church hall, gasping for breath. His time was running out. Connie was already seated at the organ tip-toeing her fingers up and down the keyboard in the way that Henry found so endearing. She swung around as he approached.

"I was beginning to think you weren't coming. Thought maybe you were in the brig or something after that disgusting exhibition with Reg."

"So you heard about it?"

"Of course, that was what I was talking to Reg about on Saturday. The poor man was quite humiliated by the whole thing." Henry couldn't bring himself to tell her why he had acted in the way he did, she probably wouldn't believe him anyway.

"I am sorry. Sometimes the way those private school snobs talk makes me see red."

"His swollen eye didn't help him in his cricket either. Although he seems to think you had more to do with his getting out than that."

"I tried to get going in a partnership with him but he didn't seem to want to co-operate. He was being obnoxious, like the day I lost my cool with him."

"No excuse to act like that. I abhor violence in all forms. Besides his grandfather is seriously ill you know. He may not even make the final of the cricket."

"I did know that and I have been seriously admonished by Captain Coulthard."

"I know Reg can be quite uppity at times and I don't admire that, but he can't be held responsible for the way he has been brought up any more than you or I can."

"Yes, and Reg sure lets us know about our shortcomings in that department."

"Well, we may not have his privileged background but that doesn't stop us caring for others regardless."

*Connie was one of those people who seemed to find good in everyone. That's a relief.* He was like that himself until he joined the Army. Everything was so competitive in his life now, it was hard for him not to wish ill on his opposition.

"Are you coming to the final of the cricket on Saturday?"

"Do you want me to come?"

"Of course I do. It is quite an important match for me. It will determine whether I get selected in future Battalion teams or not."

"Well I will certainly watch closely this time. It's time I learnt a bit about the game." *Maybe after the game I'll get a chance to tell Connie how I feel about her. It certainly isn't the right time just now.* He wasn't confident she'd be interested. Reg was still a threat.

⚒

"Hey Henry, wait on there." Sergeant Cooper came up behind him from the direction of the Rec hut as Henry walked through the camp gates.

"Hi Serg, How goes it?"

"I have just had some news you might be interested in."

"Don't tell me you know when we are getting out of here."

"No, but it might be something that will please you almost as much. Young Wentworth's grandfather has died."

"I am sorry to hear that. Even though he and I don't actually think much of each other, I don't wish him any misfortune." Henry's words belied what he was thinking. *Maybe Reg would have to stand on his own two feet now.*

"Yes and rumours are going around that his grandfather may not have been as affluent as most people thought. Apparently he was rather fond of a bet and his horses haven't been going too well lately."

"Well, that may bring an end to his uppity ways, eh Serg."

"Yeh, bring him back down to our level. I imagine that won't leave you unhappy, Henry."

Henry felt a bit guilty about his delight that Connie's benefactor had passed away and now her career might never get off the ground. *She is so talented she is sure to be discovered by someone. The time was almost right for me to declare myself.*

There was an eerie silence in the morning light. Henry couldn't sleep and was walking around the camp. The sun hadn't yet shown its colours but he could tell it was going to be a beautiful day. The army huts were standing to attention against a backdrop of the velvet curtain of dawn. Henry loved this time of day. It reminded him of home. Winning today's game could set up his career in the army –they looked after the stars of this elite game. He didn't know if it was the "old school tie" association with this sport of gentlemen or just rivalry between the battalions that made it such a big event in army life. He also intended to make the most of his opportunity and usher Connie away somewhere quiet to declare his love for her.

The morning bugle sounded and soldiers spilled out of their huts like ants; some all spruced and ready for morning roll-call and some still struggling with their uniforms as they hurried to the parade ground. Henry never had any problem rising in the morning - he had been conditioned by his early life on the dairy farm. As a member of the Battalion cricket team he was excused from early parade on the day of such an important game. He strolled to the mess hut for the early sitting of breakfast. He knew the camp cooks were keen followers of the team so he would receive special attention this morning. By the time he reached the players' dressing room he was feeling very relaxed and confident. The players huddled for the pre-game prep talk from the Captain. Their whites were freshly washed and pressed and their equipment gleamed. The room was stark with wooden benches along each wall, open showers with concrete floors, peeling paint on the window sills surrounding cracked glass. Not quite the Lord's he dreamed about but he was enjoying the moment. He was ready.

"Well boys, this occasion is probably as important a part of army life as all the training. A show of team spirit will help mould us together as a fighting unit. Let's get out there and show them what the 2/3rd Pioneers are made of." Captain Coulthard turned and led his team out onto the ground.

The crowd was gathering, soldiers from the camp as well as the townspeople were there in large numbers. It was common knowledge that the current batch of recruits was about to be deployed. The locals took a proprietary interest in the boys who trained in their town and there was a carnival atmosphere. Numerous refreshment stalls, run by the local ladies, were dotted around the grounds. It was their way of wishing the boys luck, both in today's game and in the dangerous task everyone knew was ahead of them. Connie would normally be helping too but as Henry's guest she was seated in the VIP part of the main grandstand. He looked up and his heart swelled with pride as she waved enthusiastically.

The 2/3rds had won the toss and sent the 5ths into bat. They scored a creditable 225 off their allotted overs. Henry followed the Captain out onto the field when it was their turn to bat. He had held his position as opening bat in Reg's absence. When the final winning run was scored Henry and the Captain were still not out. Sportingly he let the Captain score the last run. He could have taken an extra run off the previous ball but he thought it would be in his interests to let the Captain take the accolade. They walked off the ground to resounding applause.

"Well done, son, I think we are going to make a formidable opening pair for some time to come." Connie rushed down as they walked up the aisle between the grandstands and lent over the rail to join in the congratulations.

"Well done Henry. You were fantastic."

"Join you soon." Henry mouthed to her as he passed. He wasn't even sure she heard him over the noise.

"Come on Henry, no time to lose. We've got some serious celebrating to do." Henry was swamped by his fellow players, shaking his hand and grabbing his arm, pulling him towards the dressing room. Captain Coulthard had also stayed on in the dressing room which was unusual, so Henry felt obliged to stay too. He stayed as close to the door as he could, straining to hear the voices of their supporters still outside celebrating their win. He couldn't see them from the dressing room and he couldn't identify Connie's voice amongst them. *I should slip outside for a while to see if she is still there.*

"Come on Henry, get over here and enjoy your moment of triumph. This will help your future in the Army you know. We look after our stars." Captain Coulthard appeared to be showing the effects of the celebratory drinks. Henry had a momentary pang of regret about Connie but allowed himself to be carried away with the occasion. He took the drink offered to him and joined the raucous singing. He felt that Connie would understand.

When Henry finally came out of the dressing room an hour later there was no sign of Connie. *Well, that's the end of that. How could I be so stupid?* He threw his kit-bag onto the back of the team truck with more force than usual and strode back into the dressing room.

"Fill'er up." He said in a slightly slurred voice, handing his empty glass back to his mates. *May as well enjoy myself.*

# CHAPTER 16

# DEPLOYMENT

*"Now the only real infantry battalion encamped at Cowra, the 2/3 Pioneers stole the show. A thousand strong, they were obviously out to take the marching honours, and the big crowd was not slow to realise the merits of their performance. As company after company turned into the straight they preserved a beautifully straight line. On they came,  platoon after platoon, in columns of threes. These men, whose job of work in war demands that they shall be tough in the real sense of the word, revealed the secret of the new A.I.F. step. With right arms swinging waist high, they marched with the rhythmic perfection of ballet dancers. In the easy looseness of their tread was the same supreme adequacy without waste of energy that marks out the dancer."*

THE COWRA GUARDIAN. MARCH 2, 1941.

Henry hardly heard Captain Coulthard's words. Henry and Tom were lined up in the front row of the group of dishevelled soldiers who had been hauled out of bed much earlier than usual. He was feeling slightly under the weather from the celebrations last night. He didn't drink that much usually and it had affected him more than the seasoned drinkers. There was a buzz of excitement amongst the men; Henry knew that this was it before being told. They were about to be deployed. He was feeling very contrite about not talking to Connie after the game and was convinced that now there was no chance of her agreeing to wait for him.

"Well troops, congratulations on completing your basic training. I know you are all anxious to know where you are headed. For security reasons I can't tell you that at this point but I can tell you that you will leave at first light tomorrow."

"Did you hear that Henry? We leave tomorrow. How did you go with Connie, yesterday? I hope you popped the question – won't get a chance now." Tom nudged Henry in the ribs. There was no response.

"All personnel will be confined to base from 1300 hours today. If any of you have any business to do in town, you will have to be back in camp by then. We will be given the honour of a march past to the Showground this afternoon. Let's show them what a fine fighting unit you have turned into. Parade dismissed."

Henry and Tom sat in the mess hut finishing their breakfast. Most of the other recruits were so excited they had gulped down their breakfast and had already left to make their final preparations to leave Cowra. Henry let out a huge sigh and buried his head in his hands.

"It is exciting isn't it Henry? When do you think they will tell us where we are going?" Henry was totally oblivious to his friend's attempt at conversation. *Damn it. I am not even going to get to evening service tonight. That will be the final straw for Connie. I doubt she will even speak to me again.* He was feeling quite sick in his stomach.

"What am I going to do Tom? I won't even get to see her before I leave."

"You should have taken your chance when you had it. You knew this was coming."

"Yes, I know. That damned Reg was always between us even when he wasn't in camp."

"Well, if you left now and got the bus, you could just about be back before lock-down."

"Do you think so Tom? I would have thought there wouldn't be enough time for that."

"I will make some excuse for you if you don't make it. You will never forgive yourself if you don't at least make one more try."

"You're right Tom. Cover for me with Serg will you, I haven't got a moment to spare."

"Ok, but make sure you are back in time. You know how much Captain Coulthard wants to show us all off in this march past this afternoon."

Henry turned on his heel and hurried towards the camp gate. He had a feeling of doom but he had to go. He reached the stop as the bus into town was pulling away from the kerb. He jumped from the roadway to the steps of the bus. He almost stumbled, caught his boot on the non-slip rubber on the bottom step and tumbled forward almost landing in the driver's lap.

"In a hurry are we mate? Can't be that important to risk your life catching a bus. "

"I have something important to do before I leave Cowra. We've been deployed you know."

"I heard that. I think you should save your energies for where you are heading. You'll be taking bigger risks then."

"This is every bit as important to me as the war."

"I'd better get you there safely then."

By the time Henry alighted from the bus he had regained his outward composure but he was still churning inside. He walked jauntily down the tree lined avenue where Connie's grand-parents lived. Henry had time to think while he was on the bus and he was flush with excitement. He didn't know where they were going. The Army hierarchy liked to keep them in suspense until the last possible minute. He was convinced it was their way of keeping the new recruits under control. But to Henry, at this moment, it did not matter – they were finally on their way and he was on his way to see Connie. His heart raced as he mulled over in his mind what he was going to say:

"Connie, there is something I need to ask you."

"Connie, I have to leave in the morning and I can't go without letting you know my true feelings." *Damn. Damn. Damn. How am I going to say it?*

Henry arrived at the front gate still ruminating over his intended words. As he was about to round the back corner of the house, he heard voices. He stopped in his tracks and felt a lump forming in the pit of his stomach. Connie's tinkling laughter greeted him like a musical serenade.

*No, not now – don't let it be him! He's supposed to be still in Sydney for his grandfather's funeral.* He hesitated. Should he charge around the corner and demand that she chose between them? Or should he be more casual and stroll around there as if it was the most natural thing in the world for him to be there? He stopped as close to the corner as he could without showing himself and craned his neck to see what was making Connie so cheerful. There she was seated on *their* love-seat with Reg, his arm around her shoulders, her face upturned to his, those beautiful sparkling blue-green eyes that had gazed so longingly into his in the same place not that long ago, now focussed on that namby-pamby womanising son-of-a-bitch! He felt as if his world had suddenly collapsed around him. For one second he was tempted to interrupt their little tete-a-tete and tell Connie what Reg was really like. *I would probably end up taking another swing at him.* Common sense came to his rescue. He swung around and headed back to the bus stop. *At least I have my career to fall back on.*

CHAPTER 17

# DARWIN

The Bedford truck rumbled back and forth on the makeshift road. Henry and Tom were wedged side-by-side. With each bump their knees jolted into their chins. The red dust and bareness of the landscape was a complete contrast to Cowra. The rail journey had taken them south through Young and Cootamundra before crossing into Victoria and on to Adelaide where they spent the night housed in the local jail. That was the lap of luxury compared to this!

"We must be almost there by now Tom. If we don't get off this bloody truck soon my teeth will have been shaken so loose that I'll need a new set."

"Yes, two days on a train from Adelaide to the Alice was bad enough but two more of being tossed around like a cork in the ocean is not what I was expecting."

"We should have joined the Navy and then we could have been leaning over the deck rail with a sea breeze in our faces."

Henry wiped away the red dust that stuck to every exposed part of him like seaweed to driftwood. With the sweaty red smears across his face he looked like a war-painted Indian in a B-grade cowboy movie.

"Once we get there it shouldn't be too bad. At least we will be doing something real instead of playing those damn war-games."

"Don't count on that too soon Tom. I was talking to Sergeant Cooper about it and it looks like this camp will be another waiting game. The real action is in the Middle East. Who knows if we will ever get there?"

87

"I don't care where we go as long as we get some action."

"At least we will be away from that clown Reg."

"I didn't notice him on the train and he certainly wouldn't be travelling in these conditions!"

"I don't really care where he is as long as he stays away from me! If we are going to see some real fighting the rules should be different," Henry said slamming his fist into the canvas side of the truck.

"Don't get your hopes up. We are still in the Army."

"I would hope that in a fire fight ability would count more than connections."

"Geez Henry, I'm not sure I would like to be under fire just to get him out of our hair!"

Henry stared at the clouds of dust billowing in their wake and tried to conjure up a vision of his lost love. He felt a sharp ache in his heart. He let out a big sigh that drew the attention of the other soldiers around them. A muffled laugh from one of them jolted Henry back to the present and he turned to Tom.

"Now that I know I have no future with Connie, all I want to do is to get myself promoted in this class-ridden Army so I can do something about the causes of these conflicts. Too many good people are dying just to satisfy some sort of nationalistic notion that some races are better than others."

"You better not let any of the brass hear you talk like that Henry or you will be on report for insubordination in no time."

"Don't worry Tom I will be very careful. Now that we are out of Captain Coulthard's command, I will find out who I have to impress and do everything I can to get noticed."

As they alighted from the filthy truck and looked around the rough clearing that was going to be their home for the near future, rain started to fall. It gave some relief to the clammy, sweaty heat that was thumping away at Henry's temples but now the red dust streaks were starting to run like little rivers down his face. He and Tom looked at each other and burst out laughing.

"You sure are a sight Henry. Wonder what Connie would think if she could see you now?"

"You look like more like Bozo the Clown than a hardened fighting man."

"I think we are going to have to get used to harsher conditions."

"Yes, no more Cowra luxury for us."

Around makeshift buildings, small groups of soldiers were hurriedly putting up tents to escape the incoming weather. Tall gum trees that would have once soared high above the dusty terrain had been cut down and were piled to one side. Six-foot-high elephant grass ringed the campsite, tufted purple plumes weighed down by the rain water, greeted the soldiers with bowed heads. Henry nodded his head in the direction of the kowtowing stalks.

"I don't think this is going to be as welcoming a place as they make it seem."

"All right you lot. No time to stand around and admire the scenery. Get to work." Sergeant Cooper's familiar booming voice rang out.

"Hi Serg. Didn't expect to see you here."

"They have re-organised things from HQ. You'll see some more familiar faces around here soon."

"As long as that idiot Wentworth is not here I can handle anything."

"Well, you won't get your wish there. He'll be here soon enough I hear."

"We thought we had escaped him when he didn't come with us when we left Cowra."

"He'll be here in the next couple of weeks, as will Captain Coulthard. He's been promoted to Major and is the new 2/3rd Battalion Commander."

*At least my place in the cricket team should be safe.* He rushed over to help Tom who was still struggling to put up a large tent. *That damn Reg may still be a thorn in my side though.*

Sharing a tent with your best mate sure made things easier to handle when you were so far from home. Having Lofty and Squibby share with them was a delight. They reminded Henry of Abbott and Costello, both in looks and how they acted at times. Lofty was tall and skinny and Squibby was short with a rounded body and there was never a dull moment with these two around. Some of the recruits were frustrated because the camp was five miles from Darwin but Henry liked that. He was amazed at the number of different nationalities that were represented in the local business people. Ities, Huns, Japs, Chinks and every kind of half-caste you could imagine. *Aren't we supposed to be at war with some of these blokes?* Henry preferred to stay in camp and enjoy the company of the Australian aboriginals. He loved the story telling around the campfires by these proud people and was annoyed by the condescending way they were treated by the townsfolk.

"Did you expect it to be like this when we got deployed, Tom?"

"Not likely! I thought we would be out on patrol, keeping watch on the coast and things like that. Building huts for the brass to sleep in was not what I pictured."

"We will move on to command and supply centres after that so Serg tells me."

"We'll be sleeping in tents for some time yet."

"A few of the men aren't too happy about that. I can see it causing some problems down the track. Some are showing disrespectful attitudes towards their officers already. "

"It's the class thing rearing its ugly head again Henry."

"If I become an officer Tom, that is one of the things I am going to try and change. I will always put my men ahead of my own needs."

"We'll see. Haven't you noticed how some men's personalities change when they get some power?"

"I can sympathise with the recruits." Henry was prepared to bide his time. Major Coulthard was expected any day and then he could put his plan into action. He needed to get some duties where he could show his skills.

— ⚔ —

Henry sat on a log and looked around at the bush surrounding him. Brightly coloured parrots fled the huge cross-cut saws; butterflies took flight and seemed to disappear into the clouds. Huge centipedes and scorpions scurried away along the ground trying to flee the boots or gun butts of the soldiers. *Why don't they save it for the real enemy? Not that I would like to find a scorpion in my bunk, though. And the mossies are huge!* The aboriginal helpers around camp delighted in telling stories of twenty foot crocs – he wasn't too keen to meet them either but for now he enjoyed the warm sun on his back. He let out a big sigh.

His reverie was broken by the arrival of a convoy of vehicles. Out of the first shiny new jeep stepped the newly promoted Major Coulthard. Henry wanted to rush over and greet him but out of the other side stepped Reg. His uniform was crisp and unwrinkled, not a hair was out of place. Henry would have loved to have that wiped that smirk off his face with the sticky red dust that hung in the air all day. They could never get it off even after a long scrub in the nearby stream. Henry stopped in his tracks. Reg had three bars on his sleeve. *I can't believe it. He's a Sergeant! How could he be promoted? He's been on leave for weeks. Surely you have to do something to earn your stripes?*

⚊✦⚊

It was the day of the first battalion cricket game since they came to Darwin. A slight breeze  rustled through the leaves of the surrounding gum trees as Henry walked to the mess tent. He was dressed in his whites even though it didn't start for hours. It was only a practice game but he loved the prestige of being in the Battalion team.

"Thompson, I need to talk to you." Henry swung around to face the Major. *Must have some last minute instructions about today's game.* "There's a bit of a last minute change for today. I am re-instating Reg to the opening bat position. I'm afraid that will relegate you to twelfth man."

"But we made such a good team."

"There are some things in the Army that you will have to accept without question Thompson."

"But he hasn't played for months and then he wasn't really doing that well – that hardly seems fair."

"I thought you prided yourself with being a team player. If you don't look out you will be off the team altogether." The Major turned on his heel and strode out.

Henry looked around the mess tent and it seemed that everyone was watching. A smirking Reg appeared not to be looking in his direction but Henry knew he would be enjoying this. Henry looked down at his breakfast. He had lost his appetite.

# CHAPTER 18

# PROMOTION

Sweat poured from Henry's brow after a hard day of tree felling and stacking. Flies buzzed around his face. He was looking forward to a cool dip as soon as he was off-duty.

"Major Coulthard wants to see you right away". A fresh faced recruit came up to Henry with an air of importance. *My bath will have to wait. Major Coulthard won't.* He strode purposefully to the tent that was temporary Command Headquarters. A smile broke out on the Major's normally quite stern face when he saw Henry. *That's a good sign. Doesn't look like I am in trouble.*

"Good afternoon Thompson. I've just been looking at your record. Have you ever thought of becoming more than just one of the foot soldiers in this war?"

"I think about it all the time, sir."

"We need to appoint someone to look after the supply hut – keep records of what comes in and goes out – things like that. It seems that you are one of the few amongst this rough lot who has the skills. Interested?"

"Most definitely, but I hope it won't put me offside with the other men – I am starting to make some good friends."

"The one thing that you will have to learn very quickly if you want to rise through the ranks in this Army is that you can never get too close to the men that you are commanding. You want their respect, yes, but friendships can get in the way. Getting the job done means you have to be obeyed without question."

Henry was not sure that he agreed with this philosophy. He would always have his men's welfare at heart, but he kept this to himself for the moment.

"You will start on Monday and be attached to Brigade Headquarters but you remain a member of your own company. It means a promotion to Corporal – an honorary position really – NCOs only get a little more money but it does give you some authority over the other men, which you need when dealing with the issue of supplies." As Henry walked back to his tent, he was feeling pleased with himself. *I'm on my way.*

Most of the Company were on overnight leave in Darwin and it was still early. Henry was on guard duty. He lay back in the sentry box and gazed into the clear night sky. He felt almost alone in the universe. *Just what was out there beyond those twinkling stars and shining planets?* He had been taught about Adam and Eve at Sunday school and in church but it all seemed quite illogical. He was jolted out of his reverie by a truck hurtling down the road. Henry snapped to attention and stepped out into the path of the vehicle with his rifle cocked and ready.

"Halt – who goes there?"

The vehicle screeched to a halt and his mate Lofty put his head out the window. Henry could see Squibby in the driver's seat.

"For heaven's sake Henry, let us pass, we need to be tucked up in our beds as soon as possible! All hell has broken loose in town. We got into a fracas with the local Militia at the Victoria Hotel and now the MPs are rounding everyone up. We weren't in town tonight, do you hear. We have been here in camp all night."

Henry opened his mouth to reply when another vehicle approached in a similar fashion. By the time Henry turned back towards the original offenders they had disappeared into the camp. This scenario was repeated several times over the next hour. Henry knew his responsibilities. He made a mental note of the men returning this way - he knew them all!

They should all go on report but he knew it would mean trouble for them. Just when he thought it was all over a slower vehicle pulled up. Out jumped a thunder-faced Major Coulthard. Henry broke out in a cold sweat. He knew what he was about to do would have repercussions but he wasn't going to identify his mates.

"Well Thompson I hope you have a list for me of the men who charged back to camp in the last hour."

"W.w.well sir, it was hard for me to see them in the dark and they all came through so quickly, one after the other."

"They will all need to go on report. I will expect to see it on my desk as early as possible tomorrow." As usual Major Coulthard was gone so quickly that Henry hadn't even had time to reply. *I need to think about this.*

⚜

Henry stayed in bed as long as he could. After night duty he was not expected to report again until late afternoon. He rolled himself up tightly in his scratchy blanket on his uncomfortable stretcher and kept his eyes tightly shut so anyone glancing his way would think he was fast asleep. The sun was streaming through the flap of the tent and an occasional flash of blinding light picked up the metal of his shiny rifle propped up against his kit-bag. Henry prided himself on keeping his equipment scrupulously clean. It made him feel more important and set an example for the men under him. He restlessly turned to face away from the light.

"Thompson – rise and shine – the Major wants to see you immediately."

Henry rolled back and saw an  orderly silhouetted in the open space. This was the moment he dreaded. He rose and dressed slowly, turning over in his mind what he was going to say.

When Henry entered the command hut Major Coulthard looked up without changing his expression and gestured at the straight-backed, uncomfortable chair beside his desk. The Major looked very much like the scrub turkey that had led to his nick-name, Scrub. When he was in front of a parade he flung his arms about as if he was taking off. He cleared his throat and opened the red covered report book in front of him and started tapping his pen ominously.

"Well Corporal, have you decided to do the right thing and identify the men involved in last night's disgusting exhibition?"

Henry stiffened his back against the hard chair, squared his shoulders and looked the Major straight in the eye.

"As I told you last night it was too dark for me to identify any of the men involved – they came rushing back into camp in large groups and almost ran me over as I tried to stop them. I wasn't able to follow them back into camp to identify them as I am not allowed to leave my post – isn't that the unbreakable rule?"

⊷ ⊷

Henry was back on his second night of guard duty – he noticed the roster had been changed and now he had guard duty for the whole week – unheard of unless the person involved was being punished in some way. *Oh well, if that is the way it is going to be then so be it! I am not going to dob in my mates.* A noise made him step outside his sentry box. He was confronted with two of the guilty culprits of last night, Lofty and Squibby. They were trying to sneak back into camp unnoticed.

"What do you two think you are up to?"

"We just had to go back into town to square up with some ladies we left in a bit of a hurry last night."

"You know that all leave has been cancelled so this time I am going to have to put you on report."

As Henry filled in the required paperwork, the Major strolled up. "I suppose Thompson, you are going to tell me you don't know these men?" The sarcasm in his voice was not lost on Henry.

"No sir. I am just putting them on report."

Scrub turned towards Lofty and Squibby who were now looking very sheepish, "And what do you two have to say for yourselves?"

96

"Please, sir," said Squibby timidly, "we thought the pickets in town may have needed some help rounding up the AWOLs so we appointed ourselves pickets."

Scrub's expression made him look as if he had swallowed quite a large helping of his namesake – in one piece! Henry chuckled to himself as he added to the AWOL charge another of self-appointed pickets – a much lesser charge than they would have faced over the events of last night! He was quite pleased that he had reached a successful compromise between loyalty to his men and showing his authority.

# CHAPTER 19

# RESPONSIBILITY

"Thompson, the major needs you in his hut now!" *Damn it. I thought I would get a sleep in. I've just done a whole week of guard duty!*

He dragged himself out of bed and was standing in front of Major Coulthard within five minutes. "Well done, Thompson. I know you have had a hard week but that's the way it will be from now on."

"It's ok sir, I'm up to anything you can give me."

"We have a bigger picture to look at now. We have to get this lot battle–ready."

"They're good men sir. I am sure they will rise to the occasion."

"Well, we will soon find out. I am sending you out in charge of a group tomorrow to engage in a bit of a war game."

Henry's heart gave a little jump. *Wow, some action at last. Better than chopping trees and checking on wayward soldiers.*

"I'm ready sir. Who will be our opposition?"

"I thought it was time you and Wentworth went head-to-head. I know how both of you are keen to impress."

Henry's euphoria took a dive. *Won't I ever get away from that man?* He could see a twinkle in the Major's eye. *He's enjoying this. I'll show him. This is my big chance to impress and make Reg look as incompetent as he really is.*

"I'm ready for anything he can throw at me, sir."

"Good for you Henry. I knew you would be up to it."

⚊ ▰◆▰ ⚊

Henry and his troops were high on the ridge above Rapid Creek. He scanned the landscape with his binoculars for a sign of their opposition amid the thick scrub. Nothing was visible except the fast flowing water below. He spotted some movement in the trees on the other side of the stream. *Damn that Reg. We will never beat them now. Mustn't let the men sense that I have given up.* He turned to his men. "Well boys, it looks like they are well ahead of us."

"We'll never catch them if they are already over the other side." Tom sounded dejected.

"Our only chance is if we can find a quick way to cross and then take a shortcut though the swamp."

"But there's no way across other than the one they have already taken." Lofty chimed in.

"We'll find one. Let's get down a bit closer to the water."

Henry's little band careered down the side of the gorge, slipping and sliding. There seemed no way across the torrent. Henry looked around the surrounding trees with their overhanging branches covered with lawyer vines.

"Ok fellows, this is what I think we should try. I think if we can get hold of some of those vines, we may be able to swing ourselves across to that sandy spot over there."

"That's very risky. We don't even know if that sand is firm enough to hold us." Tom was not convinced.

"I'll go first."

"No Henry, that's not how it should be. One of us should try first.

"No Tom, I'll go. I wouldn't ask one of my men to do something unless I knew for sure that it was safe."

Before anyone could try to stop him Henry had grabbed one of the vines and started swinging back and forth to get enough momentum. *I must be mad to try this.* He let go and thudded into the sand on the other side. His men let out a cry of anguish when they heard the crack as he landed.

"Are you all right Henry?" Tom called over the roar of the water. Henry was rolling around on the hard sand clutching his ankle.

"The sand is hard enough, that's for sure," he yelled back to his men. "Think I have done myself a bit of an injury though. You boys had better take the long way round and pick me up on your way back."

"No." They cried out in unison.

"I am ordering you to continue without me," shouted Henry across the water. "I'll put you all on report if you disobey me."

"Good luck," called Henry as the men reluctantly turned their backs on him.

Henry propped himself up on his back-pack on the hard sand. As the sun fell behind the steep walls of the gorge, he felt the chill of the evening air. He was still damp from his escapade across the stream and his injured ankle was throbbing. He removed his boot and saw it was swollen and bruised too. *I hope it's not broken. That will put my plans in total disarray. There's an important cricket game next week. How Reg would love it if I couldn't play! I've only just managed to force my way back into the team.*

It was unlikely his men would get back to him before dark so Henry decided he should find some cover for the night. He dragged himself to his feet and pushed his way through the undergrowth until he found a small clearing that was covered with a soft mulch of decaying leaves. The canopy of trees would give partial shelter if it rained during the night. He laid his waterproof sheet on top of the accumulated undergrowth and settled as comfortably as possible. He consumed the rations in his kit and lay back to contemplate his predicament. His mind was churning. *Perhaps I was a bit foolhardy to have attempted that river crossing without knowing what the landing was like. I hope my men respect me for it.*

As he lay in the forest and listened to the noises that accompany nightfall, he started to think of Connie. *I wonder what she would think of me now my career has started to take shape.* He still had long and passionate dreams about her. *Maybe if I come back from war alive and a hero, or as a decorated officer she might then think as highly of me as she does that fool Reg.* His biggest fear in this war was that he would come back so badly injured he would be of no use to the Army, Connie or anyone else. The sounds of the forest were different to home. The Aboriginal trackers around camp had delighted in scaring the "city boys" with tales of man-eating crocodiles and pythons that could swallow cattle whole. Henry could handle the creepy crawlies like scorpions and centipedes, small tropical snakes and the huge mozzies that were buzzing around in the twilight. He just wasn't so sure about the large reptiles. Every slight movement in the undergrowth made his heart rate jump and he wondered if he was ever going to get any sleep. He decided that his best move was to stay as still as he could. He slept fitfully. He had no idea of the time as he had no light to look at his watch. After so long fixed to one spot he felt cramped. Once he had broken out in a cold sweat when these unfamiliar sounds were accompanied by rustling in the undergrowth. All sorts of strange thoughts raced through his mind. *Some leader I am! Maybe I don't have what it takes. Maybe I should just stick to being one of the boys and let someone else take the risks.*

He dozed on and off as the early morning light tried to force its way through the thick canopy. Another crackling noise in the undergrowth snapped him to attention. *Something a bit bigger this time.* He started to think he should find some higher ground  when a torch was shone straight into his face.

"Well, well, well. Look what we have here boys. Country boy Henry all curled up in his little nest."

*Damn that Reg. Why was it that he always seemed to be around in my most embarrassing moments?*

"Well Thompson, have the crocodiles taken your tongue?"

"I am happy to see you. It has been quite a night," squeaked Henry. His voice almost deserted him.

"Major Coulthard would be really impressed with his protégé if he could see him now. Real officer material." The other men in the group became visible. *Should have known it would be that private school lot. They look like smirking gargoyles.*

"Come on men; let's get this idiot back to camp. It looks like we are going to have to carry him. Cut down a few of those saplings so we can make some sort of stretcher."

*That's right Mr Efficiency as well. Why can't he be the one caught out for a change?*

# RECONNECTING WITH CONNIE

Henry stared at the pile of paper work on his rough wooden desk. He rested his leg on a box. He still had to get up often to change his position. Stacked in boxes at the back of the hut were daily food rations, along with limited supplies of toiletries and stationery. Uniforms, boots and kit bags and a small supply of rifles were kept in a locked cupboard in the corner. Henry felt honoured to have all this responsibility and now they had added Paymaster to his duties. Still, he longed to get back to active duty. Sorting the dispatches and mail as it came in helped him to escape this daily grind. His imagination took over as he examined delicate female handwriting. *Were they love letters? I'm never going to get any of those.*

When a letter in a hand he didn't recognise arrived, he was nearly jolted out of his chair. He stared at the name again. *It is for me.* He slowly turned it over. Beside the sender was her name: Miss Connie Foster, 14 Smith St, Cowra. He held it until his palms started to sweat. He couldn't open it. He feared what it contained. He put it aside and tried to resume his work. His eyes kept returning to where it lay on the end of his desk. He picked it up several times to check it. *It was from her all right.* He had sent his orderly to deliver the eagerly awaited letters to the men in the Rec hut before he took his letter into his trembling hands. He fumbled the letter opener and slowly unfolded the single sheet of paper.

*"Dear Henry,*

*I was very disappointed and hurt that you left Cowra without saying good-bye."* [What was I supposed to do? You were making doe eyes at that rat Reg.]

*"I have decided to write to you in the hope that we may keep in touch as friends during your absence."* [Friends? How can I ever think of you as just a friend? I thought you were the girl I had been waiting for all my life.]

*"My grandmother's health has taken a turn for the worse and I am now her full-time carer. My dreams of a career as a concert pianist have been put on hold for the time being."* [I know how important that is to you but at least now you won't need to keep Reg onside to get his family's help. Doesn't mean I have much hope though.]

Henry had almost forgotten he'd also received a letter from his mother. He had no trouble ripping it open.

*"Well Henry",* she started without any preamble, *"you seem to have started something with this going to war business. Your sister Anne has gone off and joined the Medical Corp to train as a nurse. She has promised me that she will stay on home soil and not go off overseas to some unknown danger like you seem intent on doing."* Henry chuckled. [Just shows how much she knows. If the brass decided Anne was needed overseas, she would have no choice but to go.] He wasn't going to upset his mother needlessly. Things must be getting really tough for her now with two of us gone. Henry was very fond of his sister. She had only just left school and always wanted to be a nurse. [This war has allowed both of us to fulfil our ambitions.]

*"Your father loves his new job and I think he may have finally come to accept his responsibilities. Stewart seems to be enjoying his*

*job too and has been given a nice little pay rise from next month."
[That is better news.]*

*"Allan and Lawrence want to know how many Germans you
have shot so far. I told them they shouldn't worry their young heads
about you. You will take care of whatever is necessary and the good
Lord will bring you home safely to us. I get them to say an extra
prayer for you both at each Sunday service." [I sure hope He is
listening. He will be getting a lot of requests like that.]*

*"You will be careful, won't you Henry? I don't know how we will
all bear it if anything happens to you. Ginny asks after you often
but seems to be pre-occupied with the new young curate. I am sure
it is only because you are out of reach." [Yeh, sure. That young miss
wouldn't waste any time finding herself a replacement even if we
were committed.]*

⊷ ⧉ ⊶

It was a sticky night and Henry and Tom had left the tent flap open to
pick up any breeze. Henry enjoyed this time of day with his mate. He
missed not being a part of the active duty scene and he liked to hear
what was happening. Henry lay back on his bed with his injured ankle
propped up on his kitbag. He could walk without crutches now but he
still needed to get off it as often as he could.

"I got a letter from Connie today, Tom."

"Wow, that should have cheered you up."

"It was only short – not much more than a note really. Probably
shouldn't read too much into it." Henry gave big sigh and swung his
legs back over the side of his bunk, sat up and faced Tom.

"Are you going to reply?" said Tom.

"Don't know. She wasn't exactly that encouraging. I think she may
have felt that she was doing her bit for the cause."

"Writing to a poor lonely soldier? Yes I have heard that is being
encouraged."

"I really want to know how she feels about me but I am afraid it might not be what I want to hear."

"Do you want to go to war not knowing? I think you should at least answer her and see if she continues to write."

Henry thought about this for a while and pictured Connie in that dress at the dance. A wave of desire swept over him. He swung himself onto his stomach, grabbed the few sheets of paper that he had snuck out of the supply hut and started to write.

*"Dear Connie,*

*I was quite surprised to receive your letter. I am sorry that I didn't say good-bye before I left Cowra but we were made to leave on very short notice and had no time for good-byes." [No point in letting her know now that I saw her and Reg together.]*

*"I would be very pleased to receive an occasional letter from you. We don't get much news from home up here. I would also like it if you could send us some reading matter. Doesn't matter what it is, newspapers, magazines, paperbacks. The Army doesn't supply us with any of that. I was sorry to hear about your grandmother. You must be disappointed about your career plans. Perhaps you will get the chance at some later date." [No point in mentioning Reg's involvement in her future plans. The less she thinks about him the better.]*

*"I have had a bit of an accident with my ankle so have been confined to paperwork for a few weeks. I am hoping it may lead to a step up in my career as I have been given quite a bit of responsibility. Look forward to hearing from you soon.*

*Your friend, Henry."*

He sat back up, folded the sheet of paper carefully and placed it in an envelope. He felt quite deflated as it was not the love letter he had dreamed of sending her.

"Finished already?" Tom was lying on his bunk flicking through the pages of a tattered magazine. "Hope you asked her to send us some reading, these old Pixes are getting past it.

"Yes, I did. Will give her an excuse to write back. Didn't want to get too personal yet, might frighten her off. "

CHAPTER 21

# MORE COMPLICATIONS

Since he received Connie's letter, Henry could not help thinking of her. It helped him pass the long hours at his desk. Sometimes, just for a moment, he would lose himself to those thoughts.

"Hello Henry, day-dreaming about something pleasant I hope." Major Coulthard had come silently up behind him. *I wish he wouldn't keep doing that.*

Henry sat up straight and instinctively reached out for the pile of papers in front of him. "Just about to get started, sir."

"It's ok, we are not that tough in the way we treat you men are we?"

"No, of course not sir. But there is a lot to do."

"We're not overloading you, are we?"

"I can handle it. Just get a bit restless now that I am almost fit again."

"That's what I came to see you about. Are you ready to start cricket practice? We are having a bit of a trial game on Saturday. I'd like you to come along if you are ready to play again. We have an important match coming up."

"I sure am, sir. I will be there nice and early."

⋯ ⋯

Henry covered his eyes to avoid the light streaming through the open tent flap. He was not feeling at all enthusiastic about cricket. *This heat is worse than usual - think I'll go down to the creek to cool off a bit.* He

108

staggered as he took his first steps. The whole tent seemed to revolve in front of him. He sat down to regain his balance. He managed to reach the stream and lay there letting the refreshing water course over his body. *Could stay here all day but can't miss cricket.* He forced himself back up onto the bank and somehow reached the front of the Mess hut.

He tried to open his eyes and focus on the blurred shadow looming above him.

"Where am I?" The Medical Corp officer leaning over him started to take shape.

"You're in hospital. It looks as though you have come down with a nice old dose of malaria."

"What do you mean? I was all right last night; I think it is just this darn heat. I have cricket practice today."

"I don't think so. You spent a night in the open recently didn't you? Any mossies bother you?"

"Yes but that was ages ago."

"It can take a while to affect you. We are going to keep you here until you are fully recovered."

*This can't be happening to me. Have I done something to displease Him up there or something? Why doesn't something go right for me?* Henry floated off into a fitful sleep.

"Come on , you poor thing , I'll give you a bit of a sponge down to make you more comfortable and then we will find a bed in a nice cool spot for you."

*Is that you Connie? How did you get here so quickly?*

Henry allowed himself to be gently sponged down, swallowed the foul tasting liquid he was given and then sank down into the soft mattress. Connie was still there looking longingly into his eyes, slowly wiping her soft hands across his fevered brow. Palm trees waved their fronds over them and the lingering notes of one of his favourite songs wafted soothingly around him. His arms reached up to pull her down towards him.

"Come on Henry. We will have to change your clothes and bedding. Your fever has broken. Can't leave you lying around in wet things. Might catch a chill."  Henry opened his eyes and looked into the smiling face of his young nurse.

"Where's Connie? She was here."

"Now then, you have been thrashing around for hours. You have been delirious."

"But she was here, I know she was."

"You will have a few more bouts of high fever before you get over this. You will probably get another visit from her then," chuckled the nurse. Henry rolled over contently. *Bring it on then.*

Henry had been confined to the makeshift hospital tent for several days and had lost count of Connie's visits. He was starting to feel better as each day went by. The nursing staff had been wonderful and the oh so realistic visits from Connie made him almost sorry that his fantasies were becoming less frequent. *What a pity she was tied down looking after her grandmother or I could suggest she train as a nurse and get posted up here so I could really see her.*

"Well Henry, you are certainly looking better today." Betty, his favourite nurse had just come on duty. "Connie was here again, I take it?"

"Not quite so often." Henry wiped an imaginary tear from his eye.

"We will miss her when she stops coming." Betty giggled,  "but it will mean you are getting better."

Henry turned to tell Betty how sorry he would be to leave this group of special people when he was stopped in his track. There behind her was the smirking face of the person he least wanted to see. Reg. He felt like wiping that look off his face.

"Hello Henry; thought I would call in and see how you were getting on. Heard you were quite ill." *Not half as sick as seeing you makes me.*

"It was good of you to be concerned for my welfare." Henry's voice was heavy with sarcasm.

"Well, you don't look too bad to me. Sure you're not just keeping yourself here to avoid having to compete against me again?"

"He has been a very sick man. No-one could fake an illness like that. Better hope you don't come down with it." Betty came to his rescue. "I think it is time for you to leave. Our patient's welfare is important."

As Reg stomped towards the door of the medical hut Henry called out to him. "I have certainly been getting plenty of sympathy from Connie."

Reg swung around and stood looking menacingly back at Henry. "What do you mean?  How can she know of your predicament?"

"Come Sergeant Wentworth, out you go." Betty pulled him by the arm towards the door.

"She heard about my ankle injury from her brother-in-law who is up here with the 5th Battalion. She has been very concerned. I have had several letters. Have you?" Henry took a chance that he hadn't heard from her. The look on Reg's face told him the answer. Reg wrenched his arm from Betty's grasp and stormed out.

"What an unpleasant man. Sounds like he has it in for you."

"We have crossed swords on several fronts, but don't worry I think I am starting to get to him." A cheeky grin crept over Henry's face. *Thank you Connie, you have given me the strength to keep fighting him.*

# CHAPTER 22

# NEWS FROM HOME

Although Henry was tired of being confined to the supply hut, he had to admit advantages. He knew right away when Connie had written to him. As he carefully placed each letter into its correct pile the now familiar writing of Connie seemed to leap off the paper and thump straight into his chest. He put the latest letter carefully to one side and hummed as he sped up his sorting.

Holding Connie's letter with reverence Henry took it outside and sat on one of the sawn logs used as benches around the camp. Most of the recruits were out on war games so he had the camp almost to himself. He slowly opened the envelope and unfolded the two pages inside. *A bit longer than last time, that's promising.*

*"Dear Henry,*

*I am sorry to hear about your mishap with your ankle and your bout of malaria. Hope things are going better for you now."* [They are now that I have heard from you.]

*"I had a surprise visitor yesterday. Your sister Anne. She found out about me from some of the permanent staff out at the base. It is wonderful that she is training as a nurse. I only wish that I could do something like that."* [I wonder what she would think if I told what part she had already played in my recovery.]

*"It seems to me that your family thinks there is some sort of*

*relationship happening between us. I wonder where they got that idea." [Cheeky girl. Maybe there is some hope for me.]*

*"I am a bit concerned about what she told me is happening back home. It seems that your father is causing some concern. Your mother must be a very strong person to be able to cope." [What on earth is she talking about? No-one had told me anything.]*

*"I really think you should try to be granted some compassionate leave. My brother-in-law Paul gets it all the time for much lesser events than those happening in your family." [Just what has been going on? Why can't she tell me the details? I suppose she thinks I already know. I guess Dad's drinking is causing problems again.]*

He was starting to panic. Henry strode back to the communications hut to send off a telegram to his mother. His hand was shaking as he wrote it out.

He had just arrived at his desk the next morning when one of the newest recruits, a young Italian named Romano, came charging into the supply hut. He was breathless from his obvious exertion.

"Serg wanted you to have this as soon as possible. He knew you would be anxious." Henry snatched the piece of paper from Romano's hand with such force that it ripped in two.

"Sorry mate, I am really concerned about what's in this."

"It's ok. I understand what pressure events at home can put on us." There was conviction in his voice.

"You have problems on the home front too?"

"My Dad has just been rounded up and sent to the prisoner of war camp in Cowra."

"Why would he be sent there? Aren't you naturalised Australians?"

"The rest of us are but Dad didn't think it was that important and he didn't want to cut ties with the old country altogether. Aren't you going to read your reply?"

Henry pieced together the torn telegram. It read:

"All well. Money being received. No new problems." Henry pondered this cryptic message for some time before he turned to Romano.

"It looks like I worried for nothing. All is well. Let me know if there is anything I can do to help you with your problems."

"Thanks. Not sure there is anything anyone can do." Henry thought what a nice young man he seemed. Henry's family's problem seemed trivial compared with Romano's.

Henry made a mental note to ask Connie in his next letter what it was that made her so concerned about the happenings in his family. Something didn't quite add up. Connie wasn't the sort of person to exaggerate but on the other hand his mother was. So having Connie alarmed to the extent that she suggested he apply for compassionate leave and his mother say everything was ok made him wonder just what was going on.

*Was Connie playing some sort of game with him? It was not like her. Maybe I don't know her as well as I thought. Are women are all the same? He was thinking back to the little games Ginny played with him back in Murwillumbah. Why couldn't life be just a little bit simpler?*

⋯⋯ ≍✦≍ ⋯⋯

Henry tossed and turned in his narrow bed all night. He greatest wish was still to go places in the Army but he was starting to think that might not fit in with family life. He was being pulled in too many directions at once. He hauled himself out of bed. Spring was approaching and it was sticky all night. He had so much on his mind and his recent illness had left him feeling quite lethargic. At the first available opportunity he would talk to Major Coulthard and ask whether it was possible to stay in the Army and be moved to a desk job. His opportunity came sooner than he thought.

He was on his way to the mess tent for breakfast when he ran into the Major. "Good morning Henry. I was going to send for you later. I have something I want to talk over with you. Come over to my hut as soon as you get your morning duties out of the way."

"Of course sir. I need to talk to you as well." Henry puffed out his chest as he couldn't help noticing a number of recruits watching with interest. He was pleased to be singled out by the Major. It gave him a certain air of authority. He looked on the Major as a father figure. Most of the other men were quite frightened of Scrub but Henry was fond of him and thought that his gruff manner hid a very caring nature.

Henry rushed through his early mail sorting. He locked up the store and was on the Major's doorstep by 10.30 am. He took a quick look around the camp to see if anyone was watching him enter the command hut.

"Come on in Henry." Scrub's usual impatience was in his voice.

"Sorry sir. I was just reflecting on how much things have come on around here since we arrived. We have really made a difference."

"We sure have and I am very proud of you all. I am particularly pleased with you Henry. Your devotion to your duties has not gone unnoticed."

"Thank you sir. I do enjoy Army life even when I am not on active duty."

"You said you had something to talk to me about."

"Well sir." He was hesitant and had a dull feeling in the pit of his stomach. "I have been enjoying the work that I have been doing and I was wondering if I could be given that sort of job permanently."

"You don't say that with much conviction, Henry. Are you nervous at the prospect of being sent into some real fighting?"

"No, it is not that. Quite the contrary but my family are not keen on my taking too many risks as they rely on my allotment to keep them going."

"What about that girl in Cowra? Connie, that was her name wasn't it?"

"Well I have just heard from her again. I have hopes for our relationship."

"Don't you want to know what I wanted to see you about?"

"Of course," said Henry.

"I have been talking to Brigade Headquarters about you. They have asked me to recommend several of my battalion for special training in intelligence."

"You mean spying?"

The Major chuckled and Henry felt embarrassed that he appeared so naive. His face reddened.

"No Henry, not like in the movies if that is what you are thinking. It is more like handling security mail, decoding messages, map drawing and things like that."

"I think that I would like that. I do have quite a fine hand you know."

"I have noticed how meticulous you are with your reports."

"Would I have to be taking risks? More than if I was just on active duty?"

"Yes, there would be times when you would be required to undertake reconnaissance missions which could take you right into enemy territory."

Henry felt a tingle of excitement. *That's the sort of thing I could really get into. I wonder how Mum and Connie would handle that.*

"Of course most of your duties would be top secret, not even your family would be able to be told. You could either go over to the Intelligence Corp full-time or you could be posted back to your own unit after you completed your training."

"I'm not sure if I could keep that sort of thing from my family."

"Well, you won't make it through training if you can't do that. Think about it and I will call you in again in a couple of days."

Henry walked slowly back to his post in the supply hut. How on earth was he going to decide? He thought he was going to solve all his problems but he came away from his chat with Major Coulthard with a bigger dilemma than he had before.

# CHAPTER 23

# A CHANGE OF DIRECTION

*BERLIN, GERMANY, MAY 4, 1941*

*"We know that a large share of this success is due to our Allies. In particular, the fight sustained for six months in the most difficult conditions and with the greatest sacrifices, which Italy waged against Greece. But I must also speak of the enemy who planned and started this fight. As a German and a soldier, I think it undignified to vilify a brave enemy; I think, however, that it is necessary to protect the truth from the bragging of a man who, as a soldier, is a wretched politician, and as a politician an equally wretched soldier. Mr. Churchill, who started this fight too, tries to say something here which, sooner or later, can be falsified into a success. I don't consider this honourable, but I find it understandable, coming from this man. If ever anyone else had experienced so many defeats as a politician and so many catastrophes as a soldier, he would not have retained his office for six months. Mr. Churchill can dupe his own countrymen in this way, but he cannot do away with the consequences of his defeat. A British Army of 60,000 or 70,000 men was landed in Greece, although before the catastrophe, this same man pretended that there were 240,000. The aim of this army was to attack Germany from the south, to inflict defeat on her and to terminate the war from here, just as in 1918."*

*EXTRACT FROM AN ADDRESS BY CHANCELLOR ADOLPH HITLER TO REICHSTAG.*

Henry was excited by his intelligence training; the map reading and drawing, code cracking, Morse code signalling, camouflage. He could now recognise the equipment and aircraft of different nations as well as basic commands in German and Italian. He was even getting some up-to-date information on what was happening on the war front; he hadn't had much news about the front line since arriving in Darwin except the propaganda stuff that was being fed to the nation through the local newspapers. Those in positions of power seemed to want to keep the lower ranked soldiers from finding out what was really going on. London was still suffering badly at the hands of the Luftwaffe and the British and Australian forces had been evacuated from Greece to Crete and Egypt. They don't seem to be handling the all-out German offensive in North Africa very well either.

He was troubled by not being able to give his mates this information. It also made letters home difficult. He didn't enjoy being secretive. It was toughest of all with Tom. They had always shared things. He stared at the charts and maps that were still hanging on the wall contemplating how he would now be able to really get involved in the logistics of this war. Excitement welled up inside him.

"Are you enjoying the training Henry?" Major Coulthard was right behind him.

Henry jumped to attention. "Sorry sir, you startled me." *No wonder he knows everything that goes on here.* "Yes, I love it but..."

"But? What's this about Henry? You did seem distracted when I came in."

"The British don't seem to be doing very well in Europe and North Africa."

"You have to keep a cool head when you receive information about what is happening on the front line. You need to learn to put everything into perspective."

"It worries me when things are going badly for us those at home are been given a rosier picture."

"Keeping our troops' morale up is one of our jobs Henry. We don't need anyone getting cold feet. Defeatist attitudes can sometimes be self-fulfilling."

"Well, I am troubled by not being able to tell my family what I am doing."

"You must realise that security is most important."

"Sir, we have always shared things in our family. I would also love to be able to tell Connie. It would impress her I'm sure."

"Thompson, I would hope you are not doing this because you think it will get you brownie points with others. You need to be really dedicated and believe in what you are doing or you may as well give up now."

Henry was quite taken back by this dressing down by the Major. He stiffened his back and looked him straight in the eye. "If it comes to a choice between my family and my job sir, I can assure you my duty will come first."

"I'm glad to hear that. It is the way it must be."

⚬⚬⚬

It had been an exhausting few weeks for Henry. He was now facing three days of exams. He hadn't done any formal exams since high school. How he wished he had been able to complete his education. His stomach was churning, his head was spinning and he thought at any minute he would pass out. The four others waiting for their exam paper were chattering away in anticipation but Henry couldn't bring himself to talk to anyone. He had made no mention of things to his mother and Connie. He had decided he would wait until he saw how he went in these exams. If he failed them badly, which he thought was very likely, he was not going to say anything to them at all. *There has never been a more defining moment in my life. Perhaps failing may be the best thing for me. That would save me from having to deceive Mum and Connie.*

Just as he thought he was going to have to get up and go outside so he could breathe properly, the door opened and Scrub marched in. He slammed the folder he was carrying down on the table in front of him.

119

"Well boys, this is your moment of truth. Don't be too over-awed by it all. You'll get another chance later on if you don't make it through this round."

*No way, I'm going to get this over with first go. I'm not going to go through this again.* Henry reached out to accept the paper handed to him by the Major and tried to put all else out of his mind.

"Good luck." The Major's voice was audible only to him. Henry's spirits lifted. He gave a hardly visible nod to the Major, followed by a cheeky grin, put his head down and started to read the paper.

⚜

*This has been the longest week in my life.* Henry was seated back in the exam room waiting for the appearance of Major Coulthard. The results of their exams were ready. At least now he would know where he was heading. It wouldn't be so bad going back to work with his mates again. He had missed them and it would certainly get him off the hook at home and with Connie.

"Well men, before I give you these results I want to make it quite clear to you that a failure at this point will not necessarily mean the end to your intelligence careers. You will be given another chance to re-sit in a few weeks time."

*Softening us up; if I don't find out soon, I think my head will explode.* The Major started reading:

Johnson: 2 passes, 2 failures.

Smith: 3 passes, 1 failure.

Jones: 1 Credit, 3 passes.

Allan: 2 credits, 2 passes.

Thompson: Well Henry, sorry for leaving you till last." *This is going to be really bad.*

"Thompson: 4 credits – congratulations. That's the best result I can remember from anyone in this course for some time. Well done." Henry was staring at the Major, almost in a trance.

120

*I'm dreaming. They must have got me mixed up with someone else.*

"Well aren't you going to say anything, Thompson?"

"I just don't know what to say sir. I thought I had failed."

"We are going to have to work on this lack of confidence you seem to have developed. You have no reason to doubt yourself."

Henry walked back to his tent with a smile on his face. Tom threw a bundle of letters at him as soon as he entered. "Plenty of mail for you today, Henry." On top was that familiar feminine hand-writing. His happy state evaporated almost immediately.

*How am I going to deal with Connie and Mum now?*

# CHAPTER 24

# CELEBRATION AND HIGH JINKS

Henry came rushing into the tent. He ducked under the tent flap and had to stop to catch his breath.

"Whoa there Henry. Are we about to be bombed or something?" Tom looked up quizzically. Henry took a few deep breaths and waited until his heart rate returned to normal.

"You know what Scrub tells us about rushing around the place. Better be important." Squibby chimed in.

"I've been promoted. Sergeant Henry Thompson at your service."

His mates rushed over and all tried to shake his hand at the same time. "Hey look fellows, it's probably not that big a deal. But it means a lot to me."

"What do you mean not a big deal? We're proud of you mate." Tom threw his arm around his best friend's shoulders and hugged him with such force that they lost their balance and tumbled around on the ground, laughing.

"Now you'll have no excuse for not coming into Darwin with us tonight to celebrate."

"You know what fellows – for once I am going to take you up on that."

"There's a new contingent of American service women in town and we need to check them out before the 5th divvy boys get to them!"

"Trust you to have a female in your sights Lofty."

Henry felt euphoric as he jumped into the back of the truck for the trip to town. A momentary pang of guilt flashed through his mind. *Hope Connie doesn't mind.*

He looked around the crowded bar. He was glad he came. *Wonder why Mum thinks people enjoying themselves like this could anger God in any way. Anyway she is not going to know.* There was so much noise that Henry could hardly hear the person next to him.

"Haven't seen much of you since you have been engaged in these top secret goings on of yours", yelled Lofty into Henry's ear.

"Will be that way for a few more weeks yet."

"Are you going to tell us what it is all about it?"

"Can't do, sorry. But you will find out some things soon; you will be involved."

"Stop talking in riddles Henry." Tom had more than a little annoyance in his voice.

"There is one thing I can tell you. I will be attached to Brigade Headquarters from now on but I will still be part of the 2/3 Pioneers."

Before anyone could answer, their attention turned to an American WAF as she passed close to their table. The tall brunette stopped and seemed to single Henry out for a long, lingering gaze.

"Looks like you might be going to get lucky Henry. Best follow her now or one of these other would be Romeos will cut you out." Squibby chuckled.

"Watch yourself Henry, you've already had too much to drink." Tom was always trying to steer his mate away from trouble.

"I think I could use a bit of female company. I can look after myself, you know." His voice was starting to slur. Henry lurched across the room to where the lady in question was leaning against the bar.

"Evening, pretty lady." Henry bowed elegantly. "Sergeant Henry Thompson at your service m'am. Can I buy you a drink?"

"Why certainly, sir. Tammy Whitegate is ma name and ar do like a man who knows what he wants. Please join me."

When the music began and couples started to join the dance-floor, Henry held out his hand to Tammy. *Better not let go, feeling a bit woozy. Must be the lack of air in here with this big crowd.*

He started to croon one of his favourite love songs into Tammy's ear. "My, my you are a romantic one aren't you Henry?" Tammy whispered. "I think you may have done this before". She pushed her ample body against his. Henry felt a surge of desire. He pulled her even closer. Connie was not in his thoughts at the moment.

Henry rolled over to avoid the light. He let out a groan and tried to focus on what had happened to make him feel like this. He remembered going into Darwin last night with the boys and that there was a girl involved. *What was her name? Did I even ask her? Oh my God, what have I done this time?*

He pulled his rough blanket back over his head. *Why do I get into these situations? Some intelligence officer; I can't remember what I have done from one day to the next. I am going to have to ask Tom. He wasn't happy with me last night. Perhaps I am carrying this secrecy thing too far. No, of course I'm not – he's going to have to get used to that, security comes before friendship. Hope Connie doesn't find out about this.*

"Well, how is our lover boy going this morning? Feeling unwell?" Henry sat up quickly and there looming in the opening, with a smirk on his face, was Reg.

"Go to hell, you bastard. You are the last person I want to talk to."

"Saw you having a very cosy time with that American WAF last night. Wonder what Connie would think of that?"

"If you breathe a word of this to her I won't be responsible for what I do to you, you rat-faced scum." Henry was shaking uncontrollably and if Tom hadn't appeared behind Reg at that moment he may have done something he would be sorry for. Tom shoved Reg out of the way and turned to Henry.

"Come on Henry I think you better go get something to eat. Don't waste your energy on this piece of garbage."

"You will be sorry you ever crossed swords with me Thompson, mark my words." Reg turned and glared at Henry before he strode away.

"He's going to ruin everything for me, Tom. Why does he always have to be around when things go wrong for me?" Henry choked back tears.

"Come on you'll feel better with something in your stomach."

"What did happen last night, Tom? Is there anything he can nail me for?"

"Well you certainly had a bit too much to drink and that sexy little WAF did come on very strongly. You attracted a great deal of attention."

"I don't think I can eat anything and I really don't want to face anybody after making such a fool of myself."

"Hey, don't stress yourself. You didn't leave with her. I brought you home and put you to bed."

"Thank goodness, but Reg will make a good story out of it I am sure."

"Maybe you should write to Connie and tell her before he does. He won't have so much over you then. Better start working on your excuses."

<hr>

Henry was on duty but things were particularly quiet so he decided to tackle those letters home. He had been putting it off. He was going to write to his mother and Connie. He had to tell them something to explain his promotion.

"Just tell them you are doing extra training in communications and that you have been promoted to Sergeant as a reward for showing a real flair for it." Major Coulthard had suggested. *He does have a way of putting things in perspective. If only I could be in his position one day. Then Connie would surely look at me in a different light.*

Henry sat there for a long time contemplating the Major's suggestion. In the end he decided that he would start with his mother. She would accept it without question he knew, because she would be able to crow about it at the church auxiliary meetings. He grabbed his pen and began to write.

*"Dear Mum,*

*Things have finally started to happen for me in the Army. I have been doing some extra training in communications and it seems I have a real flair for the work. We have had a few little tests."* *[Sounds better than exams – not so suspicious.]*

*"I have done really well in them. I have now been promoted to Sergeant. I do quite a few extra duties too, like paymaster and mail co-ordinator. It is quite satisfying work but I do miss mucking in with the boys."* *[That shouldn't alarm her too much. She will probably think I am taking less risk. No need to worry her about what it will mean once we are posted to a war zone.]*

*"I am really glad Anne is training to be a nurse. She will be very good at it. It is very satisfying to be in the service of your country in these uncertain times. It is good she won't be going overseas though. I hear it can get fairly rough in some of the areas where they are fighting."* *[No need to point out to her at this stage that Anne will certainly end up seeing some live action. That is where the nurses are desperately needed.]*

*"I am glad things are going along so well at home. I hope you are telling me everything. My ankle has recovered now and I seem to be over my bout of malaria. I have been warned the malaria will come back from time to time but it can be kept under control with the daily dose of Quinine that we are all having now. You can tell the boys that I am certainly not shooting anyone at the moment. You know how I hate that part of all this madness.*

*Your loving son, Henry."*

Writing to Connie was a much different proposition. Henry knew she would ask more questions as she was familiar with Army protocol. He made a number of starts at telling her about his night in Darwin.

*"The boys and I went into Darwin the other night to celebrate my promotion. We all had a bit too much to drink. I think I may have done a few silly things – you know what I am like when I drink." [No, that would make her suspicious. Sounds like I am making excuses for something that I don't know if I did or not.]*

*"The boys and I went into Darwin the other night to celebrate my promotion. We drank a lot. There were some American WAFs there and we had a few drinks and a couple of dances with them. They seemed very nice girls." [That wouldn't do! Almost admitting I did something with one of them. I think I will just take a chance and hope that Reg doesn't follow through on his threats. No point in owning up to something if she never finds out.]*

*"My dear Connie,*

*Thank you for your letter. I am glad you have met Anne. She is a compassionate girl and you two should get on well. I am a bit concerned about your comments about my family. I have contacted Mum and she tells me there is no problem. Are we all getting our wires crossed somewhere?*

*Things have finally started to happen for me in the Army. I have been doing some extra training in communications and it seems I have a real flair for the work. I have done really well in the exams. The work I am doing has involved my getting access to some high level communiqués so I can't really talk about that part of it. I also have a few extra duties as paymaster and mail orderly. They are not that much different to the duties I had at the quarry where I worked back home. I have been promoted to Sergeant. I get a bit of extra money to send home so that will ease the burden a little for them.*

*Thank you for the magazines and newspapers. I passed them on to the boys when I finished with them and they say thank you too. Sorry this letter is a bit short I have a lot of bookwork to catch up on. We had a large shipment of supplies come in today.*

*Your dear friend, Henry."*

# Chapter 25

# Friction on the Home Front

Henry loved receiving Connie's letters. But today was different. He looked at the envelope and her flowing handwriting, and lifted it to his face to take in its fragrance and wondered if this letter would signal the end of any chance he had with her.

*Well, I had better find out my fate. I shouldn't put it off. Face up to it Henry.*

He slowly slit the envelope open and withdrew the carefully folded sheets of paper. *Two pages this time – is that good or bad? I do like that perfume.*

"My Dear Henry," [*Well, that sounds a bit warmer. Maybe I was worried for nothing.*]

"Congratulations on your promotion. It must be very satisfying for you. I knew you had it in you." [*I love it when I impress her.*]

"I received a letter from Reg yesterday. I was a bit distressed about his account of your night in Darwin. Why didn't you tell me yourself? Did you have something to hide?" [*Bugger you Reg!*]

"If you are going to play around with overseas service women, wouldn't it be better for your career if you chose one with a bit of class rather than a trashy girl like that?" [*Trust Reg to play up the fact that Tammy (that was her name – so Tom told me) was obviously lacking in morals.*]

"I don't think I could commit myself to someone who was going *to lapse like that at the first opportunity." [Don't recall us actually talking about being committed. Not that I would mind. Not much chance of that now by the sound of things.]*

As he worked through his sorting, replied to several communiqués from Brigade Headquarters and ensured the day's stores requisitions were recorded correctly, he couldn't stop thinking about Connie's letter. What did she mean? Did she mean she had been committed to him and now she wasn't sure? Should he tell her that nothing really happened and that Reg was making mischief? He was still frowning when it came time for his break. He stood up and walked back towards his tent deep in thought. *I wonder what Mum would advise me to do. I never really talked about things like that with her. Maybe I should have.* He had an unread letter from his mother in his pocket. *I should read that now. It shouldn't be so hard to understand.*

*"My darling son Henry," [She's received my letter all right, she only calls me that when she is pleased with me!]*

*"Henry I was so pleased to hear you are doing so well in the Army. The ladies at the auxiliary were very impressed." [Knew that would happen.]*

*"You father is up to his old tricks again." [She never could bring herself to say it out loud. His father was an alcoholic!] "I think that low-bred woman down at Bryant's leads him astray. He says they are just friends but I think she would like it to be more than that. He seems to be coming home later every night." [It really is sad that Mum and Shirley can't be friends. Shirley does try to discourage him from drinking so much.]*

*"Now that you have a low risk job it might be easier to get some leave. It would be good to have you home for a while." [Low risk? Wonder what she would think if she knew the truth. I should try to get home soon but I would rather go to see Connie.]*

He still had time left in his break so he took up his pen and wrote.

*"Dear Mum*

*I wish you had told me before this that Dad had slipped into his old ways. I had a feeling you weren't telling me the truth. I think you are being a bit hasty with your assessment of Shirley. She seemed to be a nice lady and she is concerned about Dad's welfare. You could do worse than going to see her and enlist her help."* [*I know Mum won't do it but it might give her something to think about. No need for her to know that I had poured my heart out to Shirley before I joined the Army.*]

*"My new duties keep me very busy but I will have some leave due soon and I will try get home for a few days. It is a long way to come, so I would only be able to stay a day or so before I had to head back. Sorry this letter is a bit short but my work load seems to be increasing every day. I think we may be going to see some action soon."* [*Need to get her used to the idea of my going to a war zone.*]

*"Your loving son, Henry."* [*Well, if nothing else this new job gives me plenty of excuses for not writing.*]

⋅—⋅ ▣◆▣ ⋅—⋅

Henry was lying on his stretcher staring blankly at the pole along the top of their tent. He was having his first day of leave for some time. The rest of the boys had gone into Darwin for the weekend but he decided that he would stay in camp. He was still trying to answer Connie's letter. *I don't know what to say. Oh hell, what have I got to lose?* He rolled over and grabbed paper and pen.

*"My darling Connie,"* [*That should give her some idea of how I feel.*]

*"I am sorry you had to hear Reg's one-sided version of the Darwin incident. My memory is quite hazy. I had a lot to drink. Tom and the boys brought me back to camp and put me to bed.*

*They assured me that other than some rather provocative dancing, I didn't do anything that would have given you any cause for alarm. The tone of your letter surprised me as I wasn't aware that you thought of us as committed in that way." [Ok I have broken the ice. May as well go all the way now.]*

*"As you know I have been doing extra training in communications. I am attached to Brigade Headquarters now and am also involved in some important work. I am afraid I cannot give you any more detail than that. We will be posted to an active war zone before long." [Better not say any more than that or it won't get through the censor.]*

*"I have been thinking about my future often of late and you are very much a part of it. I was going to declare myself to you in Cowra but I thought you would probably reject me because of your attachment to Reg. I felt then that I was in love with you and that hasn't changed. I can't offer you any more than a promise that I will keep myself for you until after the war if that is what you want." [Hope this doesn't come as too much of a shock to her. ]*

*"All my love to the sweetest and most understanding girl in the world, Henry."*

That should leave her in no doubt about how I feel.

Henry placed the letter into the dispatch bag, locked and sealed it. He called in Romano, who had been assigned to help him with the copious quantities of mail that were flooding into the camp.

"Here Romano, get this over to transport before you knock off." *That will stop me having a change of heart.*

CHAPTER 26

# DECLARATION OF LOVE

Henry was sure a reply from Connie would come today but his day's work had ended and still no letter. It had never taken this long before. He felt sick. Perhaps he had misread her last letter. He had felt sure that she was inviting him to declare his feelings for her. *Maybe I should go into Darwin and drown my sorrows. Probably just as well anyway. I am not in a position to offer a woman any security for the future.* Romano came rushing in as Henry changed his clothes. He was going to try to catch the boys before they left.

"Serg, you are needed back in the Coms hut. A late batch of mail has just come in and some of the boys are quite anxious. The Major would like them to get theirs tonight." He was off duty and he could have easily made them wait until morning but he walked quickly down to the hut with Romano, trying not to let him see his own agitated state.

He didn't have to wait long. There was that delicate feminine hand addressed to him. He felt like running out of the hut and back to the privacy of his own tent immediately but the men were lined up waiting for their mail. He added a letter from his mother to his little heap. Finally he could rip Connie's letter open. *Come on, slow down. Can't change anything now.*

*"My darling Henry"* [Good start.]

*"I didn't think that Reg's version of that night in Darwin sounded*

133

*like you. I am beginning to wonder why I ever regarded him as a friend. I guess it was the carrot that he held out about being able to help my career."* [*How did I ever doubt her judgement?*]

*"We are a great pair aren't we? Why did we waste so much time in Cowra? I have felt from the moment I met you that you were going to be the one for me but I sensed reluctance from you to get involved. It is quite a relief for me to be able to say, I love you."*

Henry's wildest dreams were leaping off the paper in front of him. His heart was singing. He felt like running out into the camp and yelling to anyone who was around, "She loves me. She loves me."  *I can handle anything Reg can throw at me now. But is it wise to expect a girl wait for him, for who knows how long, to return from a war that was showing no sign of ending?* He decided to ignore the voice of caution in his head.

When he returned to his desk the next morning he saw the unopened letter from his mother. *Forgot that!*  He slowly opened it hoping that it didn't contain anything that would spoil his joyful state.

*"My darling son,*

*I'm so excited about the news that Anne gave me about the girl you met in Cowra. Why didn't you tell me about her. Anne says she is a lovely girl."* [*Well, well, I never thought she would be so excited about my falling in love with someone she had not chosen for me.*]

*"I always thought you would meet a nice pious girl and settle down. Anne tells me she plays the organ in the local Methodist church."* [*She would be impressed with that. I wonder how she will feel when she finds out how independent Connie is.*]

*"I guess this will now make you realise that taking risks is not what a man with responsibilities at home does. She sounds as*

*if she would be the sort of girl who would fit into family life in Murwillumbah very well. You should try to get out of the Army as soon as you can."*

*[So, that's what she's up to. She's going to use Connie to get me to settle down back on the Tweed. I'm not going to let that put me off. I'm going to write to Connie this very day and ask her to wait for me.]*

It was several days before he finally had time to sit down and write to her. *Things are really starting to heat up around here. I've never been so busy.*

*"My darling Connie,*

*You can't believe how relieved I was to receive your letter. I had convinced myself that I had misunderstood you. This Army mail service leaves a lot to be desired. I will have to remember not to jump to conclusions just because you haven't answered my letters.*

*This war is creating all sorts of problems with relationships. But I keep reminding myself that if it wasn't for this war I wouldn't have met you at all. I can't imagine my life without you. Anne has written to Mum and she is very excited about you. I am not sure that her reasoning is sound. She seems to think that you may in some way influence me not to go to a war-zone. I don't think she really understands the serious situation that exists in the world at the moment. I know that you understand as we talked about it in Cowra. I may not be able to right all the wrongs that are happening but I hope to be able to make some small contribution. It may mean that I have to take greater risks but I feel that if I don't try I will never be able to live with myself after the war is over. Those in control in this mad world must come to their senses and realise that war is not the answer.*

*I will do everything in my power to come back safely but you have to realise that this may not happen. I know I can rely on you to explain things to my family if this is the case. You have given me something to fight for. I want to make things better for our children. We will have plenty of those, won't we?" [Getting a bit cheeky now, but I know how she longs for children of her own.]*

*"Your devoted Henry."*

Henry and Tom were enjoying a cold beer. They hadn't seen much of each other in the last few weeks.

"Well Henry, it is nice for us to get some relaxation time together. I was beginning to think that our friendship was at an end now that you have all these secret duties."

"I'm sorry Tom. I know I have been a bit slack lately but I have been flat-out."

"Don't forget who your real friends are when the flag goes up as they say."

"I won't. And that will be quite soon as I am sure you realise."

"Yes and I do know there are things you can't tell us."

"I am glad you understand. I have some good news though."

"Not another promotion?"

"No, nothing to do with my career but it could affect it down the track."

"There you go, talking in riddles again. Let me have it."

"Connie and I have come to an agreement. She has told me that she loves me. Can you believe that?"

"What happened to that rat Wentworth? I thought they were all but engaged."

"Well, in a way he brought it to a head. He wrote to her and told her about that night in Darwin. His version anyway."

"And that brought out a declaration of love? I would have thought she would have been annoyed."

"She was, well and truly. So I wrote back to her pretending that I didn't think she really cared what I did in my spare time."

"That made her declare her love?"

"I did tell her that I had strong feelings for her and she finally admitted she cared about me too."

"Wow. You are one lucky bloke. Gives you a reason to fight. Someone to come home to."

"Could be some complications. I am going to be taking more risks when we are posted overseas but I look on it as chance to make things better for all those left at home. Make our future more secure."

"Very noble thoughts Henry. I just want to be around when Reg finds out about you and Connie! Will make my day."

"I just hope I am making the right decision Tom."

# CHAPTER 27

# DEFENCE OF LOVED ONES

Henry knew that something big was about to happen but he was ready for it. His new understanding with Connie had given him the confidence to deal with anything. He entered the Rec hut and looked around for Tom and his own group of friends. His enthusiasm died as soon as he saw Reg approaching.

"Well, well look who's here. It's the soldier who doesn't know how to fight. How is it going in that safe little office world of yours?" Henry felt briefly the urge to take a swing at that scornful face but he now knew this was not the way to handle such an annoying individual.

"Connie is very happy with the way things are going for me. We are as good as engaged you know." *That look on his face gives him away – he certainly didn't know. I think I may be finally getting the better of him.*

"Of course, if you don't mind being associated with women of such loose morals you should be satisfied. I don't think that there is much difference between her and that little American piece of trash you entertained in Darwin. Girls like that are all right to fool around with but you could never really consider settling down with them."

That was all it took for Henry to forget his resolution never to let Reg get to him again. He covered the short distance between them and landed the best right hook he had ever thrown. Reg dropped to the floor like one of the huge gum trees that they had been felling. Henry turned on his heel and strode out, knowing that there would be repercussions.

Henry took a long walk around the camp before going back to his quarters. He had so many things on his mind that he couldn't think straight. *I hope this doesn't affect things with Major Coulthard. We are getting on very well. I am bound to get another reprimand from Connie too.* He threw back the tent flap impatiently. Tom was lying on his bunk reading.

"Hey, what's the hurry? These magazines are great. Don't forget to thank Connie for me when you write."

"Gee Tom, I think I have done it again."

"What have you done? Can't you keep yourself under control?"

"Wentworth went too far this time. Called me a coward and then insulted Connie again. I got him a good one this time."

"I just saw Sergeant Cooper having an animated conversation with him outside the Rec hut. He was holding the side of his face."

"I told you I got him a good one."

"He certainly deserves it. But you mightn't have to worry this time."

"Why? I don't think the Major is going to be too happy with me."

"Well Reg certainly didn't look as though he was getting much sympathy from Serg. He marched off in a huff."

"I will just have to wait and see. Hopefully the Major will see it my way too."

⚜

Henry felt like a fugitive as he skulked around the camp making himself as inconspicuous as possible. He avoided any part of the camp where he could run into Major Coulthard. He knew he was only postponing things as there was no way that Reg would let him get away with it. Any day now they were going to be posted. Things were very tense around the camp.

"Well Henry, I thought I had better come here if I wanted to see you. You seem to be avoiding me. You and I need to talk."

Henry jumped to his feet. "Sorry sir, I didn't hear you come in. I have been quite busy the last few days. A lot of messages have been coming through."

"You are well aware what is going on. You realise that you can't tell anyone about the details yet. It's classified information."

"I do know that sir, and you can be sure that I will keep it confidential."

"I have no doubt of that Henry. Your credentials in that department are impeccable these days. There's only one aspect of your training that I am concerned about. You know what that is, don't you?"

"I guessed you would hear about the incident with Reg yesterday. I am sorry sir but sometimes that man just pushes me too far."

"I have his version of it but I have also spoken to Sergeant Cooper who overheard the whole thing. You were provoked but that still doesn't excuse your behaviour."

"I have not forgiven myself for letting go like that."

"You realise Henry, that if you are going to succeed in intelligence you are going to have to keep your emotions in check. Not just with the likes of Wentworth but when you are on assignments it will be necessary for your own safety."

"I will try to work on it sir."

"Glad to hear that."

Henry felt the Major was on the verge of divulging some important information when Romano walked in. "Why the glum looks? It's a great day outside. I'm beginning to get used to this place."

Major Coulthard glared at Romano. "Oops, sorry, I'm obviously interrupting something important. I'll come back later."

"It's ok Private. I am just leaving." He turned back to Henry. "Come and see me when you are off duty." He turned and strode out as abruptly as he had entered.

"What was that all about? Something is about to happen, isn't it?"

"Yes but I really can't tell you about it."

"I'll find out soon enough. Wouldn't mind getting involved in your sort or work one day Serg."

"Think carefully before you commit yourself Romano. There's more to it than just taking messages and sorting mail."

Henry and Romano worked their way quickly through the pile of mail.

"Ok that's it. You had better get that lot over to the men before they start banging the door down." Henry jumped up and headed for the door. He didn't want to keep the Major waiting any longer.

"Letters to and from home are very important. My mother starts to panic if she doesn't hear from me every week." Romano let out a long sigh and slowly pulled himself to his feet.

Henry was excited about going to a war zone but he felt it was also going to be an important time in his relationship with Connie. *I hope it is going to work out for all of us.*

The Major sat behind his desk staring at the large chart on the wall. He turned abruptly towards Henry as he barged through the door without knocking. There were pins of different colours and sizes all over the map. Henry couldn't help notice the cluster of them around the North Africa region, the Middle East as they had come to know it.

"Come in, sit down Henry. Before you fall over and injure yourself again."

"Sorry sir. I should have knocked. I have lot on my mind at the moment."

"We all do my boy, but just slow down a bit. We need to be cool and calm about all this."

"Shall do sir. I know how important all this is."

"Well, I guess you know what's about to happen, don't you."

"Our overseas deployment is about to come through isn't it?"

"The next couple of days will sort things out for us. I would like to be informed as soon as the news comes through. Even if it is the middle of the night."

"I'll certainly do that if I am on duty."

"You'll be on duty all right. You are not going to get a lot of sleep until this breaks."

"I'll be ready for it. The camp is buzzing with excitement. I think they all know something is in the air."

"I can't stress enough the need for secrecy on this. It will be highly classified information."

"Don't worry. I won't let you down."

"I know you won't Henry. You have become a very important member of our team."

He straightened his back and looked the Major straight in the eye.

"I am very proud to be involved at this level, sir. Just wish I could share the thrill with my family."

"That day will come Henry, when this is all over. Now go get some sleep, you are going to need it."

CHAPTER 28

# OVERSEAS DEPLOYMENT

*"My fellow Americans*
*The Navy Department of the United States has reported to me*
*that on the morning of September 4 the U. S. Destroyer GREER,*
*proceeding in full daylight toward Iceland, carrying American mail.*
*She was flying the American flag. Her identity as an American ship*
*was unmistakable. She was then and there attacked by a submarine.*
*Germany admits that it was a German submarine.*
*Five days ago another United States merchant ship, the STEEL*
*SEAFARER, was sunk by a German aircraft in the Red Sea 220*
*miles south of Suez. She was bound for an Egyptian port. Four of*
*the vessels sunk or attacked flew the American flag and were clearly*
*identifiable. Two of these ships were warships of the American Navy*
*The important truth is that these acts of international lawlessness*
*are a manifestation of a design which has been made clear to the*
*American people for a long time. It is the Nazi design to abolish the*
*freedom of the seas, and to acquire absolute control and domination*
*of the seas for themselves.*
*When you see a rattlesnake poised to strike you do not wait until he*
*has struck before you crush him.*
*These Nazi submarines and raiders are the rattlesnakes of the*
*Atlantic. They are a menace to the free pathways  of the high seas.*
*They are a challenge to our sovereignty. They hammer at our most*
*precious rights when they attack ships of the American flag-symbols*

*of our independence, our freedom, our very life.*
*The time for active defence is now.*

*Extract from radio address by Franklin Roosevelt*
*concerning the attack upon the destroyer GREER,*
*September 11, 1941*

Henry now worked in the communications hut full-time and messages were coming through at an alarming rate. He snatched a rest when he could on the camp stretcher in the corner. He was just about to open his latest letter from Connie when the familiar beep sounded.

Excitement rippled through his body. This was what they had been waiting for. He deciphered the message as quickly as he could, locked up and walked briskly to the Major's hut. He felt like running but he didn't want to alarm any of the men who may have been watching. Henry knocked softly on the door, hoping he could wake the Major without making too much noise. He need not have worried, the door opened immediately.

"Come in Henry." The Major quickly closed the door behind him and eagerly grabbed the paper from Henry's grasp. The light of the kerosene lamp flickered as the Major hurriedly skimmed through the pages.

"Well Henry, this is it. The Middle East. Rommel is trying to push his way through. We will certainly see action there."

"It is going to take all the forces that the Allies can muster to win this one, isn't it?"

"Yes, it sure will. It looks as though the United States is going to be joining the party soon. The Germans are getting a bit too aggressive towards their shipping."

"They have a bit of opposition in their own country to joining the war, don't they?"

"That should turn around very quickly if the Germans keep attacking their ships, especially the civilian ones."

"Will I be involved in the fighting sir?"

"Well, that depends on what we decide to do with you. We have big plans for you."

"Am I going to have a say in it?"

"We have two choices for you Henry; I want you to consider things carefully. One of them will put you in extreme danger. The other could be considered to be about as safe an active war job as you could have."

"That doesn't put me off. Let me have it up front sir. I need to know."

"If you stay attached to intelligence you will be in charge of the communications area. A very responsible job but essentially we would not be putting you in any danger as this aspect of our battle plan is too important to let it fall into enemy hands."

"That would probably make those I leave behind happy. Not sure if it would be my choice though. What's the other one?"

"You could stay attached to your own unit but be sent out on risky field missions. Reconnaissance, mapping, getting as much information about the enemy as you can."

"That sounds very exciting sir."

"There are risks but I think you may be very well suited to it. You have made an impression with your superior analysis and mapping skills. You have also shown that you can handle yourself in a crisis and make good decisions on the spur of the moment. You can have a few days to think about it if you like."

"I would like to know a bit more about what I will actually be doing in both roles sir, if that is possible?"

"We are having a full briefing at 0900 at Brigade HQ. You should be there. You can ask your questions then."

※◆※

Henry had managed a few hours sleep, read Connie's letter (a nice chatty one – no dramas this time) and even had time for a quick breakfast. He entered the front door of Brigade HQ. The officer behind the desk jumped up and ushered him over to the door of the large operations room.

"They are waiting for you – go straight in."

Henry looked around at the array of brass seated around the big conference table. He was startled by how many high ranking officers were present.  They all turned towards him and Henry stopped in his tracks. Major Coulthard moved over next to him.

"Come on Thompson. Don't be nervous, this is a big day for all of us."

He turned to the assembled hierarchy. "This is the bright young man I have been telling you about."

*They look like a line of magpies sitting on a fence.* The brass on their uniforms shone so brightly Henry almost reached up to cover his eyes. No-one seemed to be moving; they were staring unblinkingly at him as if waiting for him to turn and run (he did consider it.) Never in his wildest dreams had he ever thought he would be facing a line up like this. *Some of those insignias I have never seen before. They must be very serious brass.*

"P...p...pleased to meet you all."

The General at the end of the table stood up and offered his hand to Henry. "Pleased to meet you too Sergeant. I am General Blamey."

*Our Commander–in–Chief no less.*

The General proceeded to introduce Henry to the seated officers, one at a time. Henry could barely hear the names he was so over-awed and he was certainly never going to remember them all. There were several other Generals (fewer stars Henry noticed), a Brigadier, a Major General and at least four Colonels. Henry slipped into the offered seat about halfway down the side of the table with the lowest ranking officers.

"So you are going to do some Intelligence work for us, are you?"  A Colonel on his side of the table broke the ice; the one with the bald head and shoulders the size of a front rower.

"Well, I think so. I hope I am up to it."

"So do we, you will have a vital job to do whatever course you decide on." The Brigadier spoke with a voice like thunder from the other side of the table.

"Let's get down to business," Major Coulthard interrupted. "What Henry wants to know is what is entailed in each of the choices you are offering him."

"A full-time job in communications means a lot of written work and a good working knowledge of our radio network." The colonel with his glasses hanging off a long pointy nose examined Henry with piercing eyes.

"I've had almost three months doing that sir. I want to know what risks I will be taking."

"I hope you realise that war itself is a risk," huffed the Brigadier. "No Sunday school picnic outings available." *Don't think I would want to mess with him.*

"Henry knows what he has to do and he is capable of either job," said Major Coulthard coming to his rescue again.

General Blamey interrupted, "Look, the way I see it that the full-time intelligence job is one that can be done by a number of our trained officers but our field staff are specialised. Of course they take more risks but at the end of the day they are ones who contribute the most to our operations. Where do you think you stand in this Thompson?"

" I really want to make a difference in this crazy war. I want to do all I can to protect our way of life. "

"We don't need any statements of national fervour, we just need to know if you are up to the job. You can have 24 hours to think about it if you want to," said the General impatiently.

"Don't think I need it sir. I would like to try the field job. My family are not going to know about it anyway and I think this will be my best contribution. Besides I would like to stay near my mates."

"I am glad you think this way Sergeant. I think you will do an outstanding job."

Henry walked slowly back to his communication post. *I hope I have made the right decision.*

Henry had to keep the news of their deployment to himself for three days. He must have seemed very stand-offish to his mates as he tried to avoid any talk about the issue. The whole camp was buzzing with excitement. They knew something was imminent. It was especially hard for Henry to keep the news from Tom.

Henry lay awake thinking about Connie. He was scared of where he was headed but knew in his heart what he had to do. The early morning bugle sounded. He jumped up – he knew this was the day – the boys were going to be told.

A jovial air was flowing around the men as they assembled on the parade ground. Major Coulthard, in his full dress uniform entered the compound and a hush fell over the assembled men. Henry let out a big sigh of relief. It was quite audible in the eerie silence. Henry looked around in an embarrassed way but none of the men seemed to notice. They were all focussed on the Major. *Thank goodness I can now talk to my mates about what was in store for them.*

The Major strutted to the dais erected for this occasion looking every bit like the scrub turkey that he got his nickname from. He cleared his throat.

"Well boys, I guess you all know what this is about. It has finally happened. You have received your marching orders. Tomorrow we leave for Sydney, and then after 10 days leave we embark for an overseas posting. I am sorry that for security reasons I still can't tell you where you are actually going but I can tell you it will be quite a long sea journey on the illustrious Queen Mary."

A groan rippled through the assembled men. A voice from behind Henry could be clearly heard. "The bastards still aren't going to tell us where we are going. What are we supposed to tell our families?"

Scrub went on about being proud of his men and the sacrifice they were about to make for their country and the free world but his words were lost on the disgruntled men. Henry found it hard to concentrate on what the Major was saying through the muttering of voices around him.

Tom, who was standing next to Henry, whispered, "You know where we are going don't you?"

"Please don't ask me. You know I can't say anything. You won't find out until you are actually on the ship. Don't you think you should listen to what you are being told?" He nodded towards the front of the assembly.

Tom turned sulkily to Henry as they walked back to their tent to get organised for their departure the next day. "Are you going to be one of us or are you going to hang out with the brass?"

"I will be with you where the action is most of the time but I will also be assigned to other duties from time to time. That's all I can tell you."

"You know that bastard Reg has been spreading rumours that you are a coward and have only taken up these new duties because you are afraid to fight."

"I think he is still smarting from the fact that Connie has chosen me. I am not going to let him faze me. The only worry I have now is how much I am going to be able to tell her."

"Do you think it is fair to ask her to wait for you when you don't know when or if you will return?"

"That is something I am going to have to deal with before I leave. At least I am going to be able to see her before I go and have a serious talk about our future."

He still didn't know what he was going to say to Connie. *It is much easier to write something in a letter than it is to say it to her face. Is she still going to think she loves me enough to wait? Perhaps she is just enjoying the idea of having a man in the armed forces. My mates say there are some girls like that. A soldier boyfriend is more like a status symbol than a true love for them. Connie wouldn't be that dishonest with me.* It had been nine months since he saw her and they certainly weren't on intimate terms then. He had never even kissed her! He had dreamed of it often but it suddenly came home to him that he had never held her in his arms.

A letter wouldn't arrive before he did so he had sent a telegram. She had replied, she would be in Sydney at her sister's when he arrived. *How am I going to get through this?*

# CHAPTER 29

# BREACH OF SECURITY

"It's great that we are taking the northern route to Sydney isn't it Henry?"

"Yes Tom. We do need to see our families before we leave for the action." The troop train rumbled along through the dry brown countryside of western New South Wales.

"You are very excited about this overseas tour of duty aren't you?" Tom watched Henry squirm in his seat, unable to keep still.

"Well, aren't you? At last we are going to do what we have been trained for."

"Not sure I like the idea of being shot at with live bullets. Those blanks in training were scary enough."

"Don't worry, I hear that most of the fighting in the Middle East is long range stuff. The heavy artillery regiments will bear the brunt of it." As soon as the words were out of his mouth Henry realised what he had said. He broke out in a cold sweat. At least it was only Tom.

"So that's where we are going. Don't know why it had to be such a big secret."

"Please Tom, forget I said anything. I could be in big trouble if the brass finds out. Where we are headed needs to be kept under wraps or we could become sitting ducks."

"So they don't trust us. Can't see why you get all this information and not us."

"Look Tom as far as you and the others in our company are concerned

I am just one of you. I may be sent out on a few special jobs now and then but for most purposes I am just an ordinary soldier like you."

"How much are you going to tell Connie and your family?"

"Nothing at all.  No problem with Mum as she thinks I have a desk job and is happy about it. Connie is a different matter. She has grown up in military circles and knows the ropes."

Tom stood up to stretch his legs. He sat back down so abruptly that Henry was almost jolted off his seat.

"What's the problem?" Tom raised his eyebrows and gestured to the seat behind them. Henry slowly turned his head. *Bloody hell! Can't I ever get away from that bastard?*

The look of sheer glee on Reg's face told Henry that he had heard. Henry felt as if he had something caught in his throat. *That's going to be a problem for me. He won't keep it to himself. I will never make it in the intelligence game if I can't keep my mouth shut.*

⚬⚬⚬

It was a beautiful spring day in Casino and the townspeople had come out in force to greet their brave boys. The soldiers pushed and shoved each other at the windows as the train slowly pulled into the station. Most came from around this area so the crowd that awaited them on the platform was full of relatives. There was a brass band and children waving Australian flags. It was a picnic atmosphere. They were allowed to alight from the train but were not permitted to leave the station area. MPs took up positions at all the exits. *That brings us back to reality. Do they think someone is going to make a run for it? No picnic where we're going.*

Henry spotted his parents before they saw him. He was pushing his way through the crowd when he was grabbed by his arm. He swung around and there was Shirley. He looked around nervously hoping that his mother did not see them together.

"Henry, I was hoping to get a minute with you. We are all very proud of you."

"Shirley, how good to see you. Tom was right behind me but he must have got swallowed up in the crowd." *Damn, why should I care if Mum does see us.* He reached out and gave her a quick hug. Her grip tightened in response.

"I know you want to spend time with your Mum and Dad so I won't keep you. Your Dad is doing very well at the moment. Don't worry about him, I will keep an eye on him for you. Your mother is still giving him a hard time."

"That's never going to change. Thank you."

"Good luck and please return safely to us."

She slipped away into the crowd just as his mother came pushing through. Henry was relieved she did not seem to have seen Shirley's departing back.

"Oh Henry, my darling boy. It is so long since we have seen you. I have missed you so much." His mother enveloped him in her arms. Henry could not remember her doing that since he was a small child. *If only she had in recent times we may have saved a lot of arguments.*

"Well, my boy, all ready for the task ahead?" His father finally caught up with them and as Henry held out his hand to him he took hold of it in both of his own hands with such a firm grip that Henry winced a little. He felt tears welling in his eyes. *If things go wrong, this could be the last time I see them.*

"Where are the kids? I thought they would all want to be here to see their big brother off to war."

"Oh yes, they wanted to come all right but your mother thought it was best that only the two of us came. She didn't want them getting too upset."

"I would have liked to see them."

"I tried to tell her that but she wouldn't listen – that hasn't changed." Henry could see the old hurt still there in his father's eyes. He felt guilty.

His mother had missed this exchange as she was pushing her way through the crowd towards a rickety bench at the far end of the platform. She was now waving frantically at them. Henry and Arthur had no choice but join her.

"Henry, I can't tell you how happy I am to hear about your desk job. That will keep you out the firing line won't it?"

"For heaven's sake, Myrtle let the boy go and do what he feels he has to. There can be no guarantees, war is a dirty game."

"Yes Mum, I really can't tell what lies ahead but you can be sure I will not take unnecessary risks. I won't run away from the action if I have to fight though. We all have to do the best we can to bring this war to a satisfactory conclusion so we can all get on with a peaceful way of life."

"This girl, Connie, that Anne has told us about, she still part of your future plans?"

"Very much so, Mum. I am going to ask her to wait for me until the war is over."

"Good for you Henry - nothing like a little bit of soft flesh to dream of when the going gets tough."

"Don't be so vulgar Arthur. By all reports she is a good church-going girl and very suited to you Henry. She should make you a fine wife one day, before you leave even."

"I don't plan on getting that far ahead of things Mum. I don't think it is fair to marry and then take off into who knows what dangers. She may not even agree to wait."

The whistle sounded for the men to return to the train. Henry gave his mother another quick hug. He turned to his father. "Don't worry Dad, I will try to do you proud. If I don't make it back, you'll take care of everyone, won't you?"

"She'll be right lad, you just get over there and wipe the bastards out before they head this way."

Henry regained his seat on the train. He couldn't pick out his parents or Shirley in the crowd but he waved anyway. He closed his eyes and felt the train slowly gather speed. *Things are never going to be the same again. Please God, let it all turn out right in the end.*

For an hour or so the train seemed to be crawling. At one point, as it neared the top of the ridge after they had crossed the Hawkesbury, Henry thought they were going to start rolling backwards. Normally he enjoyed this beautiful country-side and marvelled at the engineering feat that had allowed a train to even move through this terrain. The huge cuttings that had been made through solid rock showed the different layers built up over centuries. All Henry could think of was getting to Sydney and Connie.

"Can't they speed it up a bit?"

"Won't be long now. You'll get there soon enough," said Tom from the seat beside him.

"What if she isn't there Tom? What am I going to do? I may not even get to see her before we leave."

"She will be there Henry. And if she isn't I am sure she will get there as soon as she can."

⋯ ⊱✦⊰ ⋯

Henry craned his neck to see if he could pick Connie out in the crowd at Central Station. There weren't many people there. *Where was she?* They were officially on leave now and did not have to report back to their barracks for ten days. Henry and Tom walked down the steps of the station into the street outside.

"What do you want to do?" asked Tom.

"I guess we will have to see if we can get a bus into the city and find our hostel. Not much point hanging around here." *I don't care what we do. I just want to curl up somewhere and lose myself.* A cab screeched to halt in front of their bus and out jumped two young ladies who appeared to be in a great hurry. Henry only gave them a cursory glance until Tom grabbed his arm and pulled him back down the stairs of the bus.

"Well, aren't you going to catch up with her." By the time Henry realised that it was Connie and her sister Dottie, the two young women were almost running up the stairs of the station.

"Connie, wait on," he yelled as he hurried towards them. He thrust his backpack at Tom and took off after them.

Connie and Henry stared at each other across the dingy tea room in Pitt St. "Like to show me around, Dottie?" Tom grabbed her hand and pulled her out onto the street.

"What was that all about?" Connie watched their disappearing backs.

"I guess Tom thought we needed a bit of privacy."

"I was surprised when I got your telegram. You hadn't told me anything like this was about to happen."

"Well, we weren't allowed to tell you anything. You realise that security issues come into it."

"When Dottie's husband Paul left for overseas, she knew weeks before. You haven't even told me where you are going."

"I'm afraid I can't tell you. There is a security black-out on that information until we actually embark."

"You mean you don't even know where you are going."

"Look, I don't think we should be even discussing this. I have to watch what I say these days."

"I can't really understand why you can't tell me at least a few details. Paul seems to tell Dottie everything. "

"Paul is not in the position I am in."

"So this is obviously to do with these security issues you keep referring to in your letters. Does being in communications mean you are privy to secret information?

"You have to understand that I can't divulge these things to you."

"Well, that's going to be a problem for me. I will never know where you are or what you are doing."

"You will have to trust me."

"I would have thought that the trust that exists between us now we are committed would mean you could at least tell me."

"That won't be possible. Our mail will be very closely censored and if you want to hear from me at all you will have to be content with no actual war details. Is that is going to be a problem for you?" said Henry, starting to sound annoyed.

"Yes it probably will, perhaps we should rethink this whole commitment thing. Leave it until you get back or something. If you get back that is." Connie turned her head angrily and looked down the street.

"Perhaps we should go find the others and decide what we are going to do tonight." Henry placed his hand over Connie's and gave it a squeeze. "Come on, let's not dwell on this too much. We only have a few days before I leave. Let's have some fun." Outwardly he looked to be taking the whole thing very casually but inside he was in turmoil. *How am I going to get around this?*

# CHAPTER 30

# DEMOTION

Henry was shown into the Major's office. He had never seen Scrub looking so serious. Henry stood to attention and saluted him. He could tell from the look on his face that this was not going to be pleasant. When he saw the official envelope handed to him by the doorman at their hostel last night he knew he was in trouble. He had no defence. *This may be the end of my intelligence career. Perhaps that may not be a bad thing. I could just go back to being an ordinary soldier. Connie would be happier. She didn't thaw out at all last night.*

"Thompson." *No friendly first name greeting. Not a good sign.*

"I think I know what this is about sir."

"Well at least you are starting to recognize when you break security now. Would you like to tell me your side of it?"

"Nothing to tell sir. In the excitement of the moment when we were travelling on the train, I let it slip that we were going to the Middle East. Only to Tom mind you, in a private conversation. It was not intentional. There will be no security problem with him."

"Didn't even occur to you that someone else may be listening?"

"Just my luck that it was that bastard Wentworth. He has it in for me you know."

"Perhaps it was just as well it was him. At least he knows enough about military protocol to know how dangerous such slips can be."

"Yes and how necessary it was to run to you with it."

"Now, Thompson. No need for nastiness. Sergeant Wentworth did the correct thing."

"I do regret the whole thing and I am being very careful now sir. Connie's not happy about it."

"That is something you are going to have to learn to live with if you are going to make a go of a career in intelligence. I have to discipline you this time. You will be demoted back to Corporal immediately. Any more indiscretions and I will have no option but to remove you from intelligence duties altogether. Dismissed."

Henry walked slowly out of Army Headquarters and wandered aimlessly around the surrounding streets. He had never been to this part of the city before and had no idea where he was. He stumbled on a bench in a little park and sat down. It was a clear spring day and the surrounding trees were starting to open their leaves like a new chapter was unfolding in their lives. *Just as it should have been for me. But now I have stuffed it up. Why do I always have to be so impulsive? Will I be able to hold myself together in a crisis?*

"'ello mate." A shabby old tramp sat silently beside Henry. "Gosh a bob or twosh forsh shomeone down on hish luck?"

Henry turned with a start to look at this sorry figure. "Gee, wish I did but I have just arrived from Darwin. Haven't been paid yet."

"Ish alrish. I should be helping yoush bloshes whash fighting for ush all. Wissh I could have enlishted. Toosh old and toosh late now."

"What happened in your life to bring you to this sorry state?"

"Welsh ish a long shtory mate. Jush take my advishe and donsh be afraid to take rishks when yoush have shomeshing offered, the safe way ish nosh alwashys the besht in the end." The old man pulled himself up off the bench and staggered away across the park. Henry thought of his own father and his alcohol problem. *Is this a message from God almighty himself?*

Henry closed his eyes and tried to focus on his own dilemma. The easy way out would be just to go back to being an ordinary soldier and follow orders. *No, I want to do something myself. I want to be the one remembered for making a difference.* He walked around for hours, thinking how he could overcome this setback to his career. He thought of his father. *Am I as weak as him? Will I be able to deal with the situations that are bound to occur in a war zone?*

When Henry finally arrived back at his lodgings he walked slowly up the stairs. The old presbytery building had been turned into a hostel, and with its peeling paint and shabby furnishings, made Henry feel determined to do something about his own future. *This would be the sort of place I would be condemned to for the rest of my life if I don't make a go of my Army career.*

"Where on earth have you been? I have been so worried about you. I thought you were with Connie but she called in here looking for you several hours ago." Henry stood with his shoulders slumped, unable to look Tom in the eye.

"I've been demoted."

"Why? Is there something you haven't told me?"

"No, it's all over that incident on the train."

"So Reg couldn't help himself."

"Of course he wouldn't miss the chance to get me into trouble."

"What are you going to do?  Are you going back into the trenches with us poor bastards now?"

"No, I'll have to watch myself though. I don't think I will get another chance."

"Don't get too serious about things. It is unhealthy for us to bottle up our emotions going into the strife that we are facing. We need to let off steam now and then. You would think the officers would understand that."

"I just know that I will not allow anything to come between me and my career from now on."

"Even Connie?"

"Yes, even Connie."

"The boys are going into the city tonight; I think you better come with us for a bit of relaxation. We aren't going to get much of that where we're going."

"I am going to see Connie and tell her the bad news. She is not going to be impressed so I will most likely join you later. I think I am going to need a drink after facing her with this."

⊷ ⊷⊱⊰⊶ ⊶

Houses and business premises whizzed by as the train rattled on. Henry usually loved train travel. Some of the oldest parts of Sydney were on the Canterbury–Bankstown line. Run-down and grimy factory buildings, federation style houses with peeling paint and untidy backyards, all crammed in to a limited space. Not much money around for maintenance in war time. But this time he wasn't interested. *How am I going to tell Connie about my demotion?* He alighted from the train at Canterbury station and walked slowly to Dottie's house. As he unlatched the rusty catch on the gate the front door opened and out rushed Dottie's four-year-old son Jerry.

" 'lo 'enry." He threw himself into Henry's arms. They had  met for the first time only days ago but already the young boy regarded him as some sort of hero.

"Come on Jerry." Dottie grabbed him by the arm. "Let Henry come inside, he wants to see Aunt Connie, not you." Jerry latched onto Henry's hand and pulled him towards the front entrance to the house.

"Come on 'enry . Mum says you better marry Aunt Connie soon or one of these Yanks in town will snap her up. They all keep chasing her."

Henry was saved from a reply by the appearance of Connie in the doorway. She was wearing his favourite blue dress which emphasised the fragile porcelain colour of her skin and enhanced her blue-green eyes. Desire coursed through his body. *How could a beauty like this give me a second glance?*

"I have been looking for you Henry. I called in at your hostel earlier today but no-one seemed to know where you were."

"Sorry about that. I had some business at HQ that I had to deal with."

160

"It's all right, you don't have to give me any details. I had a long talk to Paul last night and he has told me what an important part communications play in the war."

Henry opened his mouth to tell Connie that he might not be in intelligence much longer but he couldn't get the words out.

Connie kept talking quickly as if she had to get it all out before Henry could speak. "I understand why you can't tell anyone the details of what you are doing. I know that breaking security would put the lives of thousands of men in danger. Can you ever forgive me for being so insensitive?"

Connie held out her arms to Henry and he couldn't help drawing her gently towards him. *I will leave it a little while before I tell her my news. I am enjoying this too much.*

After dinner, they sat on the hard cushions of a faded horse-hair sofa in the lounge. It was a sparsely furnished room but to Henry it could have been heaven. Connie looked at Henry closely. "I know this special service thing will put you in more danger than most of the other soldiers, Henry but do you know what I would like?"

"No but don't say anything you might regret." *Hope she is not going to suggest that she join the Army too or something. She probably has more of what it takes than I have.*

"I would like us to get married before you leave for overseas. It will give me something to remember while I am waiting for you to return."

"Connie, please. That is out of the question. I wouldn't ever put you in that position not knowing if I will be coming home." Connie snuggled up closer to Henry and ran her hands up and down his thighs in such a provocative way that it was all Henry could do to stop himself from taking her then and there.

"Please Henry, you do want me, don't you?"

"If it is just a bit of fooling around that you want, we could go away somewhere for a few days. I still have five days left." Connie pulled herself abruptly away from Henry and he could see her back stiffen.

"I can't believe you would suggest that. What do you think I am? One of those loose women who follow soldiers around, excusing their behaviour by saying they are making them forget the danger that they are going into?"

"I'm sorry Connie, I certainly don't think that. All the more reason for us to leave the marriage business until after I return safely."

"I think it is time you left. Maybe you are right; rushing into anything in these uncertain times would be a big mistake."

# CHAPTER 31

# THE BRAWL

The servicemen's bar in the Oxford Hotel was decked out with bunting of all colours in a sort of party atmosphere. But it didn't conceal the shabbiness of the place. Army, navy and air force men from Australia and abroad packed the small public area. Henry looked around as he pushed his way into the crowd. *The Yanks are the noisiest, as usual.* He stopped in his tracks when he spotted another raucous group gathered in the corner. Reg was holding the floor as usual. Henry saw Tom and the boys over in the opposite corner and decided to take the long way round. He came up behind Tom from the other direction and tapped him on the shoulder.

"God damn it Henry. Did you have to creep up behind me like that? Look what I have done with my drink." He pointed to the darkening patch on his dress uniform.

"Sorry Tom, I just didn't want to go past that lot over there."

"Well, we have already had a bit of an altercation with them tonight. Reg was making rude remarks about your demotion. Made out it was because you are a coward. I had to pull Lofty away from him."

"Don't get involved in my fights Tom. It's not worth it."

"We are used to defending our own and we are not going to let a weasel like him get the better of us. How did it go with Connie?"

"As usual things didn't go as planned. She wants us to get married before we leave. Her offer took me by such a surprise that I ended up suggesting we have a few days away together instead."

"How did she handle that?"

"She threw me out."

Tom chuckled. "Always thought that girl had a bit of class. You are not going to let her get away are you?"

"I don't know how I am going to get back in her good books. I couldn't bring myself to tell her about my demotion."

"Look, I am going to have to go to the men's room  and try to clean this mess up. Want to come and give me a hand?"

"Sure, as long as we don't have to go that way," said Henry nodding towards Reg and his mates.

"Follow me." Tom led the way through the packed bar area, keeping as much distance between them and Reg's group as they could.

Henry was helping Tom swab the spilled drink off the front of his uniform when the door the swung open. They jumped apart abruptly.

"Well, well, well. What have we here?" Reg's smarmy voice rang out in Henry's ears. *What have I done to deserve this? Am I ever going to be free of this man?*  "A pair of nancies? I wonder what the delectable Connie will think of this."

Henry lunged at Reg and hit him on the nose with such force that blood immediately spurted all over them. The door opened again and in came the rest of Reg's followers. They grabbed Henry and pinned his arms behind his back. "Come on Reg, give it to him. He deserves what is coming this time."

Tom opened the door and yelled to the rest of his mates. Before long the room was filled with soldiers. They spilled out into the bar area and the place erupted into an all-in brawl.

Henry came to on the floor as he heard the loud shrill of the MPs' whistles. An open window caught his eye and he quickly squeezed himself though it into the back alley of the hotel. He mustered up what little energy he had left and ran as fast as he could. He didn't know where he was headed. He came to a seat under a big fig tree and guessed he must be in Hyde Park. He slumped down and tried to recall what had happened. He ran his hands gingerly over his body. He ached all over. *Someone has given me a good work-over, that's for sure. Who's going to believe I wasn't in the thick of things if I turn up in this state? Maybe I should just go to Dottie's place.* As he started to limp towards the railway station, a figure emerged from the darkness. He looked familiar. Henry racked his memory. It was the tramp of several days ago. He was carrying a sack in one hand and a brown paper bag in the other. Henry was about to turn and flee when he realised the old man's stagger did not appear to be a drunken stupor. As he reached Henry he fell flat on his face on the ground. Henry propped him up on the park bench and gently patted his face. The old tramp opened his eyes and squinted in the poorly lit park.

"Don't I know you from somewhere?" he said in a cultured voice, without slurring.

"Yes, we have met. Are you all right?"

"Well, I have felt better my good man. What brings you here at this hour of the night?"

"That doesn't matter. I think we need to get you some medical help."

"No-one will want to help someone like me at this hour."

"I know there is an all night mission around here somewhere. Can I help you there?"

"What a nice young man you are. It is a long time since anyone was concerned about my well-being."

It took Henry about half an hour to find the Methodist church mission he had visited with his father some years ago. His companion was semi-conscious and Henry was worn out from carrying, half dragging the obviously very ill man. He knocked on the front door and it was opened by a fresh-faced young man.

"What have we here?  Not Joe again. Drunk again I see."

"No I don't think so; I think he could be quite ill."

"Better bring him in then." Henry and the mission officer helped Joe into the warmth of the church hall. The young man pulled some blankets from a stack in the corner and carefully wrapped them around Joe. He settled him on one of the few bunk beds that remained unoccupied.

"We won't be able to get him any help until morning but he seems quite comfortable now." He held his hand out to Henry. "John's my name. You must be a caring sort of soldier. I thought most of you would be still down at the pub. I hear you ship out pretty soon."

"Turn the damn light off, we're trying to get some sleep in here." A cry came from the middle of the sleeping men.

John ushered Henry out to a small room at the back of the hall and carefully closed the door. "You look as though you have been through a bit yourself. Want to talk about it?" Henry hung his head in his hands. His body started to heave in convulsive sobs. John placed his arm gently around Henry's shoulders. "I think you better stay the night too. There's a spare bed in the store room that you can have if you like. We can talk in the morning."

Henry was woken the next morning by the sound of clatter from the kitchen next door. For a short while he wondered where the heck he was. He recalled the events of the previous evening and the old feeling of despair rolled over him. He carefully opened the door leading to the kitchen to find John and several young women hurriedly preparing breakfasts.

"Is there something I can do to help?" He felt guilty about taking up a bed last night that could have gone to someone in more need.

"Sure." John was as cheerful as ever. "Take these plates out to the hall. They start to get a bit impatient if we don't get their food to them early. Once they have slept it off they get very hungry."

Henry loaded one of the heavy metal trays with as many bowls as he could and pushed his way backwards through the swing doors. Seated at the long wooden table was an assortment of dishevelled men. They swung around to stare at Henry as he approached with the steaming porridge. "Come on there, we haven't got all day, you know." A grimy old man gave a raucous laugh and then lapsed into a coughing fit.

"Yeah, we need to get out there on the street to start our begging. Don't want to miss the rush hour." Another joined in with a cackle.

Henry saw Joe seated at the end of one of the tables, looking decidedly better than he did last night. As Henry approached, Joe reached out and placed a warm hand on his arm.

"Thank you for last night. I don't think I would have made it without you."

"You feeling ok today?"

"Well, still not quite right but John's getting a doctor friend to have a good look at me today. Hopefully it will be something they can fix."

After they finished serving the last of the breakfast Henry helped John clean up. The girls who had been helping earlier had left. They had families to look after, John told him. Henry was astounded that so many people were willing to help those less fortunate than themselves. They all probably had a family member serving overseas.

"Thank you for your help. Now do you want to talk about what is troubling you?"

"I don't want to involve you in my tawdry affairs."

"No matter how big our problems seem they are always easier to deal with if you talk to someone about them."

"We had a bit of a to-do in the city last night at the Oxford. "

"I heard about it. There's not much that goes on in this city at night that we don't hear about."

"I have my reasons for it not being known that I was there. It is very important for my future."

"That sounds quite ominous. These sort of brawls have become quite common with so many servicemen in town. The authorities tend to overlook them as long as the damage is not too great."

"My career could be on the line if my CO finds out I was there."

"How are you going to get away with it?

"I was only involved in the early stages and then I think I was unconscious for a while. When I came to it was in full swing, so I climbed out a washroom window and ended up here."

"Surely with such a small involvement you would be better off admitting being there and explaining how you left to avoid further trouble."

"You don't understand. There were some people there who would love to get me into trouble over my part in it. Some may even say I started it."

"I still think you would be better to face up to it. It will be worse for you if they find out about it later."

"I have been thinking that I should get someone to alibi me; say I was with them all night."

"Well don't ask me to do something like that."

"My girl might do it for me. I think I'll go see her before I report back to my lodgings"

Henry caught the early morning train to Canterbury. There were only two other people in the carriage – neither of whom acknowledged Henry's presence. Henry was happy about that. The noise of the heavy wheels thumping along on the metal tracks and the hiss of the steam from the engine were the only noises piercing the Sunday morning silence. Looking out through the dirty smoked covered windows he could make out a few people scurrying off to early morning church services. A couple of horse drawn trailers wended their way down the narrow streets. He had cleaned up at the mission but he still looked the worse for the wear. His uniform was crumpled and covered in bloody patches even though he had tried to sponge them off. One of his epaulettes had been ripped from his shoulder and was hanging by a thread. He hadn't removed his Sergeant's stripes but it looked as though Reg and his mates had tried to do it for him.

The train jolted to a stop before Henry realised it had reached his station. Looking around the now empty carriage he hesitated before he dragged himself up. As he stepped across the gap from train's steps to the platform a nagging doubt crept into his mind. *Should I risk all by bringing Connie into this or should I just go to Major Coulthard, confess and throw myself at his mercy?*

Connie looked very surprised when she opened the door to Henry's loud knock. She looked him up and down with contempt. "Well, what have you been up to? I hope you weren't present at that fracas at the

Oxford last night. We have just been hearing about it on the radio news. Most who were there were arrested and thrown in the brig."

"I was there earlier, but when the going got rough I decided to get out and climbed through the washroom window."

"Look at your uniform. Looks as though you did more than climb out a washroom window."

"Ripped my jacket on the frame and ended up cutting myself on a cracked pane of glass."

*My, I am getting good at thinking on the run.* The story flowed off his tongue like he had rehearsed it. *Maybe I have what it takes to be in intelligence after all. Just have to learn to keep my cool when I am telling untruths.*

"Are you sure you are telling the truth Henry? Those stripes of yours look as though they have been ripped off by someone."

"Must have got caught up when I tried to free my jacket. You know I wouldn't lie to you Connie."

"Aren't you worried that you may be caught up in the aftermath just by being there?"

"Well, yes and it will not look good on my record. Most of the guys there were so drunk they are not going to be able to be reliable witnesses."

"You had better do something about the state of your uniform before you report back or that will give you away."

"I was hoping you could help me there and I thought you might even be able to give me a bit of an alibi while you are at it. You could say I was here with you all night."

"Henry Thompson, I can't believe your hide. First of all you turn down my offer of marriage with an indecent proposal and now you want me to lie for you."

Henry's heart gave a bit of a jump. *Boy, do I have a lot to learn about the ways of women. I just can't seem to get it right. Oh well, may as well go all the way and totally stuff things up.*

"I thought that a woman who says she loves a man would do anything to get him out of trouble."

"Maybe if that man had showed some commitment to the woman she would. But that is hardly the case with us is it?"

Henry could feel the situation slipping away from him. He could see himself losing not only his career but Connie too. In desperation he took a deep breath reached out and pulled Connie into his arms and whispered in her ear. "I really do love you with all my heart. I was taken by surprise yesterday. I think you were right, we should get married before I leave." Henry felt Connie relax in his arms.

"You do, do you? Well I would need to be sure that you were going stop and think a bit more before you acted."

"Connie, if I knew you were here waiting for me when I return, I would be thinking about that every day and I certainly wouldn't risk that for anything."

"Oh Henry, you don't know how long I have dreamed of you saying those words. There is nothing I would like more." She pulled her head back from his shoulder. She reached up and the kiss she tenderly planted on his dry and grimy mouth told him everything he wanted to know. As she pulled away she looked longingly into his eyes.

"Of course you were with me all last night. We had just become engaged, hadn't we?" Henry melted under this seductive gaze. *Can't disappoint her now by telling her about my demotion. There will be plenty of time for that later. After I have really made her mine.*

# CHAPTER 32

# A Quick Fix

*It's my wedding day. Who would have thought?* Henry rolled over on the camp bed in Ted's little cottage and squinted into the bright sunlight that was streaming through the window. Connie's brother wanted to preserve as many of the traditional trappings of the marriage ritual as possible for his sister in these austere times. She didn't want to see Henry on their wedding day until she arrived at the altar.

*What a beautiful day. Please God let it all turn out right.* Henry was starting to feel excited at the thought of marriage to Connie but there was a cloud hanging over the day. He couldn't help worrying what Connie would say when she knew the truth. He hadn't reported to Ingleburn as he was supposed to yesterday. All leave was over and all personnel had been ordered to the Army Base to prepare for embarkation. He knew they would now be in lockdown and any absence without leave would be treated as desertion. He decided that going AWOL was still his best option. *I should be able to convince Major Coulthard that I had forgotten when I had to report back as I was so excited about getting married.* He was finding it easier to lie to cover himself.

Ted banged on his door. "Come on Henry, up you get. Connie would never forgive me if I didn't get you there on time." Ted burst into a loud rendition of "Get me to the Church on Time." Henry joined in and by the time they had danced their way down the hall to the kitchen he was starting to feel as he should on such a day. *To hell with what happens tomorrow!*

As Henry stood at the altar waiting for the appearance of Connie and Dottie he was feeling nervous. His guilt built up inside him. He and Ted were resplendent in their full dress uniforms. Henry's had been restored to its former glory by Connie's loving hands and still had his Sergeant's stripes. *I wonder if it is an offence to misrepresent myself like this.* The churning in his stomach increased.

He was staring blankly at the ornate carvings on the wall at the front of the little Methodist Church in Canterbury when he felt a gentle arm around his shoulder. "It will be ok lad." The kindly old minister, Reverend Smith, said in a soothing voice. "Everyone gets cold feet about now but it will work out in the end. God will watch over you." *If only he knew.*

The organ broke out in the bridal march and everyone turned to watch the girls in their slow procession down the aisle. Dottie led, dressed in lovely dusky pink linen frock and then followed Connie on the arm of her brother Ron. Her father had abandoned the family when Connie was a little girl and had never been seen to this day.

*She is a vision of loveliness. How had she managed to pull together such a lovely ensemble at such times when even everyday clothes were hard to come by?* Her simple frock was in Henry's favourite cornflower blue, its yoke decorated with delicate, hand-embroidered white daisies. The girls had hinted that they might have to settle for something from the church jumble sale but they had surpassed themselves. Henry knew he was marrying a very clever woman and now he was seeing just how resourceful she could be. As she glided down the aisle towards him Henry felt a surge of desire. All other thoughts were forced from his mind as he watched with pride this lovely young woman moving towards him. *I will never let her down. I will make her proud of me. Please Lord, don't let her regret this day.*

⚊⚊ ❈ ⚊⚊

Henry propped himself up and gazed at his wife sleeping peacefully beside him. He couldn't remember ever being this happy. Her newly suntanned skin glowed against the white pillow slip. *She has never looked more beautiful. My Brownie.* He had managed to book a room at a small Bondi hotel recommended by Ted. The curtains and the bedspreads were faded and the furniture in the room was pure church jumble sale material but everything was spotlessly clean. The view from the window of the rolling waves thundering onto the white sand was worth every penny of the rather inflated price that the feisty old owner had extracted from him. Henry decided to go down to the lobby to check if he could have breakfast delivered to their room.

As he reached the bottom of the ornate carved staircase the front doors of the hotel burst open and in marched two MPs. "Henry Thompson?" They confronted Henry. Before he could answer, the angry proprietor came charging over from behind the desk.

"What's going on? We don't have no criminals staying here."

"It's all right." Henry tried to placate the agitated man. "I'll sort this out." He turned to the MPs. "I know what it's all about. I was going to report in later today. I got married yesterday you know."

"Sorry mate, but we can't take that into account. We have been sent to round up all the AWOLs and we got a tip-off that we would find you here." *No mention of the brawl. What's going on? Must think of some excuse.*

"AWOL? I'm not AWOL. I'm not due back until tomorrow."

"Not according to our list. You should have been back 48 hours ago."

"Geez, I must have lost track of time in the excitement of getting married. I will report in immediately. Just give me time to go back upstairs and tell my darling wife."

"Sorry, can't do. You will have to come with us now. Can't let you out of our sight – you might do a runner on us. "

"Please, it is important. Can't you just trust me? I'm an honest man."

"Yeh, they all say that." The larger of the MPs grabbed Henry from behind and the other clasped on the hand-cuffs. They pulled Henry kicking and struggling out to the waiting jeep. Just as the door was about to close behind them Henry glimpsed Connie standing on the stairs, still dressed in her floating white nightie. *Damn, what is she going to think now?*

CHAPTER 33

# EMBARKATION

The paint on the ceiling was peeling and the cornices were mildewed above the wooden bunk at the Ingleburn military stockade. *How on earth has it come to this? Only a few weeks ago everything was rosy.* Henry gave out a big sigh and thumped his fist into the grimy pillow he was holding tightly to his chest. He rolled over to face the wall to shield his moment of weakness from the other prisoners. It wouldn't do to turn into a blubbering idiot in this sort of company. He would bear the brunt of their frustrations in no time at all. Just as Henry was almost choking in his efforts to hold back his tears, the cell door swung open and an abrupt voice called, "Thompson, front and centre. Visitor for you. Important one at that. Get a move on."

Henry jumped to his feet and hurriedly followed the MP as he pulled the door closed with a resounding clang.

"You look a bit young and naive to be in there with that lot. What happened? Did you get cold feet?" Henry was about to stutter a reply when the officer flung open the door of a small interview room. Henry felt a lump forming in his throat when he saw Major Coulthard waiting for him. He slowly lowered himself onto the chair the Major had pointed to without uttering a word, and tried to look him straight in the eye without flinching.

"Well Thompson, I really don't have to tell you how disappointed I am in you."

Henry felt a jolt in his chest as he realised that the easy going relationship he had cultivated with his commanding officer had disappeared. "I am sorry sir, I just seem to have the knack for finding new ways to stuff things up."

"I had big plans for you. I thought you had all the attributes to make a first class intelligence officer. You must realise that this is a major set-back in that plan."

"I don't know what made me do it sir. You know how infuriating that Reg can be. Sometimes I just can't help myself."

"What did Wentworth have to do with it? I thought you went AWOL to get married. You should have known that was unnecessary. You would have been given permission"

"That's not quite how it happened sir."

"How about you tell me just what happened."

"I know you will have heard about that fracas at the Oxford. I had a bit of an altercation with Reg in the men's room and don't remember much after that. I woke up on the floor to find the whole place in an uproar and I thought I had better get out. Was sure I would get the blame, so I went to Connie's place."

"Wait a minute, you were at the Oxford? First I have heard of it. Anyway we decided no further action would be taken as too many high profile officers were involved."

"You mean too many private school boys with connections?"

"Well, you know how it is with these boys with backgrounds, we can't be seen to be too harsh on them."

"Nothing has changed."

"No need to get narky about it. We agreed before that we would work around it. Anyway what has this all got to do with your going AWOL?"

"When I got to Connie's, she wouldn't give me an alibi as we weren't committed. So on the spur of the moment I asked her to marry me. After that things moved so quickly that I plain forgot that I was due at Ingleburn on Tuesday. It looks as though I made a wrong decision again, doesn't it?"

"That may be true but getting married is a drastic way of creating an alibi."

"Yes, especially when it looks as though I didn't even need it."

"You realise that going AWOL is a very serious offence and that you can't expect to get off without punishment."

"Yes sir, I do realise that but it is just that I am so committed to my intelligence career that I thought another lapse would be the end of it for me."

"Normally it would have been, but in view of the circumstances I will recommend that you just be temporarily suspended from those duties and that you be demoted to private.  Of course you will get no more leave before embarking.

"Can't I even get some time off to see Connie and explain?"

"No I'm sorry that is just not possible. Your hearing will not be until we are well under way on the high seas. It is just not permissible to release you in the meantime. You will have to rely on doing it by mail and even then you will have to be careful what you say. Your mail will be very heavily censored while you are in any way involved with intelligence. You will have to get used to that."

"Maybe it wasn't such a good idea to get married after all."

"We normally don't encourage it amongst our intelligence personnel serving overseas. Puts too much pressure on them when they have someone at home to worry about as well as their duties." The Major stood up abruptly and left the room, leaving Henry to contemplate the mess he had made of things.

***

It was only half an hour before the Queen Mary embarked for the Middle East. Henry had been transferred from the land-based stockade to the brig on the ship the night before.  Now here he was, standing next to the MP who had been allowed, after a special order from Major Coulthard, to escort him on deck for their departure. He hadn't been allowed to dress in his full military uniform and was clothed in rather drab prison fatigues. He didn't care —he needed to be where he could see the people crowding the dock. He was scanning the throng of people below. *How did this many people know that they were leaving today? It was supposed to be a secret* They were mostly women and children waving colourful flags with signs of encouragement and farewell. Henry hoped somehow Connie had heard about their departure and would be somewhere amongst the morale boosting crowd below.

Connie was nowhere to be seen. He was sure she would know that they were leaving. He felt she would be there to wave him off but it looked like he had totally misjudged this situation too. He was about to turn to his guard and ask to be escorted below as he didn't want to stand there any longer seeing the other men waving frantically to their loved ones. One more scan of the crowd and his scowl evaporated. There she was with a huge sign that read:

I LOVE YOU HENRY
PLEASE COME BACK
SAFELY TO ME.
CONNIE.

Henry waved frantically as he clambered to the highest point he could; the top of a pile of mooring ropes that were being slowly wound up in preparation for departure. The MP called urgently to him from below. "Thompson, get yourself back down here. If you fall from up there you will hold up everyone's departure."

Henry pretended he couldn't hear and tried to climb even higher – up onto the deck railing where he had to hold onto a stay rope that cut into his hand. He still couldn't be sure Connie could see him and he had nothing to wave at her. *She won't even recognise me in this clobber.*

He was still clinging to his high vantage point as the Queen Mary slowly pulled away from the dock. As the boat swung around to head seaward he could no longer see Connie or her sign but still maintained his position. His MP guard was becoming quite agitated below till eventually Henry lowered himself to the deck. The old feeling of helplessness overcame him; that familiar rock was forming in his stomach.

The MP grabbed hold of his arm and roughly dragged him towards the manhole that led to the brig. "If you pull a stunt like that again Thompson you won't get any more privileges even if you do have friends in high places." Henry meekly followed the angry guard. He didn't really care what happened now. He had one last glimpse of her. *Please God let her understand and don't let that be the last time I ever see her.*

# CHAPTER 34

# THE VOYAGE AND PUNISHMENT

*Q.M. DAILY*
*EDITOR: CPL. S.N. WILLMOTT.*
*EDITORIAL ADDRESS: H.Q. ORDERLY ROOM DECK AFT.*
*No. 3 WEDNESDAY NOV 5, 1941. PRICE 1D.*

Welcome to the "Queen Mary". You will find life on board not entirely devoid of pleasures. You may be travelling in much more crowded conditions than Her Majesty's peace-time passengers but you will find many activities which are intended to relieve the boredom of a long sea voyage. This daily newspaper will keep you well up to date with shipboard and international news. Functions of various kinds will be held in the various messes.

Meals are generally quite good (see sample menu below.)
Sunday, November 9, 1941.
W.O.'s & Sergeants.

DINNER
Creme Duchess
Fillets of Trumpeter, Menuniere
Roast Quarters of Lamb, Mint
   Sauce
Green Peas
Boiled and Roast Potatoes
Roast Sydney Duckling
Anglaise, Delaware Pudding
Ice Cream and Wafers

Henry looked around the small damp cell. He knew only the names of his three cellmates. Conversation was almost impossible. He had nothing in common with these men. He passed his time reading what newspapers and magazines he could get his hands on. He glanced scornfully at his companions. *Not much competition from them. Doubt that Mick can even read.* The smell of human excrement filtered up his nostrils even as he tried to hold his breath. The slops bucket was emptied each time it was used and every day their cell was scrubbed out with carbolic but this didn't seem to overcome the lingering offensive odour. *It must soon be time to go up on deck. Where the hell are those MPs? We are supposed to be taken up for 20 minutes each day.* He looked at the onboard newspaper that had been slipped under the cell door. At least his mates were having a better time than this. He had seen the prim and proper Englishmen who were the stewards. They dressed like they were still on a cruise ship rather than a troop carrier. *And look at what those damned officers are getting to eat! A bit better than the sausages with bread and butter; maybe some cheese and pickles; that we are being fed.*

⸻ ❖ ⸻

The Queen Mary was six days out of Sydney when it pulled into Fremantle. Henry heaved a sigh of relief as she dropped anchor 200 yards from the dock. They had encountered some heavy seas crossing the southern ocean and two of Henry's cell-mates had been violently sea-sick. The stink from this coupled with the other smells in their confined space had Henry on the verge of joining his companions in their frequent upheavals. To make things worse they had not had their daily promenade on the deck for two days due to the rough seas.

They were finally allowed on deck. Henry watched with interest at attempts to load supplies onto the rolling ship. The Western Australian contingent of troops, including Voluntary Aid Detachment nurses, who were trying to join the ship from launches, was continually thwarted by the winds and choppy seas.

"Get yourself a bloody row boat," came the ribald comment from the soldiers on deck.

"Here darlin', jump and I'll look after you," said a large Sergeant, leaning out over the railing towards the nursing contingent.

Finally from the bridge of the great ship, "Anchor the bloody thing and I'll come alongside you!"

Henry was finally called before the Military Tribunal two days out of Fremantle. It was a great relief for Henry to be escorted to the small state-room that served as a court. He had to duck his head to enter the door but once inside he was surprised how elegantly it was furnished. A mahogany desk surrounded by regal, padded chairs. On one side of the desk sat three officers. On the other side were two similar chairs, one of which was occupied by a younger looking officer who Henry found out was his appointed legal representative.

"Well, Corporal Thompson it looks as though you have been quite foolish on your last few days of leave." One of the serious looking officers broke the uneasy silence.

"Would you like to tell us your side of the story?"

Henry looked apprehensively at his lawyer. He didn't know what to say. He was out of his depth and didn't want to say anything that would contradict the story he had concocted for Major Coulthard. He didn't know what information was already before them.

The young officer put his hand on Henry's arm. "Don't look so worried, you will be treated fairly. Just explain how you came to be AWOL. We have Major Coulthard's testimonial on your behalf. We just need you to back that up in your own words."

Henry stood with his shoulders back and his head held high as he repeated his account just the way he had told the Major, playing up the excitement he felt at getting married and forgetting what day he had to report back. The Tribunal members listened, unmoved. Henry injected as much passion as he could into his words, even wiping a tear or two from his eyes as he went.

"You're lucky you have some high ranking officers vouching for you. Normally you wouldn't have even made it onto this ship after such an action. You would have been in the stockade for the rest of the war and then you would have been dishonourably discharged." The first of the seated officers glared at Henry over his horn-rimmed spectacles.

"I really do regret my actions sir. You can be assured that I have learnt my lesson and there will be no repeat."

"Well, apparently you have shown a great deal of promise in the intelligence area and heaven help us, we are going to need your services where we are going."

"You will be detained in the brig until we make landfall and then you will be provisionally re-instated to your position in intelligence, as a private of course. Any further misdemeanour will see you take no further part in any live action and you will be shipped home at the first opportunity." The most senior officer delivered the decision then stood up gathering the papers in front of him and looked at Henry with an air of derision that left him in no doubt that he was being dismissed. Henry turned around so quickly that he almost knocked over the elegant chair he had been standing behind.

As Henry was leaving the room the young officer leant towards him and whispered in his ear. "Well done, but just a word of warning. Someone has it in for you. That's how the MPs knew where to find you. They were tipped off." *Bloody Reg, I'll bet. Would Connie have told him where we were going for our honeymoon? I'll have to keep my eye on him.* In spite of this revelation, he felt a wave of relief as he was escorted back to his cell. *That was easier than I thought. I always have been able to spin a good yarn. Nothing will get in the way of my career from now on. Even Connie will come second.*

Henry was about to slump down on his hard bunk when the MP turned to him. "Just grab your things and come with me."

"I thought I was going to be confined until landfall."

"You will be, but in better accommodation than this. Orders from above. You sure have some friends in high places but I know better than to ask questions."

"I don't really know what this is about but anything will be better than there." He nodded at the confined space he had just left. He followed the MP to a small cabin.

"Here you are. Still not luxury but you will be on your own."

It looked like a converted storeroom. The bunk took up almost half the space but it had some sort of mattress on it which was going to be welcome. There was a small table and an uncomfortable looking chair in the corner. He even had a small porthole where he could get a glimpse of blue sky although every now and then a wave splashed up against it. He had moved upwards in the ship but still hadn't reached the level of the free soldiers. Henry turned to his escort to ask if he could be issued with some writing materials when a figure loomed in the doorway.

"It's ok Corporal, I'll take over now."

Henry was so surprised to see Major Coulthard that when he opened his mouth to thank the Major for intervening on his behalf it came out sounding a bit lame.

"Sir, I um um want to thank you for your um um help.'

"No need for thanks my boy. Besides, after you see what we have in store for you, you may not want to thank me."

"This is all a mystery to me sir. I thought I was going to have to prove myself before I was re-instated."

"That would normally be the case but we are going into such a precarious situation we are going to need you for some very important assignments almost immediately.

"That sounds pretty ominous."

"It is and you are going to need all the skills I know you have, and a few others that we have yet to teach you."

"I hope I am not going to let you down sir."

"So do I my boy, so do I. We have put you in here as we have some important documents that you will need to familiarise yourself with. You will probably have to spend the rest of this voyage reading."

"That should be better than the way I thought I was going to finish our journey, with that lot down there."

"Couldn't let you stay there. I can't emphasise enough the importance of some of these documents. Utmost secrecy needed."

"I will be able to write some letters home, won't I? "

"Sure, but you realise that you won't be able to mention any of this."

"Of course sir. You can rely on me. This is very important to me. I really do want to contribute something useful to this wretched world upheaval."

"Glad to hear that. I knew my instinct about you wasn't wrong." The Major left in his usual abrupt manner leaving Henry to ponder this turn of events. He was elated but at the same time afraid of what was coming. He hoped he could handle it. He resolved to write to Connie at the first available opportunity. What he was going to tell her he still needed to think about.

# CHAPTER 35

# APPROACHING THE WAR ZONE

*"We were in consultation all day yesterday with the French Government and we felt that the intensified action which the Germans were taking against Poland allowed no delay in making our own position clear. Accordingly, we decided to send to our Ambassador in Berlin instructions which he was to hand at 9 o'clock this morning to the German Foreign Secretary and which read as follows:*

*"Sir, In the communication which I had the honour to make to you on the 1st September, I informed you, on the instructions of His Majesty's Principal Secretary of State for Foreign Affairs, that unless the German Government were prepared to give His Majesty's Government in the United Kingdom satisfactory assurances that the German Government had suspended all aggressive action against Poland and were prepared promptly to withdraw their forces from Polish territory, His Majesty's Government in the United Kingdom would, without hesitation, fulfil their obligations to Poland. Although this communication was made more than twenty-four hours ago, no reply has been received but German attacks upon Poland have been continued and intensified. I have accordingly the honour to inform you that, unless not later than 11 a.m., British Summer Time, today 3rd September, satisfactory assurances to the above effect have been given by the German Government and have reached His Majesty's Government in*

*London, a state of war will exist between the two countries as from that hour."*

EXTRACT FROM A SPEECH BY THE BRITISH PRIME MINISTER NEVILLE CHAMBERLAIN IN THE HOUSE OF COMMONS ON SEPTEMBER 3, 1939.

Henry poured over the documents delivered daily to his new quarters. He was starting to realise what this war was all about – land and its resources. He hadn't realised how far the Germans and their allies would go to control as many countries as they could to impose their own agenda. The Germans and Italians were now forging their way deep into Northern Africa and Henry's battalion was going to join the allied forces that were trying to push them back. The struggle in the Middle East was important to the peace and prosperity of his country. His job was going to be pinpointing enemy positions. The allied troops were attempting to prevent the enemy from continuing their march through Africa to the Middle East and its oil rich lands. Controlling these resources would indeed give the winning country an expansion base that would reverberate through the whole world economy. Henry wondered about the morality of such policies but realised he couldn't express such thoughts until he was in a much higher position. Maybe this was the area in which he would one day be able to make a difference.

⚔

It was a bright clear day in the middle of the Indian Ocean. Henry looked out of his porthole and took great comfort from seeing the Queen Elizabeth and their escort ships in close proximity. He was still gazing at this majestic site when his MP arrived to escort him to his daily session on deck.

"You're early today Serg."

"The Major thought you might like some contact with your friends in A Company. They are having a bit of relaxation at the moment at the intercompany Boxing Championships."

"That's thoughtful of him. Things are getting a bit warm down here now we are approaching the equator. My shirt is permanently stuck to my back."

"Make the most of it. When we get closer to land you will probably be confined to your quarters. There's quite a bit of traffic out there now and it's not all friendly!"

"Yeah, I believe Sydney has left us to return to Fremantle."

"How did you know that? It was supposed to be hush-hush."

"I am privy to some classified stuff, you know."

"Actually I don't know. Just what you're all about is being kept quiet."

"Is it now? Well it's not for me to disclose anything."

They stepped onto the lower deck and Henry spotted Tom leaning up against the railing on one of the higher decks. Henry felt a surge of pleasure at seeing his old friend.

"Is it ok if I go up there? I can see one my mates."

"Sure. Just don't move out of my sight."

Henry bounded up the steps to the upper deck with such haste that he almost stumbled to the deck at Tom's feet. His friend looked so tanned and relaxed.

"Henry, what a relief to see you." He grabbed Henry with such force that he could hardly get his breath to answer him.

"Jeez, mate. Go easy on me. I'm not in as good a condition as you."

"Sorry. I can see that. You're all skin and bones. What the hell have they done to you? No-one will tell us anything." Tom held up his hand before Henry had time to speak. "Yes, I know, you can't tell us. But they had better start looking after you or some of us will have something to say about it."

"Thanks for the concern Tom. Maybe one day I will tell you all about it. I really miss being in the thick of it with you blokes. What do you all get up to out here on the ocean blue, other than acquiring a suntan?"

Tom chuckled. "Can be pretty boring at times but there are some amusing moments."

"Tell me about it. I have no idea what is going on up here."

"Well, we had a bit of a commotion the other day. The beer strike they are calling it."

"What? Did they cut your beer off?"

"No quite the opposite. We refused it."

"Was there something wrong with it?"

"No. Our thirst is so great out here in this stinking heat that we would drink almost anything."

"I can relate to that. Only I don't get any relief at all!  Come on tell me about it."

"They have set up these "wet canteens" but they are in completely unsuitable places on the ship and can only hold a few men at a time."

"That must have brought on a bit of a bun fight."

"They march us there platoon by platoon, at designated times. The blokes hate it! Drinking by numbers, they call it. So C Company initiated a strike! They were marched to the canteen and the stewards began to pour but the men refused to drink."

"Bet that didn't last long! "

"Eventually the heat and intense thirst won the day and a compromise was worked out."

"I would have loved to have been there. I would have drunk their beer for them. Haven't had one since we left Sydney."

"You really are being punished aren't you?"

"Things aren't that bad. Food has improved a bit of late."

"Ours is really good. The other day in the mess an orderly accidently poured tea into a soldier's meal.  A food fight erupted with rock cakes, sauce bottles and any uneaten food hurtling around the room."

"That must have been a sight to see. How did things get under control?"

"Major Coulthard was called to deal with the situation and received a slop bucket over his head for his trouble."

"How did he take that?"

"Well the sight of him, with tea leaves spitting from his mouth, surveying his ruined, freshly pressed dress uniform was enough for the whole mess to erupt in laughter, including stewards and fellow officers."

"I can picture the look on his face." Henry could hardly control his amusement and started to chuckle himself.

"The Major, with his usual ability to see an opportunity, pulled himself up to his full height, stuck out his chest in his best scrub fashion and bellowed, "Ok Men, a free beer all round if this place is cleaned up in 15 minutes." Of course there was a stampede to do just that and the fight ended harmlessly with no injuries or permanent damage."

By the time Henry returned to his quarters he was feeling refreshed even though he had a pang of regret after hearing these tales. He felt left out. *Why did I have to muck things up the way I did?* His guilt about marrying Connie in such haste resurfaced. *I really need to get in touch with her. I should give her a chance to opt out of our marriage.* They had only one night together and now he realised how selfish he had been committing to her without telling her the truth about his army duties. He swung his legs off his bunk, took the single step that was needed to get to his desk in the corner and took up his pen and started to write.

*"Dearest Connie,*

*I am so sorry that things ended the way they did in Sydney. I owe you an apology for not telling you the real reason that I was taken away on our wedding morning. I had overlooked the fact that I was due back at HQ the day before. I was actually picked up for being AWOL. The alibi that I had asked you to provide was unnecessary as there was no action going to be taken in relation to the brawl at the Oxford. There were too many high profile soldiers involved (including Reg Wentworth) so the brass decided to turn a blind eye.*

*I feel that I married you under false pretences. I am sure that we could have the whole thing annulled if you wish. It was not a smart thing for me to do when I was about to leave for a war zone, not knowing if I would even return. You need to get on with your life without having to worry about me and I need to be able to get on with my job without being concerned about you. I have spoken to Major Coulthard about it and he can organise it for us." [That doesn't sound convincing but it is the best I can do. It is going to break my heart to release her. I will never find another girl like her but it was not fair to ask her to wait when I am going to be taking such risks.]*

The need to get out there and do something about this stupid war was engulfing him. He didn't need to be distracted by anything else.

—+— ▬◆▬ —+—

As the convoy continued on its way across the Indian Ocean Henry felt he was quickly becoming an expert in Middle Eastern and North African culture and politics.  At his own insistence he was furnished with phrase books in the languages of the region, although he wondered what use this would be as he became aware of the number of different dialects each language possessed. By the middle of November they had reached Trincomalee, a naval base in Ceylon. There was no shore leave and all the troops were to see of the place was the view from the ship. Henry was enthralled by the beauty of the surrounds. Distant palm trees swayed in the breeze as gentle waves rolled onto the sand. This belied all that Henry knew of the history of the place and its bloody past, with the many years of battle between the Dutch and the British over sovereignty of this island colony. As Henry came on deck the ship was quickly surrounded by natives in outrigger canoes. The troops on deck, expecting the natives to dive for coins, started throwing pennies overboard. The jovial natives laughed and shook their heads pointing to the water and the word "shark" could be clearly understood. Henry was very disappointed to leave these shores. He would have enjoyed staying here.

—+— ▬◆▬ —+—

Henry was in deep thought about the documents he was still receiving each day. It was clear to him that the holiday atmosphere that had developed on the ship was about to end. The door of his little cabin was flung open and a breathless orderly thrust a sealed envelope at him.

"The Major wanted you to see this right away."

Henry waited until the door closed before he slit open the envelope. He let out a cry of anguish as he read the contents.

*MOST SECRET:*

*"SYDNEY" - 25$^{TH}$ November, 1941.*

*"SYDNEY" has been overdue on return to Fremantle from escort duty since P.M. 21$^{st}$ November, 1941 and has not replied to instructions from Naval Board to report her E.T.A.*

*The British Tanker "TROCAS", bound from Palembang to Fremantle, reported at 1700 yesterday she had picked up 25 German Naval men on a raft in position 24.06' S : 111.40' E (about 115 miles WNW of Carnarvon), and requested guards, which have been dispatched from Fremantle embarked in four of H.M.A Auxiliary vessels. Survivors stated they were from "COMORON" which had been sunk by a cruiser.*

*Air searches over the area are being carried out this morning to locate "SYDNEY" or boats. Two flying boats have been ordered to Fremantle from Port Moresby to carry out a search along "SYDNEY's" possible track tomorrow, Wednesday.*

*All British and Allied Merchant Vessels in the area, have been ordered to proceed to the above position to search for survivors.*

*Later news:*

*1030 Tuesday 25$^{th}$.*

*Aircraft sighted life boat in position 40' South of where raft was picked up.*

*THE ABOVE MUST BE KEPT MOST SECRET AS ENEMY ARE PROBABLY UNAWARE OF SITUATION.*

Henry broke out in a cold sweat. *Holy shit, she only left our convoy a few days ago.* On the bottom of the document scrawled in Major Coulthard's bold hand was a message to Henry.

"Know this will distress you Henry. By now you must be starting to realise what a dangerous game we are about enter."

*I've got to keep my cool. This is for real. Connie please forgive me if I cause you any grief.*

As the ship approached Aden and the Red Sea, liquor was banned and a strange silence crept over the ship and its occupants. Everyone was aware they were approaching the real action of the war. Henry was on deck when land was sighted. A barren pyramid like formation, swathed in a mysterious light, rose out of the mist. It was the natural port of Aden that had formed in the crater of an extinct volcano. The troops were in a constant state of readiness as air raids were now a possibility.

The Queen Mary slipped quietly into the Red Sea under the cover of dark after bidding a silent farewell to her travelling companion, the Queen Elizabeth. Before daylight Henry was awakened by the sound of an approaching aircraft. His door opened silently and the duty officer motioned him to follow. He was taken to the bridge where Major Coulthard and several other officers were gathered.

"Come and tell us who owns this one." The Major pointed in the direction of flares being dropped by the approaching plane.

"Can't see much in this light but I would say it is probably hostile the way it is approaching. Seems to be looking for something. Probably us."

"We are under orders not to fire unless under direct attack," said the Major.

"If we can get out of its direct path it probably won't see us," said Henry.

The Captain had already started to wheel the huge ship back along her own track. The next flare landed right where she would have been if she continued on course. The plane passed harmlessly off into the gathering light.

"Well done Henry. You read that well."

"Didn': really add much sir, the Captain had already started to alter course."

"Still, I like the way you deal with these things, my boy. You will be an asset to us when we get to the real game."

A shiver went down Henry's spine as he contemplated what was ahead but he was uplifted by the way the Major had slipped back into calling him by his first name.  He felt he was well on the way to overcoming the setback following his actions in Sydney.

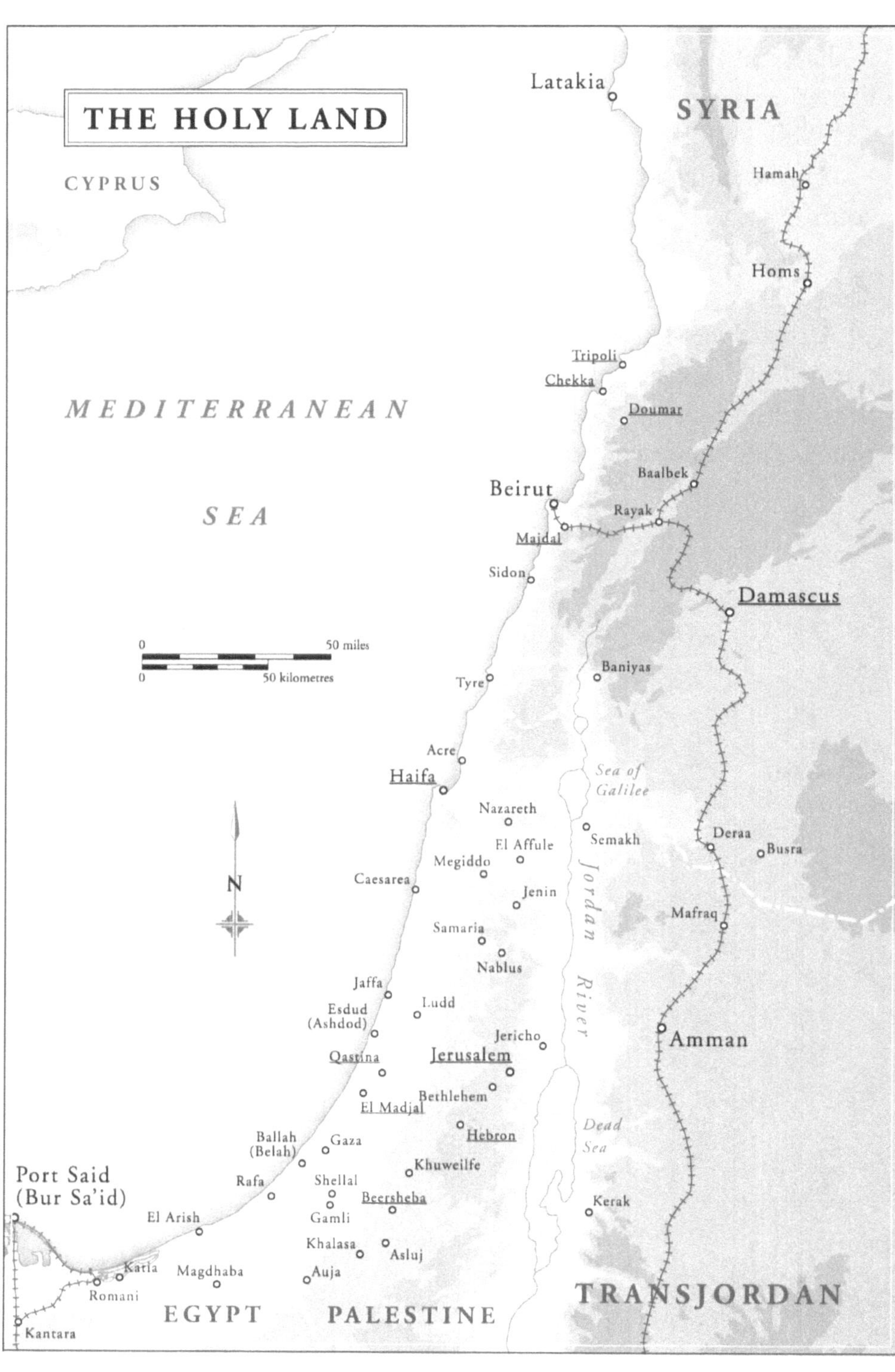

THE HOLY LAND
CYPRUS
MEDITERRANEAN
SEA
Latakia
SYRIA
Hamah
Homs
Tripoli
Chekka
Doumar
Baalbek
Beirut
Rayak
Majdal
Sidon
Damascus
Baniyas
Tyre
Sea of
Galilee
Acre
Haifa
Nazareth
Semakh
Deraa
Busra
El Affule
Megiddo
Caesarea
Jenin
Mafraq
Samaria
Nablus
Jordan River
Jaffa
Ludd
Esdud
(Ashdod)
Jericho
Qastina
Jerusalem
Amman
Bethlehem
El Madjal
Hebron
Dead
Sea
Ballah
(Belah)
Gaza
Khuweilfe
Port Said
(Bur Sa'id)
Rafa
Shellal
Beersheba
Kerak
El Arish
Gamli
Khalasa
Asluj
Katia
Magdhaba
Auja
Romani
EGYPT
PALESTINE
TRANSJORDAN
Kantara
0          50 miles
0          50 kilometres
N

# CHAPTER 36

# THE HOLY LAND

It had been a stealthy but uneventful journey from the Port of Tewfik at the top of the Red Sea to their camp at Qastina. They had disembarked from the Queen Mary, crossed the Suez Canal by punt under the cover of darkness and boarded an overloaded train, with dirty grey carriages and no glass in the windows, for the journey to El Madjal. By the time they had completed their journey by truck, Henry's euphoria about setting foot in the Holy Land for the first time had almost erased his memories of the discomfort and apprehension on the boat. He was in a war zone for the first time.

In the cold the Pioneers had stuck with the task of erecting tents and weatherboard huts, one of which he was now occupying. It made him feel proud. Conditions were abysmal and the camp had turned into a quagmire from the unrelenting rain but the troops were now housed in light and dry tents on the side of a hill. The huts that were being used by the officers and administration staff were shielded from the cold Palestinian winds by four-foot high mud walls. The slit trenches dug in case of air-raids had filled with water and the approaches to the tents and cook houses were virtually impassable. Snow had appeared on the surrounding Hebron Hills and training was continually disrupted.

In spite of all these difficulties life was fairly quiet and uneventful. Henry had been released from detention as soon as they arrived in camp. There didn't seem any point in keeping him under guard when there was no way he could escape. He had been assigned to the communications hut to keep watch for incoming messages but nothing much was happening. The prevailing feeling amongst the troops was that the war in the Middle East had been all but won by the Allies. Two days after their arrival at Qastina their first lot of mail arrived but there was none for Henry. He felt deflated at the waiting and the lack of information getting through to the Pioneers.

Henry was on the verandah of the communications hut surveying his surroundings, digesting a hearty lunch. *Nothing much seems to happen around here. Don't know what they are doing with us. The men are not going to put up with this much longer.* A commotion at the bottom of the camp made him sit up quickly. A jeep had sped into the compound and soldiers were spilling out waving what looked like a newspaper. Henry slipped rather than ran down the steep, muddy slope.

"What's happened? Where have you blokes been? What's all the fuss about?"

"We've just come back from leave in Jerusalem. The bloody Japs have bombed Pearl Harbour." A breathless private from C Company spat out the words as Henry snatched the newspaper from his hand.

"Let me see that."

*THE PALESTINE POST*
*Monday, Vol. XV11 No. 4787*
*December 8, 1941 Price: 10 Mils.*

# Japan makes war on America!
## Air attacks on Pearl Harbour and Manila!
### U.S. to Declare War Today Following Tokyo Declaration Against America and Britain.

President Roosevelt is expected to ask Congress today (Monday) for a
declaration of war. This message from Washington received at 3 a.m.
this morning (Palestine Time) followed close on the heels of a White
House report that Imperial Headquarters in Tokyo had announced that
Japan entered into a state of war with the United States and Britain
in the

Western Pacific as from Sunday.

The first news that came through reported Japanese attacks on
American naval bases in Hawaii and the Philippines and on American
shipping in the Pacific. Four hours later cables named Pearl Harbour and
Manila. These announcements came as a climax to series of cables
flashed by Reuters from America and the Far East which began
arriving some four hours earlier.

"Jesus Christ! It's going to be on for one and all now." Henry flung
the newspaper back at the startled soldier and took off back up the
hill to his hut. *Why did I have to hear about this from a bloody wog
newspaper?* He continued up the hill to HQ and pushed open the
door.

"Don't you know how to knock?" Major Coulthard looked up from
a pile of papers in front of him.

"Sorry sir, but why wasn't I told about the Pearl Harbour attack?
Nothing has come through on the radio."

"Have only just found out about it myself. Not much information
out yet."

"This could change the whole course of the war."

"Yes Henry, but we need to keep our eye on the job at hand. We have
only just arrived here."

"The men are becoming restless already. The buzz around camp is
that we are not needed here and will be headed home soon."

"We are going to be needed soon enough. Rommel is starting to get
on top of the British and we will be on the move sooner than you think."

"No-one will be happy over here fighting for the British if there is any
chance their families at home are in danger."

"The threat to Australian soil is becoming very real Henry, but what is happening here is important to Australia too. We are going to need to keep on the right side of our stronger allies. God knows we are going to need their help if our country is invaded. You better get back to your post. I expect things will start to come through pretty quickly after this."  With a heavy heart Henry dragged himself back down to the communications hut. *Geez, I wish I could get some news from home. This will really be increasing the stress on everyone. Please God, keep Connie safe until this cursed war is over.*

Christmas was upon them and the continuing wet and freezing conditions made things most unpleasant for the troops. Hampers were received from home but most of the holiday season was spent re-erecting tents that had been blown down in the gale force winds. Those who were lucky enough to reach the mess tent from the cookhouse on the slippery ground without losing their whole dinner in the mud enjoyed a masterpiece of army cooking in the circumstances. On Boxing Day Henry was disturbed in his hut by yelling coming from the row of tents below. He jumped up and when his feet hit the mud as he leapt from his hut to the sloppy ground below, they flew from under him and he slid down the hill on his rear end.

"Jesus Henry what the hell are you doing?" Tom yelled at him as he torpedoed into the side of the tent that he and Squibby were trying to stop collapsing under the strain of the icy winds.

"Just trying to see if I can help." Henry yelled over the howling wind as he took the tent and the other two men down the side of the slope with him. They all collapsed into a wet muddy heap and Tom burst into a rendition of "T'is the season to be jolly".  Soon, all the men in the near vicinity had joined them and were all singing at the top of their voices oblivious to their wet and muddy surroundings.

"Thompson!!! On your feet. I need to talk to you." Major Coulthard was standing over the squirming mass of wet muddy soldiers who were now scrambling to their feet. Henry made several attempts before he was standing somewhat unsteadily before the Major.

"Sorry sir, just giving the boys a hand to re-erect this tent."

"As soon as you are cleaned up present yourself to my quarters. We have a war going on you know." The glint in his eye and half smile told Henry that he saw the funny side of things too.

It took Henry almost half an hour to get cleaned up. The shortage of fuel for hot water meant he had to try to remove the mud with icy cold water in a bucket left outside the hut in case of fire. Quite ironic really, as they never got any fuel to light one! He dressed in the still damp clothes that he had been trying to dry over the back of his chair and slowly navigated the slippery slope up to the Major's hut.

"Sorry about that little ruckus sir, these conditions are starting to get to us all."

"Yes Thompson I know but we just have to make the best of things. We may be out of here soon anyway."

"The men still think we are going home."

"Well, let them think that if it helps to keep their morale up. They will need it where we will be heading."

"They are worried about their loved ones and would rather be defending them than fighting on foreign soil so far from home."

"As I think I have told you before, what is happening here is important too."

"I wish we could get on with it then. We don't seem to be doing anything."

"That's what I want to talk to you about. I have a little job I'd like you to do."

"But I'm still under suspension aren't I?"

"I've been talking to HQ about you and they have agreed that we need your full active services so you are being restored to your former position in intelligence and if it works out you will have your Sergeant's ranking restored too."

"That is good news. I meant it when I said my career is my sole purpose in life now."

"What about that wife of yours?"

"I have written to her to offer an annulment but I haven't heard from her yet. What's this job you have for me?"

"There's a bridge down near Beersheba that has been washed away. It's a very important supply route for us and C Coy has been called on to restore it. "

"How do I come into that? I'm still attached to A Coy aren't I?"

"Yes but I would like you to go along on this one and see what you can find out about the allegiances of the locals. They seem to be on our side but I never feel like we can trust these Arabs."

"I have noticed that some of our stores seem to be disappearing much quicker than we are using them."

"I want you to take that over too. You did a good job in Darwin and it will give you an excuse to check up on the movement of things around camp and beyond."

"When do I start?"

"First thing in the morning, so you better try to get a good night's sleep. I'll even sign for a bit of fuel for you tonight to warm those frozen bones of yours after today's escapade." Henry didn't normally like taking privileges that the other men didn't get but in this case he was only too happy to accept.

⚊⚌✦⚌⚊

Henry was on board the bus with its kamikaze Arab driver, hurtling down the road to Beersheba before sunrise, when it came to a screeching halt in front of a War Cemetery with a Rising Sun insignia. Their driver, in careful broken English (obviously rehearsed), informed them that this was where the men from the World War 1 Light Horse Regiment who took part in the famous charge, were buried. Included in the dead was pre-war great Australian fast bowler Tibby Cotter.

"It was reputed to be the last great cavalry charge of modern warfare." A voice from the back of the bus piped up. Henry felt a shiver go up his spine as he reverently bowed his head in honour of such brave men. He was not tempted to purchase the hastily produced tattered postcards proffered by the driver.

As C Coy set to work, Henry strolled over to the group of Arab on-lookers who followed everywhere the soldiers went. A group of boys laden with baskets of oranges pushed forward to offer their produce to Henry.

"Wanna oranges boss?" Henry pulled out his pockets to indicate he had no money and shook his head. The oldest boy pointed to Henry's rifle, obviously wanting to exchange it for some of the delicious looking fruit. They looked so good he was almost tempted to agree when he saw an adult member of the group, who was holding back behind the orange boys, hastily pull what looked like an Australian Army issue rifle back under his robes. A quick look around told Henry that he was hopelessly outnumbered and he decided to take no action other than giving the offending Arab a steely look.

Henry spent the rest of the day carefully scrutinising the Arab onlookers but he noticed no more hidden weapons. At the end of the day's toil the workers were treated to a steaming mug of strong, sweet Arab tea made by heavily robed women. It was a welcome antidote for aching limbs and numb icy feet before the hair-raising bus trip back to camp. One soldier chided the driver for his erratic driving and he promptly took both hands off the wheel and cheerfully replied "Me no drive. Allah drive." Silence ensured for the rest of the trip back to camp!

Henry wasted no time reporting back to the Major. "Most of the Arabs seem friendly enough; especially the women and children, but there were a few untrustworthy looking older men with what appeared to be Army issue rifles."

"We have suspected for some time that rifles, which were being reported as disappearing from tents when unattended, were being traded by our own men for other favours in the villages. We will have to step up our pickets until we get to the bottom of it."

"Maybe the guards can search everyone leaving camp."

"We'll be out of here soon anyway."

"Rumour has it that the 7th division is going to Malaya and that we are going with them."

"No Henry, we will be attached to the 9th division from now on and will heading closer to the action in North Africa. Rommel is proving harder to control than we anticipated."

# Chapter 37

# The Move to Syria

On January 21st, 1942 Henry received the order from Middle East HQ that the 2/3rd Pioneers were to ready themselves to move. He hurried to the Major's quarters as quickly as he could on the slippery and waterlogged ground.

"Ok Henry, this is it. Full marching orders but remember no talk on where we are headed; we still can't trust these Arabs."

"Sure thing sir. I'm very careful of my tongue these days."

"Glad to hear that."

Henry hurried down to the men's quarters with the orders. "So you're back giving the orders, are you?" said Reg, sneering at him.

"Just get on with it Wentworth or I will put you on report."

"You may have got your job back country boy but you still don't outrank me."

"Well, get this lot going; we ship out at 0600 tomorrow morning. Full marching orders."

"Aren't you going to tell us where we are headed? I hear we are going home. Will we be using the Queen again? That should be welcome after this hellhole."

"You had better get used to tougher conditions than this." Henry heard the groan from the men as he walked quickly away. Full marching orders meant each man had to carry four blankets, ground sheet, water bottle, rifle, haversack with emergency rations and all personal gear in their kit bags.

After a rough truck ride into Majdal, fourteen men to a truck, they were crammed into a bumpy train for the journey to Haifa. That was the good part of the trip! After Haifa they were herded onto another train with box type narrow gauge carriages. Eight men could sit in each carriage but the racks could only take the gear of three, so the men had to perch on top of the remainder, stowed on their seats with their heads hardly fitting under the racks. After much grumbling the train headed off and passed over the river Jordan into Syria. All Henry could see out the glassless carriage windows were rugged and barren mountains. As they headed higher into the mountain to Daraa, the blizzard picked up, and it was colder than anything they had encountered in Palestine. Groans could be heard coming from every carriage.

At 10.30pm as they entered Damascus they were greeted by hordes of Arabs selling liquor and food of dubious quality. The potent brew of cherry brandy offered was welcomed by the soldiers in the cold and draughty waiting rooms. Buses soon arrived to take them to their new quarters but many were well and truly under the weather before then. Henry's A Coy was the first to leave. They headed for Doummar, a quaint village five miles from Damascus. As their old rattly bus rumbled through the cobbled streets Henry was enthralled by the eerie night landscape. Under half blackout, with the blue tinted street lights bouncing off the sleet and rain, it was like something out of a Boris Karloff movie.

The accommodation in Doummar was a complete surprise, the flat roofed mud huts were the best they had encountered in their tour of duty. The camp, with its beer garden overlooking the waterfall on the Barada river became the envy of the rest of the 2/3 rd Pioneers. By early February the whole Battalion was here and the Pioneers were to meet up with their British allies for the first time. Hot showers were achieved by some ingenious B Coy engineers using the steep slope to erect boilers, fuelled by a mixture of oil and kerosene, above the showers immediately below. Drainage was simple – the water just ran down the hill. When the British moved in nearby, the officer in charge offered the Pioneers the use of their Mobile Bath Unit every five weeks. He was laughed out of the administration hut. When told of the Australians' arrangement he made overtures for his men to use the facilities too. Colonel Busby offered to show the British how to make their own. This offer was refused and the British continued to use the five-weekly Bath Unit, amid much cat-calling from the Aussies.

Henry resumed all his old duties, and at last, received a long letter from Connie. She wrote lovingly, refusing his offer of freedom and saying she would wait for him, her love for him was going to last a lifetime. In the same batch of mail was a letter from his mother. She was very excited about Connie and couldn't be more pleased with Henry's choice of life partner. Although Henry felt safe and loved, he was restless. *What were they really doing in this part of the world?* He knew other Aussies were doing it tough in North Africa and he felt guilty that his unit was not still seeing any action.

***

Henry received message after message about the pressure the Allies were being put under by General Rommel, now known as the Desert Fox, in North Africa. He had just delivered the latest communiqué to Major Coulthard.

"Things are not going well for us, are they sir?"

"No. Rommel is starting to become a real bogeyman to our allies. He is certainly a force to be reckoned with."

"Why are we being kept here building defences like this Barze Fortress when we could be helping in the real action?"

"Apparently Churchill has a real fixation about keeping control of Suez. He thinks the Germans may come through Turkey and attack the canal."

"By the time they do that we could have not only lost the battle but also the war."

"We are under operational command of the British now, as you know, and I got the impression when I chatted to General Auchinleck on his last visit here that some of the high ranking British generals are not happy with their Supreme Commander, one Winston Leonard Spencer Churchill."

"Can't General Morsehead pull us out of this and get us into some real action? We don't want the sacrifices our mates are making in Tobruk to be for nothing."

"You have a good tactical head on your shoulders Henry but I am afraid that at the moment our hands are tied. I believe our own PM Curtin doesn't get on with Churchill either but he has the handicap of being in a minority government."

"Well, it was Churchill's inaction that caused the fall of Singapore. I think we should be back defending the home front."

"You are certainly taking careful note of things, Henry. I think our PM wants us back home too but we will be so dependent on Britain and America if we are attacked we have to let them determine these things."

"I wish these people in power could have a look at the human suffering this war is bringing to all the countries involved. There must be an easier way."

Henry was deep in thought as he walked back to his post. *How long is it going to be before I see my homeland again?* He felt a tight knot forming in his stomach as he slowly pulled his hard chair out and looked down. He could hardly believe what he saw. An urgent message had arrived in his absence.

*H.Q. DARWIN Feb 19, 1942*
*Attention all Units:*
*At 1000 hours Darwin bombed by Imperial Japanese forces. Heavy damage to installations. Casualties unknown. Preparing for more raids.*

"The bastards! When will this madness end?" He jumped to his feet and retraced his steps to the Command hut to deliver this unwelcome news.

# CHAPTER 38

# FRUSTRATION

*PRIME MINISTER'S DEPARTMENT.*
*CABLEGRAM.*
*DECYPHER FROM: Dated – 22nd Feb, 1942 . THE SECRETARY OF STATE FOR  DOMINION AFFAIRS, LONDON.*
*MOST IMMEDIATE.*

*Following from the Prime Minister for the Prime Minister.  (Begins):-
We could not contemplate that you would refuse our request and that of the President of the United States for the diversion of the leading division to save the situation in Burma. We knew that if our ships proceeded on their course to Australia while we were waiting for your formal approval they would either arrive too late at Rangoon or even without enough fuel to go there at all. We therefore decided that the convoy should be temporarily diverted to the northward. The convoy is now too far north for some of the ships in it to reach Australia without refuelling. These physical considerations give a few days for the situation to develop and for you to review the position should you wish to do so. Otherwise the leading Australian Division will be returned to Australia as quickly  as possible in accordance with your wishes. (Ends).*
*Copy to War Cabinet Mr Shedden. 23/2/42.*

When the news came through that Churchill had asked for the leading division of the returning Australian forces to be diverted to defend Burma, Henry was relieved to hear that Curtin had firmly refused. When Curtin learned on the afternoon of 22nd February that Churchill had temporarily diverted the convoy, his response was swift and decisive, forcing Churchill to give way. These vitriolic exchanges taking part between Churchill and Curtin were very disturbing to Henry. *We are being used as pawns in a political game. Here we are sitting around playing soldier and no one is at home to defend us from the increasing threat from Japan.*

By Anzac Day the 2/3rd Battalion were the only Australian troops left in the area around Damascus. Henry's frustration grew. He had started to attend Arabic classes at Garrison HQ in Damascus but had to stop after he had been set upon by Arabs one night on his way home. He received a couple of nasty knife cuts on his forearms but his fitness allowed him to escape more serious injuries. Mail from home was trickling in slowly and Henry spent much of his off-duty time writing to Connie and his family. He tried to write something to Connie every day even though the mail was heavily censored and he couldn't tell her anything about their movements or the fighting. The Home Office took care of all the news releases and a far rosier picture was being constructed for those at home.

Finally in mid May the whole Battalion was once again bundled into uncomfortable train carriages to be taken to Chekka, a small village some 20 miles from Tripoli. This frustrated Henry even more as they were now further from the action in North Africa than they had ever been. Their surroundings were once again quite pleasant. They were housed in tents carefully erected under the trees in a large olive grove and the men were becoming quite jovial as they were now sure they would be going home any day. They were only 200 yards from the beach, pebbly and without surf but a pleasant change from the rain and bitter cold of the Syrian hills.

Unlimited leave was granted into the village and organised leave into Tripoli was available at set times. Here the soldiers were able to attend the theatre and sample an abundant supply of American beer. Relations with the mainly Christian Arabs were very cordial. They enjoyed having the fun-loving Aussies in their midst. Henry thought it was more like a holiday camp than a war zone!

Ninth Division HQ was set up in a fine mansion near the heart of Tripoli. Henry was transferred there to continue his communication duties in very comfortable quarters. For the first time since they reached the Middle East he had a bed with a comfortable mattress, with clean linen and even a pillow! He should have been very pleased with his situation but that was a long way from the truth. When news of the Japanese submarines entering Sydney Harbour came through on 31st May Henry became despondent.

Henry was assigned to dress as a local and, using his limited Arabic, go into the streets of Tripoli to see what he could find out about the underground activities of the Arab natives. Some were known to be hostile to the Australians. A number of raids on local villages revealed a surprising number of stolen weapons in the wrong hands. Henry decided there was no real threat to the soldiers themselves; the locals were mostly catering to their own fears of future attacks from either side. On a number of occasions he spied Reg and his cronies living it up in Tripoli's nightlife. He made sure they didn't recognise him. During one of these encounters Henry heard Reg boasting in a loud voice about how we had won the war and would be on our way home soon. *Hope I am around when he finds out the truth. He seems to be receiving special privileges again. Some of the men had not been able to secure even a single visit into Tripoli!*

The closest Henry had come to seeing any action was when he was sent to investigate a report that German subs were firing on the shore near the Chekka tunnel that A Coy had been assigned to guard. He rushed to a vantage point high on the cliff overlooking the ocean. It soon became clear that there was indeed a German submarine attacking a small coastal ship less than half a mile from shore. Henry heard three shots – then shots four and five were direct hits and a fire broke out on the coaster, followed by several explosions. There were no allied air or sea units in the area so the submarine escaped into the distance as the small ship sunk to a watery grave. *Wow, some excitement at last. Is that all the war we are going to see?*

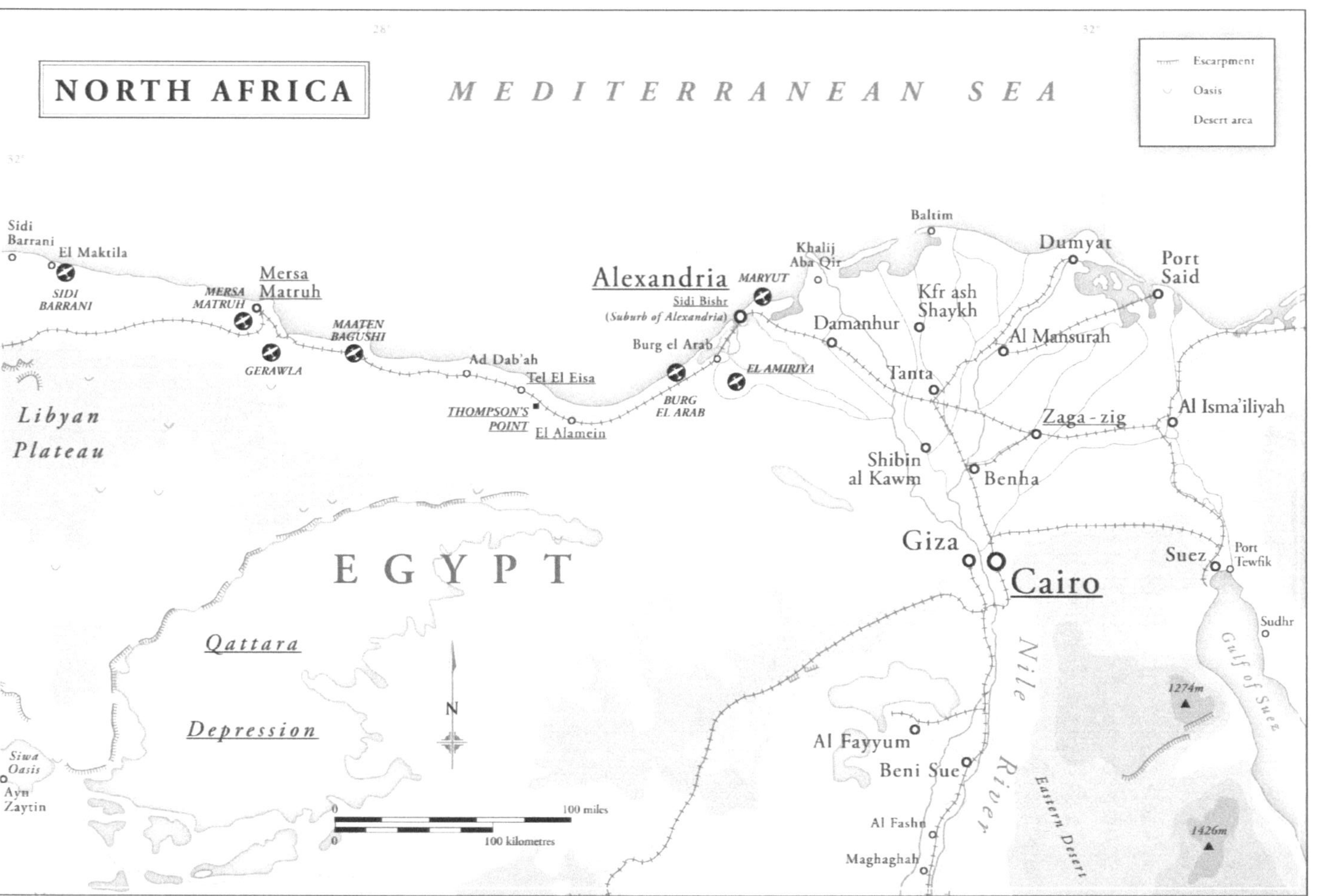

NORTH AFRICA
MEDITERRANEAN SEA
Escarpment
Oasis
Desert area
Sidi Barrani
El Maktila
SIDI BARRANI
Mersa Matruh
MERSA MATRUH
GERAWLA
MAATEN BAGUSHI
Ad Dab'ah
Tel El Eisa
THOMPSON'S POINT
El Alamein
BURG EL ARAB
Burg el Arab
EL AMIRIYA
MARYUT
Alexandria
Sidi Bishr
(Suburb of Alexandria)
Khalij Abu Qir
Baltim
Dumyat
Port Said
Kfr ash Shaykh
Damanhur
Al Mansurah
Tanta
Zaga-zig
Al Isma'iliyah
Shibin al Kawm
Benha
Giza
Cairo
Suez
Port Tewfik
Sudhr
Libyan Plateau
EGYPT
Qattara Depression
Siwa Oasis
Ayn Zaytin
Al Fayyum
Beni Sue
Al Fashn
Maghaghah
Nile River
Eastern Desert
Gulf of Suez
1274m
1426m
N
100 miles
100 kilometres

# Chapter 39

# Into the Desert

June was almost over and Henry's unit was still ensconced in Tripoli. He was taking out his frustration with his best cartoon yet. He was using the plentiful supply of paper he had received courtesy of the British, an irony that made Henry chuckle. He had drawn a German tank with one track over a prostrate Aussie soldier, slouch hat askew, the British PM, cigar in hand, ample midriff hanging over the top of his pinstripe suit pants, kicking the soldier in the rear end. The caption read "Come on you lazy son-of-a-bitch, you are not going to give in without a fight are you?"

"Ahem. I wouldn't leave that lying around here Henry." Henry stood up and almost fell over his chair into the arms of Major Coulthard who was standing right behind him with a wry smile on his face.

"Jeez, sir I didn't hear you come in."

"Obviously. I can understand your frustration but things might finally be going to happen."

"I didn't see any message to that effect."

"This didn't come through the usual channels. It has just been hand delivered. Too important to be sent over the air-waves. I want you back in camp to ready your men for a move south."

"Full marching orders sir?"

"More than that. Here's a full list of gear they have to carry. All excess equipment has to be packed into their kitbags. No slouch hats are to be visible. The utmost secrecy is to prevail."

"Where are we going?"

"This time Henry, I can't even tell you. But we will be crossing the Nile under total blackout conditions."

"The troops still think they are going home."

"That's why I want you to travel with your company and do what you can to keep them as quiet as possible. And keep an eye on those damn Arabs. They will probably see it as a chance to add to their supplies."

"How long is all this going to take?"

"We will be going by truck to Haifa and then onto trains for the trip through Palestine to the canal. That will have to be done mainly at night as the enemy has started air-raids on the railway yards. Then it will be across the canal again and back onto trains for the rest of the journey. We'll probably be on the move for several days and nights."

"That's going to upset the boys. I think they've had life a bit too easy around here."

"You're right about that."

"No beer or smokes either," called the Major over his shoulder as he left.

⸻ ❈ ⸻

There was not a sound as the small railway carriage edged slowly into the station. The tension in the air was unmistakeable. Henry could feel the sweat on Tom's forearm as he pushed over him to stare out into the dark silence.

"Where the hell are we Henry? Why is everything so quiet and blacked out?"

"This is the middle of Egypt mate. Zaga-Zig."

"Who are all those Arabs piling onto that train over there? They look like they are fleeing from something. What the hell are we being dumped into now?"

"We're at war, don't forget. It looks like we are finally going to see some action. I don't think the locals believe we're going to stop Rommel."

214

"Reg kept telling us that the fighting was all but over and we would be on our way home soon."

"Well, now you know he was totally wrong. The British have been struggling to contain the Fox for months now."

"Did you know the truth?"

"I knew things were not going well but I didn't know until now what our involvement would be. I did know that going home was never an option."

"That's what really pisses me off about this bloody Army. The bastards back there in their safe little offices just throw us out into God-knows-what without so much as a word about what's in store for us."

"Yes, I know Tom and it has always been a burden on me when I know things in advance and can't talk about it with you men. It's all about security you know. In this sort of warfare surprise is our best weapon."

"I don't blame you Henry, you are just doing your job. I just wish they would let us know a bit sooner what ours was."

The Pioneers disembarked at Sidi Bishr, a small army camp on the outskirts of Alexandria. The night was dark and still. There was not a soul in sight. All Henry could see in the light from the horizon was a few tents erected on a sandy beach. "Ok men, just bunk down wherever you can and we will sort it out in the morning." Tired and disgruntled men fell into whatever vacant tent they could find.

Henry had just fallen into a deep sleep when the sound of gun-fire rang out over the camp. Tent flaps were thrown in the air and half–clothed men poured out, stumbling as they rummaged around for their weapons. Searchlights could be seen clearly from the direction of the port but the gunfire was quite muffled.

"Come on men, it's too far away to worry us. You need to get some sleep. We still have further to go tomorrow. Welcome to our war!" said Major Coulthard as he struggled down the hill from his tent, pulling on his uniform.

The men were in quite a jovial mood as they were served a piping hot breakfast. Henry walked into the makeshift mess tent. *Good to see the old Aussie spirit bouncing back.*

"Morning Serg, when are we going on our fox hunt? We'll get the bastard for them."

"These bloody Poms couldn't hit a rat stuck in a drain if they had a machine gun."

"We'll show 'em how an Aussie gets the job done."

"Bring it on. We'll have Rommel runnin' home to Adolf with his tail between his legs."

They were soon back on trucks heading through the streets of Alexandria. Henry was awe-struck by the beauty of this ancient city with its well laid out gardens surrounding high class homes stretching along tree-lined avenues. The amazement was short-lived. The true meaning of war soon became  apparent as they entered the dock area. Silence fell over the long line of troop-filled trucks. Stretching along the sides of the docks were rows of disabled and burnt out tanks and motor vehicles. As they passed on into piles of rubble and ruined buildings, the hushed silence gave way to mumbled gasps.

Tom nudged Henry in the ribs and leant towards him. "Is there anything left for us to save? I think we should have been here sooner."

"Has been my concern for some time mate. Let's hope we can still make a difference and stop some of this wanton destruction."

As the city turned into desert, traffic on the road built up and they passed ambulances, trucks and transporters of all sizes moving slowly in both directions.

"I guess we are in the midst of it now, Henry."

"Sure are Tom. Look over there." He pointed to the sign at the intersection of the Matruh and Cairo roads that declared the beginning of the Western Desert.

"What's that?" Tom pointed to the enormous ditch running north-south.

"That's the anti-tank ditch –the last line of defence before the canal."

"And we're going past there?"

"Sure are. I think you could say we are now on active service."

The tar road soon ran out and clouds of dust filled the air. The trucks stopped on top of a small rise and the men were ordered to alight. Major Coulthard appeared beside the gathered group and pulled himself up onto a large rock.

"Ok, this is going to be your base for the time being."

"Where the hell are we?" A voice came from the dense throng of men.

"This is El Amiriya and no-one can get to Alexandria without coming through here. It's our job to defend this territory so the Allied forces can be kept supplied and have an escape route if things go wrong."

"But there's nothing here." The same voice from the crowd rang out.

"Come on, when has that ever worried us before? That's why you men have been given the job. You have done it so well in the past." Henry pushed to the front of the crowd and turned to face the men.

"Come on then, let's get on with it. Let's start digging in while we are waiting for the rest of our supplies to arrive."

Henry looked towards the long, bare, rocky ridge running west from the Cairo-Matruh road junction as it gave way to undulating sand covered with low scrub. Muffled gunfire could be heard in the direction of Alamein and the noise of planes taking off from Amiriya echoed around them. Gusts of hot air from the desert blew clouds of fine sand into eyes and hair with monotonous regularity. Henry wished he was feeling as confident as he sounded.

# CHAPTER 40

# THE ACTION BEGINS

The first siren split the quiet air. The sun was about to disappear behind the hills that masked the western desert. Henry was sitting on an empty ammunition box outside the tent that served as Battalion HQ. It was in the quarry at the top of the ridge. He turned towards the east and could see the search-lights lighting up the skies over Alexandria. Soon he would be able pick up a German plane or two. *There's one, a German Junkers JU 88 twin engine bomber. It sounds like it is conking out but isn't; it is just slowing down to drop its payload. Not very accurately, thank goodness.* Soon the British Tomahawk fighters would take off and engage in their nightly dogfight with these unwelcome visitors.

The Pioneers had been camped here for nearly three weeks and had settled into a routine of nightly patrols and look-outs. Rommel had to be pushed back into the desert to keep Alexandria in Allied hands. Henry called it the "dawn and evening stand-to." It seemed almost ridiculous to some of the Pioneers, so far from the action, that they should have to go through these paces every night. Henry knew there were two brigades between them and Rommel's Axis forces but he also knew that the Fox had a knack for getting behind opposing forces and hitting from unexpected directions. He tried to impress the seriousness of this tactic on his men. He drew their attention to the constant stream of ambulances passing along the road below. Burnt out tanks and vehicles being towed became more frequent. Henry had become quite frustrated at being kept so far from the action but he never let the other men see how he felt.

The morning all clear had sounded in the last week of July, 1942. Henry was lingering over the remains of his breakfast when a breathless orderly charged into the mess tent looking around as if he had urgent business. He made a beeline for Henry.

"Sgt. Thompson, the Major wants you at HQ immediately."

"Whoa there, Corporal. Running around at that pace is not a good idea at this hour of the day. You could get mistaken for the enemy. Some of those still on guard duty are just itching to get a shot at someone, anything!"

"Well, it's important. You should have been on duty by now. The radio has been going off like a clucky hen for almost half an hour. The Major is manning it himself so I would get up there quick smart if I were you."

Henry had made the trip up the escarpment to the command tent in very quick time in the past, but never as quickly as this morning. "Sorry sir, I was day-dreaming. Not a lot has been happening around here lately."

"Well it's happening now."

"Most of the Pioneers are going to be urgently needed at the front. The Fox has managed to inflict heavy casualties on our British friends and we have to plug some gaps in their ranks. "

"I'll be happy to see some action."

"You'll be staying by the radio. Communications are going to be more important than ever. They need anti-tank gunners as well as some mine specialists."

"It sounds like Rommel has cranked things up a bit."

"Yes I think we are heading into one of the most defining moments in this war. We can't afford to lose this one."

When the order to move the 9th Division towards the front line came through Henry felt a surge of excitement. They were to replace the 2/43 Battalion right in the middle of the Alamein Box. It was not a move that took any great time to complete but it brought about a great change in their contribution to the fighting. For once they did not have to establish the defensive positions; they took up already established reinforced positions consisting of concrete pillboxes connected by a series of underground passages and rooms. Henry and his equipment were very safely housed in one of these rooms and he felt secure. The Pioneers had been given the task of defending the main bitumen Mersah-Matruh Road. Henry could see down the sloping ground towards Alamein Station. He had a clear view of the continuous stream along the road; trucks and troop carriers of all sizes, tanks, including the fast moving Crusader, anti-aircraft guns mounted on carriers and many other mobile weapons. Henry knew how vital this supply corridor was. As they headed west to the front they looked bold and brave, flying flags of the various units, and they were greeted with much excitement as they passed by the Pioneers. But all too often the flow of traffic was also eastern bound in retreat; a sorry sight of damaged and disabled equipment, badly in need of repair but suffering from a lack of spare parts. The mounting number of ambulances joining these processions alarmed Henry.

"Gee Henry, it looks like we are being dumped on again." Tom had come up beside him and followed Henry's eyes.

"What do you mean? We are still not seeing any real action."

"The bloody Germans seem to like taking a pot-shot at us whenever they want to."

"We are dug in well enough and our camouflage seems to be working. They are not really damaging anything and we haven't had any casualties yet."

"Yeah, I suppose Churchill wouldn't have risked his arse with that visit yesterday if there was any real danger. Not that we were allowed near him. The rumour is that he has come to Africa to give Auchinleck the boot. "

"I'm not privy to any of that information Tom, but he must be up to something to come this close to the front lines."

"I wish I was in a position to shoot back at the bastards. I'm sick of waving to passing brass as if we were all at a Sunday school picnic."

"Your chance may come sooner than you think. The Poms are taking a bit of a hammering at the moment and we are going to be needed as reinforcements any day."

"Are you coming with us?"

"Well, I'll be with you but I will still have to man the radio. Communications are a vital part of the campaign."

"Reg will have a field day with that. He never misses an opportunity to brand you as a coward."

"I'm used to that. We'll see how things pan out when we get some real action."

*"On 6th August Churchill made the decision to appoint General Alexander, Commander Middle East and Gott, Commander 8th Army. Next day while flying to Cairo to take up his appointment, Gott's aircraft was intercepted by two German aircraft and was shot down. And Gott was killed. It was under these circumstances that Montgomery was selected to command the army with which his name will always be linked.*

*Alexander reached Cairo on 9th August and was given a brief directive from Churchill: "To take or destroy at the earliest opportunity the German-Italian army commanded by Field Marshall Rommel, together with all its supplies and establishments in Egypt and Libya."*

*Montgomery arrived in Egypt on 13th August. After a conference with Alexander he went to the front to look around. He did not like what he saw and decided to take immediate command."*

CHAPTER *20 HOLED UP IN THE DESERT*
*THE DESERT CAMPAIGNS 1940–1943. RAY HAYWARD.*

The Pioneers had been settled in their new position for two days when Henry was summoned to the Command bunker. Major Coulthard and several generals and a number of high ranking British officers were seated around a low table covered with a large map of the Alamein Box.

"Come in Henry. Have some bad news. Gott has been shot down by the Krauts before he even got to Cairo."

"What's going to happen now? Here we are under the command of the British 8th Army and they have no leader."

"Well, Thompson," the closest of the British officers turned towards him with a chill in his voice, "Churchill is going to have to replace him quick smart."

"If he had done what we wanted in the first place we wouldn't be in this position." Another of the officers grumbled.

"That's enough, Blacksure. No need to air our disagreements here."

"It's ok. Sergeant Thompson is well versed in what's happening behind the scenes in both our countries' politics." Major Coulthard jumped to Henry's defence.

"Is he now?" The British General raised his eyebrows and turned to Henry with a look of disdain.

"He's not only our radio operator; he's one of our most highly trained intelligence personnel. Besides that he has a good tactical head on his shoulders."

"Well, well. How about that? Why do you keep him hidden away then?"

"That's part of our security arrangements. We don't want the enemy knowing who our key operatives are."

"Interesting tactics. Anyway let's get back to the task at hand. Yes, Thompson, it looks like some of your Company are finally going to see some real action."

General Richie held up his hand to the Australian Major in a motion that left no-one in doubt who was calling the shots. "We are going to need some of your boys to start mounting night patrols around our perimeters. There is every chance they will come under enemy fire."

"I'd be quite happy to lead some of those patrols sir." Henry's heart was in his mouth and he felt a tingle of excitement run through his body. *Action at last.*

"Well my boy, from the sound of things you are too valuable around here to be exposed to such risks. I am sure there are other NCO's in your unit to do the job."

It was with a heavy heart that Henry wended his way back through the concrete structures to his radio post. *I'll get my chance soon, I hope.*

# Chapter 41

# Some Relief for Henry

*"The enemy is now attempting to break through our position in order to reach Cairo, Suez and Alexandria and to drive us from Egypt. The Eighth Army bars the way. It carries a great responsibility and the whole future of the war will depend on how we carry out our task. We will fight the enemy where we now stand; there will be NO WITHDRAWAL and NO SURRENDER. Every officer and man must continue to do his duty, we cannot fail: the opportunity will then occur to take the offensive ourselves and to destroy once and for all the enemy forces  now in Egypt. Into battle then, with stout hearts and with the determination to do our duty. And may God give us victory!"*

LIEUT.-GENERAL B.L. MONTGOMERY. AUGUST 15TH, 1942.

The harsh desert conditions were taking their toll on both the Allied and Axis forces. The sand, rock and scrub were inhospitable and would have made even the most hardened soldier despondent. The battleground was bounded on the south by the Qattara Depression which was below sea level and almost impassable. It formed part of the sand sea of the Libyan Desert, itself desolate and waterless. To the north high limestone cliffs rose to a height of 500 feet above sea level. There were few formed roadways and warfare took on a whole new complexion. The mobility of the forces was vital. Early in the conflict the

British tanks were far superior to the Italian ones but now the Germans had arrived in the desert and their Panzer tanks were much more suited to the conditions. Rommel, a brilliant tactician, was now on the verge of overwhelming the Allies and morale was low.

Henry was continually being told he was a vital part of the Allied campaign but he was far from happy. He aired his frustration about his lack of involvement in the real war to Major Coulthard and he was given extra duties. He was re-instated as Supply Officer and also had again taken over the role of Battalion Pay Master. These duties were so routine that they only took up a small part of the spare time he had sitting in front of his radio waiting for messages.

One of Henry's roles was to see the troops were kept well-supplied. All water, food, ammunition, fuel and spare parts had to be brought in from elsewhere and had to be in place before any assault started. Each soldier was allowed only one gallon of water per day to cover washing, cooking and drinking, so a tight rein had to be kept on its stocks. Henry felt the ultimate irony in all this was that the more successful your army was and the further forward you forged, the further supplies had to be brought.

Henry hoped that the appointment of General Montgomery to the command of the 8th Army would step up the campaign. He sat and liaised with the commanding officers, listened to them make decisions that put the front line troops in increasing amounts of danger, while they themselves stayed out of harm's way. Henry refrained from expressing his thoughts on this. He should have been well satisfied. His career was well and truly on-track; he was mostly well out of the way of any danger from enemy fire and received many privileges that the other men in his unit didn't. Perhaps this was the problem. He felt guilty listening to the guns pounding in the distance as he sat here in his safe little cocoon, in his dry comfortable clothes with plenty to eat and drink. The members of his company were now being sent out on nightly patrols.

Each morning he anxiously watched the men file back into camp dragging their feet, a bedraggled lot showing signs of lack of sleep.

Henry tried not to let his mates see him doing his daily head count as they passed. A member of B Company had already been killed while on patrol and Henry was thankful that all his closest friends were still unscathed.

Suddenly his heart lurched as a stretcher party appeared on the path below their camp. He rushed forward and tried to hide his dismay when he recognised one of the youngest members of his company. Private Doug Campbell was a special favourite of his and seeing the heavily blood-stained bandage on his head which was slumped to one side, dark eyes staring unseeingly into the morning light, Henry felt like throwing up. He grabbed the arm of one the stretcher bearers. "What are his chances?"

The soldier holding the stretcher just looked at Henry with tears rolling down his cheeks and shook his head.

Henry walked slowly back to his post, trying to hold back his own tears. What a waste of a young life. He was so enthusiastic about joining the army. That lovely young girlfriend he showed me the snap of only a few nights ago, is going to be shattered. He resolved to go and see this girl if he came safely out of the war. He wanted her to know how brave Doug was. Henry sat at his post contemplating his own situation. Maybe I should ask to be transferred back to a field company. I can't keep sitting here out of harm's way while my mates are risking their lives every day.

"Well, how is Sergeant Yellow Belly in his safe little bunker? Hardly a hair out of place I see. The real diggers are recovering from the battle against Jerry and are looking a bit the worse for wear."

Henry took a deep breath and turned to face Reg lounging nonchalantly in the doorway of the communications bunker. What was going through his head was very different to his words.

"It is just as well we have men like you then. I'm a married man now. I'll do whatever I have to do to get back safe and sound to my wife. She's worth going back to don't you think?" Henry hoped he sounded convincing.

"What makes you think she is sitting around waiting for you to return? I hear the Yanks are in Sydney and all the women throw themselves at them, married or not."

"Good try Reg. I know that Connie isn't like that but you can keep trying to unsettle me if you think you can."

"Keep thinking that way if you like but just remember, war can make people do some desperate things. Absence doesn't always make the heart grow fonder when temptations are on offer and the future is uncertain."

Henry felt the anger rising in him but still he kept his cool. "Could you just piss off? I have some very important work to do and I am sure General Messinger wouldn't want any unauthorised personnel sitting in on it."

Reg huffed as only someone of his own perceived superiority could and turned on his heel and strode out.

⎯⎯ ⋈ ⎯⎯

Henry was thinking about Connie and longing to feel her in his arms again when he was called up to Command HQ. He walked into the small concrete bunker. All the top commanders were present.

"Sit down Thompson." General Messinger gestured to a chair at the end of the table.

"You must be aware that things are not going that well for us at the moment."

"I have noticed how demoralised the troops are when they come back to camp. It does worry me."

"We are not keeping up with the Fox in the way we would like. The Axis forces are getting alarmingly close to our front lines and Rommel seems to be going in for an all out attack. We have to make sure he doesn't get any closer to Suez. If he takes control of that we could probably say we had lost the battle."

"What has this got to do with me? Have I slipped up in some of my message deciphering?"

"On the contrary, you have done such a good job we would like to entrust you with a very important mission."

"I have been a bit frustrated with being kept so far from the fighting. I would really like to make a more positive contribution."

"Well, this could be your chance. We need someone with mapping skills to get as close as they can to Rommel's position and send accurate information back to HQ so we can deploy our forces. We seem to be missing the target quite often."

"I would be more than willing to try."

"Good man. You realise you will be going into grave danger. If you get trapped behind enemy lines you will need all your skills to get back to camp."

"Will I be alone on this mission?"

"Yes, I am afraid you are all we have at the moment. There are some newly-trained recruits coming in on the next troop ship but they will arrive too late."

"I will give it my all sir. "

Henry walked back to his post like he was walking on air. *This is what I have been waiting for. Please God let me be successful.*

# CHAPTER 42

# ENCOUNTER WITH THE ENEMY

Leaflets dropped by enemy aircraft over Australian positions at Alamein on 22$^{nd}$ August. A platypus over a boomerang was the 9$^{th}$ Division's vehicle sign.

Henry was tired on the morning of his mission. He had stayed up late the night before being briefed. He slept in his clothes so he wouldn't wake Tom and the others when he left early. Dawn was appearing on the horizon as Henry moved silently across the open space between the sleeping quarters and the communications bunker area. He stopped to pick up some leaflets that had obviously been dropped on their camp overnight. *The bastards, they will stop at nothing to try to demoralise us. I wonder if we are doing the same to them.* Henry was having trouble coming to terms with this side of war.

He picked up the backpack that had been prepared for him the night before. The officer on duty was slumped over his radio, a position familiar to Henry. He was well away from the encampment before he relaxed and started to breathe normally again. He had made it out unnoticed.

Henry moved quickly through the sparse undergrowth on the edge of the desert, keeping low. It would take him longer but open spaces would make him a sitting duck for enemy patrols. He consulted his maps of the minefields that had been laid by the members of D Company and carefully manoeuvred through the safe zones. He travelled for two hours before he came across the first sign of enemy activity. He made his way through a small gap in a rocky outcrop and there below him, in a small convoy, were a number of armoured vehicles and several tanks. Henry found a hidden vantage point between two large rocks. Something was very different about one of the tanks. It was moving quickly and easily across the rocky terrain. It was nothing like any that Henry had encountered in his studies. It looked much heavier than the Panzers that the Germans used extensively in Europe and it seemed to be reinforced with much heavier armour-plating in the front area. It had a higher and fully mobile gun turret. He pinpointed their position. The convoy also seemed to be travelling in a totally different direction than he expected. It looked as though Rommel might be embarking on one of his famous tactics – striking the enemy from an unlikely position.

Henry had repacked his gear when he was startled by a noise on the track he had just used. He managed to cram himself back into the narrow gap in the rocky outcrop as a German patrol passed several feet away from him. He held his breath and hoped that his pounding heart would not alert them. It sounded like the percussion section of a symphony orchestra to him. The patrol passed without a glance in his direction. Henry considered whether he should call it a day and make his way back to camp with his startling discovery. *They must be bringing in a secret new tank. It looks like it could be a force to be reckoned with.* He had strict instructions on the area he had to cover and as he was alone he decided to continue on his mission. *You need two men to do this job properly.*

For the rest of the day Henry continued this same process several times, but he was more vigilant in  looking for patrols. He had finished his mapping tasks by mid-afternoon but decided to wait until the light faded to start his long trek back. When he finally came over the last ridge he sat down for a few moments and thought about what he had just been through. He was feeling proud of himself and exhilarated about his success but he still felt a nervous flutter in the pit of his stomach when he remembered how close he had been to being picked up.

⊷⊷ ▤◈▤ ⊶⊶

Henry sat brooding in the mess tent when Tom came over and sat beside him. There was no-one else around so they could speak freely.

"You look a bit down in the dumps, Henry."

"I wish I could tell you Tom. Things are getting a bit on top of me these days."

"I know you are involved in classified activities so I won't even try to get you to tell me the problem."

"It's not the work I am doing that is the problem. I enjoy that but it's not being able to talk about it or tell them at home that makes it very hard."

"Here, have a smoke. I know you were one of the few who refused the packets they gave us on the boat but I find it relaxing."

"I couldn't even consider it Tom. It's one of Connie's pet hates. She's asthmatic and she's quite paranoid about not having anyone near her who smokes."

"One now and again is not going to hurt you. Besides it is going to be a long time before we are anywhere near home."

"If it would help me deal with that bloody Reg, I suppose I could give it a try."

231

"Has he been giving you a hard time again?"

"His still seems to want to interfere with Connie and me. He keeps putting ideas into my head about what she may be doing while I'm here."

"The bastard. You would think he would have given up by now."

"Well, I think he just can't accept that Connie preferred me to him. He's also trying to rub in the fact that I'm not part of the battlefield action – branding me a coward."

"He is probably jealous of your contact with the top brass. We all know your work is vitally important, even if we don't know the details."

"Here, give me that smoke." Henry grabbed the lighted cigarette from Tom and placed it between his lips.

"Don't try to inhale too deeply at first. You will learn how to handle that later."

Henry felt the warm smoke swirl around in his mouth before he slowly inhaled it. It was pleasant. By the time he and Tom had silently finished off their cigarettes Henry was feeling relaxed.

"Thanks Tom, that was good. I think I will issue myself a pack or two. There'll be plenty of time to get it out of my system when I am not under so much pressure."

When Henry was back at his post a short time later he had already consumed half the pack he had signed out. He didn't think that such a little thing could relax you so much.

·—·—≡◆≡—·—·

It was 9 am and Henry was relaxing with his fifth cigarette of the morning. He found his intelligence work stimulating but fear lingered in the background and kept him in a state of high tension. He had just stubbed his butt in the overfull ration tin that he was using as an ashtray when an orderly stuck his head in the door.

"Major Coulthard would like to see you right away."

"Sure," said Henry "would you like to take over here while I go. You have security clearance for it, don't you?" He hoped he sounded more casual and

232

confident than he felt. Whenever he was summoned these days a shudder went through his whole system. It usually meant another mission. He was increasingly nervous about his assignments. He was taking more and more risks to satisfy the demands of his commanding officers.

"Sure do. Anything in particular you want to know about as it comes in. By the look of the officers waiting to brief you, I would say you will be gone a while."

"No, just use your discretion." Henry tried to remain casual. *What on earth have they got for me this time? Is this really what I want to do with my life? Am I going to be able to make a difference anyway?*

He knocked softly on the door of the command hut. He seemed to be acting like he was on assignment all the time these days, so automatic were his covert actions. He slowly opened the door, checking the occupants of the room as each one came into view. Major Coulthard, as expected, General Messinger who seemed to be at all his briefings these days. There were two other men in the room who Henry did not know.

"Come in Thompson." Major Coulthard pushed Henry forward.

"Meet General Montgomery." The short British officer with an unmistakeable air of authority stood up and held his hand out to Henry. Henry was so in awe of being the presence of the great "Monty" himself he was a bit slow in taking it. When he did, his own hand was shaking so much that he could hardly hold it still enough to return the firm grip.

"Pleased to meet you young man. I have heard a lot about you and I have certainly seen your results. We are very proud to have you on our side. That information you gave us on the new Panther tank certainly saved many allied lives." Henry's chest puffed out with pride. *If only Mum and Connie could see me now!*

"So it was a completely new tank. I thought so."

"Yes, much lighter and faster than their Panzers. Able to handle rough country and shoot from a much longer range. More than a match for our T-34s. We could have been really caught with our pants down."

Major Coulthard turned to the other man in the room and pushed him towards Henry. Henry had hardly taken his eyes off General

Montgomery and had forgotten about the other person. Henry looked carefully at this young man in an Australian Army uniform. *Do I know him? Not much of an Aussie look about him. More middle eastern with that dark swarthy skin and jet black hair.*

"Meet Romano Cesaro. He is going to be joining you in your next few missions."

Of course, the young Italian he had met briefly in Darwin. He felt an instinctive wariness of this steely eyed young man.

By the time they walked back to the communications tent Henry had relaxed a little. Romano seemed to be very personable and he certainly had skills that Henry didn't. He could speak both Italian and German.

"How did you come to be so fluent in both languages?  Have you lived in Australia long?" Henry asked cautiously.

"Was born there mate," Romano answered with an exaggerated Aussie accent and a hint of a laughter in his voice. "Actually my family has been out here for about 25 years now but we still speak Italian as our main language at home."

"What's with the German then?" Henry was suspicious.

"Well, I did study it at school then picked it up again as part of my intelligence training."

"How does your family feel about your being over here fighting against their home country?"

"My father has been incarcerated in Cowra as a prisoner of war for over a year now."

"Yes, you told me about that in Darwin. What did he do?"

"Nothing. All Italian men who hadn't taken Australian citizenship were rounded up."

"What about your mother?"

"She obviously isn't regarded as a threat and she has my three younger brothers to look after as well as a farm in Queensland."

"That seems a bit rough. I wasn't aware that was going on. Hardly seems fair."

"It certainly isn't and my blood boils every time I think about it. Here I am fighting for this country and my family is being persecuted back home."

*I am going to have to watch him like a hawk. His allegiance could change at any time.*

# CHAPTER 43

# MIXED ALLEGIANCES

*"The main British assault was pushing west from Tel El Eisa towards what previous reconnaissance had identified as the main Axis force. The Italians were moving in from the south and the allies had set up a forty-mile defence line between the sea and the Qattara Depression. Motor vehicles were useless in this terrain but the allies didn't have any problems on their flanks; they were defended by nature. General MacArthur Onslow, to whose Composite Forces A Coy was now attached, had misgivings about how far away from the coastline that the "Fox" had moved his forces. Montgomery had refused Churchill's entreaties to attack before his forces were fully replenished and reinforced. MacArthur Onslow was worried that this also gave the Axis forces time to do the same."*

MUD AND SAND: 2/3 PIONEER BATTALION AT WAR.
J. A. ANDERSON & G. JACKETT.

Henry and Romano were concealed in tall grass on the ridge above the German camp. They had been sent out to check for enemy positions north of Thompson's Post and towards the coast. They watched the enemy erect camouflage nets over the convoy of equipment and weapons that was rolling in below them. They needed to move closer but there was too much activity. Henry pulled a packet of cigarettes out of his pocket and lit up.

"For Christ's sake Henry put that bloody thing out. You could tip them off to our presence."

"Don't be stupid, we are too far away. Besides it keeps me calm and relaxed, you have to be in this job."

"You won't be bloody calm and relaxed if you set fire to this grass. It will go up like a bush fire."

"Look here mate. I'm the boss in this two-man outfit of ours and don't you forget it."

"I'm not going to stay around and let you put me in danger. Report me if you want to."

"I wasn't happy when they assigned you to me. I'm still not sure where your allegiances lie and I've heard blood ties are a big thing in Italy. I won't hesitate to put you on report if you don't follow orders."

"Come on mate, it is silly for us to be bickering like this. We are on the same side you know. You may need me more than you think. I have an ace up my sleeve if we get caught. You will have to trust me to do all the talking."

"Yeah. That would be convenient wouldn't it? I wouldn't be able to understand a word you said. You could be selling me out for all I knew. What ace can you produce that will save us?"

Romano reached inside his jacket. Henry instinctively raised and cocked his rifle in his direction. "Settle down mate. Look what I have here. A friend of mine back home did it for me."

"What's the big deal about a passport?"

"Have a closer look. It's an Italian one. It may come in handy if we get captured. I'll pass myself off as a spy for them or something. You'll just have to shut your mouth."

Before Henry could answer a loud report sounded from below. Henry trained his binoculars on the entrance to the camp but his view was obstructed. He turned to Romano and signalled him to follow him back from the edge and up an unusually large acacia tree about fifty yards away; high enough to get a much better view of the full camp. The young recruit didn't hesitate and Henry gave a sigh of relief. *We have to work together on this but I'm still going to keep close tabs on him.*

The gunfire was only a brief volley of shots. An enemy patrol passed right underneath their tree but the men were laughing and jostling each other. When they had passed Henry turned to Romano.

"That was only a bit of sky-larking I think. They certainly weren't looking for us."

"Hadn't we better get on with things before it gets too dark?" Romano answered nervously.

*He's getting a bit jumpy. Not sure I will be able to rely on him if the going gets rough.* "Yes, but we need a few more details on equipment and numbers of troops."Henry replied as calmly as he could.

"We better get moving then," said Romano.

Henry could see that the Axis forces had moved in far more heavy equipment and big guns than his superiors had supposed. It was important to get these details back to HQ as soon as possible. They were ten miles from camp but one of them needed to get back with the details of this build-up and soon. Henry tried to lay out their hastily sketched maps in front of them. He had to resort to his torchlight to read in the failing light but managed to conceal it under his jacket. He laid down his binoculars and signalled to Romano to follow him to the ground. They slithered silently through the tall grass towards the edge of the ridge. The camp was a hive of activity, drowning out any noise they made.

Henry whispered to Romano. "You go that way to get a better view of the other side of the camp and I will cover this side." The young Italian's body stiffened as Henry pointed in the direction he wanted Romano to go.

"Can't I just stay with you?"

"No, it is better to cover both sides of the camp and then get out of here – we must get this information back to HQ as soon as possible. Move it!"

"Where will we meet up?" Romano still hadn't moved.

"Look, in this game you can't plan too far ahead. You will have to use your common sense – you may even have to find your own way back to camp." Henry turned abruptly and moved away, his own hand shaking on the backpack he was carrying – it would not do to show his own fear.

Henry moved stealthily around to the eastern side of the saucer-like valley in the rolling sand dunes. The camp was well concealed. A movement on the other side of the camp caught his eye - a German patrol was coming around the perimeter of the ridge.  His first instinct was to try to find Romano but he then realised that one of them had to make it back to camp at all costs. With his heart in his mouth he silently dissolved into the sparse wood-land that was all that lay between the opposing sides and headed back to camp. His stomach churned when he heard the shouting from behind him – it sounded like Romano may not have been so lucky.

Henry hurried to the mess tent the next morning. He looked around anxiously hoping to see Romano but there was no sign of him. Henry gulped down his breakfast and turned up at his communications post about an hour earlier than necessary.

"Well, good morning Henry," said night duty officer. "Did you fall out of bed?"

"I just couldn't sleep worrying about Romano. I take it that he hasn't shown up."

"No, nothing from him at all."

"He wouldn't try to contact by radio so close to enemy lines."

"I have been instructed to post him as missing in action if he doesn't show up by nightfall."

"That will be a blow to his family. His father is locked up in Cowra you know."

"No I didn't. What did he do?"

"Nothing it appears, other than still being an Italian citizen."

"Yeah, I had heard they were doing that. But you would think that he would have volunteered for some sort of service for Australia. I believe that gets them out."

"Romano didn't mention anything about that. He enlisted before his father was arrested but apparently that didn't get taken into account."

"I would keep an eye on him if he does come back. He could have a grudge against us all."

"Don't worry, I intend to. You may as well go to breakfast now. I will take over here."

Henry was tempted to try to contact Romano by radio but he knew that would not be wise. He was feeling guilty about leaving him on his own but he still wasn't sure that Romano would put his duty as an Australian soldier first.

# Chapter 44

# Accolades for Henry

Henry sat at his radio post mulling over whether he should write to Connie. His mail was heavily censored and he didn't like others reading his letters before she did. *I would like to tell her how I long to hold her in my arms and whisper words of love but a short note will have to do; I'm ok and thinking of her.*

He was still at his post when Major Coulthard walked in. "I hoped you would still be here Henry."

"I am getting a letter or two off home while I have the chance."

"You don't have much time for that now we are keeping you so busy. We are pleased with the responsible way you are approaching your work these days."

"It's what I am here for. I really do want to get stuck into this crazy war so it will be over and we can all get back to our lives."

"General Montgomery is very impressed with your dedication. In fact it is on his recommendation that we are going to recommend you for an M. I. D."

"Who me? Mentioned in Dispatches? I wouldn't have thought I deserved that."

"If Monty wants you to be mentioned in dispatches then mentioned in dispatches you will be."

Henry felt a rush of satisfaction. It was some time since he'd had accolades from his superiors. "Why, thank you. I wasn't expecting it. "

"We always reward vital service."

"Any word on Romano, sir? "

"You will hear about it when it happens."

"I am worried about him."

"We all are Henry, but these are tough times and we have to learn to deal with setbacks." The Major took his usual abrupt exit and left Henry thinking. *If only I could tell Connie and Mum. At least I have one up on Reg.*

Henry decided to reward himself with a new uniform. As he was returning to his post he saw Reg leaning up against a pole outside the medical tent chatting to one of the newly arrived soldiers. He had his sleeves rolled up, shirt unbuttoned and looked more like he was trying to impress a lady friend than a new recruit. Changing direction Henry walked confidently up to the pair with his head held high and his brand new jacket with its pristine white stripes gleaming in the bright sunlight.

"Hey Reg, if you want to change that old uniform how about calling in when I am on duty and I'll see what I can round up for you. Several of the others who have been sergeants less time than you have been promoted and have handed in some of their gear. None of these uniforms are made to last as long as you have been asked to wear it."

The look on Reg's face as he turned to Henry was pure venom. "At least I haven't been rewarded for fraternising with enemy sympathisers. "

"If it's Romano you are talking about, at least he has got where he is by virtue of his own skills, not because of who his father is."

Henry saw Reg's back stiffen. *At least I am hitting him where it hurts.* Henry's face lit up.

Reg's eyes narrowed even further. "I've heard that his father is an enemy POW. I don't think that we should have to serve beside someone with those sorts of connections. Besides there's a rumour going round that he has deserted."

"I wouldn't believe everything you hear. There are some things that just can't be told for security reasons."

"I'm sure that little tart of yours would like to hear of your good fortune. Anyway, security will preclude you from telling her anything about it." The malice in his voice was hard to mistake.

Henry nodded at the young private who stood there with his mouth open and a quizzical look on his face, then turned on his heel and headed back to his tent. *That should give the new digger something to think about. Reg showing his true colours. Don't think he will be impressed with that display of insolence.*

Henry was lounging on his bunk later that day thinking about his encounter with Reg. *Hey, wait a minute. How did Reg know all that stuff about Romano?* Intelligence officers are not supposed to have anything like that on their record. They are just meant to be ordinary members of their own units. Maybe he should go see the Major and broach the subject with him.

Henry jumped up and almost ran to the command hut and knocked on the door. It was opened by General Messinger.

"Hello Thompson. I was just leaving. You seem to be in a hurry young man."

"It's ok, sir. I'll come back later."

"No need. I was just leaving."

"Come in Henry." The familiar gruff voice called from behind the door. "You must have something important on your mind to be in such a hurry. Has there been some news?"

"W…w…well no sir. I'm just pretty worried about Romano. You know he still hasn't returned." *Better not voice my reservations about Reg straight out.*

"Don't worry about him. He is a very resourceful young man. There may be some surprises about him. He's had special training."

"All that worries me is that if he has been captured, my information may not be worth much if he talks. They could change their whole plan of attack."

"Romano will manage to get news back to us if that happens I am sure." *So Romano is some hot-shot intelligence agent is he? Could he be so good he has them all fooled?*

"There's something else I think you should know about sir."

"Well, out with it lad. I knew there was something more on your mind."

"I had an encounter with Reg Wentworth today that I think you should know about."

The Major gave a big sigh. "My God, Henry, you haven't hit him again have you?"

"No sir, nothing like that. It's just that he was sounding off in front of one of the new recruits about Romano being the enemy and rattled off a whole lot of details about his home life and his father."

"Most of that is common knowledge around camp Henry. I don't like the enemy comment though. He's probably just having a go at you. "

"Should he even know I'm working with him?"

"Not officially but I am sure any observant member of our unit would have seen the two of you coming and going together."

"I hope we can trust him."

The Major let out a loud guffaw. "Gee Henry, you are taking this secret business a bit too far aren't you. Wentworth is very trustworthy, coming from his family background."

"I just wanted to be sure. I'm the one taking the risks. The less others know about what I am doing the better."

"Sure Henry, I'm aware of that. If Romano doesn't return soon we may have to assign someone else to you. Maybe Wentworth would be a good choice seeing he knows so much already."

Henry felt like he had been hit right in the pit of his stomach but he looked up and saw the twinkle in the Major's eye. *He's testing me. I'm not going to let him see how much the thought of that fills me with dread!*

Henry strode off to his tent. *Blast that damn Reg. He really tipped me in it this time. How could I be so stupid to think he was a spy or something. The Major made me feel like an idiot. I still have to do something about Romano. I need to know what happened to him. I just can't wait around for news. Maybe I should do a little reconnaissance of my own. I am not due back at my post for 48 hours so maybe I could sneak out tonight and be back before anyone missed me.* His mother always told him he had some sort of sixth sense about impending danger. He always knew in advance when he was going to get the short end of the stick with her anyway! Now he had this gut feeling that Romano was actually in grave danger or that he was a grave danger to Henry and maybe all the Allied forces. He was not sure why but the hairs on the back of his neck were tingling. He couldn't just let it rest. He had to know!

# CHAPTER 45

# SECRET MISSION

Henry sat on the side of his bunk watching the sun disappear behind the distant brown and rocky hills, brooding about what he should do. Tom, seated with his back facing Henry, jumped when he tapped him on the shoulder. The writing paper on his lap flew sideways as he grabbed his ink bottle.

"Geez Henry, don't creep up on me like that. You scared the shit out of me. "

"Sorry mate. I'm going back to the communications tent for a while. Have some work to catch up on."

"Thought you had a few days off. You don't get any thanks for busting your gut in this army."

"Yeah, I know but it will make things easier for me when I get back to it. Don't wait up for me; I could be there all night."

Henry slipped silently into the gathering dusk and walked in the direction of the communications tent. As soon as he was out of sight, he looked around furtively before diving between the supply hut and the mess tent. He grabbed the backpack he had hidden earlier in the sparse undergrowth and didn't stop until he was well out of sight. He changed into his camouflage clothing and headed towards the last known enemy position. Several hours later, after having to change course several times to evade patrols, he was back on the ridge. Below were remnants of the previous heavily armed encampment. A small convoy of trucks and some light artillery vehicles were lined up to head east. Henry took out his binoculars and trained them on the only source of light, a small camp fire burning on the edge of the clearing. His heart leapt as he focussed on the men seated around the fire. There, laughing and joking with the Italian officers, was Romano. *I need to get closer. Can't see any guards. Nothing strategic around to guard anyway.*

Henry moved stealthily around the perimeter of the camp until he was in hearing range. *Damn, they're speaking Italian. What the hell should I do? Stay and see what is going on or get back to camp and report. I have to be back before daylight or I'll be missed so I had better go now.* He retraced his path to camp without encountering any patrols. There should have been some around. He feared the enemy must have already moved out and not in the direction supposed by his superiors.

⚔

Less than an hour after Henry had slipped into the safety of his bunk, he was up again and heading towards Command HQ. It was still early and no-one was stirring. The soldiers on overnight guard duty were leaning on their rifles smoking and hardly even looked in his direction. He hadn't had any sleep. He still didn't know what to do. He couldn't really tell his commanding officers what he saw as he hadn't been authorised to be out of camp. He had to think of a way to get them to send him out to check on the enemy positions.

He arrived at the command hut just as Major Coulthard was coming out the door. "Henry, I was just coming to find you. Come inside, we have something to talk about."

"I was just coming to see you myself." As they entered the hut Henry saw that General Messinger was already seated inside. *Must be something important to get him out of bed this early.*

"Good morning Thompson. Sorry to get you out of bed on your day off."

"No problem, I was already up and around."

247

"We intercepted some messages overnight that seem to indicate that the enemy is planning some action in the next few days. We may have to send you out to check."

"I think I should go and check that camp we found a few days ago."

"We don't want you to go in that direction; we want you to check to the south west. We cut them off going north to Suez but we think they may be heading there from another direction."

"With all due respect sir, I don't think that is the case. I think that they may be going north east."

"There's no way they can get through along the coast Henry. Our Air Force and the British Navy have that covered."

"The Fox has been known to do the unexpected." Henry knew they weren't coming south as he would have encountered them on the way home last night. North east was the only way they could be headed.

"I think we can leave the strategy to those in command, Henry," Major Coulthard interrupted.

Henry kept quiet. Once he got out there he could make his own decisions on which way he went and explain himself later.

"Certainly sir, I would never disobey orders. I assume we haven't heard from Romano." Henry tried to stay calm. He knew that he would not be allowed out if he told them what he planned. He had to find out what Romano was up to.

"No, but we can't risk our whole campaign strategy by wasting time trying to rescue him. He knew what he was risking when he took on this job. Just as you do Thompson." The General was emphatic. Henry knew he would brook no questioning of his decisions.

Henry left camp at dusk. There was a lot of clear ground to cover. He moved quickly around the southern side of the camp and just as he was about to double back and head north he heard an allied patrol coming straight towards him. He dived into a clump of bushes close to the track as the group of heavily armed diggers rounded the corner chatting among  themselves.

"Well at least we haven't found any of those Krauts heading our way."

"Command is going to be happy with that."

"We should be able to take them by surprise this time."

*Not if you are heading west.* It could be a total disaster for the Allies if they were headed in the wrong direction. It wasn't a time to worry about his career. As soon as it was safe, Henry took a deep breath and continued on his way north.

From the top of the ridge just south of Thompson's Post he would have a clear view of the coastline north and south. The coincidence of this place's name was not lost on him, as that was just what it was going to be, his post. He was almost there when he spotted two shadows coming towards him. He was becoming skilled at clambering up trees and deftly flew up the only tree large enough to give him cover and held his breath as two figures passed only a few feet underneath him. Their camouflage gear was different to his. *An enemy surveillance mission coming from the north. So I am right. I can't stay and deal with them. I'll just have to hope that one of the Allied patrols picks them up.*

He travelled steadily for several hours, stopping at regular intervals to check his position and listen for enemy activity. He started to think he had been wrong when an armed vehicle appeared, speeding towards him. There was no tree to climb so he threw himself to the ground and crawled quickly behind a rocky outcrop seconds before the vehicle pulled up on the track, so close he could almost touch it. The occupants spoke excitedly in Italian. They seemed to be looking for someone – he hoped it wasn't him. He was sure he hadn't left any signs. Eventually they moved off in the opposite direction. He waited for 10 minutes before he moved north again. As he came over the top of the next outcrop of rocks he stopped abruptly in his tracks. The whole Axis convoy was lined up below ready to move north east!

*Jeez, worse than I thought. Less than an hour to dawn. No time to get back to camp on foot. I'm going to have to use my radio. We are going the wrong way! I have to risk it.* He headed towards a high ridge silhouetted against the dawn sky. He sent his message as quickly as possible and then looked around for an escape route. *Think I'll go in the opposite direction to camp, that may throw them off the scent.* He found a rocky outcrop with a cave-like recess that gave him a good view of any approaching traffic. *I could sure do with a smoke but I'll have to settle for this chocolate bar.*

Henry dozed fitfully in his uncomfortable rock cocoon. He dreamt of Connie and the life they would have after this war was over. He could see

a lovely little place in the country, far from the hustle and bustle of the city with laughing children playing happily in the sun and Connie smiling at her little brood. He would have a nice comfortable job in town.

As the sun rose Henry felt hot and uncomfortable. He forced his mind back to the job at hand. He had not seen or heard any patrols so decided to risk another look at where the enemy was headed.  He hid his radio and other equipment behind a pile of loose rocks. It was so well hidden that he fashioned a small arrowhead of rocks pointing to it, so he could retrieve it later.

He reached what he thought was the ridge he had climbed to send his message. It was hard for him to get his bearings in the bright daylight. *Damn it, why did I leave my compass in my backpack?* There was no sign of the Axis forces; just clear space in every direction. Using the sun as a guide he decided to move towards a distant outcrop that was about 500 yards to what he thought was north east of his position. He was halfway across the open space when a speeding jeep came hurtling through a gap in the rocks. He threw himself to the ground and rolled into the only depression he could find. He stayed perfectly still keeping his head down and hoped he hadn't been seen. He could tell the vehicle was getting closer by the increasing vibrations on the hard ground. Just when he thought it was safe to raise his head to take a look he felt a sharp stab in his back and excited voices broke out in Italian. Henry could not understand the fast gabbled words but he did pick up "Inglaise" so he rolled over, sat up and reached his hands in the air. His last thoughts as he held his head high and looked straight into the eye of his captors were of Connie. *Please forgive me my darling for such foolishness. I only hope one day you will find out how deeply and truly I loved you.*

# CHAPTER 46

# CAPTURED

Henry's hands and feet were tied and he was thrown face down into the back of the jeep. The Italians became agitated when he couldn't understand their questions. The jeep bumped its way across the rough terrain for what seemed like hours. Henry was afraid to lift his head and his forehead kept bouncing off the floor of the jeep. He was sure he would be covered in bruises. He closed his eyes and tried to ignore the searing pains. *Why would anyone put themselves through this just so grown men could see how many of their fellow men they could kill?*

The jeep finally pulled up and Henry was pulled roughly to his feet. He looked quickly around. He had been brought to the remnants of the camp he had spied on the night before. The heavy artillery and the tanks were nowhere to be seen but Henry recognised the makeshift shelters surrounding the clearing. Several officers in German uniforms came striding towards the small group that had gathered around the jeep. Henry looked directly into the steely eyes of an SS General and shuddered. *Please don't turn me over to them. I won't survive the night.*

An officer pulled Henry roughly to his feet, spat in his face and let out a torrent of what Henry guessed were German expletives. *Perhaps it's better I don't understand.* He involuntarily let out a little grunt. This was answered by a series of open-handed slaps to Henry's face. The General grabbed hold of the officer's hand.

"Nein, halt! Nehmen ihn entfernt." *Thank goodness one of them has some decency.*

With an SS officer on each side of him, Henry was dragged to a makeshift outdoor compound. Huddled inside were a blood stained and grubby assortment of allied prisoners with hardly enough room to stand comfortably, let alone sit. Beside this compound Henry noticed a hut with a roof and outer walls of wire-netting. There were only a few prisoners inside and they had canvas camp chairs to sit on. Henry thought these men may have been the German's own defectors when his eyes came to rest on a bedraggled figure sitting against the wire-netting. Romano! Henry's gasp must have been loud enough that the British soldier in a torn and dirty uniform, standing next to him, leant towards him and whispered:

"Important prisoners that lot – won't let them mix with us rabble out here."

"Are they from our side?" asked Henry.

"Don't know. They get taken away at intervals and come back looking worse for the wear."

"I need to get as close as I can to the one near the fence.

"I'll see what I can do for you."

After a small number of casual manoeuvres by the men in the compound, Henry was positioned only a few metres away from Romano.

"Romano," Henry called as loud as he dared. He kept his back to the guard at the other end of the compound and was shielded by the group of British soldiers. Henry repeated his call several times before Romano finally turned in his direction. He gave Henry a blank stare and Henry noticed he had bruises on his face and one eye was almost completely closed. Without another glance in Henry's direction, Romano stood up and walked to the other side of the covered enclosure.

*What on earth is he up to? Has he been tortured, has he has lost his memory or is this part of a double game he is playing? 48 hours ago he was laughing and talking to the same Italian officers who were now his prison guards.*

As the days passed in the compound, the prisoners were becoming very disconsolate. They were fed stale bread and cracked, foul-tasting cheese. They had no blankets for the cold desert nights even if they could lie down anywhere. The only toilet was a bucket pushed through a small opening in the fence and only emptied when it was filled to overflowing. Henry tried to ignore his dirt encrusted clothing, the stench of sweat and the putrid buckets. He silently watched everything that was going on in the surrounding camp. Romano was no longer in the compound next door. *If only he could talk to him.*

Henry was deep in thought when the gate of his compound opened. Two Germans in SS uniforms scanned the rancid mass of squirming bodies until their eyes rested on him. He tried to look unconcerned as they pushed their way through the tightly packed prisoners and grabbed him on either side. He had never felt this scared in his whole life but he stiffened his back and looked them straight in the eye.

"You, Inglaise, come." The bigger of the two menacing German soldiers commanded in heavily accented English. *Well at least they haven't found out who I am. Romano hasn't disclosed that.* He tried to brush aside the hands that gripped his arms tightly.

"I come willingly. There's no need for that." But the grip on his arms only tightened more until Henry finally gave in and winced with the pain. He was half-dragged, half-marched to a tent at the far end of the camp, well out of sight of the prisoners. He was pushed through the open flap which was immediately dropped down behind him.

As Henry's eyes became accustomed to the dull light, he shuddered at what he saw. A table in the middle of the tent was stacked with what he immediately recognised as implements of torture. Batons, chains, an assortment of lethal looking knives plus several hand guns. Either side of the table stood the two biggest men Henry had ever seen. Henry's mind was racing. He had heard about the methods and equipment used by the Germans to extract information from their prisoners but seeing it made him cringe. *I need to formulate a plan before I am in such a state that I will tell them anything.*

As he was hauled up onto the table, Henry steeled himself for the pain he knew was coming. He was chained to all four corners of the table by his arms and legs and the chains were slowly tightened. The flap was pulled up and they were joined by the SS General who had halted Henry's abuse previously. The officer put his hand on Henry's torturers to again stop their actions. He turned to Henry with a look that could only be described as murderous.

"Theese not having to happen, you know. Tell us you know about British positions and we let go," he said in broken English.

"I know nothing about the British. I am an Australian – got lost on my way back to camp and separated from my unit. I'm just a lowly foot soldier taking orders."

"So, Australie are you?  Well same thing – you fight with British. Where Australie forces going?"

"I told you I am only a private. No idea where we are headed until we start." The General nodded to the officers and they slowly tightened the chains on Henry's arms and legs. Searing pain shot through every inch of his body, as if his arms and legs were being torn off.

"You like that? Make you much taller." The General laughed as he gestured to his men and the tightening continued. Henry tried to make his mind go blank and ignore the pain. Wouldn't do to crack just yet. Eventually it all became too much and he cried out:

"Ok, please stop! I will tell you what little I know." Henry's mind was churning as he tried to concoct some positions that were as far from the Allied forces as he could remember. He hoped the Allies had now received his message and were headed north.

"Please, all I know is that when I left camp there was lots of talk about how we were going to head south to cut off the Italian forces that were moving up to reinforce your tank divisions. "

"I theenk not. Our planes see your guns and cavalry moving north to coast."

*Well that's a relief. How can I explain that?* " That is just a diversion to keep you from knowing our real purpose. We are using some of Rommel's own tactics – attacking from an unexpected direction."

"Ha. You not Major. How you know those things?"

"Those in command keep us in the dark but we keep our eyes and ears open. A lot of those guns you see are fake you know."

"Yes we find that out. Which ones the real ones? That's what we need to know."

"All I know is that those ones we set up along the coastal ridges are all fakes."

Henry hoped that that would send them in that direction as he knew that the Allies were targeting the coastal strip north of the railway line in order to stop the Axis forces from going any way other than along the ridge line that was well and truly covered by strategically placed anti-tank brigades and mine fields.

The General was looking scornfully at Henry. "You Australie, not so tough eh? "

He turned to the officers and spoke. Only when he was pushed roughly through the gate did Henry realise he had been taken to the other compound. He settled down in a corner as far from the outdoor compound as he could get and closed his eyes and tried to ignore the pain that still racked his tortured body.

# CHAPTER 47

# RESCUED

Henry slept fitfully. He grabbed a smelly blanket thrown in the corner and at least he had room to lie down. There were bruises on his arms and legs and he could only guess what a mess his face was in. There were fewer prisoners now and there was definitely no Romano! Henry kept to himself as much as possible as he didn't want to be asked questions. None of the other prisoners came from any units that Henry recognised. He wafted in and out of sleep and as the sun came up over the distant horizon he discarded his tattered blanket. Even though he had been in North Africa for almost a year he was still amazed at the difference in temperature between day and night.

*What are the Germans going to do when they find out I misled them? Will I be tortured again? I hope they kill me instead. Maybe then Connie and my family will remember me as a hero rather than a failed intelligence officer.*

As soon as he had finished the stale bread and the mug of warm, dirty water that was thrust at him through the fence, Henry's tormentors from the day before came thundering into the compound and without a word grabbed him and dragged him once again to the tent at the end of the camp. From glimpses of the sky, Henry guessed it was around midday. *This was not looking good. Surely they couldn't have checked up on things yet.*

The SS General was standing with his arms folded, a thunderous look on his face. Henry felt his stomach tighten into a knot. "Vell my little Aussie soldier. You sent us on a, how you say, an old goose chase. Vhat do you have to say for yourself?"

"Please sir, I only gave you the last known position of my battalion. It has been several days since I last saw them. They could have changed plans since then."

"Vell, they sure did move very quickly. Other sources put them hundreds of miles from your information."

"I warned you that I didn't know anything useful." Henry's spirits were buoyed by the thought that perhaps he had bought the Allied forces some time.

"Vhy I vaisting time on you, you little smart bum." The General turned impatiently to his other officers. He barked out some orders in German and stalked out of the tent. The only word Henry understood was "executionie". His lifted spirits took an immediate dive.

Henry was tied to a chair in the interview tent with a lone SS officer left to guard him. He knew his luck had run out. He had heard that when someone faces death their whole life flashes before them. All he could think of was Connie and his failed ambitions. How could he have been so stupid to think that he, a poor country boy with limited education could make a name for himself by changing the way people of different cultures looked at each other? Oh, how he would love to be back in Connie's sweet arms right now. He couldn't hold back the sob that racked his body. His guard jumped to his feet and cocked his rifle in his direction.

"You, Aussie – stop trying escape. Shoot you now, no wait."

Henry's head slumped to his chest and he closed his eyes tightly to hold back the tears. A feeling of calm came over him when he started to think about meeting his maker. His religious upbringing had taught him there was peace and contentment after death and he felt a wave of tranquillity engulf him. He pictured angels floating around him and he could almost hear the harp music. Just as Henry reached out to be taken by the hand by one of these celestial beings, his peaceful vision was interrupted by a steel grasp on his shoulder.

"You come now, you Aussie liar." His ankles were unshackled and he was pulled roughly to his feet. He was marched by six armed SS officers out of the tent and in the opposite direction to the prisoner compound. They reached a small clearing and Henry was stood against a lone palm tree. One of the guards attempted to tie a blindfold around his head. Henry pulled it from his grasp and threw it on the ground beside him. He stared straight into the eyes of his captor.

"Look me in the eye when you shoot me you bastard."

The SS officer shrugged his shoulders and without looking at Henry scooped up the discarded blindfold and strolled back to the waiting firing squad. Henry stiffened his back, looked straight at his executioners and took one last deep breath as the rifles were raised in unison in his direction. A vision of Connie and his family wafted over him. *May we all meet up again in more peaceful surroundings.*

At that moment an explosion rang out from the direction of the camp and loud voices yelled excitedly in German. The firing squad turned as one in the direction of the noise and in a split second Henry was grabbed on the arm and whisked behind the palm tree. The familiar voice of Romano whispered,

"Come on Henry, no time for explanations. Just follow me and run like you have never run before."

Henry needed no second invitation and even with his arms still tied he followed the young Italian at breakneck speed through the arid countryside. As they crossed about 50 metres of open ground to the nearest rocky outcrop, Henry noticed Romano was wearing an Italian officer's uniform. They slumped to the ground breathless and as Henry opened his mouth to speak, Romano put his finger to his lips. He gestured to Henry to follow him as he squeezed through a narrow opening in the rocks. Romano quickly rolled a waiting boulder across the opening to the small cave as they heard the Germans in pursuit. Henry felt a squeeze on his arm as Romano silently cut away his constraints. He took few quick breaths before settling down for what could be a long silent wait.

Romano handed Henry a water bottle and a small package of army rations. Still no conversation passed between them. When the sliver of light that was squeezing through beside the rock had almost faded, Romano slowly removed the rock. It seemed to Henry that it took forever before they could see outside. The desert night was descending, creating an eerie scene. Filtered light from the new moon was trying to escape from the confines of a cloud and was throwing strange shadows over the rocky terrain. A light breeze whispered through the sparse undergrowth creating quivering ghost-like images that startled Henry as he slowly followed Romano out into the early evening.

Romano gestured to Henry to follow him up the face of one of the larger rocky hillocks. They could see for miles in every direction. There were several lights blazing from the German camp but they couldn't make out any movements, even with the binoculars that Romano produced from his small knapsack. At last Romano broke his silence.

"Well Henry, it looks as though they have stopped looking for us for the moment."

"Romano, I don't know how to thank you. I thought I was a goner."

"Save your words Henry. We need to be well away from here before morning when I am sure they will start looking for us again."

"I really need to retrieve my gear before we head back to camp."

"Are you sure that is necessary Henry? It will cost us time and is very risky."

"Yes, there are some maps of enemy positions in there that I need to get back to HQ. I think they have totally misread where Rommel is headed. I can't be sure they received my radio message. Our efforts could be in vain if we don't let them know. I can go on my own if you like."

"Oh no you don't. It was splitting up that led us into all this trouble. I'm going to keep you where I can see you this time."

It seemed that Romano had assumed leadership of their two man team even though Henry out-ranked him. Normally that would have drawn a rebuff from Henry but he owed this young man his life so remained silent.

Henry and Romano sat in the only bit of cover from the bright moonlight that they could find, huddled close together under some Spinifex-type bushes clumped as if they also felt their unity would help them cope.

When the moon was high in the sky and there had been no sign of enemy movement for several hours, they moved stealthily over the desert terrain to where Henry had stowed his equipment. He was relieved when he rolled back the rocks and found everything as he left it except for a thick coating of desert dust.

"Well, Henry we have your precious equipment. Where to now?" Henry was relieved that Romano had now relinquished command back to him.

"We must get this stuff back to HQ as soon as we can. Lives could be lost if they take our troops where I think they intend to." Henry wished he was feeling as confident as he sounded.

"Chances are they will be long gone when we get back."

"They will keep someone there waiting for us, I am sure. I did manage to get one brief radio message back to them."

"Yes and that is what got you captured," Romano replied cynically.

"I know but I thought the risk was worth taking. Now it is vital that I get all the details back to them."

"We are going to need all our skills to keep ahead of these Axis forces. They are moving at an alarming rate. I wish we knew what was happening at the front."

"So do I Romano, so do I," said Henry with a big sigh.

⚬ ⚬ ❈❖❈ ⚬ ⚬

It was almost dawn when Henry and Romano heard approaching vehicles. They dived quickly into the undergrowth. A fast moving jeep, followed by a truck full of soldiers, was upon them almost as soon as they had moved. The dust engulfed them and it was all Henry could do to stop himself from lapsing into a coughing fit. There was very little cover for hundreds of yards in every direction except for a large rocky outcrop in the opposite direction to where they were headed. It looked like their only chance.

The German vehicles had pulled up on a small rise about fifty yards past their hiding place. The occupants of jeep were standing in the back scanning the terrain through binoculars. Henry gestured towards the rocky outcrop and Romano nodded. The vehicles started to move off so Henry and Romano started to run across the bare earth. They had almost reached their destination when shots rang out. The bullets bounced on the hard surface around them and showered them with dry earth. Henry turned to Romano to point to where they should go next and he saw him sprawled face down on the ground. *Oh my god, he's been hit.* Henry quickly covered the ground back to Romano and dragged him to the safety of the rocks as the two vehicles sped in their direction.

# CHAPTER 48

# ABANDONED

Henry was shaking as he pulled Romano to the safety of the rocky hillock. He ripped off his grimy shirt and tied it tightly around Romano's leg. No blood was flowing from the wound but Henry could see a gaping hole and knew the blood would soon follow. A trail of blood would give them no chance of evading the Germans who were now pursuing them on foot over the rough terrain. Henry could see them cautiously shielding themselves behind the rocks. *So they think we are armed! If only they knew.* They only had one small pistol and the last few rounds of ammunition were in its chamber. Henry was not going to give away their position by firing. Romano was now starting to regain consciousness and Henry looked frantically around for somewhere else to hide. On the other side of their rocky hill was a small but rather heavily wooded area. *They'll expect us to head there.* Henry noticed an opening in the side of a rock pile similar to the one they had hidden in before. After rolling a few rocks away Henry realised that there was a small cave behind. He dragged Romano quickly, yet gently into the space and succeeded in rolling several rocks back in front of them. He had to lie flat on top of Romano with his hand held over his mouth to keep them hidden and silent. Romano squirmed at first as he struggled with his consciousness but then went still, so Henry relaxed his hold.

The Germans were quite close. Henry hoped Romano was able to hear what they were talking about. Henry waited until he felt it was safe enough to raise his head and look around. He was abruptly pulled back down by Romano just as the Germans returned to their vehicles and drove off.

"Wow, that was close," whispered Henry.

"I don't think they'll be back. They think we got away through the trees and they have urgent business back with their forces."

"I guess they think we are not that important."

"They didn't have any idea who we were so they didn't want to waste any more time on us."

"It has been a real bonus for us that you speak the language. I wish I had taken the time to learn myself."

"My father wanted us to learn other languages."

"I thought you must have learnt it as part of your training."

"I did take it to another level then. "

"Have you ever regretted becoming an intelligence operative?" said Henry cautiously.

"It has certainly been a lot riskier than I thought it would be."

Romano winced. Henry reached over and touched gently him on the arm. "Don't worry, we are going to make it – it is too important for us not to."

*There's no way he's going to make it on his own and I'm not going to leave him here. I owe him too much for that. I should have never doubted him. He is a remarkable young man.*

Henry moved Romano to the shelter of the small forest behind their rocky hideout. Romano's condition was deteriorating and he was lapsing in and out of consciousness. They had no medical supplies but Henry had managed to dress the wound with the cotton wadding he carried with his radio. He had stopped the bleeding but had nothing to give Romano for the pain. He wasn't complaining but Henry knew he must be in agony. His flesh had been blown away down to bone and his whole leg was burning. As Romano lapsed into periods of delirium, Henry could not even spare any of the small amount of water that was left to wipe his fevered brow. He knew that if Romano's leg wasn't removed soon, infection would set in and there would be no saving him. In lucid moments Romano had tried to talk Henry into heading back on his own. Henry would not listen to him. He had made up his mind that he would stay with Romano as long as he was alive. He owed him too much to let him die out here alone. They had enough food for another meal each and about half a cup of water to go with it.

On the second morning Romano pulled Henry down beside him and handed him the sharp pocket knife that he always carried. He pointed to his leg and whispered in his weakened state: "Please, you are going to have to do it for me. I haven't the strength. It has to come off. I can't stand the pain anymore."

Henry felt his stomach tighten and as he removed the makeshift dressing he saw the tell-tale pus oozing out of the wound and he knew Romano was right. The leg had to come off. "I don't know if I can do it Romano."

"Please Henry. I know it will not save me but it will ease the pain."

Henry took a deep breath, gave Romano the case from his radio to bite on and started to cut. He was surprised how easily the red hot flesh yielded to the sharp blade. By the time he had reached the bone Romano had passed out. Henry managed to saw a groove all the way around the brittle fibula and then used the butt of his pistol to crack it enough to remove the whole lower leg. Henry quickly used Romano's belt as a tourniquet and then dressed the wound with cotton wadding.

Henry picked up the foul smelling limb and buried it in a shallow hole that he managed to dig with the blade of Romano's knife. The ground was rock hard. He hurried back to Romano's side convinced that the smell of rotting flesh would stay with him for the rest of his days.

Romano recovered consciousness long enough to reach out and grab Henry's arm with a feeble grip. "Thank you. We are no longer in each other's debt. Now I want you to go and get that information back to HQ otherwise all our efforts will have been wasted." Henry turned away from Romano so that he couldn't see the tears now rolling down his face. When he composed himself enough he took Romano gently in his arms and gave him a hug.

"I know you are right. I have to go. I will never forget you. We are true mates." Romano sighed, closed his eyes and slumped back onto the makeshift bed of foliage that Henry had fashioned for him. Henry gently placed the remainder of their rations and water as well as the pistol with its few remaining bullets next to the now peaceful figure. With a heavy heart he picked up his backpack, took out his compass and commenced his journey in what he hoped was the right direction.

⊷⊶⊷

Henry had been walking for two days when he finally entered the clearing where he expected to find his battalion. It was now quite dark. There had been a bit of moonlight earlier so he had kept going, using the night as his cover. Dawn was fast approaching and the moon had now sunk below the horizon. Eerie light cast vague shadows around the clearing. There was not a single vehicle, tent, hut or soldier in sight. Romano was right. They had already moved on. What on earth was he going to do now? He had no food or water, no gun and no idea what direction to take to catch up with the Allies. He slumped on the ground against one of the spindly palm trees that surrounded the former camp. He closed his eyes and tried to compose himself.

"Come on Henry Thompson get a move on." He imagined the voice of his mother when she was ordering him to walk faster as a child. *Oh my God, I haven't given my mother a thought in months. What's she doing in my head now?* He tried to conjure up a more pleasant picture of the delectable Connie but his mother kept imposing herself. *Was this my retribution for defying her to join the army? Was God finally punishing me for neglecting my family? Or have I finally lost my marbles? They say too much time in the desert can play havoc with your sanity. Am I even in the right clearing?* Henry slumped over, his head on his chest and lapsed into a deep sleep.

Henry woke up with the sun high in the sky and he was bathed in sweat. He slowly pulled himself up from his uncomfortable position against the palm tree and looked around the abandoned camp. There were few remnants of his fellow soldiers' occupation. All he found was a water canteen partly concealed in the sparse undergrowth. Henry turned it upside down in a vain attempt to extract even the smallest drop of moisture. He threw it away in disgust.

*Should I send a radio message? No, that would not do. The last time I did that look what happened.* He slumped back on the ground, placed his head between his knees and started to sob.

# Chapter 49

# Unexpected Encounter

Henry stared at his desolate surroundings. The country as far as he could see was dry and dusty; rolling hills covered with small bushy shrubs and an occasional copse of trees. He twirled his compass around in his hand. Should he try going east and see if he could make it to Alexandria? Or should he head west towards the front line. Not really knowing what the situation was in the west he decided to try to catch up with his own battalion. He hoped it was headed north east to confront Rommel head-on. He stuffed the empty water canteen and his compass into his rucksack and headed away from the setting sun.

Henry knew it was only a matter of time before he reached the vast desert plains. He could hear guns booming in the distance and allied and enemy planes came and went overhead. He knew the Axis forces couldn't be too far away. Romano told him how he had overhead the German generals laughing about how the Allies were so easy to fool. He needed to find his unit soon. By late afternoon Henry started to feel light-headed. It was 36 hours since he had anything to eat or drink. His lips were chapped and his stomach had sunken into its cavity as if it was being sucked away by some unseen parasite. He knew he could not go on much longer. His thoughts turned to Connie. How he had failed her! Not only would he not be returning from this senseless war but he wouldn't have achieved anything to change the course of events either. What would his family think? There'd be no bragging about their hero now! He had let everyone down.

He arrived at another rocky hillock and decided to rest there for the night. He rummaged around in the few small bushes nearby, trying to decide if any were edible or contained water. As he parted the foliage of one of the largest, a distant image caught his eye. *I am going off my head. Starting to see mirages now.*  He saw an oasis with green palm trees. He quickly averted his gaze and sat down in the shade of the largest bush. He tried not to think about it but he couldn't stop himself from parting the foliage and having another look.

The light was starting to fade, but the vision was becoming clearer. As the shimmering heat haze started to disappear, the image seemed to rise out of the desert landscape and beckon him. He pulled his binoculars out of his backpack. He could see the palm trees swaying gently in the evening breeze. *If they are real I could reach them before the light goes completely.* He tried not to stare too intensely as he crossed the open space but every time he looked, the apparition appeared clearer. He eventually started to run, gathering strength until he came charging into the centre of his dream. He threw himself headlong into the murky water. As his lungs started to fill with the dirty liquid he came up spluttering. He drank greedily, gulping the water down so quickly that he almost choked.

"Take it easy, young man. Make youself ill." A vaguely familiar voice with a heavy German accent split the desert silence. He was frozen with fear.

Henry pulled himself back from the water and slowly turned around. His heart started to beat so fast that he thought it was going to jump out of his emaciated body. There was the one person he did not ever want to see again. The SS General, who had ordered his torture and execution, was propped up against a palm tree, with a rifle pointed directly at Henry.

"Vell, vell if it isn't my escaping Aussie spy." Henry was rooted to the spot in fear. When he opened his mouth to reply, no sound came out. He was still shaking when he realised that the SS General was injured. Although his rifle was pointed at Henry he winced with pain each time he moved. Henry's mind was working overtime. Should he wait until the next bout of pain and make a run for it? It was unlikely that the officer would be able to follow. There appeared to be no one else in the vicinity. Henry hoped the officer had not noticed his furtive glances around the small clearing.

"Don't try anything. I may be injured but I am good shot. You wouldn't make first tree." Henry still hadn't said a word to his tormentor.

The General gestured with his gun to Henry. "Come sit here. I really would like talk you. I don't want hurt you." Henry stood his ground. It was very hard to sit down and have a chat with someone who had recently inflicted so much pain on you.

"I know you not trust me but we both in much trouble. I think we help each other. Don't have to like."

Henry walked slowly over to the seated General and lowered himself to the ground. The prostrate figure winced again and Henry could see fresh blood oozing through the loosely arranged bandage on his upper right arm. The gun was held in the crook of his left arm. Henry tried to cast his mind back to the scene of his torture. *Was he left-handed?* The steely blue eyes that had mesmerised him back then were fixed on him again. Henry decided to risk it and lunged out and neatly grabbed the gun from his grasp and quickly pointed it in the General's direction. A low chuckle was squeezed from the pain-racked man.

"No bullets. Nice try." Henry turned to walk away from the seated man.

"You not getting far without my help." Henry stopped in his tracks. He knew that the General was right.

"Here, have some my food. Not much left but will share if you spare me."

"Why should I do that? I could take it all if I wanted to." Henry finally croaked out his first words. He had stopped shaking but he was not going to socialise with this bastard.

"I have something you need."

"I could take whatever I want and you couldn't stop me."

"What I can help you with not lying around somewhere."

"There's nothing you can do for me."

"Don't you want get back to own forces?"

"How can you help me with that?"

"I can lead you around Axis checkpoints."

"Why would you do that for me?"

"I have been left here to die. Only hope is for someone help me out here. When you are safe I will be closer some help myself."

"I don't know if I can trust you."

"I feel same way about you but I think we both no choice. My name Heinrich, what yours?"

"Henry – English version of yours, I think. Perhaps there is a reason we have been thrown together like this." Henry looked skyward to the stars that had appeared in the night sky as if to ask the Lord for some guidance.

Heinrich pointed to a pile of things just out of his reach. "Lamp and some matches there. Light, then we eat." Henry realised he had no choice.

Henry's state of exhaustion had caught up with him. He sat out of reach of Heinrich, watching him carefully in the flickering lamp-light. They had split one ration pack between them and Henry had brought some water from the oasis and held it to Heinrich's parched lips. Heinrich fell into a fitful sleep, interrupted only by an occasional start that Henry guessed was caused by pain.

Henry had done his best to clean Heinrich's wounds with the medical kit that he found among the small cache of supplies. There were still some jagged pieces of metal protruding from the wounds. Henry wasn't able to remove them for fear of setting off more bleeding. Heinrich told him his wounds had come from shrapnel from a bomb that was dropped on their convoy by circling British planes. *Hopefully that was because they got my message.* They were on their way to the front line so he was left with all the supplies they could spare. They promised him they would contact their support services to come and pick him up. That was three days ago.

Heinrich stirred and opened his eyes and looked straight at Henry. He grabbed the rifle with no bullets and held it between them.

"I no threat you know. Can't get to my feet." Heinrich was struggling for breath as he forced the words out.

"Is there anything else I can do for you?" Henry asked with genuine concern. If he had only been meeting this man for the first time he felt as though he could have even liked him.

"Not unless you have surgical instruments to cut this shrapnel away." After taking several deep breaths as if to regain some strength to continue, "Are you married?" asked Heinrich.

"Yes," said Henry.

"Children?"

"No, we only married three days before I embarked for this God-forsaken country."

"Most difficult. I have wife, and four children. Married ten years."

"You miss them?"

"Of course. Don't know if I will see them again. Didn't ask to get in this war. Curse that Hitler and Churchill."

"I sometimes feel that way about them too. They seem to keep themselves dry and safe while we go out and do their dirty work. Why the SS?"

"In German Army no choice. Do as told or suffer consequences. Disobey orders and…." Heinrich then made a cutting motion across his throat with his flattened hand. Heinrich winced again and Henry walked over and covered him with a grubby blanket he had found.

"I think we should both try and get some sleep and see what we want to do in the morning." Heinrich had already closed his eyes so Henry lay down on the ground-using his backpack for a pillow but propping the rifle up against his shoulder and covering it with his free arm in such a way that it would wake him if anyone tried to remove it. Sleep quickly engulfed him.

Henry woke up with a start in the middle of a nightmare about his torture. He was in a cold sweat. He looked around. The sun was just starting to rise behind the distant sand hills and he didn't feel as if he had slept at all. He rose slowly and went over to check on Heinrich. The way he was slumped over with his head on the side made Henry think that maybe he wasn't going to have to worry about him anymore. Just as Henry bent down, Heinrich groaned weakly and opened his eyes, rubbing them as if to help them in their efforts to stay that way. Henry pulled back quickly.

"Hoping you were saved the trouble of disposing of me, were you?" Heinrich said slowly as if every word was causing him immense pain. Henry gave a start as he had weighed up his chances of finding his way back to his forces on his own but he knew he needed Heinrich. His Christian upbringing had taught him to forgive his fellow man no matter how badly they had sinned and he knew that he wouldn't have been able to kill him anyway, even in self-defence.

"You may not believe this but I am glad you are still with us. I wish death on no man, no matter how badly they have treated me. God is the only judge of a man's deeds."

"Religion played no part in my upbringing but have always felt a being more powerful than man existed. I pray a little sometimes."

"I could debate the subject with you all day but I think we should start thinking about what we are going to do."

"See bushes over there," pointing at a brown clump of desert undergrowth about 30 yards away, "go look behind."

Henry walked cautiously in that direction. As he got closer he could see a camouflage net had been thrown over something, Henry circled the site several times, poking the ground with the empty rifle that he still carried with him (why he didn't know). He finally stretched out from as far away as he could and slowly lifted the net. Underneath he could see a jeep. *How did I miss that?* He walked briskly back to where Heinrich had not moved.

"Why didn't you tell me about that last night? We could be well on our way now."

"Were you trusting me then? I think not. You my enemy too you know. Waited to see what happened during the night."

"Do you have much fuel?"

"They leave me enough to get back to camp if I recover enough to drive."

"Well, if we are going to get out of this God-forsaken place we had better get started."

Heinrich held out his hand to Henry with a set of keys. He also gestured to a jacket folded up on the ground.  "You put that on in case we spotted by patrol. "

Henry loaded their few possessions into the back of the jeep, fashioning a bed out of the softer things and then, as gently as he could, lifted Heinrich and laid him on top. Heinrich made no sound but Henry knew he was in great pain and admired him for his strength in not showing it. Henry jumped into the driver's seat, still holding that damn useless rifle. Somehow he regarded it as the symbol of his position of authority over this once powerful man.

"Which way?" Henry turned to Heinrich.

"Go straight through there," he said, pointing through the palm trees in the direction of the morning sun. Henry crunched into first then second gear, and steered the jeep to weave through the sand dunes. *Best keep out of sight as much as possible.* He gripped the wheel tightly, still feeling apprehensive. *Maybe Heinrich will turn me over the first chance he gets.* Heinrich moaned. Henry glanced over his shoulder at his pale sweaty face. He feared that Heinrich would not survive for that much longer. Henry hoped they would be close to his own unit when that happened. He straightened up, shifted into third and put his foot down, speeding along a flat section towards some dunes a few miles up ahead. If Heinrich died it could be the end of the line for him too.

# CHAPTER 50

# TRUSTING YOUR ENEMY

The hot air of the desert was blowing straight into Henry's face. His eyes were becoming very irritated. He estimated they had been on the go for about six hours. He pulled out the remaining piece of cotton wadding that he was carrying and wiped the sweat from his grimy face. He had wrapped his compass in it to protect it from the harsh desert conditions so he quickly checked their direction.

"It's all right my friend. I not lead you into trap." Heinrich was paying closer attention to him than he realised.

"Well, we don't seem to be going in the right direction. We are still going due east."

"So you not tell me truth about where your forces are? I suspect so."

"So you are leading us straight to yours? I didn't think you had any forces in this area. There's not anything strategic here. We are just going further into the desert."

"Ha ha. You should know never to expect the Fox to do what is expected of him. We should start coming across some patrols soon."

"What, your patrols? I thought you were going to get me back to my unit."

"Be patient, I do as promised."

The jeep spluttered as it crawled up and over the top of a steep sand dune. Henry pulled it to a slow stop as they sighted a number of vehicles displaying the red and black swastika flag of the German Third Reich, coming straight towards them.

"Leave talking to me." Heinrich whispered to Henry.

Heinrich started talking very rapidly to the German soldiers who had alighted from their vehicles and waved the approaching jeep to stop. Heinrich chatted casually to them for several minutes. They made no complaint as Henreich motioned Henry to move off.

"What was that all about?"Henry said when they were a safe distance away.

"Nothing of consequence. They are on their way back to their camp. They say there are no enemy forces in the area and they are hoping to have a day off." Henry started to feel very uneasy. *No British or Australian forces in the area? Where on earth have they gone? I hope they got my message.*

They continued on, passing a German patrol almost every hour; each as jovial as the first. *We must be miles from any of my units. We haven't even come across a checkpoint.*

⸺ ⊱❈⊰ ⸺

At last they saw a number of vehicle and tents under a small copse of trees about 300 yards ahead. Heinrich waved to Henry to take a track that took them around a hillock well away from the assembled group. As they sped off across a new stretch of dusty open terrain Henry paused to look back and there was no sign of anyone pursuing them. They had not been noticed. The terrain became more rugged and Henry had to slow down. More trees appeared and from the position of the sun he decided they were now heading north-east. He didn't want to let Heinrich see that he was getting anxious about their situation so he avoided another look at his compass. He stopped at intervals to check on Heinrich who appeared to be weakening.

"Would you like to rest in the shade for a while?" They were approaching a wooded area.

"No," said Heinrich emphatically. "Keep moving." He was covered in dust but Henry could still make out the pallor of his skin. His eyes looked like sunken black holes, rimmed with red and then white. His lips were cracked and parched even though they had plenty of water.

"Why are we going around the checkpoints when we are getting past the patrols so easily?"

"It would slow us down too much."

"They must see us sooner or later and then we may have some tough questions to answer."

"There is another checkpoint just on the other side of those trees. We are going to have to go through  as there is no way around. Just let me do talking and we be ok."

The desert had given way to rocky ridges. Henry knew they were getting closer to the coast. But where on the coast? The Allies thought they had captured the entire coast between Alexandria and El Alamein so where on earth were they? Heinrich directed Henry towards a group of vehicles that were blocking the entrance to some sort of canyon. His heart began to pound and his mouth felt dry. *It's too late now. If Heinrich is going to turn me over this will be it.* Heinrich managed to pull himself up to a sitting position in the back of the jeep. Henry noticed he had used some of their precious water to sponge the worst spots on what was left of his uniform and had wiped most of the caked dust from his face. He looked almost regal in his appearance as he sat stiffly propped up. *He's one tough son-of a-bitch.*

Henry rolled the jeep to a stop. For several minutes Heinrich spoke with two soldiers who stood to attention as soon as they saw the remnants of the General's stars on his tattered uniform. They held their rifles stiffly and Henry wondered if he could grab one if he had to make a break for it. He needn't have worried. One of the soldiers disappeared into the small tent behind them and when he came back out he handed a small package to Heinrich who signalled Henry to move off through the narrow canyon.

"See, told you we'd be right. Even managed to get some more food for us."

Henry started to relax. He turned to thank Heinrich and jumped out of the jeep when he saw him slumped over with his head on his chest.

Henry held a canteen to his lips; he was burning with fever and thirstily gulped the offered water.

"Try to have something to eat," stuttered Henry knowing that it was really no use. Heinrich was dying.

Heinrich put a burning hand on Henry's arm "You save food for youself. It's water I need. Please keep going, we almost there." His voice was weak and trembling; he slumped back and closed his eyes. Henry looked back towards the checkpoint and one of the guards seemed to be pointing in their direction. What was he going to do if Heinrich died? He stole another look back and decided it was time to get out of there. He sped up and careered the jeep through the narrow canyon as quickly as he thought was safe.

An occasional groan came from Heinrich but Henry didn't stop. He didn't know why Heinrich hadn't turned him in then and there. It would have been in his own best interests. He looked around and noticed dust from a vehicle not that far behind them. *Are we being followed or are they just going the same way?* Heinrich appeared unconscious. Henry increased his speed again.

Looking ahead over the next rise Henry noticed a greener tinge in the vegetation and more of it. The canyon had given way to open ground. About 500 yards to the right he could see a small hill covered in some quite large trees, interspersed with bushy shrubs. Henry pulled up, checked behind him but there was no sign of the other vehicle. Maybe he was worried for nothing. He trained his binoculars on the surrounding horizon.

*Damn there's another checkpoint at the end of the canyon.* Heinrich hadn't told him about that. Heinrich's breathing was laboured and his head was slumped to the side unnaturally. Henry tried to force some water between his parched lips but he was too weak to swallow. Henry jumped back into the driver's seat and headed for the wooded hill as fast as he could. It was as if he got there quicker he would be able to keep Heinrich alive longer. The jeep was at times almost airborne as it flew over the rough terrain. They arrived at the last rise before the end of the woods as the engine began to splutter. Henry felt the jeep lurch forward. *Damn, we are out of fuel.* Henry slapped the gearstick into neutral and managed to turn the jeep towards a small patch of shade and it came to its final rest with Heinrich sheltered from the setting sun. Henry had feeling of déjà vu as he looked at his passenger who was barely alive. *Am I going to have to abandon another human who had risked all to save my life?  I have to get back to our forces as quick as I can. Romano's sacrifice would have been in vain if I don't.*

Henry gently lifted Heinrich out of the jeep and placed him in a more comfortable position in the shade of the tallest of the thorny acacia trees. He laid the empty rifle across his chest (a symbolic gesture more than anything) and the radio by his side (that was going to be no use to Henry either as he couldn't risk using it). He gathered as much of the equipment as he could carry, including the remaining food and water. With one last peaceful gesture, he carefully swept a dust laden lock of Heinrich's hair away from his eyes. *I hope that Romano was treated humanely by whoever found him.  This senseless waste of life can't go on.* He turned his eyes skyward. *Please God bring this madness to an end soon.*

As Henry reached the edge of the clearing he turned and took one a last look at Heinrich. He took out his compass and turned to the north. He decided that he was probably not that far from their previous base at El Amiraya. He slowly turned and started on his way, his shoulders slumped forward and his eyes staring down at the dry ground ahead.

CHAPTER 51

# JOURNEY TO SAFETY

Henry trudged on, barely looking at his compass, putting one foot after the other, not even glancing up to see if anything had changed ahead of him. *Am I ever going to get back to my unit? Where on earth am I? Can I be sure I am headed in the right direction? Even If I do get back to my own unit, what is going to happen to me? Could I be court-marshalled for disobeying orders? What will Connie think of me then? My mother will certainly disown me. I hope Connie somehow gets the full story if I don't get out of here. I should have written her a letter and left it somewhere to be found but the enemy could have found it and that could have made them start looking for me. I seem to have been walking for hours. How do I know what time it is in this long twilight?*

Henry slowly lifted his head. The countryside had turned into a broad expanse of green. Wooded areas were dotted all over the terrain. Henry took a deep breath. He felt a difference in the air. He spotted some small cottages and what looked like fruit or olive trees surrounding them. *Maybe I could find some shelter and food. But what sort of reception will I get? Would they be sympathetic to our side? I am going to have to take the chance. I have no other choice. Please don't desert me now Lord.*

Henry was about to make a run for it when he heard a vehicle approaching. He ducked behind a tree with large trunk covered in some kind of prickly leaves. The sharp points dug into the side of his face as he pressed himself up against it. His hands started to shake. *They must have seen me standing on top of the rise. I would have been clearly silhouetted against the setting sun. I should have been more careful.*

When he saw the blue and gold British uniforms a feeling of euphoria came over him and he felt like bursting into song. There were four men in the jeep, two in the back, a Captain and a Corporal and another Corporal and a Sergeant in the front. He ran out onto the roughly formed track waving his arms. The jeep came to an abrupt halt and those on board jumped out and surrounded him with their guns cocked, the officers with hand pistols and the other two with rifles.

"It's OK – I'm an Australian. 2/3rd Pioneers, 9th Division," Henry yelled as he threw his arms in the air.

"What's with the Third Reich gear then, mate!" said the Corporal in a cockney accent, with a sarcastic emphasis on the "mate".

"Oh shit, I forgot about that." Henry ripped off the German Officer's jacket to reveal a ripped vest underneath.

"That's not too convincing either son," drawled the Captain with an upper-class accent. "I think you better come back to camp with us. Tie him up Serg."

The Sergeant started to push Henry towards their vehicle with his hands held firmly behind his back as another vehicle arrived.

"What's going on here?" A British Colonel swung himself down out of the jeep and walked purposefully towards them.

Henry fumbled around in his backpack and found his dog tags. He handed them to the Colonel who slowly turned them over in his hand. "What's an Aussie Sergeant doing out in the middle of nowhere in a German uniform?"

"It's a long story sir but if you can get me back to my unit, I will get my commanding officer to explain it to you."

"Special forces, eh. I'm afraid we are going to have to keep you under guard until we confirm all this."

"That's no problem. I would have been surprised if you did take my word. I must be some sight!"

"You sure are. Can't wait to hear your story." He reminded Henry of Major Coulthard. Gruff yet fair.

Henry's hands were tied together and  he was pushed in the back of the jeep between the two British officers. The Sergeant in the front seat was turned around to watch him closely. He had his rifle at the ready. Henry felt degraded but knew they had no choice. He decided to tell them about Heinrich. He hoped they would understand. "How would you like to take a very important German General prisoner?"

"Are you telling us now that you are a German General?"  Said the straight-laced Colonel, with a touch of sarcasm in his voice.

Henry chuckled, "Of course not, but I know where you can find one and you won't have any trouble taking him prisoner, he is badly injured."

"Ok, tell us about it." A hint of resignation had crept into his voice.

"I was helped to escape by an SS General who needed assistance as he was injured. He had a jeep but couldn't drive. I needed to get away in a hurry so we came to an arrangement."

"Where is he now?"

"Well, the jeep ran out of fuel a few miles back and he was too ill to continue. I made him as comfortable as I could and continued on foot. It won't be too far away by jeep."

"What do we have to gain by retrieving him?"

"He would be a very important prisoner for you. A high ranking SS Officer."

"If he is so ill, will he really be any use to us?"

"I was hoping we may be able to save his life. I owe him mine."

"What about enemy patrols?"

"Haven't seen any for hours. Besides they all seemed to be going in the other direction."

"Let's give it a try then."

It took the jeep only 15 minutes to traverse the short distance back to the wooded copse. *Geez, I must have been going around in circles. I thought I came much further than this.*

The Corporal slowed down as they approached the trees. "Where was this checkpoint you were telling us about?"

"Back there over the rise. You should be able to see some sort of light if they are still there."

"Go check it out Sergeant – hold your positions the rest of you. Lights off." No one moved once this authoritative voice had spoken.

The Sergeant was back in five minutes. "No sign of anything down there sir."

"Let's get on with this then."

The jeep was still where Henry had left it. The Sergeant cocked his rifle and had it pointed straight at Henry. "I hope for your sake this is not a trap. You will be the first to go." The Sergeant had stayed with the jeep as the other British officers slowly approached the jeep with guns drawn.

"There's no-one here sir."

"He's over there." Henry pointed to the shadowy figure slumped over just as he had left him.

"It's too late," called back the Corporal, "this guy's a goner." Henry felt a pang of guilt and turned to the Sergeant.

"Can I please go over and pay my last respects? In spite of the fact that this bloke treated me badly and was our sworn enemy I somehow feel responsible for him."

"Well don't be too long over it. We need to get out of here and back to base before we are seen," interrupted the Colonel. *I could get to like this man.*

Henry walked slowly over to Heinrich. He could see that he hadn't moved and he had a peaceful look on his face. Henry laid his hand on Heinrich's now cool forehead. He said a silent prayer and wiped away a tear that trickled down his face. *Blast this useless war. How many more lives are going to be wasted before it's over?*

The Colonel caught hold of Henry's arm. "Come on mate, we have to get out of here."

"Can't we bury him or something?"

The Sergeant chipped in. "What do we want to do that for. These bastards wouldn't do that for us."

"This one would have, I think," said Henry in a barely audible voice.

"Come on. We haven't got much time. We have nothing to dig with but if we lay him over here," the Colonel swung his lantern around the wooded area, "we should be able to cover him with those loose rocks. That will give him some sort of resting place. Maybe his own will find him if we put this rifle in as a marker."

It only took the group of men a few minutes to complete their task and as they piled back into the jeep, Henry couldn't help looking back one last time. The rifle protruding from the pile of rocks sent a long shadow away from the jeep's lights. A sort of monument to the futility of war, he thought. He kept watching until the image faded slowly as the jeep moved off and was lost in the darkness of the night. Henry wondered again if Romano was afforded the same dignity in his resting place.

Henry was free to move around the British camp but was closely shadowed by Sergeant Campbell. They had been unable to get in touch with Henry's unit to confirm his story. Apparently the fighting at El Alamein was in full swing and there was not much news coming back in this direction. These British forces were being held in reserve in case things didn't go to plan. There was a lot of activity in the camp this morning. Henry took an early morning walk and was sure that something was about to happen. He noticed his watch dog Sergeant casually leaning up against a jeep watching him and enjoying an early morning cigarette. It had been so long since Henry had a smoke that he was sure he was cured of this habit but the temptation got the better of him.

"Don't suppose you could spare me one. " Henry nodded at the smouldering cigarette in the Sergeant's hand. The Sergeant looked at him with his steely grey eyes. Without saying a word he held out the packet to Henry who eagerly took one and put it into his mouth with such haste that he almost devoured it.

"Been a while, has it?" The sarcastic tone of the untrusting Sergeant was obvious in his voice. Henry ignored the spiteful quip.

"What's happening around here? I get the feeling that something is going down."

"Yes, you would like to know wouldn't you? Well I'm afraid you won't be part of it. In fact I was just about to come and round you up. The Colonel wants you locked up for the duration."

"What could I do even if I am the enemy sympathiser you think I am? I have no weapons or radio. I think I would have probably been better off still out there in the desert than here with you untrusting lot."

The Sergeant pulled his pistol and pushed Henry in the direction of a makeshift compound at the other end of the camp. As they approached Henry could see that there were several German and Italian prisoners already locked up. "Hey, you're not putting me in there with that lot are you? I'll be lucky to get out alive."

"Well if you don't I will be the first to apologise," sniggered the unlikeable Sergeant. He pushed Henry through the gate being held open by two armed guards. "Go on, get in there you would-be German l over."

Henry stumbled to regain his footing and turned to see an approaching convoy of vehicles. There were two heavily armed trucks in front followed by a covered field vehicle and another two trucks behind. As they approached Henry felt his heart beat quicken. "Hey that's Monty himself! He'll be able to vouch for me you know – I have worked with him."

"Yeah, sure. Next thing you will be telling me you're really the King of England. There's no way you're getting near the great man. He's the reason we are locking you up. Can't take any chances with him."

"Please," pleaded Henry, "at least tell him that Sergeant Henry Thompson from the 2/3rd Pioneers would like a word with him and let him make up his own mind."

"Hey Serg," interrupted one of the guards, "perhaps you had better give him a chance to prove himself. You are going to look pretty silly if he is who he says he is."

"Just lock him up, will you. I'll speak to the Colonel about it."

Henry had been in the prisoner compound for less than an hour. He endured the other prisoners talking to him first in German and then in Italian – he couldn't understand a word. Henry became  agitated. He looked around for some possible means of escape. Then he heard the familiar calm voice of the Colonel.

"Let him out. Monty wants to see him." The relief Henry felt made tears well in his eyes.

"Thank you sir. I knew I would eventually get through to someone who knew me but I didn't think it would be the great Monty himself."

"Sorry we doubted you. But you had better be genuine or I will turn you over to Serg to deal with if you make a fool of me."

The Colonel had no need to worry. The minute Henry was hustled, still with a gun trained on him, through the door of the tent that had been specially set up for the occasion, General Montgomery came over and took him in a great big bear hug. The Sergeant was standing holding back the flap of the tent and Henry caught his eye over the General's shoulder. There was no hint of remorse or no sign of any apology there. Henry couldn't help thinking that there were good and bad men on both side in this conflict.

"Henry my boy, how good it is to see you. We thought we had lost you."

"You don't know what a relief it was for me to see you sir."

"You can't blame my officers for doubting you – you are quite a sight you know." The General said with a hint of laughter in his voice.

"Well I haven't actually been carrying a mirror around with me." Henry replied jovially.

"I need to sit down and go through some things with you." The General's voice had suddenly taken on a serious note.

"It will be my pleasure sir but don't you think we should wait until we are back with my command and we can go through things together.

I have some really important stuff on troop numbers and equipment and where they are heading." There was a long pause before the General answered.

"I have some bad news for you Henry. You unit suffered severe casualties early in the battle for El Alamein. Those who were left unscathed have already been sent home."

Henry felt as if his whole world had collapsed around him. A knot formed in his stomach. He opened his mouth to ask about some of his closest friends when the General put up his hand to stop him. "Don't get yourself worked up. I will get you a full casualty list when we get you back to HQ. You will be coming with us when we leave here later today."

Henry hung his head to hide the tears that were welling up in his eyes. "I will never forgive myself. I have failed everyone."

Monty came over to Henry and gently placed an arm around his shoulders. "Don't blame yourself son. We won't win all the battles but we are getting on top in this one. That radio message you got through saved many lives. We ARE going to win the war."

Henry let out a heavy sob. "But how am I going to face them at home. They expected so much of me."

"Come on now the important thing is to get you home as soon as possible. Things won't seem so bad then."

CHAPTER 52

# HOME AT LAST

*"Officers, warrant officers and non-commissioned officers and men of the Australian Imperial Force; these great days we are living in are in a time for deeds rather than words, but when great deeds have been done there is no harm in speaking of them. And great deeds have been done. The Battle of Alamein has made history, and you are in the proud position of having taken a major part in that great victory. Your reputation as fighters has always been famous, but I do not believe you have ever fought with greater bravery or distinction than you did during that battle, when you broke the German and Italian Armies in the Western Desert. Now you have added fresh lustre to your already illustrious name. Your losses have been heavy indeed and for that we are all greatly distressed. But war is a hard and bloody affair, and great victories cannot be won without sacrifice. It is always a fine and moving spectacle to see, as I do today, worthy men who have done their duty on the battle field assembled in ranks on parade, and those ranks filled again with young recruits and fresh reinforcements. There is a hard and bitter struggle ahead before we come to final victory and much hard fighting to be done. In the flux and change of war individuals will change. Some will come; others will go. Formations will move from one theatre to another, and where you will be when the next battles are fought I do not know. But wherever you may be my thoughts will always go with you and I shall follow your fortunes with interest and your successes with*

*admiration. There is one thought I will cherish above all others –
under my command fought the 9th AUSTRALIAN DIVISION."*

*Extract from: Address made to the A.I.F.(M.E.)
by General Hon.Sir Harold R.L.G. Alexander, K.G.B., C.S.I., D.S.O.,
M.C., Commander in Chief, the Middle East Forces
at a parade of the A.I.F. held in Palestine on 22nd December, 1942*
*in commemoration of fallen comrades.*

Henry paced the deck of HMS Carlisle. The British Cruiser was bringing him home. As it neared the dock in Sydney Harbour, Henry was glad to be here but his hands shook as they held tightly to the railing. He had no idea how he would be received. His head and heart were throbbing and his stomach was turning cartwheels. He scanned the small crowd on the dock but could see no sign of Connie. He had not been in contact with her for almost two months. He didn't even know if she knew he was on his way home.

Henry turned to a British officer standing at the railing and said, "You'd think that a state of the art boat like this could dock a bit quicker than this."

"Well young man, if it was docking in a state of the art wharf, maybe it would."

"Sorry sir, "he said sheepishly, "I'm just a bit impatient that's all. I was listed as MIA and I don't really know if word has got through yet that I have been found. Don't know how you can put up with travelling under radio silence all the time."

"It's better than having those crazy Japs take pot-shots at us. Sinking us would be a real prize for them."

"It was a shock to us when Sydney went down. She was escorting us only a few days before. A lot of good men are losing their lives in this war. Makes you wonder if it is all worth it."

"I read the report of the praise that the Commander in Chief gave your division as they left the Middle East. That 9th Division must have been one hell of a fighting unit."

"Yes I read it too. I regret not being there with them. Too many of them made the ultimate sacrifice."

"I won't ask you why you weren't there but I know Monty thinks highly of you. You intelligence blokes do a vital job. "

"No-one at home knows about it and I can't tell them." Henry let out a big sigh and turned away so his companion couldn't see his pained expression.

"Perhaps that young lady jumping up and down and waving her arms is someone you know," said the officer pointing to the far end of the dock.

Henry turned abruptly back and scanned the wharf below. He could hardly contain himself. She was wearing his favourite blue dress. "Yes, that's my darling wife." *How could I ever leave her again? Maybe I should consider leaving the Army altogether.*

Henry couldn't wait any longer. He jumped up and over the ship's railing and landed half way down the gang plank with such a thump that the whole thing almost gave way. He turned to the waiting British officers, waved and said, "Sorry fellows. Can't wait." Connie had seen him and was pushing her way through the crowd. They arrived at the bottom of the gang plank at the same time. The waiting crowd applauded as he swung her off her feet with such force that she had to grab her hat to stop it falling in the water.

⚜

Henry and Connie looked out over the waves breaking onto Bondi Beach. They had been inseparable since catapulting into each other's arms at the dock a week ago. The sun was starting to disappear and long shadows were creeping their way towards the clear blue water. There were still a few surfers splashing their way through the even swells. Afternoon walkers were strolling here and there amongst late sun-bathers. Henry couldn't remember ever being this happy. His arm was around her smooth shoulders and she was resting her head gently against his. They had sated their physical desire with long hours of passionate love-making in their honeymoon suite and now an air of contentment engulfed them as they sat taking in this peaceful scene.

Henry had managed to block out most memories of his recent experiences. He avoided any discussion of them with Connie because he didn't really want to remember. But somehow as hard as he tried he couldn't quite put them aside. He had been thinking about how good it would be if this war was over and this could be the start of the rest of their lives. Connie turned her face up to his and said wistfully. "Oh, how I wish that this war was over and we could just stay like this forever." Henry gave a start when he realised how in tune their thinking was. *We are meant to be together. How could I have ever doubted it?*

It was comfortable on the train. It had reached the top of the hill before the swift run-down into the lovely Hawkesbury Valley. They were on their way home to Murwillumbah. Henry looked longingly out the window. He tightened his grip on Connie's shoulders as if he was trying to stop her from going anywhere. He looked down at her now suntanned skin which looked as perfect in its golden glow as it did in its previous milky state.

"My darling Brownie, you don't know how much I would give to be able to enjoy this sort of scenery every day for the rest of my life. I have really missed all this."

"I can't wait to meet the rest of your family. I hope they like me."

"How could they not? Anne has told them all about you and my mother is as excited as you are. She has always wanted to see me settle down with a nice girl."

"Well that's going to have to wait for a while yet."

"It is only another 15 hours or so and we will be there."

"I didn't mean meeting your family. I meant the settling down bit. We are still at war and you are still in the Army."

"I am trying not to think about it. I don't really want to go back for more of that. I have really had my fill of war."

"Is there any way you could get out of the Army now?"

"I would love to but I am not sure how to go about it."

"I'd love it too but that wouldn't really help solve those world problems you always talk about."

"Yes, I know Connie. In my heart I still want to make a difference in this mixed-up world but doubt that will happen now. I screwed up in the Middle East. I shouldn't have disobeyed orders."

"I know you can't talk about it but is there any way you could get a desk job at home or something?"

"I don't think so. Once you enlist, unless you get killed or wounded, you are there for the duration."

"Dottie says Paul is going to ask for a discharge on compassionate grounds and it looks as though he may be granted it."

"What compassionate grounds does he have? His own fear of fighting?"

"Apparently because they now have three children and she is having trouble coping with her medical problems, it is possible."

"Her medical problems? More likely her not being able to cope is because she is out on the town with those Yanks so often, she doesn't get enough sleep. Is Paul sure that those kids are all his? Better check his dates I think."

"That's unfair, Henry. She is only trying to do her bit for the cause."

"Well, if I ever found out you were up those little tricks I would lock you up and throw away the key. How they can bring children into the world at a time like this I don't know. Then to use it as an excuse to get out of fighting is like deserting your country in its hour of need."

"Don't you think our needs are important too?"

"If everyone deserted the cause we would be overrun in no time."

"I don't think I can bear your being away so long again but I know what you are doing is important to the future of our nation. I will just have to be patient."

Henry looked into her beautiful eyes. *How can I deny this woman anything?* "You're a wonderful woman Connie. I don't think I really deserve you." He pulled her towards him, not caring who saw them and gave her a lingering kiss on her soft lips. She pulled her head away and snuggled her face into his shoulder but not before Henry saw the tears welling.

The jolt as the train pulled into the station at Murwillumbah roused Henry from a fitful sleep. "Wake up darling, we are here." Henry lightly shook Connie and she sat bolt upright.

"Look there's Stewart."

"Which one? The one in the check shirt? He looks a bit like you."

"No, over there, the good looking one waving his hat at us."

As they alighted, Stewart pushed towards them and pulled Henry towards him in a great big bear hug. "Whoa there mate. Leave some breath in me – I'm still a bit fragile."

"Geez, Henry you are all skin and bones. What did they do to you over there?"

"Hang on, time for that later. Meet my darling Connie." He propelled her towards his brother and Stewart's face started to turn the colour of the red shirt he was wearing.

"I'm sorry. That was quite rude of me. Can I give my new sister a hug?" Connie's smiled broadened as she held out her arms and gave her brother-in-law a warm embrace.

"Come on you two. She's my missus Stewart. You go find your own."

"Not too many like her around here Henry." He turned to Connie. "You got any sisters at home?"

"Come on Stew, give her chance to get to know you first. Tell me how things are at home. You sounded a bit worried on the phone."

"Things are not too good Henry."

"What do you mean? Is Mum giving Dad a hard time again?"

"Well she is struggling to cope. Dad's taken to the grog again."

"Geez, I thought things were going well. Mum's letters said he had started to face up to things."

"Yeah, he was until you were posted as missing in action and he just went off to the pub and didn't come home until closing time. He's hardly been sober since."

"Why didn't someone tell me? "

"How were we going to do that? You were missing remember."

"I've been home for a couple of weeks now. Hasn't he settled down yet?"

"No. In fact I think that's where he is now."

Henry sighed. It was like a dark cloud descending over the battle field in the middle of a bombing raid. "Let's get home to Mum and see what needs to be done."

Myrtle was waiting on the verandah as they turned into the familiar yard of the Peter St home. Henry couldn't help notice the run down state of things. The front gate was hanging off its hinges, paint was peeling from the weatherboard walls and several of the front steps almost dislodged as he bounded up them towards his mother. Tears streamed down his mother's face as she wound her arms around him and squeezed him tighter than Henry ever imagined she could.

"My darling boy, I thought we were never going to see you again."

"Gee Mum, you'll break my ribs if you don't let go." Henry turned to Connie who followed closely behind him and gently shoved her forward. "Here's my reason for returning home safely Mum." Myrtle took a step backwards, wiped the tears from her eyes with the bottom of her apron and reached out her arms to the smiling Connie.

"Welcome to our home and our family Connie."

⚬—⚬ ▰◆▰ ⚬—⚬

Henry walked into the familiar surroundings of Bryant's Hotel. Connie and his mother were getting on famously. They had happily settled down in the kitchen for a nice cup of tea, his mother's answer for everything. Henry had taken the opportunity to go and look for his father. The first person he saw was Shirley.

"Welcome home Henry. It's good to see you back in one piece." She came over and patted him gently on the arm.

"Hey, that's not much of a welcome."

"Don't want to set tongues wagging any more than I have to."

"Thinking of everyone else as usual. Ok, where is he?"

"Out back." She nodded towards the small room behind the bar. There he was stretched out on an old faded couch that Henry suspected Shirley might have put there just for this purpose. His mouth was open and spittle was dribbling down and off his chin onto his grubby, wrinkled shirt. *What a sorry sight. Surely I can't be responsible for this.*

"Come on Dad, we've got to get you home." He shook his father more roughly than he would have dared in the past.

"Henry? Ish thash you? Home at last." Henry saw tears running down his cheeks as he struggled to get to his feet.

"Hang on there, let me help you. We'll get someone to take us home."

As Henry struggled through the doorway into the bar with his father propped up in his arms, he saw that Shirley had the situation well in hand. "This is Joe, one of our new staff members. He'll drive you home."

Henry bundled his father into the back of the old black Plymouth that he knew Shirley had scrimped and saved to buy. *That's what the world needs, not wars, a few more people like Shirley.* Henry looked down at the man passed out on his shoulder and felt a wave of disgust. He could feel his father's thin bones against his own war ravaged body. He worried about his laboured breathing.

***

Henry sat with his mother at the kitchen table. After a morning cup of tea Connie had gone for a walk saying she wanted to see more of this lovely country town. She knew Henry had things to talk over with his mother.

"Connie is a lovely girl Henry. It would be wonderful for all of us if you could bring her to live up here near us."

"After the war that could very well happen. But things are far from over you know."

"But surely they can't expect any more from you after what you have been through."

"I only have six weeks leave and then I will probably be sent into action again. The threat from the Japanese in the Pacific is growing by the day."

"But I need you here. Your father can't seem to handle the thought that you may not come back at all. Many local boys have been killed you know."

"Don't you think I know that? Remember I was in the thick of it but my unit was recalled from the Middle East to deal with the threat to Australia from the north."

"Those that survived, that is. Can't you get a desk job or something? You are not much of a soldier anyway if you got lost in the desert and missed the boat home."

Henry felt a pang of guilt. If only he could tell her what he had really been doing. He had even started to blame himself that so many of his friends died in battle in North Africa. His mother lowered her head into her hands and her body started to shake with loud sobs. Henry had dealt with this before but now he had the added burden of his father's health to worry about.

"Ok, I will have a talk to my Commanding Officer when I get back to Sydney and see what can be done." He put his arms around his mother and gave her what he hoped was a comforting hug. His heart wasn't really in it.

⋯⋯⋯

Henry was quiet on the train on the way back to Sydney. Connie turned to him with an irritable look on her face.

"Well, aren't we going to even discuss it Henry? I know you have something on your mind."

"If you must know I have promised Mum I will look into getting out of the Army."

"I thought you said you couldn't do that?"

"I might be able to use the situation at home to avoid being sent to the front."

"But you said the Army needs every man they have to combat the Japanese threat."

"They do, but maybe I can get a non-combat role or something."

"I thought you were looking towards a fulltime career in the Army after the war. How will you be able to support a family and any children we may have if you haven't got a career?"

"I might even contemplate a new career. Go back and finish school and become a teacher."

"I would really like that but I think you should wait until you talk it over with Major Coulthard." Henry looked at Connie quizzically. *Why is she now trying to talk me out of it? I thought she wanted me to leave the Army.* He hadn't seen Reg since he arrived home but doubt gnawed away at him. *Why has she stopped talking about him?*

# CHAPTER 53

# FAMILY VERSUS DUTY

When Henry walked into the Sydney office of his Commanding Officer the first thing he noticed was the extra pips on his shoulder. The newly appointed Colonel Coulthard sat perfectly straight behind his mahogany desk. He shoulders were squared and the papers on his desk were neatly arranged. Behind him was a large painting of what Henry thought was the Battle of Waterloo. Maybe Napoleon was his hero. He carried himself the same way Henry imagined the great General would. If Henry didn't know this man so well he would be terrified by now.

"Good morning Henry," said the Colonel with a broad smile.

"Congratulations on your promotion sir," said Henry, "no one deserves it more than you."

"Thank you Henry. It is good to see you look so well again. You must be doing something that agrees with you."

"Yes, I am well rested now and Connie is a very good cook so I have fattened up a bit. I've been home to see my family."

"You wanted to see me urgently? You have several weeks leave left I believe."

"I have something important I would like to ask."

"Come on, get it out. You look as though you think I am going to berate you."

"Well, my mother and Connie are getting very nervous about my going back to the front line and for their sake I said I would check up on the possibility of getting an early discharge."

"Is that what you want for yourself, Henry?" The Major looked over his spectacles at him like a concerned father.

"I am rather disillusioned about this war. The senseless killing seems to be not getting us anywhere."

"We didn't start it Henry. Don't you think you should be thinking about the future of your country? For us to give up now would be like surrendering."

"I met a few of the enemy face to face on my little adventure. They are human beings just like us, with the same dreams and aspirations for themselves and their families. I have not had to kill one of them yet and I doubt that I ever will be able to."

"To protect our way of life and that of our families we MUST fight to the end."

"How about a desk job then? I was offered a full time job at Intelligence HQ when I was training in Darwin. Would that be still possible?"

"Absolutely not. Your unit will be leaving for jungle warfare training in a few weeks prior to being sent into action in New Guinea. Your services will be needed in the field more than ever. We have very few people left with your training and experience. Romano is still missing in action you know."

Henry felt a resurgence of guilt. "I had no choice but to leave him. Neither of us would have made it out if I had stayed with him."

"I am not blaming you Henry. You had no choice. You followed your training well. Your information was a great help to the Allies' cause. They kept the enemy forces away from Suez. It has been acknowledged that the Ninth Division was a vital part in the Allied win at El Alamein."

"That makes me feel better but I still hold myself responsible for his death. If I hadn't let myself get captured he wouldn't have had to take such risks to save me. I didn't get into this business to get accolades for myself. I thought it was going to be for the good of mankind. I'm beginning to doubt that I can make a difference at all."

"If it will help, you could bring Connie in to see me and I could explain how important you are to our efforts. Without giving any secrets away that is."

"I don't think that would do any good, sir. She is a very strong-minded you know. How long have we got before this becomes general knowledge?"

"Not long now. You will be called in the next week or so to be briefed."

Henry left the Major's office deep in thought. He was pleased his work had made a difference in the African campaign but he wasn't sure that Connie was going to see it that way. *She would rather have me home for good. Or would she?*

As Henry strolled back across the grounds of Command Headquarters in a day dream about the few days he had left with his wife, he walked right into Reg before he saw him.

"Well, nice to see you back on home soil Thompson. Sorry we couldn't wait for you to get back from your little sojourn in the desert. We had some real fighting to do."

"Look, mate I don't want to pick another fight with you. Can't we just keep out of each other's way until this bloody war is over? Then if we both make it back, if you want to settle it once and for all, I'll be quite happy to explore pugilistic skills with you."

"Big words for a country boy," Reg quipped sarcastically. "How's that delectable wife of yours?"

"She's very well, thank you. We have had a lot of catching up to do."

"She was quite happy for me to look after her when she thought you weren't coming back. We had some great times together."

"I know you are only trying to inflame me again but I am not buying it. I know how Connie feels about me and there's nothing you can do to interfere with that. I suggest you move on and find someone who is really interested in you. Shouldn't be too hard for you with your money!"

"Just ask her about New Year's Eve. She sure didn't seem to be missing you then. We all had a bit too much to drink but she was not acting like a good little wife pining for her husband missing in action."

"You bastard. I told you this kind of talk won't work. Connie and I are committed to each other, now and for the rest of our lives."

"She knows I'll be around for her too. Better watch out when we get back into action, you'll never know when or where I'll pop up. No medals for cowards who run away from the fighting." And with that Reg turned on his heel and walked briskly into Command Headquarters. He's up to something thought Henry. *I'll have to watch myself from now on. He's not going to get me into trouble again. I was at the front for over a year and didn't kill a single enemy soldier. Does the number of enemy kills you make determine your worth as a member of the Armed forces?* Again Henry's moral code had reared its head.

⊶ ⊱⊰ ⊷

Henry was called in to HQ to be briefed on the New Guinea deployment. Things were getting serious up there. His battalion was heading for the Atherton Tablelands in Queensland to undergo jungle training before being sent north. They were going to be called on to help take back the base the Japanese had established at Lae. The Pioneers were normally a support group sent in to prepare for Allied occupation but this time they were to be part of the fighting.

Henry was leaving HQ to go back to Dottie's house where Connie was waiting for him, when Tom came up to him.

"I heard you were safe. I wondered when I was going to see you."

"I've been busy sorting things out with Connie."

"I've been home with Mum and Dad. I felt I needed some time with them before we head to New Guinea."

"Who told you that?"

"You wouldn't tell us, that's for sure. It seems Reg is circulating some rumours about it."

"Hey, let's change the subject. You know I can't talk about those things."

"Ok. How are things with Connie?"

"Well, they were fine but that bastard Reg seems to be interfering again."

"I wondered what you would think of that."

"So you knew about that, did you?" Henry's eyes narrowed as he glared at Tom.

"Not that there is anything to know. I did see them around together a bit."

"I think she's hiding something from me. But she won't tell, says I should trust her."

"Maybe you should. She did marry you after all."

"I'm not going to sit around and let him try to move in whenever I leave town. If that's her attitude, he can have her."

"Are you sure that's what she wants. She may be trying to pull you into line by making you jealous."

"I still haven't told her about our new deployment. Not sure she will be happy. I had committed myself to trying to get out of the Army."

⸻ ▆◆▆ ⸻

Henry arrived at Dottie and Paul's place in Canterbury as the sun was going down behind the workers' houses. It was a grimy industrial suburb but Connie's sister's house was neater than most, with a fancy railing and a carefully tended flower garden. Dottie had told him that Connie had worked diligently in the garden while Henry was overseas. It was lovely and Henry was filled with pride. He bounded up the front stairs until he was almost knocked over by four-year-old Jerry. Henry scooped him up in his arms and threw him onto his shoulders. The boy wriggled but Henry held him firmly in place.

"Look out unca 'enry, Judy is gonna get me." Connie's niece was trying to reach her brother high on Henry's shoulders when Dottie came through the door.

"Come on you two. Let Uncle Henry have some peace and quiet. He will think he is still away at war."

"It's ok Dottie; I've got to learn the ropes. Connie and I hope to have a brood of our own one day. At least I thought she did."

Dottie turned to Henry with a puzzled look on her face. "Connie wasn't expecting you; she has just gone round to a friend's place."

"Well, she won't find him home, he's in at Headquarters," said Henry in a sullen voice.

"Who's in at Headquarters? I've just come from Mrs Finch's place, one of the elderly widows I keep an eye on." Connie had come up behind them. As Henry turned abruptly to her, his face turned red. He held out his arms but she turned her head away from his offered kiss.

Jerry ran back into the room. "Hello Aunt Connie, where's Uncle Reg? He promised me another tank."

Connie blushed. "I think you had better leave us alone for a while, Dottie. Henry and I have a few things to clear up." She pulled Henry down onto the old rusty garden seat, not yet restored, that she had rescued from the tip. With that no-nonsense look on her face that Henry was becoming used to, she said, "Well, want to tell me what that was all about?"

"How about you tell me? I ran into bloody Reg today."

"So, is that supposed to mean something to me?" Connie said sharply.

"You haven't seen him since he got back from the Middle East then?"

"Of course I have. He came to see me to tell me about your not coming home with the rest of your unit."

"And that's the only time?"

"He's been at a few social functions I have been at. What's this inquisition all about? "

"What about Jerry? He's obviously seen him."

"For heaven's sake Henry, he brought a toy tank with him for Jerry when he came to see me when you were missing. It was quite thoughtful of him. The boy is quite fond of you; he thought it would distract him."

"He says you two got quite cosy on New Year's Eve."

"Henry Thompson, if you are going to be like this and not trust me when we are out of each other's sight, maybe we should re-think our whole future."

"It seems that when you thought I wasn't coming back you didn't waste any time seeking comfort in another man's arms."

Connie moved as far as back as she could from Henry. She squared up her shoulders and stuck out her stubborn chin. "I will explain myself to no man, even one I'm married to. Love, honour and obey, forsaking all others, isn't that what I promised? "

"It doesn't seem like you are taking those vows seriously." Henry's anger started to take over from his guilt. *She is acting like someone with something to hide. Am I ever going to be able to trust her?*

"I have nothing more to say to you Henry until you come to your senses on this." She stood up and pushed the front door so hard that it almost came off its hinges. Then she slammed it with a bang that shook the wall. Henry looked at the closed door. He was in no mood to back down on his position. *She has to make up her mind once and for all about who she really wants.* He turned on his heel and stormed off down the street towards the railway station.

⊷ ⊷ ⊷

Henry was pacing the platform at Central Station, puffing away on what was probably his 20th cigarette of the day. He had two hours until the train to Atherton was due but he had nowhere else to go. He had never felt so despondent. He was about to leave Sydney without seeing Connie since the night they quarrelled. He had one last go at talking to her before he left but she refused to see him. Dottie told him she'd had a visit from Reg the day before and now she was refusing to talk to anyone.

"I've never seen her like this," said Dottie. "Apparently Reg told her about some misdemeanour of yours in the Middle East." *If I ever get the chance to get my hands on that bastard he will need more repairs than the German Army after El Alamein.*

He felt a hand on his shoulder. "Come on mate, it can't be that bad." He turned around abruptly to a familiar face.

"I think I have lost her altogether this time Tom. Bloody Wentworth is causing problems again."

"We all have our ups and downs with our women in these unstable times."

"I just can't seem to get the bastard out of my life."

"I heard a rumour that he is not going with us. Apparently he is staying on in Sydney for some sort of special training. He will make the most of that chance I'll bet."

"He has told a whole lot of lies to Connie about what I did in the Middle East."

"Henry, if she really loves you she will wait and if she doesn't then she is probably not worth the pain she has put you through."

"If we get back in one piece from this hell hole we are headed for I will try to make it up to her. We are meant for each other but we are both strong-willed and stubborn."

"Yes, we are going to need our wits about us to keep these little yellow bastards out of our country."

"You know Tom, I met a few German soldiers when I was captured in the Middle East. They are not that much different to us. I imagine the Japs are much the same."

"We didn't ask to get into this war and I am damned if I'm going to start feeling sorry for anyone who is trying to blow my brains out and take over my country," said Tom testily.

"They are taking orders just like us Tom, and sometimes we don't like what we are asked to do but we still do it. Maybe the soldiers on both sides should stage a revolt and stand up against the heads of government who risk our lives while they sit in their safe offices in no danger at all."

"You really are getting a chip on your shoulder aren't you?"

"I just want this bloody war over with so I can get back to my normal life."

"We all want that Henry. Perhaps if we kill the buggers off quicker that will bring things to an end."

"There has to be some other way, Tom." Henry lit another cigarette and starting to puff furiously on it.

"I thought Connie didn't like you smoking."

"Well, she's not going to damn well know is she? Unless you are going to be like that bastard Wentworth and tell tales too."

"Come on Henry, let's go down to the pub and have a few beers, that will cheer you up. We have plenty of time before the train leaves."

"Yes and maybe we can play some two-up too. That will complete the whole circle of vices for me. My mother will disown me when she finds out the poor excuse for a man I have become."

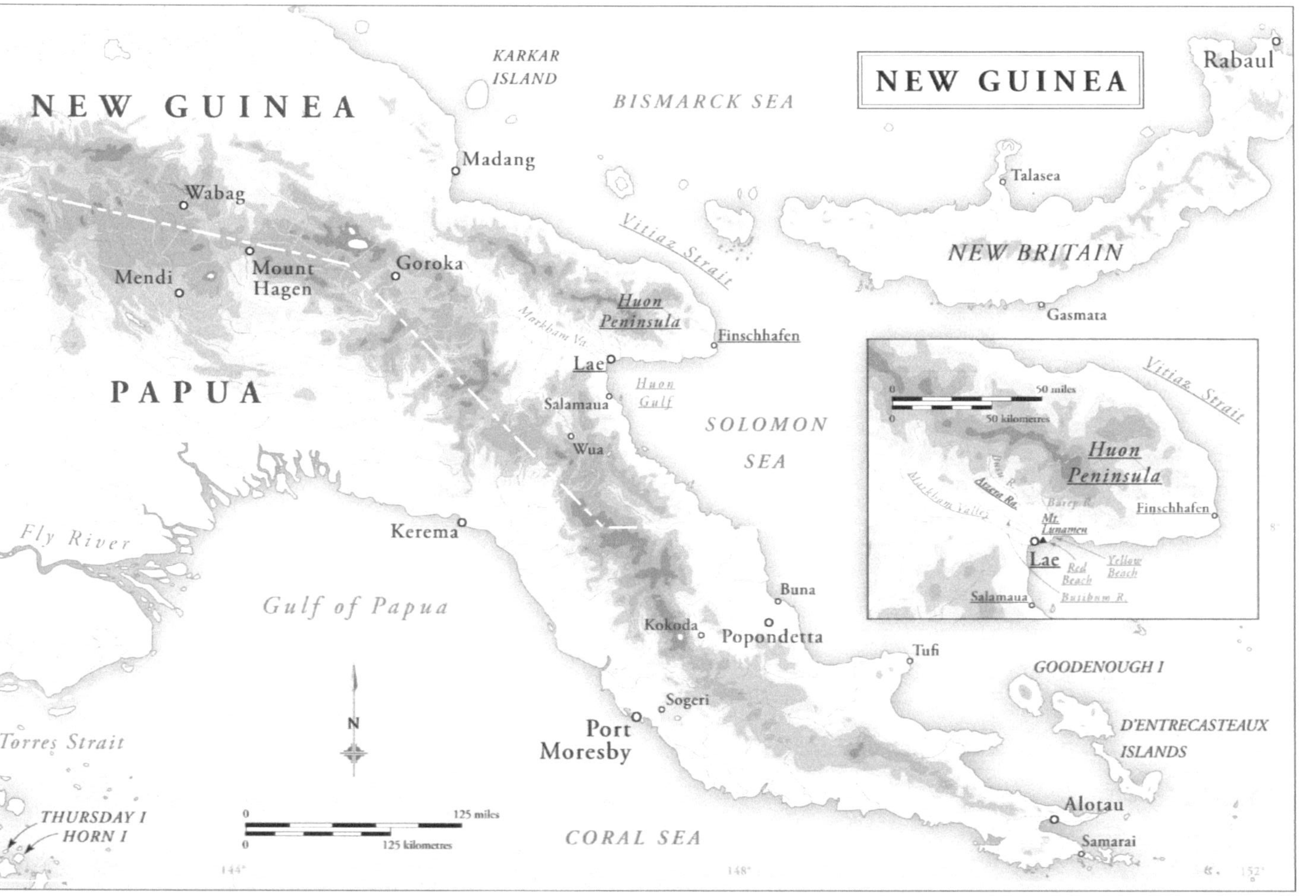

NEW GUINEA
NEW GUINEA
PAPUA
NEW BRITAIN
Rabaul
Talasea
Gasmata
BISMARCK SEA
KARKAR ISLAND
Madang
Wabag
Mendi
Mount Hagen
Goroka
Markham Va.
Huon Peninsula
Finschhafen
Lae
Salamaua
Wua
Huon Gulf
Vitiaz Strait
SOLOMON SEA
Fly River
Kerema
Gulf of Papua
Buna
Kokoda
Popondetta
Tufi
Sogeri
Port Moresby
GOODENOUGH I
D'ENTRECASTEAUX ISLANDS
Alotau
Samarai
Torres Strait
THURSDAY I
HORN I
N
125 miles
125 kilometres
0
0
CORAL SEA
144°
148°
152°
Vitiaz Strait
Huon Peninsula
Markham Valley
Atzera Ra.
Busu R.
Barep R.
Finschhafen
Mt. Lunamen
Lae
Red Beach
Yellow Beach
Busibum R.
Salamaua
50 miles
50 kilometres
0
0

# CHAPTER 54

# JUNGLE WARFARE TRAINING

*"Tropical North Queensland played a crucial role in the Australian war effort during World War II. These were fraught times. The Japanese had pushed the Americans out of the Philippines and the British out of Singapore; they occupied most of South-East Asia. Australian troops were engaged in a life and death struggle in the jungles of New Guinea and naval battles were lighting up the Coral Sea, the thunder of the guns audible in Cairns. Meanwhile, Japanese squadrons were bombing numerous towns right across the Top End, including Darwin, Katherine, Townsville and Mossman. Invasion seemed imminent.*

*General Thomas Blamey, Australian Commander-in-Chief of the Pacific War theatre, decided the Atherton Tableland  was ideal both as a tropical training ground for soldiers preparing for the war, and a rehabilitation zone with field hospitals and convalescent facilities for the returned casualties, sick and wounded. Between 1943 and 1945 the Tableland was the biggest military base in Australia. Up to 300,000 troops from various army divisions were stationed in camps and training facilities across the region – in small towns such as Kuranda, Kairi, Atherton, Ravenshoe and Herberton."*

THE BATTLE FOR NEW GUINEA. JUNGLE WARFARE.
AUSTRALIAN WAR MEMORIAL, CANBERRA. *1944.*

Life in Atherton wasn't unpleasant for the Pioneers. They were gearing up to join the rest of the 9th Division in the task of deflating the air of invincibility that the fanatical enemy had assumed since Malaysia and Singapore. The Japanese had proved themselves masters of the jungle and the 8th Division were badly mauled due to lack of experience in jungle warfare.

Henry resumed communication and mail duties and apart from the nasty things that crept, crawled and grew around the rain forest, life was uneventful. Several men came down with Scrub Typhus and others sustained festering and agonising sores from the Gympie bush "stinging tree". The shade of the lush tropical trees may have looked inviting but was soon treated with caution by the Pioneers.

Henry sat at his desk as the early morning sun filtered down through the towering black kauri trees surrounding camp, the fingers of light appearing as slithers of liquid gold. He sighed and turned back to the pile of mail he knew the men would be clamouring for as soon as they rose. He was in a trance as he put the letters into piles for the different platoons but he stopped abruptly when he saw familiar handwriting. His heart jumped. At first he felt relief that she had finally broken the silence between them until he focussed on the letter burning a hole in his hand.

*Sgt R Wentworth,*
*"A" Coy 2/3 Aust Pnr Bn,*
*AIF Northern Aust.*

Henry's heart almost stopped beating. The constriction of his chest made it almost impossible for him to breathe. His cry of anguish was so loud it would almost certainly attract attention in the early morning silence. He flew out of the mail room and charged into the mess tent looking for Reg.

Tom was coming off night guard duty and came running to his aid. "Henry, Henry what's up mate?" He said, taking him by the shoulders and giving him a good shake. Henry collapsed against the rickety table in front of him, and held his head in his hands.

"Have you had bad news?" Tom continued.

Henry looked despairingly at his friend, "Th...th...that bastard. He's finally won."

"What are you talking about?"

"That bloody Wentworth. He's stolen my wife. I'll kill him when I get my hands on him." Henry jumped up from the table knocking a pile of empty plates to the ground. He started to march towards the open doorway. Tom quickly grabbed him by the arm. Henry shook Tom off and stormed back to the mail tent. Tom came running after him. Henry was already hurling things around the confines of the small tent when Tom caught up with him.

"Come on mate, calm down. Let's not do anything you will be sorry for."

"I can't help it. Let me go and find the rat. Damn the consequences."

"Whoa there. Don't forget he hasn't even arrived here yet."

"Maybe that is just as well."

"Here have a cigarette and let's talk this through. Is it worth wrecking your career over?"

"You just don't understand. Connie is writing to him. Her letter has just come in."

"I don't know how you are going to deal with this, but think before you act."

Tom placed the already lit cigarette in Henry's shaking hand and with the other hand deftly picked up the chair that had been knocked over and gently pushed him down onto it. Henry closed his eyes, took several deep breathes and slowly started to draw on the comforting cigarette.

"Look mate, you are going to have to get used to having Reg around. Rumour has it that he is not here because he is in intelligence training."

"Jesus Christ – that would be the last straw. How could I ever work with him? I can't believe they would do that to me."

Henry sat in the far corner of the Rec Hut. It was late and most of the men had retired. He was surrounded by empty beer glasses and an ashtray overflowing with smouldering cigarette butts. Tom tapped Henry on the shoulder.

"Come on Henry, I think you should call it a night. These blokes need to pack up." Henry gave a start and peered through bleary eyes at his mate.

"You know Tom, you are the best mate a man could have," he said with alcohol-fuelled emotion. "If it wasn't for you I think I would have called this whole thing quits by now."

"It's pretty depressing at times for us all but we know we have to get on with it for the sake of those at home."

"I know Tom, but I just can't get used to the idea that we are hell bent on killing each other. There has to be a better way."

"Well you won't find the answer at the bottom of a booze bottle or by puffing non-stop on those ciggies."

"Yes, but they are the only comfort I have these days. I haven't got Connie anymore."

"But you are not going to give her up without a fight are you?"

"I think the battle is over. He's won. I just haven't got it in me to try any more. Not with all the rest of this crap going on."

"Why don't you just write to her and tell her how much you love her and want to sort things out when you get home?"

"That's all very well to say but it's a very hard thing to do now that she obviously seeking comfort with him. And now I might have to work with the bastard too."

"If you don't let her know how you feel Wentworth will have a clear run with her. I think you should give it another try."

With a quick nod at the bar staff who were watching with great interest, Tom pulled his mate to his feet and helped him back to their tent. "Come on, let's get you to bed and we will talk more about it in the morning."

⊷ ⋈✦⋈ ⊶

Henry stood contritely with his head down in front of Colonel Coulthard. His head was throbbing from his over-indulgence the night before.

"Well my boy, what have you got to say for yourself? I know you haven't been yourself since we arrived here but you really must set a good example for the men you know."

"I am sorry sir. Things have got on top of me a bit lately."

"We all feel that way at times but the sign of a good soldier is one who can put aside personal problems and pull his weight for his country."

"I can do that all right but I have some issues with war as a solution to the world's problems. And now that I have to deal with Wentworth as well, I sometimes wonder whether I am in the right place."

"If you continue in this irresponsible way I am going to have no choice but put him in charge of your little unit. There is too much at stake to rely on someone in an emotionally fragile state."

"You mean I am going to have to work with him? I don't think I'm going to be able to do that."

"You won't have a choice if that's your orders." The unusually harsh tone of the Colonel's voice snapped Henry to attention.

"He has moved in on Connie too, you know."

"I thought you had finished with her anyway."

"I thought I had but somehow I just can't get her out of my mind."

"Does she know this?" The softer side of the Colonel was re-emerging and Henry felt that the bond that had formed between them was coming to the fore again.

"No, I can't bring myself to write to her. Not while I still have risky business to attend to. I feel that maybe she will be better off without me until then."

311

"Sometimes Henry we all need something to fight for. Despair in a soldier is almost as dangerous as cowardice at times."

"I know how important my work is to the Allied cause but I sometimes doubt if we are settling our differences in the right way."

"My boy, I know exactly how you feel. We can never be certain about these things but I do know that not doing anything would be tantamount to surrender. We have to fight for what we believe in. The way of life we take for granted is under threat."

"You can be assured I will give it my utmost sir and I will do my best to work together with Wentworth."

"I am pleased to hear that Henry. Wentworth may be a bit obnoxious at times but he's a good soldier."

"He's going to have to be if we are going to pull this one off."

"He is going to be here soon. You both need to be briefed. Soon enough we will back in the thick of things and you will have to put your differences aside. I think you should lay off the grog for a while and get plenty of rest. You're going to need it where we are going."

⚊ ⚎⚏ ⚊

Henry and Tom were relaxing in the Rec hut after the final jungle warfare challenge. It had been a hard six weeks, but satisfying. The cooler autumn months were coming to the tropics but it was still humid as the rainy season was not yet over. They were continually wet, if not from the frequent showers, then from the perspiration that poured out of them whenever they exerted themselves. The bush with its thick undergrowth and clinging vines was far different to the sparse desert landscape. The men still didn't know exactly where they were going but Henry knew that Japanese bases in New Guinea were springing up at an alarming rate. Rumours were rife in the camp but Henry had no trouble keeping things to himself until Command HQ felt it was right to tell them.

"Let me buy you a drink Henry," called Lofty from across the bar. "It's been good to have you back with us."

"Sure thing," said Henry. "It's always good to be back with your mates."

"But you won't be out on the front line with us, will you?" Tom muttered to Henry in a low voice as Lofty pushed his way through the jovial crowd to their side of the bar.

"Look, Tom you know I can't tell you about my special duties but you can be assured I will be doing everything in my power to make your job easier."

Henry felt a healthy thump on his back as Lofty arrived and slammed a pint of the best lager in front of him. "Here you are mate, get this into you." Henry grabbed the large glass and threw it down in double quick time. He wondered what his mother would think of these new found vices. Drinking, smoking and gambling; "dancing with the devil" she called it. But Henry found it relaxing and soothing to the nerves. A dig in the ribs from Tom brought him back to reality.

"Don't look now but you will never guess who has just walked in?"

"Don't tell me," said Henry, quite inebriated by now, "Vera Lynn. I always dreamed she would find me one day."

"No such luck, it's Wentworth." Even in his alcohol induced euphoria Henry felt like an electric current had coursed through his body, such was the jolt.

"Bloody hell," groaned Henry as he thudded the palm of his hand into his forehead. "Am I never going to be free of that bastard?"

"I think you should stay well away from him."

"I'm not even going to ac...acc.. , oh damn, who's taken my tongue? I'm not even going to speak to him!"

"I think it would be a good idea if you came with me right now and we put you to bed."

"You sound like my mother, or Connie. I'm not answerable to either of THEM."

"Look mate I think this is going to lead to more trouble for you. But I need my sleep. We have an early start tomorrow."

"I'll just have one for the road and then I'll be with you."

As Henry stumbled through the tents in the dark several hours later he didn't notice the glow of a cigarette beside the tent rope he had almost tripped over.

"Had a few too many have we?" The voice of his nemesis cut through the still night air. As Henry's eyes adjusted to the light he could make out a figure leaning nonchalantly up against the front pole of the tent.

"You bastard. Can't you stay out of my life?"

"Come on now Henry. We could be mates if you would only accept that the better man was always going to win. With Connie and in this civilized Army of ours."

"You might have got the girl but you are not going to interfere with my career too." He had started to sober up in the face of his old enemy.

"You don't know then?"

"What do you mean, I don't know what?"

"We are going to be working together in New Guinea. I have just completed my training. I'll be taking Romano's place in your little team."

"Not if I have anything to say about it you won't."

"Well, that's just it. You won't have anything to say about it. It's all settled. There's going to be no-one else but us. There will be a huge responsibility on our shoulders."

"You better learn to take orders then. I won't have any of your smart alec backchat when I am in charge."

"You won't necessarily be in charge. I have talked to Colonel Coulthard about it. We will be of equal rank so neither of us will be ordering the other around. I don't want to end up like poor Romano. Abandoned for dead."

"Watch what you say about Romano, you don't know a thing about what happened."

"I know that you came back and he didn't. Rumour has it that he was injured and you abandoned him to save your own skin."

Henry knew there was no point trying to argue with this conceited son-of-a-bitch so he turned on his heel and marched as soberly as he could in the direction of his tent.

*I'll talk to Colonel Coulthard about this. He must know it would be impossible for us to work together.*

Henry woke with another throbbing headache. He pulled himself slowly out of bed, looked over at Tom sleeping peacefully in the corner bunk, and decided to have an early morning dip in the stream that ran by the camp. He grabbed a towel and a clean shirt and shorts and walked briskly through the towering bamboo. The morning silence was broken every now and then by distant calls from the numerous tropical birds that lived in the scrub. There was not another soul in sight. Parade had been called for 10 am and it was only 6 am. He stripped off his T-shirt and shorts and dived head first into the clear water. As the cold water hit his body, it sent a shiver right through him but he soon adjusted and started to cavort like a frolicking seal. He swaggered back to camp feeling like a new man. He was now ready to face Colonel Coulthard with the questions he wanted to ask about Reg.

As he approached the Command tent Henry noticed the flap was tied back and he knew it could be no-one but the Colonel himself. He decided now was as good a time as any to tackle him. He called softly through the half opened flap.

"Come in," came the usual gruff reply. Henry saw the Colonel's expression soften and widen into a smile when he saw who it was.

"Good morning Henry. Obviously you didn't have a skin-full like the rest of them last night or you wouldn't be up yet."

Henry laughed, "Well I don't think I could lay claim to that sir, I probably had more than most but old habits of rising early die hard and besides I sobered up very quickly when I encountered Reg Wentworth on my way back to my tent."

"He's here already, is he? We weren't expecting him until tomorrow. I had wanted to talk to you before he arrived."

"And so you damn well should have," said Henry. He looked at his Commanding Officer and realised he was no longer pleased. The Colonel pulled himself up to his full height.

"Hang on there my boy, you are still under my command you know and you would do well to remember that."

"Sorry sir, I was just very upset to hear he is going to be working with me in New Guinea."

"I told you that the other day."

"I didn't realise we would be working in the field together too. You must have known that I would not be happy about that?"

"Yes, I had an inkling you would feel that way but he is the best man for the job. He was available and he did volunteer."

"So there's no way it can be changed?"

"We haven't got Romano to fall back on this time."

"I still feel guilty about him sir. You must know that."

"As I have told you before, you did the right thing Henry. It's a cruel thing war, but your work is going to be extremely important this time. Those damn Japs are getting too close to our borders to be left alone. We are going to need you to pinpoint where they are so the Airforce can deal with them."

"I could do that on my own sir. In fact I think I would do better on my own than having to keep looking over my shoulder to see what Reg was up to."

"Look Henry, he is a trained professional just like you and we have never had any problem with his performance of his duties."

"Yes, but he has other beefs with me. My wife for example."

"I'm afraid you are going to have to put your personal life aside. Your country needs you more."

CHAPTER 55

# A NEW STYLE OF WAR

*"Early in July 1943, the G.O.C. New Guinea Force, Lieut.-General Sir Edmund Herring, outlined to the commanders of the Seventh and Ninth Australian Divisions their roles in General Sir Thomas Blamey's plan for a major offensive in the New Guinea area. The immediate objective of these concentrated operations was the seizure of the airfields  in the Lae–Markham Valley area. The broad plan was less restricted, and envisaged the expulsion of the Japanese from the entire Huon Peninsula, and the consequent domination of the Vitiaz Straits separating New Britain and New Guinea. The Ninth Australian Division under the command of Major-General G.F. Wootten would strike the enemy from the sea in the first Australian amphibious operation since Gallipoli, while the Seventh Division – Australia's first air-borne division – attacked from the air. Ten days later elements of the Ninth Division planning headquarters arrived and, in collaboration with the U.S. Navy and the Fifth U.S. Army Air Force, began the intricate task of planning its amphibious operation."*

THE BATTLE FOR NEW GUINEA. JUNGLE WARFARE.
AUSTRALIAN WAR MEMORIAL, CANBERRA. *1944.*

Henry was at his desk contemplating the resumption of his intelligence duties. Now camped at Trinity Beach near Cairns, they had been taking part in joint exercises with the US Navy, involving amphibious landings. From the hut he could see glistening white sand, lined with tropical palm trees and blue water gently lapping the shore. It seemed more like a holiday location than the scene for serious preparation for grim battles. *I wonder if these blokes knew what was in store for them, would they be so happy go lucky?*

Henry knew that a full offensive was planned at Red and Yellow Beach in New Guinea in the near future and that the Pioneers would be a vital part of this operation. Henry was excited at the prospect. It had been five months since he returned from the Middle East and he had missed the excitement of being in the thick of the action. He didn't want to be a hero – just a good honest soldier doing his best for his country and his family. His heart still ached every time he thought of Connie but he hadn't given in to the urgings of Tom and Colonel Coulthard to write to her.

A letter to Reg from Connie stared him in the face almost every time he sat at his desk. There was one there now. It came several days ago. *If he doesn't come and ask for it, I'm not going to tell him it is here. Maybe I should throw it into the waste paper basket and deliberately drop a lighted match on it.* Henry was about to do just that when the flap of the communications tent was thrown open and in barged Reg.

"Well, Henry I'm here at last. Couldn't get away from those intelligence officers. They sure want me briefed on everything."

"Hope you took note of the confidentiality rules."

"Look mate, I'm well voiced in such protocols these days."

"Just see that you stick to it when we are in the field. Normal rules of engagement don't apply to us. We have to be not seen or heard." *A pretty hard assignment for someone with a big mouth like you.* Henry's eyes went straight to the letter and he had the urge to grab it before Reg saw it, but he was too late.

"Letter for me. Hey, let me have it." Henry reached over and slowly handed it to him without a word.

"Well, well I wonder who this is from. Looks private, better keep it until I'm alone to open don't you think, mate?" He said as he tucked the letter into his breast pocket.

"Closer to my heart. Best get back to HQ. They'll be waiting for me I'm sure." Reg left with a smug look on his face.

Henry banged his fist into his desk so hard that he winced. *Control yourself Henry. How am I ever going to work with this incompetent egomaniac?*

The next morning before Henry could settle down to review the overnight communications he was called to the command hut. He hoped he would get a chance to voice his reservations about Reg to Colonel Coulthard. He walked briskly over the short distance between the communications tent and Command HQ. The door was ajar and as he approached he heard a loud guffaw from within that could have only come from one person.

"Come in Henry, we've been waiting for you," said Reg greeting him as if the whole meeting was his to command. Henry shuddered as he turned away from the smirking face to greet the officers present.

"Good morning gentlemen," he said as he saluted his superiors, ignoring the grinning Reg.

"Come in Thompson. We need you to have a look at this," said General Blamey. Henry allowed himself a brief glance at Reg who seemed to miss the inference of this greeting.

General Blamey tugged on Henry's arm. "Come over here and see this."

On the table in the corner was a large relief map of New Guinea and its myriad islands. "Wow, it is going to be a hard task to patrol all that area."

"No problem, we just head to the highest ground and then we will be able to see forever," said Reg butting in with what seemed to be an air of authority.

"Not quite that easy Reg," said Henry. "Sometimes the enemy doesn't do what is obvious. Besides they usually have patrols out looking at the same places we are. So sometimes we have to take the harder route to get our information and get back to camp safely."

"If they get in our way we will just have to deal with them."

"Oh no, we won't. We have to gather information and keep ourselves out of their way so we can keep them guessing as to what we know. There'll be no unnecessary killing on my missions."

The General tapped his pointer on the map in front of them and glared at the bickering soldiers. "Come on you two. I can't impress on you how important it is for you two to co-operate. Team work is what is needed. Neither of you is indispensable and if your personal differences interfere you will both be relieved of your duties and sent back to the frontline to fight. We need to get on with this briefing. There's not much time left."

"Yes, I know that sir. Let's just hope we can be ready by the time we are needed." Henry gave Reg a look that left him in no doubt that he would be taking no nonsense from this know-it-all.

Released from their briefing, as they walked back to their quarters, Henry turned to Reg.

"Look Reg, we are going to have to forget our past differences if we are going to succeed in our task. This is a very important mission we have been given. Our results will be crucial to the success of the campaign in New Guinea."

"I know what is required of us. I have been privy to a lot of information that you would never dream of having. I have some important connections you know," said Reg.

"I don't care who your connections are. They won't be any use to you when we are cornered in some remote corner of the jungle and have to use our ingenuity to get back with our information."

"Look mate, I know we have to work together but I have superior knowledge of military manoeuvres you know. I was brought up on such discussions."

"Well, if you think dealing with the enemy is part of our brief you will have a quick fall from grace."

"If any of our missions go wrong, I can assure you I won't get the blame. There is no way my father will ever let me be relieved of my duty."

"I sure won't be taking the blame if you stuff things up."

"We'll see about that. Who do you think they will believe? A well brought up military boy or a country hick like you?"

Henry turned his back before he did something he would regret. He barged through the flap of his tent and threw himself on his bunk. Tom was seated on the opposite side of the tent.

"Hey, whoa there Henry. You look as though you could kill with your bare hands."

"Well, I hope it doesn't come to that. I sure don't know how I am going to handle working with that pompous ass."

"Rather it was you than me. It's the path you have chosen for yourself so you are going to have to wear it."

"Yes I know. It is going to be the hardest thing I have ever been asked to do."

"Have you written that letter to Connie yet?"

"No, I will see how things work out first. Can I rely on you to one day get the correct version of things back to Connie if I don't make it?"

"Stop that sort of talk Henry. We all need to be confident that we are doing the right thing in this war and hope truth will prevail."

"I know you are not a religious man Tom but I have prayed to God that we all make it back safely."

The two embraced in a fashion that in other circumstances would not have been regarded as manly but these were uncertain times.

⊱ ❈ ⊰

Henry had decided to stay in camp as he had some last minute letter writing to do. It was their last day of leave. Tomorrow they would begin their sea journey north on HMT Anhui. Most of the men had taken the opportunity to go into town. Henry, however, had to get his drinking under control and the best way to do that was to stay away from the pubs!

He wrote to his mother and his sister, Anne. He wanted to assure them that he would be safe. He thought about writing to Connie but

321

decided against it. If she wanted to communicate with him she'd had ample opportunity. There was a dull ache in his chest. He had begun to think he wasn't capable of a full-blown relationship with a woman; probably just as well in view of what they were heading into tomorrow. Henry had a feeling that New Guinea was going to make El Alamein look like a Sunday school picnic. The conditions were going to be much harsher and the enemy was already well and truly dug in. They would be part of the offensive to recapture Lae, destroy as many enemy bases as possible and push the Japanese back as far as they could from the shores of Australia.

Henry had just finished the last of his letters when Tom entered the tent. "I wondered where you had got to. I am heading into town now, want to come?"

"No, I think I will just hang around here. Still have a few things to deal with before tomorrow."

"You know Henry, brooding about it is not going to solve anything. Why don't you write to her?"

"She's not the problem, it's Reg."

"I heard that he has been crowing about how he will be in charge of your little unit. How do you think you will deal with that?"

"That's not quite the way it is going to be. He shouldn't talk so much – part of our training is how to keep our mouths shut. You know how they say 'loose lips sink ships' and that is very much the case where we are going."

"I am sure the Colonel will hear about it. Maybe you could take a leaf out of his book and dob him in like he is always doing with you."

"I tried that once before and it back-fired on me. I am very concerned about how safe I will be out there on a mission with him. I would be better off on my own."

"I don't envy you your task but I know how important your unit is to our cause. We would be in a lot more danger without you. Most of the men realise that risk taking is not only about being on the front line shooting."

"Yes, Reg has always made a big deal about my having a coward's job. I wonder how he will look at it now he's taking the same risks as me. He has a lot of work to do before I have faith in him the way I did with Romano."

"Best be off now. Is there anything I can get for you in town?"

"No, I'm right for everything. Working in supply has its advantages you know."

CHAPTER 56

# THE ENEMY FROM THE NORTH

*"Lae was a powerful base, manned by a Japanese force estimated at 7000 strong. Many well dug strongpoints, covering all approaches and sited in considerable depth, were located in and around the town itself. There was no evidence of any defences east of the Busu River, although concealment in the thick vegetation would have been simple. Unconfirmed reports placed enemy beach defences along the entire southern coast of the Huon Peninsular. The area through which the Ninth Division proposed to approach Lae consisted of flat coastal plain to an average depth of three miles, before rising into the rugged foothills of the inland mountains. The coastal plain was covered with dense jungle interspersed with patches of Kunai grass eight to ten feet high, and with mangrove swamps in the immediate coastal areas. Between the main landing beach - Red Beach - and Lae, the plain was interspersed by five rivers and numerous small streams; but apart from the Busu River they were not expected to present any real problem. There were no roads. Swamps behind the beaches allowed few exits. The immediate objective of the operation was to capture Red and Yellow beaches, secure a covering position, and establish a beach maintenance area at Red Beach. From this beachhead the advance on Lae would begin."*

THE BATTLE FOR NEW GUINEA. JUNGLE WARFARE.
AUSTRALIAN WAR MEMORIAL, CANBERRA. *1944.*

The Pioneer's arrival at Red Beach in the predawn of 4th September 1943 was an anti-climax. They were in the last wave of landing craft that scrambled ashore. Heavy rain was falling and many of the men were suffering from the sea sickness that started when they ran into the tail of a cyclone while traversing the Coral Sea. The early waves of landing craft had encountered a small pocket of Japanese who'd headed for the hills as soon as they realised the scale of the Allied invasion. The Pioneers, in spite of being cold, wet and hungry were relieved to collapse under the coconut palms that were bent over by the wind.

Their serenity was short lived. A wave of Japanese float planes welcomed them with a shower of 25 pound bombs. These weapons were small but they sent the Pioneers scattering for cover in the jungle that backed onto the black sand.

"Welcome to your new home," bellowed Captain Anderson as the Pioneers regrouped when the danger passed.

⊰⊱

Henry knew this battle would be vital in the war in the Pacific. The Ninth Division's camp was almost invisible until you were right upon it and could not be seen at all from the air. The plan was for the launch of a pincer type offensive, with amphibious forces landing east of the town, and an airborne attack from Nadzab in the west supported by the 503rd US Parachute Regiment. Henry knew the mapping and pin-pointing of Japanese positions by him and Reg would be vital to the success of the mission. The tension between them only served to increase the pressure of their duties. Henry had immediately taken up his old position as Supply and Pay Sergeant. Reg seemed to sit around all day or strut around the camp with his chest puffed out wearing a smug look.

It was early and there was only a faint stirring of activity. A slight onshore breeze rustled through the palm trees before reaching tropical jungle. When Henry peeked out of the open flap of his tent he glimpsed the sun bouncing off Pacific Ocean as the waves rolled in a constant sequence. It was so idyllic Henry found it hard to concentrate on the job at hand. The violence, carnage and destruction that Henry knew was about to be unleashed seemed to him to be like spitting in the eye of the Almighty who had created this wondrous place.

Henry mechanically sorted the mail amid his day-dreaming until he saw a letter in that oh-so-familiar writing. *Damn it. She is still writing to him. I don't really care. Our country is in real danger here. Whether I get back safely or not, I would like to think I have helped to preserve the way of life that Connie and the rest of the Australian people have taken for granted before this nightmare was unleashed.* He completed his sorting and started sifting through the pile of communications. *The all-out offensive is getting closer by the day. Where the hell is Reg? He is supposed to be here working on our strategy with me. Is he getting special privileges again?*

*There he is. About time.* "Hey, Reg how about coming and helping me with these communications? It's part of your responsibility, you know."

"Sorry, have some important messages to deliver to General Blamey. Can't leave that to anyone else. Then I have an important letter to answer. I'll see if I can help you out after that, if I have time." Before Henry could answer, Reg had strutted off towards the makeshift HQ hut. Henry was furious. *I'm not going to let that bastard get away with leaving all the work to me.*

⸺ ❖ ⸺

Henry and Reg were called to HQ in the early morning to be briefed on their first mission. They would be assessing the gathering Japanese forces before the assault on Lae started. Henry knew that the 9th Division was to be part of the advance towards Lae from the eastern front with support from USAAF and the RAAF aircraft. Reg pushed Henry out of the way and pretended he was aware of the whole plan. Henry managed to hold his tongue. He knew Reg had not even looked at the relevant maps and battle plan. *How am I going to be able to trust this smart arse individual with my life?*

On their way back to their quarters Henry tackled Reg. "I'm not going to let you keep getting away with misleading our superiors like that."

"Do you really think they are going to take any notice of you, country boy?"

"You better act a bit more responsibly or I will leave you to fend for yourself."

"That should go down well with our superiors. We are supposed to be a team, you know." With a toss of his head and a chuckle Reg strutted off towards his tent leaving Henry to stare after him, his mouth open. Henry felt fear rising in his stomach.

⋆⋆⋅⋈⋅⋆⋆

Henry got up with the sun. The jungle was alive with calls from the wild aviary in the undergrowth. Reg approached across the campsite, struggling under his load.

"Jesus Reg, what are you doing with all that stuff?"

"You never know when you are going to need some extra protection."

"One small pistol is all we need. You certainly don't need a machine gun!"

"I'm not going out amongst those little yellow bastards unless I can defend myself."

"We can't use those grenades – we are supposed to unseen, remember. Besides I need some help with the radio and the mapping gear."

"Well, I'm taking it all and that's final."

"Don't expect me to help you with any of it. I will have to manage all this on my own."

"It will be no problem. I'm fit you know."

"We'll see how far you get."

The jungle floor crackled underfoot as they started on their way. The trees were dripping with condensation in the cool morning air. Henry's camouflage uniform clung to his sweating body and his backpack started to feel like it was full of rocks. They had been travelling for almost three hours and had arrived at the bottom of a steep cliff when Henry turned to his companion,

"I think we should take a breather now Reg. It's going to get a lot tougher before the day is out. We don't want to exhaust ourselves too early."

"Are we going to have to find a way up there?" Reg looked up at the dense scrub that covered the way ahead. There were no formed paths to follow and they had been forging forward following the direction shown on their compasses, cutting their way through the undergrowth with their razor sharp machetes, making as little noise as possible. They flopped down under a large fig tree and sat propped up on opposite sides of the huge trunk. They consumed a small portion of their rations of army biscuits and bully beef, mindful that they might have to make them last for some considerable time.

"Geez mate, if I had known it would be like this I would have thought twice about this intelligence thing. I am sorry I gave you a hard time about it being a soft option," said Reg.

Henry looked suspiciously at Reg. He never thought he would hear such an admission from him. *I suppose if I am going to work with this bloke I had better start to be civil with him.* "Well, it was no use trying to convince you otherwise before you had tried it. It is something you have to experience before you can appreciate it."

"Don't I know that now? If it hadn't been for Connie, you and I could have probably been good friends."

"I'm not so sure about that. We come from vastly different backgrounds and I don't know if someone of your privileged upbringing could really understand someone like me. "

"When it comes to shooting Japs I don't think our backgrounds are going to matter. You can shoot, can't you?"

"You know how I feel about needless killing. This mission is going to be dangerous and there is no guarantee we will get back safely. Keeping ourselves unnoticed will be crucial to our success."

"The only good Jap is a dead one as far as I am concerned."

"Look Reg, I am prepared to put our differences aside and work together with you. Our success will be vital to the whole allied campaign. If you try anything that endangers that I warn you that I will act to stop you."

"Hey, I'm not going to be that stupid. It's just that I can't help wanting to shoot the bastards. They would do the same to us if they got the chance."

Suddenly the jungle silence was interrupted by what sounded like a herd of elephants. Henry pulled Reg behind the large fig tree they had been resting against just as five Japanese soldiers in camouflage gear came charging up the path they had just hacked out. The group stopped as they came to the end of the cleared path, chatting on excitedly as they looked at the cliff barring their path. Henry and Reg held their breath as they pressed against the trunk of the tree. Please don't let them come around here, thought Henry. Reg fumbled in his pack and pulled out a grenade but before he could pull the pin, the group had turned and headed back the way they had come.

"Put that away Reg. That would have really given us away."

"What the hell were they talking about?"

"I have no idea but I think they know we are about somewhere. We are going to have to get out of here as quickly as we can."

"I think I might leave some of this stuff hidden here. I can pick it up later." A smile of satisfaction crossed Henry's face but he resisted the temptation to say anything. After helping Reg stow his excess gear in the undergrowth behind several large trees he turned and handed him a radio pack.

"Here take some of this for me. We have to get up there to higher ground. We can't see anything from here."

"This is pretty rough country. I don't think our artillery boys are going to be able to get their big guns through here," said Reg.

"That is part of our job. We have to look into which way our forces should approach Lae."

"They could have a problem if they have to cross this river on our map. What's it called?"

"If you had done your homework you would know that it is the Busu. It is shallow but the current can be strong in this sort of weather. The Singuau Swamp may give them more trouble than that."

"The Pioneers' skills will come in handy. They will need to build some of those corduroy roads they are famous for."

"Come on. Unless we get a move on they won't be going anywhere."

They arrived at a ridge high on Mt Lunamen just as the midday sun was breaking through the dark rain clouds. They had a perfect view down the Busu river to its mouth and out over the Huon Gulf. The main Japanese camp in Lae was clearly visible in the distance. Below them the northern side of the water was a hive of activity. There were a number of Japanese vessels offshore and supplies, once unloaded from a flotilla of large landing craft, were being ferried to the large tent erected right up against the cliff face. It was shielded from the air by a thick overhanging canopy of trees. The landing craft were hardly moving in the still ocean, just bobbing up and down on the barely perceptible swell. From their high position, the khaki clad soldiers look like ants moving their food supply to a safer position in the face of a rising tide.

"That must be part of the Japanese 5th Army and they look like they are preparing for a major offensive," said Henry, handing the binoculars to Reg.

"They seem to have some sort of hidden dump down there."

"They are probably using some caves at the cliff base. I believe there are plenty of them around in these mountains."

Henry motioned that it was time for them to leave. As Henry started to stand Reg grabbed his arm to pull him back.

"Can't we just wait a bit longer? We may get a chance to put a spanner in their works."

"We need to get word of this build up back as soon as we can."

"Look at the little yellows bastards. How I would love to get amongst them with a machine gun."

"That would really be a great help to our cause," said Henry, unable to contain his sarcasm. "We really need them to know that we have found their camp and know what they are up to."

"It wouldn't hurt for us to pick a few of them off before we return to HQ. I can't look at the slanty-eyed scourges without wanting to plug one between their eyes."

"You are hardly equipped to do that. We only have pistols remember."

Henry and Reg's feet hardly hit the ground as they slid down the jungle track leading back to their camp. It was much easier than their upward journey as they now had a clearly defined path. As they approach the spot where Reg had left his weaponry, he called Henry to a halt.

"Let's leave our radio and stuff here and go back up there and reduce their numbers a bit."

"Don't you realise that what we know without them knowing we know is of paramount importance. Taking pot-shots at them for fun is hardly in keeping with that."

"You would feel like that. You've never had the stomach for the heat of the battle, have you? You can't talk them into surrendering, you know.

"I think that if we are going to all live together after this war is over, killing for the sake of killing is totally immoral."

"No wonder Connie ditched you. A girl like her needs a real man to look after her, not some cowardly skunk who runs away every time it looks like there will be a good fight."

"Look mate, if you and I are going to be able to work together in this risky business, we are going to have to keep the personal stuff out of it."

Before Reg could answer the sound of voices sent them scurrying back behind the tree. They left their equipment in the open. A Japanese patrol came running through the jungle in too much of a hurry to notice the pile of gear. Henry grabbed the back of Reg's jacket to stop him from following.

"No time to be a hero. We need to report back to HQ as soon as we can. Something is going to happen here soon."

"All the more reason for us to decrease their numbers a bit!"

"Look, I'm heading off back to camp. If you want to disobey orders and stay here playing games it's your decision but I will have to report to command on it." He slipped out from behind the tree and headed off as silently as possible into the cover of the thick undergrowth, with Reg clambering after him.

"Hey, I don't have to take orders from you, remember."

"I'm certainly not going to put my career in jeopardy to satisfy your ego!" Henry called over his shoulder as he continued on his way.

"Well, I'm not going anywhere until I have one of them in my bag!"

Henry shrugged his shoulders and headed off on his own to get back to camp. "Be it on your head then."

A gunshot reverberated through the jungle. Reg came running after Henry.

"For Christ's sake Henry, wait on. I'm coming."

Henry chuckled to himself – some hero!

CHAPTER 57

# THE BATTLE BEGINS

*"The Seventh Division pincer inland was squeezing the enemy. The first serious contact with the enemy occurred on the afternoon of the 10th September at Jensen's Plantation where the 2/25th Battalion located an enemy patrol. The Jap was quickly outflanked on both sides, and withdrew under cover of darkness.  Battalions had been moved across the mouth of the Busu by barge and folding-boat ferry. Heavy fighting developed, extending the bridgehead on the west side of the river also along the coast to take in a suitable beachhead. As soon as the line of the Busu River was secured, the dumps at G Beach and at the beachhead  on the Burep River behind the 26th Brigade were built up as the 2/3rd Pioneers established a practicable road between the Burep and Busu Rivers to supply the brigade. All stores were brought from Red Beach by small craft.  The Japanese were showing increased activity in this area and more artillery was brought up as infantry support."*

THE BATTLE FOR NEW GUINEA. JUNGLE WARFARE. AUSTRALIAN WAR MEMORIAL, CANBERRA. *1944.*

Henry and Reg had found a vantage point high in the Atzera Range to guide the Allied forces (air and sea) for the attack on Lae. Little was known about Japanese patrol activity in this area so it was important that Henry and Reg provided continual updates on these activities. Aircraft of the USAAF and the RAAF were supplying support bombing of strategic positions as the Allied troops moved in. Henry and Reg were in close contact with these forces pinpointing the bombing targets. It was their riskiest mission to date. Henry hoped Reg fully realised how important it was for them to be undetected. There would be no target practice, as Reg called it, on this mission.

"Look Reg, there are Jap patrols everywhere. They are moving in re-enforcements and supplies down the river by boat as well as overland. That's not what we were expecting."

"Weren't we supposed to have cut off their route from the west?"

"Well, well, so you are actually paying some attention to the things that matter now."

"I'd still like to shoot a few of the bastards as they pass by – to even up the odds. It looks as though we are going to be outnumbered."

"We need to try to get a message back to HQ even though it is going to be risky to use our radio."

"We are going to have to get up higher on the cliff to do that," said Reg, pointing to a ridge even further up the range.

"Yes, we'll be sitting ducks up there but we have to take the chance."

They were almost at their objective when they came to a clearing in the thick scrub. It had been fashioned on what appeared to be a plateau part of the way up to the highest ridge.

"We want to get across to the other side Reg."

"There doesn't seem to be anyone around, so let's make a run for it."

Henry and Reg were half way across the clearing when they heard the sound of soldiers approaching. They threw themselves into what seemed to be a weapons pit that had been dug out on one side of the clearing. They stayed for nearly half an hour concealed behind cases of ammunition, unable to move, hardly even daring to breathe as several Japanese soldiers leaned up against the trunk of a large tree, smoking and laughing as if they didn't have a care in the world. They were only a few feet from where Henry and Reg lay flattened on the ground. *If only they knew what was about to unleashed on them.* Henry took great care not to look straight at any of the Japanese as he didn't want to remember any faces. He knew that a large number of the enemy were going to die when the assault started so he didn't want real images to come back and haunt him. The soldiers eventually moved away to the other side of the clearing.

"We are not going to have time to get to higher ground," Henry whispered.

"Let's see if we can get up one of those giant trees we have been passing," said Reg.

"Ok, we are going to have to take a risk and send this message immediately. Let's go."

Henry was on the move as he uttered these words. They bolted across to the far side of the clearing 50 yards away from the small group and scurried up a large tree that reached right to the top of the rain forest canopy. Henry didn't know what species it was but he guessed it would have been several hundred years old.

"Ok I will cover for you," said Reg cocking his rifle.

"Remember, if we are going to get out of here alive we don't need to draw attention to ourselves. Let's see if we can get any higher in this tree. It will give us better reception."

Troops and equipment were being moved into the clearing below in a continual stream.

"Things are pretty busy down there. Hopefully we will be able to cover our sound with their noise," said Henry as he looked down. He settled himself in the fork of several of the spreading branches and turned on his radio. The tap-tapping of the Morse code seemed to echo like a base drum around the tree's thick foliage. Henry heaved a sigh of relief as the message received signal came through. He flicked off the radio and gave Reg the all clear signal just as a commotion broke out below them. It looked like they had been detected. As quick as a flash Reg dropped something to the ground below. Henry looked at him quizzically, gesturing with his hands.

The Japanese soldiers were closely examining the dropped object and after a quick look upwards they walked away back towards their camp. "Well, what on earth was that?" Henry finally felt safe enough to say out loud.

Reg chuckled. "It's an old trick I learnt in boarding school when we were trying to get out undetected. Give them something they think would have made the noise and they will invariably stop looking for the source."

"Just what was it? "

"Animal dung; not sure from what but I picked it up earlier in the day. Works every time," Reg laughed.

"Just to be on the safe side, I think we had better stay up here for a while yet," Henry said as he looked at Reg with new respect. *Maybe this bloke isn't so bad after all.*

---

Henry and Reg were still holed up in their tree when dawn broke. A group of Japanese soldiers had settled underneath them for the night so they had been unable to escape. They tried to take turns to sleep without success. While they were secure reclining on the spreading canopy of the magnificent rain forest tree, neither of them could relax enough to actually sleep.

"Let's kill the bastards while they are asleep," whispered Reg. It was just before dawn.

"Sure that would really make sense. Every Jap from miles around would be on us in no time."

"Hey, but we would probably get the VC if we took enough of them out," said Reg fumbling with his rifle.

"Look you might want to be a dead hero but I'm not going to die in this God-forsaken place, I have too many loose ends left behind that need fixing. If you want to stay here and play shoot the sleeping Jap you can count me out."

Before Reg could answer, a sound like a storm split the silence. Henry grabbed Reg's arm. "This is it, the start of our attack," he said shaking with excitement.

Soon the first wave of incoming planes flashed through the sky like lightning and this was quickly followed by the thundering of the first explosions. The Japanese below yelled and ran in all directions. The whole jungle reverberated with the sounds of bombs exploding and every now and then the sky lit up like daylight. Within minutes the enemy soldiers had all disappeared into the jungle.

"This is our chance to escape," said Henry as he grabbed his backpack and carefully edged his way down to the jungle floor.

"Let's head to higher ground," whispered Reg scrambling after him.

"Good idea. That will give us a vantage point to watch the action."

As they forged their way uphill through the dense jungle Henry was surprised at the camaraderie growing between him and Reg. He remembered something Colonel Coulthard said to him once:

"To have a mate you have to be a mate." And if he ever needed a mate it was right now.

It wasn't long before they had reached a plateau the size of a couple of football fields. "My God, who would have thought there would be something like this up here," Reg said as he gazed in awe at the vast clearing.

"Come on, let's not stay out in the open too long. This looks as though it could have been used as a supply dropping area," said Henry as he scanned the surrounds.

"Sure thing. We would be sitting ducks out here," agreed Reg.

"Over there," said Henry pointing to a copse of trees on the edge of the clearing.

From the other side of the trees they could see right down the Huon Valley. Henry estimated they were about 5000 feet up so it was a majestic sight. Just then a roar like the approach of wall of water echoed between the high mountains. It was the sound of approaching aircraft moments before hundreds of Allied bombers flew up the gorge at about 2000 feet. They were actually looking down on the planes as they roared by.

"Wow. What a sight to behold." Reg was transfixed. Henry dived on him and threw him to the ground. Japanese fighter planes had appeared high above them. As they slowly raised their heads after the planes had roared off in pursuit of the Allied planes they caught sight of a small group of Japanese soldiers on the other side of the clearing. Henry gestured to Reg to follow him in the direction of a rocky outcrop about 50 yards away at the base of a yet higher cliff face.

They reached the outcrop safely but were unsure if they had been spotted. Henry led Reg towards a group of shrubs up against the cliff face. As he pushed them aside he noticed an opening to a cave behind them. He grabbed Reg's arm and pulled him into the dark space as the Japanese soldiers rounded the rocks. Henry felt around and realised that the cave they had entered was quite large and pulled Reg even further inside. A stale musky smell permeated the air and Henry could feel Reg shaking uncontrollably.

"Come on mate. It's going to be ok. We just have to wait it out. Don't give up now," Henry whispered, his voice reverberated around the hollow cave and sounded more like a shout.

"The bastards are going to get us," said Reg in a husky voice that was barely audible. Henry held tightly to his arm to give him reassurance. The whole world seemed to be closing in on him.

*How are we going to escape this time?*

# CHAPTER 58

# TRAPPED

Henry held his hand firmly over Reg's mouth. Scratching sounds could be heard at the entrance to the cave. The bushes covering the entrance parted. In the dull light a figure loomed. Reg jerked himself away. Henry glimpsed the shape of a grenade in his hand. He threw himself on top of Reg and pinned him to the ground. The silhouetted figure disappeared as quickly as it had appeared.

"Don't you dare," Henry barked into Reg's ear at very close range. He had his forearm lodged firmly under Reg's chin. His whole body was shaking uncontrollably. "You know that I could break your neck in seconds."

More explosions echoed through the crisp mountain air. Excited Japanese voices came from all directions. Undergrowth was trampled as they fled to whatever cover they could find. Then, as suddenly as it all started, it stopped. Henry kept Reg pinned to the ground. He was now sobbing quietly, his body occasionally heaving sideways with an involuntary shudder. *Who would have thought that a once cocky, private school trained, bright young thing, with his army background, would turn into this blubbering mess?* Without releasing his hold Henry reached into his backpack and took out a length of cord and wound it tightly around Reg's hands. He then released his tight grip on his throat and tied his feet together as well. Sobs were still racking through Reg's body and they seemed to be getting louder so Henry stuffed his spare socks into his mouth and fastened the gag with another length of cord.

There were no sounds at all from outside the cave. Henry flicked on his torch to get his bearings and dragged the trussed up Reg to the cave wall and propped him up on his backpack. With the light shining straight into Reg's face Henry whispered menacingly:

"Don't you ever try anything like that again. You will stay like this until I am satisfied you are in control of yourself."

Tears streamed down Reg's face and in the torch light he had the look of a startled deer. Henry thought how easy it would be to leave him here like this and make his own way back to camp. He turned off his light to conserve the batteries and sat a few feet away from Reg. He listened until the dampened whimpers ceased. It was pitch black and any sounds that penetrated the silence seemed to echo around the cave. Henry reached out to touch Reg now he had calmed down. He knew that soon he would have to leave the cave and go outside to assess the situation.

Before Henry had a chance to stand up a flash of light came from the front of the cave and a lone figure entered the space. With his torch pointed to the ground the menacing shadow had what looked like a rifle in his hand. He advanced further into the cave. Henry pulled his knife from his backpack and circled around behind the stalking figure. He could now make out the Japanese uniform. Henry grabbed the soldier from behind locking his arm around his neck and knocking the rifle away in the same move. A single shot rang out and the bullet ricocheted off the walls of the cave several times with a ping like a score in a pinball machine. Reg let out a loud gasp as Henry sunk the knife deep into the throat of the enemy interloper. Henry quickly gathered the torch and grabbed the now limp body under the shoulders. He dragged it deeper into the cave, hid it behind a pile of loose rocks and covered it roughly with smaller loose rocks nearby. He stepped back and suddenly realised what he had done.

He had killed a man for the first time. He slumped down on the ground with his head in his hands, the now discarded light shining like a beacon on an airport runway, all the way to the back of the cave.

His stomach heaved with emotion and he vomited all over his boots and trouser legs. As he sat there breathing heavily he heard gasping sounds from Reg. Snapping back to reality, he hurried back to Reg and whispered: "I am going to turn off this light now and we need to stay perfectly still and silent until we are sure he was alone."

Henry loosened Reg's gag. "Any noise and it goes back on." The last thing Henry noticed as he turned off the torch was the accusing look in Reg's eyes. Henry's stomach still churned but he closed his eyes and leant back against the wall of the cave, alert to any noise outside, and waited.

⊷ ▣◆▣ ⊶

It was hard for Henry to tell how long they sat in silence. He could hear Reg's rhythmic breathing and assumed that he had fallen asleep with exhaustion. Henry decided it was time to look outside. He flashed his torch on Reg and saw that he was indeed asleep. He moved cautiously towards the opening of the cave and carefully parted the covering bushes. It was still light outside but it was obvious from the long shadows that night would soon be upon them. Henry slowly eased himself out, taking care not to cause too much movement. He stood up and blinked a few times to accustom his eyes to the unfamiliar light. It was still warm in the gathering dusk and the humid air brought a rush of sweat to his brow. Looking around he could see no sign of life. The skies were silent and there were no echoes of the turmoil that had hit this region only a few hours ago. It was as if all life had been eliminated and the whole area had been returned to nature.

Henry wondered if the battle for Lae was over. Reg's state of mind worried him. *Is he going to be any use to me or should I leave and try to make it out of the jungle on my own?* Henry leant against a large tree and was soaking up this peaceful scene when his attention was drawn to the other side of the cleared plateau. A group of about 20 Japanese soldiers had emerged from the scrub. Henry ducked behind the tree.

The soldiers crossed the clearing and walked only a few feet away from him. As they approached the bushes covering the opening to their cave Henry's heart gave a lurch. Should he make a run for it now, leaving Reg to the mercy of the enemy? He realised he had left all his equipment in the cave and knew he couldn't leave Reg in the state he was in. He feared what would happen if the enemy soldiers found him. He would not go peacefully.

Henry contemplated how he would rescue Reg if he fell into the clutches of the Japs. He would have to move fast if Reg did something stupid. He had no weapons so he was going to have to create a distraction. He then realised the group had walked right past the cave entrance and was relieved when there was no sign of Reg. He feared the temptation would be too great and Reg would try to attack the Japanese in some way. He then remembered Reg was still tied up.

Henry stayed behind the tree keeping a watchful eye for any movement in the clearing and the surrounding bush. When he felt it was safe he moved stealthily to the edge of the plateau to view the surrounding valley. He saw many small camp fires dotting the scrub like fireflies and realised the jungle was full of fleeing Japanese soldiers. They needed to get out of this area as soon as possible. He returned to the cave, flashed the light and saw Reg was still asleep. Henry's feelings for this man of complex character softened. *War plays on everyone's mind in the end. I just hope he comes out of this with his sanity. We are going to have to make our move at first light.*

Reg woke with a start, shielded his eyes from Henry's torch and started shaking uncontrollably. He tried to raise his arms as if surrendering. "For heaven's sake Reg, it's only me."

"Jesus Henry, I thought you had left me to fend for myself."

"That won't happen as long as you behave."

"Can't do much when you have got me trussed up like a turkey."

Henry resisted the temptation to tell him that was exactly what he acted like; a turkey. "We are going to leave as soon as it is light. This place is crawling with Japs. We need to get out of here before they find us."

"How am I going to move?"

"I'll loosen your bonds for now as we need to get some sleep. Do as you are told tomorrow and I will consider taking them all off."

"I'll do whatever you ask if you just get me out of this God-forsaken pace."

"Ok. But try to get some sleep now."

Henry spent a fitful night trying to find a comfortable spot on the hard floor. He periodically checked on Reg. Henry had finally dozed off in the early hours of the morning when he was aroused abruptly by a struggle in the cave. He backed himself up against the wall, drew his pistol and shone his light on Reg to find him writhing around on the ground with a six-foot python wrapped around his head. It was only a small reptile and Henry knew it was harmless. He had an uncontrollable urge to laugh but he realised the commotion Reg was making could betray them once and for all. "G.g.g.get this thing off me!" Shrieked Reg.

Henry could see the look of terror on Reg's face. He toyed again with the idea of making a run for it alone. This would be his ultimate revenge on his old nemesis. He then realised he had to deal with the snake situation first or all could be lost. Henry pulled his knife from his backpack, propped his torch on top of it and approached the writhing figures.

"Just hold still for a moment. The snake won't hurt you. It is harmless but I could do you an injury trying to deal with it when you are rolling around like that."

"Jesus mate, just get it off me!"

Henry managed to grab the snake behind its head and by stretching it upwards away from Reg, he deftly removed the top half of its writhing body. Blood spurted from the snake but it soon loosened its hold and dropped to the ground. Reg rolled away frantically trying to remove the thick, sticky blood from his body.

"Hang on there." Henry cut Reg free from his bonds. For a moment Reg lay motionless on the ground until he realised he was free and he picked himself up, backed up to the wall and looked daggers at Henry.

"Why don't you finish me off too?"

"If I was going to do that, I would have done it hours ago. I could have been miles away from here by now."

"Why didn't you? I've been nothing but a liability to you on this whole mission."

"If I had known you had a snake phobia, maybe I would have. Don't have too many snakes in Toffsville, eh?"

"I have always had a thing about them. They scare the shit out of me no matter how small or harmless."

Henry chuckled, "I wish I had a camera. It would have been interesting to show your mates back at camp how their hero dealt with such a minor incident."

"I don't care what you do when we get back but just get me out of this snake-infested hole. I'll do anything you ask. You're in total control now."

"Well, thanks for your confidence but we still have to get out of here. The place is crawling with Jap deserters. We need to get going."

"Point me in the direction you want us to go."

# CHAPTER 59

# FLIGHT TO SAFETY

Henry carefully pulled back the bushes guarding the entrance to the cave and after a quick look around beckoned Reg to follow him. The morning light was filtering over the high cliffs. Shafts of light beamed down through the trees like golden icicles.

Henry turned to Reg. "Just look at that mate. How could man bring such destruction into a world that can produce a sight like that?"

"It sure does send shivers down your spine," said Reg, unusually philosophical.

"I could stay and look at that forever, but we have to try to get out of here," sighed Henry.

He looked at his compass and pointed up the sheer cliff face ahead of them. "I think we should head north but we need to stay away from the well-worn paths so we aren't found."

"You're not thinking of going up there are you?" Reg looked incredulously in the direction Henry was pointing.

"Well, do you want to be dodging Nips all day? Sometimes in this game you need to weigh up the risks. We might have to do a bit of chopping but it will be safer."

"That should wake up all the snakes."

"Now come on Reg, you are going to have to get over this irrational fear of yours."

"It's all right for you; you aren't covered in the blood of their brother like I am. They'll be attracted to me."

Reg started to unbutton the torn bloodstained shirt he was still wearing, "I think I'll just get rid of this."

"Don't be stupid. The mossies will give you more trouble than the snakes."

"You can swat mossies and I certainly don't need any extra warmth in this climate." He wiped the sweat from his face with the remains of his shirt.

"If only you could see yourself – you now have blood all over your face," Henry laughed.

"Bugger," Reg frantically looked for a clean part of the shirt to re-wipe his face. "How's that now?"

"Come on. Get it back on so we can get started. When it cools off a bit I'll let you have my flak jacket to wear but for now you need that shirt." Henry turned on his heel and strode off towards the base of the cliff. Reg followed, struggling to put the remains of his shirt back on.

Sweat ran down his face and his hands had started to blister as Henry chopped his way through the undergrowth. Reg had been reluctant to help so Henry loaded him up with their gear. It was quite a load but he was prepared to do anything to avoid going first into this snake-infested wilderness.

"You know Reg, snakes are only a problem when you approach them abruptly and unannounced. With the noise we are making they will all be in Papua by now."

"The only good snake is a dead one! And even then I wouldn't want to touch it. Their slimy skin gives me the creeps."

Henry raised the machete to lop a large vine blocking their way when Reg let out a shriek and Henry got such a fright he followed through with the razor sharp blade and cut right through the toe of his boot. Blood spurted out like a fountain.

"For Christ's sake Reg, what was that all about? Now look what I have done."

"Geez mate, I thought that vine hanging down was a snake. I was trying to warn you."

Henry slumped to the ground in shock. As he tried to pull his mangled boot from his foot to see the damage he toppled forward and landed at Reg's feet. Reg quickly rolled him over and removed Henry's boot. Blood flowed unabated. Reg quickly stripped off his shirt, wrapped it tightly around Henry's foot and held it until the bleeding stopped. Every time he tried to release the pressure the bleeding started again so he secured it with his belt. Henry faded in and out of consciousness as the pain engulfed him.

"I'm so sorry, Henry, to have caused this. But don't worry, I'll get you out of here."

"I think there are some aspirin in my backpack. Could you get me a few, this pain is unbearable."

Reg shoved four of the tablets into Henry's mouth and held his head so he could drink from his canteen. "Go easy on the water mate, we don't have a lot left. "

"Can you see the damage," asked Henry in a weakened voice.

"I don't know how to tell you this but a couple of your toes are still in your boot. We are not going to be able to loosen that dressing for some time yet."

"I think you should just leave me here and go on your own. You can send someone back for me when you get to Lae. I won't be going anywhere."

"No way. You saved me from that bloody snake, so there is no way I am leaving you here to die."

"It could be the best result for you. You'd have Connie all to yourself."

"Look mate, we are going to have to have a serious talk about Connie soon but now is not the time. We have to work out a way to get us both out of here."

"One of us needs to get back as soon as possible. HQ needs to be aware of all these Jap deserters running around this jungle like loose cannons."

"There's no way I am leaving you here to fend for yourself. Besides Connie would never forgive me for that."

"Not sure she would really care."

"Like I said, now is not the time. We need a plan. Maybe we could capture a few of these wandering Nips and get them to help us."

"You really think that would work? They would be more likely to overcome us and then we would be their prisoners!"

"Well, maybe we would be better to surrender to them – pretend we have vital info for them and they might lead us out of this hell-hole safely."

"Oh, no you don't. I've had experience at the hands of their Kraut brothers. You don't get away from them –with or without information. The more they think you know, the worse they treat you!" Henry flopped down onto the wet ground. "I need to sit for a while."

Henry had a major dilemma. *Reg has become quite irrational. I hope he is not losing his mind. I need him to get us out of here. Could I trust him to go on his own? Maybe I should surrender to the Japs to create a distraction to let Reg get away. I can't seem to focus on anything.* He lifted his head to try to see what Reg was doing.

Planes buzzed overhead but they couldn't identify which side they belonged to because of the thick foliage. It would be no use signalling and then finding out that it was the enemy. Reg handed Henry a length of thick bamboo.

"Come on mate; let's see if we can get you moving with this."

"Look, you really should leave me and get back as soon as you can. I am just a liability."

"There's no way I am heading off into this snake and Jap infested jungle on my own." Reg's eyes grew wide as he stared into the undergrowth in front of them. He gently pulled Henry to his feet and they started to move slowly.

"I think we are going to have to take a chance and head back down to an easier path," said Reg with relief in his voice.

"I'll leave all the decisions to you. I'm not in a fit state to lead."

"Not me. You're the snake expert, you get us away from this snake den."

"Ok, let's get down there and see if the going is any easier." He nodded towards a level track they could see below. Henry leant on Reg as he helped him down the slippery slope. A group of planes swooped low over the top of the jungle treetops. Reg dumped Henry heavily on the ground, pulled out his pistol and started firing indiscriminately in the air. Henry mustered up his last bit of energy to fling his make-shift crutch at Reg's hand and knocked the pistol flying.

"Jesus mate, what do you think you are doing? They're ours."

"Well, they will know we are here then."

"And so will every Jap within 20 miles of us."

"Maybe the Japs will be more help to us than our own forces. They seem to have forgotten we exist."

"You seem to forget that our main purpose out here is to remain hidden and get information back without the enemy knowing."

"Well, they should do something about these damn snakes." Reg scrambled around on the ground trying to retrieve his pistol when there was a thud on the ground in front of them. It was one of the biggest pythons Henry had ever seen, twice the size of the one in the cave. Reg froze and suddenly jumped backwards. Henry fell heavily to the ground.

"Bloody hell!" said Henry.

"Shit, that's a big bastard. He's looking at us, what are we going to do?" Reg was standing rooted to the spot and growing paler by the minute. Henry eased himself slowly backwards along the ground towards Reg.

"Just lower yourself slowly down beside me. Don't take your eyes off him and no quick movements." For once Reg was happy to oblige. As he sunk down he took hold of Henry's arm with a grip that would have brought a sharp retort if his foot hadn't started to throb again. "That's it mate, slowly now, deep breaths, stay as still as you can."

Henry could feel the thumping of Reg's pulse through the hand that gripped his forearm. *The poor bugger, he really is freaked out.* Henry eased Reg's fingers off his arm and gave them a gentle squeeze. "Come on old boy," said Henry softly, "just relax." He was not sure if he was addressing the snake or Reg.

The huge snake turned and slid silently out of sight. Moments later it was as if it had never been there. Reg was still frozen to the spot. Henry continued to stroke his forearm until he finally relaxed. "Come on, I think we can sit for a while and recover ourselves. There is not much daylight left so we are going to have to spend another night out here," Henry said with more confidence in his voice than he felt. He cradled Reg as he imagined he would a baby in distress. An image of Connie flashed before him, her smiling face looking as serene as the Virgin Mary. Henry snapped himself back to reality.

"We must almost be back into enemy territory," said Henry as they came across a well worn path. "We had better keep our ears open for any sign of those damn Nips."

"I'll be keeping my eyes out for those slimy things, "said Reg tensely.

"Geez, mate. I'm getting a bit sick of this paranoia of yours. Snakes are the least of our worries from now on."

"Look, I've told you before, they scare the shit out of me and nothing you can say is going to change that."

They rounded a bend in the path and Henry let out a startled cry, "Jesus, let's get out of here." They had come into a small clearing and seated in a circle examining what looked like a map were three Japanese soldiers. Reg pulled Henry back into the undergrowth but not before the Japanese soldiers had seen them. They dropped the paper they were examining and jumped to attention, grabbing their rifles. Reg dumped Henry heavily and pulled his pistol. Henry struggled to do the same but had trouble getting to his backpack as it was out of his reach. Henry was still fumbling to get it open when the first shot rang out. Reg had felled the first Jap before he could fire a shot. A bullet thudded into the tree just behind Henry. Reg hit the second soldier right between the eyes and he dropped to the ground like a stone. The third soldier had thrown himself behind a tree but they could still see his gun protruding.

"Go after him Reg. Don't let him get away, I'll cover you from here." Henry was sweating profusely but he had managed to secure his pistol. As quick as a flash Reg ducked over to the other side of the clearing where he had a clear view of the hidden soldier. Henry fired several shots in the direction of the tree. Then Henry saw a white rag waving on the end of the hidden Japanese's rifle. Just as Henry called out, "Hold your fire Reg," a shot rang out and the body of the third enemy soldier toppled from behind the tree and lay face down on top of his rifle with its white attachment starting to turn red as blood poured from his head wound.

"I didn't see the flag," Reg said casually. "Wouldn't have been able to take him with us anyway."

"You shot him in the back," Henry cried out.

"I told you I didn't see the flag."

Propping himself on his bamboo crutch, Henry looked in silence at the bodies of the fallen Japanese.. He felt nausea rise into his throat. This time he knew that it was unavoidable but he couldn't help his feeling of abhorrence of this senseless killing. Henry slumped to the ground with his head in his hands trying to ignore the throbbing of his injured foot. He shoved the last aspirins into his mouth and took a sip from their diminishing water supply. He opened his eyes and there was Reg, still holding his pistol pointed at the dense undergrowth. There was a glazed look in his eye. A shiver ran down Henry's spine.

"Come on mate, let's get these bodies out of sight," said Henry in a soft voice, "and get out of here before we attract any more unwanted attention."

CHAPTER 60

# SAFE AT LAST

*"The 24th and 25th Brigades of the Ninth Division were ordered to push forward at dawn on 16th of September to the Butibum River and to cross if possible. At 10.45 am the same day the 25th Brigade (Seventh Division) reached the outskirts of Lae. They couldn't enter the stricken town as it was in the throes of its last pounding by the American bombers. During the morning the forward brigades of the Ninth Division had been pushed forward to control the airfield and its defences. Explosions were heard in the middle of Lae at midday and these were closely followed by machine-gun fire and the unmistakable whistling of 25-pounder shells. For two hours the Ninth Division hammered the already battered township. At 2.30 pm H.Q. Ninth Division had received a signal that troops of the Seventh Division had occupied Lae. The township had been blasted to the ground – it was no more than an evil-smelling rubbish heap. Dozens of Japanese planes littered the airstrip. Motor trucks, splintered, wrecked and overturned, lay where Chinatown had once been. Strongposts and foxholes in the hill-faces, filled with Japanese bodies, marked the enemy's last stand at Lae. The only living thing untouched was a fifty yard hedge of blooming frangipani."*

THE BATTLE FOR NEW GUINEA. JUNGLE WARFARE. AUSTRALIAN WAR MEMORIAL, CANBERRA. *1944.*

Henry and Reg managed another two hours on the jungle path. The light had almost completely faded and they had trouble staying on the rough track. Thankfully they had encountered no more Japanese. Henry still felt queasy every time he pictured those mangled bodies.

"You're very quiet Henry," said Reg.

"Yes, well I still can't get used to having to kill another human. It makes my stomach churn."

"It was them or us."

"I know that but it doesn't make it any easier. Look, I'm exhausted. We should find a safe place for the night and get an early start tomorrow."

"I'm not staying another night in this snake-infested hole!"

"You have no choice. Unless you want to go ahead on your own."

"If another of those bloody snakes comes near me I am going to jump off the nearest cliff!"

Henry shrugged his shoulders, he was too tired to argue the point with Reg. Another day and they should be at their destination. Hopefully as they got closer there would be fewer enemy troops. That was if the Allies had secured Lae. It had just occurred to Henry that perhaps the offensive had failed and they were heading towards more trouble!

Henry was resting against a tall rosewood tree. He opened his eyes to see Reg fiddling with the radio. "You can't use that. The Japs must know we are here and that will pinpoint us."

"I'm just calling our planes to get them to come and bomb the jungle to remove all the snakes." Henry reached out and snatched the radio from Reg's hands. *He really has lost his marbles. I must keep it together and get out of here for Connie's sake. Even if it is Reg she really loves, someone will need to tell her the truth about his bravery if he doesn't make it out of here with his mind intact. I will make myself do that for him.*

"Come on Reg, we need to find somewhere to rest for the night." *I need to get his mind off those snakes!*

"That looks pretty comfortable, thanks Reg," said Henry as he sank down onto the ground sheet that Reg had spread over the accumulated undergrowth on the forest floor.

"Think I'll just make an overhead cover out of some of these palm leaves." The old Reg was back.

"You know Reg, if anyone had told me a few weeks ago that you and I would be working together like this I would have thought they were crazy."

"I would have probably agreed with them. Now I need to get this roof in place so we have no more problems with falling reptiles." Reg was finally satisfied with his efforts and flopped down beside Henry.

"You know Henry there is something I need to tell you about Connie." The mention of her name sent a sharp pain through Henry's chest.

"I think I would rather leave any talk of her until we get out of here."

"No, I think you need to know something now."

*He's going to tell me how she is just waiting for him to return to get a divorce from me so they can be together.* "I suppose I may as well know now. If we don't make it I may never find out."

"You must have realised there wasn't ever anything serious between the two of us," said Reg cautiously.

"What do you mean? I thought you two were an item before I was on the scene."

"Well, I had been trying ever since I met her but never really got anywhere and after she met you, I didn't stand a chance."

"But she's been writing to you. I saw the letters."

"I wondered if you recognised them. It gave me a bit of a thrill to think you may have been stressed over them. But she was only trying to find out what you were up to."

"Checking up on me you mean?"

"No, she was worried sick about you and couldn't bring herself to write directly to you after the dust-up you two had."

Henry's heart began to flutter. "How stupid people can be Reg. I was convinced she had decided you were a much better catch than me and I was inclined to agree with her."

"Well I probably am, but she certainly didn't think so."

"Thank you for telling me Reg. It will give me the incentive I need to push myself harder so we get out of this mess." He slumped back on his soft cushion of leaves and slipped quietly into the deepest, most relaxed sleep he had had in weeks.

Henry opened his eyes to the sun filtering through the forest canopy. He rolled over on the downy undergrowth. Looking up he could see the first stirrings of life in the jungle. He was still awed by the abundance of colourful bird life in this remote part of the world. From the majestic birds of prey, Osprey and Whistling Kite, that soared high in the crystal clear sky, to the seemingly unending array of multicoloured parrots that foraged overhead. Henry could never hope to identify them all. Then down on the forest floor another world still, bush turkeys and other flightless birds scratched away in the rotting and mouldy under world. He was sure that many species of flora and fauna here were yet to be discovered and labelled. Mankind had a lot to answer for if this was what nature could produce when left undisturbed.

For a moment he lost himself in his contemplation of this seemingly peaceful and untouched world. Warmth coursed through his body and he felt more relaxed than he had in months. Reg's revelation last night had added to his state of euphoria. He couldn't believe that Connie was so worried about him. Those dreams he had of a wonderful future together after this senseless war was over may be possible after all. An image of her smiling face with those mesmerising blue green eyes, hovered closely overhead as he closed his eyes and lost himself in thoughts of her soft pliable body snuggled close, her tender touch enveloping him in a sea of tranquillity.

The sound of movement in the undergrowth snapped Henry completely awake. He eased his aching body into a sitting position and was about to shake Reg when the crunching in the undergrowth grew louder. Reg immediately jolted sideways, grabbed his pistol from his kit and jumped to his feet. The sound of crumpling undergrowth continued to grow louder and Henry and Reg stayed frozen to the spot.

"At least it's not a snake," whispered Reg. Henry grabbed hold of Reg's leg to get his attention and motioned him back to the ground. Reg lowered himself still holding his pistol cocked in front of him. The undergrowth a few feet away had started to move and Reg levelled his gun in that direction and was about to squeeze the trigger.

"No, stop." Henry knocked the gun out of Reg's hand just as an Aussie slouch hat appeared over the top of their little night shelter. A menacing army rifle was shoved right in their faces.

"Well, well what do we have here? Robinson Crusoe and Man Friday?"

"Geez mate, are we glad to see you," Henry managed to squeeze out the words. Reg stayed rigid and didn't seem able to register what was happening.

"My god, it's not Henry and Reg is it? We were told to look out for you. Thought you spy boys would be able to keep in better shape. Hey fellas, come and look at what I have found," he called back over his shoulder.

"Please, just get us out of here," pleaded Reg.

The pair stepped gingerly onto the jungle track. Reg was dressed only in torn fatigue pants covered in dried snake blood, with the upper part of his body scratched and bleeding; Henry was in a torn and muddy shirt and fatigues with one foot tightly wrapped in the remains of Reg's shirt. Their faces were streaked with dirt and dried blood, their hair was matted and plastered to their heads. They looked at each other and burst out laughing.

"We sure are a sight. But you lot are the most beautiful thing we have seen, ever, aren't they Reg?" Henry said steadying himself by putting his arm around Reg. He took a huge breath, let go and walked slowly towards the Aussie soldiers under his own steam for the first time in days. One of them stepped forward and grabbed him by the arm.

"Come on mate. You look as though you've been through enough for now. We'll make you a stretcher and get you back to Lae and some medical help."

⸙

Henry lay in a sagging bunk in the makeshift hospital on the outskirts of Lae. The air was humid and there was  no breeze. Between the tied back flaps of the canvas tent he spotted frangipanis in full bloom. *Wonder how they escaped the carnage? It looks like heaven.* Henry had been debriefed and had turned over his blood-stained maps of the enemy positions even though he wondered at their value now that the battle appeared to be over.

The army nurses made a fuss over him. They cleaned and dressed his foot with its missing toes. It was now badly swollen. The medical officer had scheduled him for surgery as soon as they could control the infection. Henry knew his army career was about to change as he was going to be unable to partake in any activities that involved putting on boots, walking or marching. He lay there, pain-free for the first time in days, dreaming about what he would say to Connie next time he saw her. He still couldn't believe what Reg had told him in the jungle - that Connie wanted him and only him. A shadow loomed. He looked up to see the welcome face of Colonel Coulthard, smiling broadly. He tried to stand to salute him.

"Stay where you are. Well my boy, you certainly gave us a bit of a fright. We thought we had lost you."

"It's good to be back in civilisation, I can tell you."

"I don't know that you can call this civilised but you both did a great job. I am sure you will not be forgotten when the accolades are handed out. You played an important a role in our success.

"It's not something I would want to go through again, sir."

"The messages you got to us pin-pointing enemy camps helped in our victory and those maps of yours will be of use to us for many months to come."

"You don't think things are almost at an end then?"

"No, not by a long way. We may have routed them from Lae but as you confirmed there are hordes of them still up there and armed well enough to make nuisances of themselves for some time."

"Hope you don't expect me to go back up there, sir."

"Of course not. You realise that your injury means you are not going to be on active duty again for some time. If ever."

"That is not going to make me unhappy sir. I sure need a break."

"It's Reg I'm worried about. Did he act normally with you?" said the Colonel in a concerned voice.

"I wouldn't have made it back without him," snapped Henry.

"That's not what I am talking about. His mental state seems questionable to say the least."

"Anyone who went through what we did will need some time to adjust."

"Yes, well his father was known for his inability to cope under pressure. He was more of a liability out in the field than an asset. That's why they retired him to a desk job."

"Look, if you think I am going to criticise Reg, you will have to think again. I am sure with a bit of time off he will be back to normal. I owe him my life."

### CHAPTER 61

# ON HOME SOIL

*"Following Lae's capture, the Australians made another landing at Scarlet Beach, near Finschhafen. The 2/3rd Pioneers rejoined the division and in October participated in the successful defence of Scarlet Beach when the Japanese counter-attacked. When the fighting was over, the pioneers reverted to their engineering role, working on the Satelburg Road and  other locations on New Guinea's northern coast supporting the Huon Peninsula campaign."*

MUD AND SAND: 2/3 PIONEER BATTALION AT WAR.

Henry looked at the four walls of his dingy room. He had returned home from another day in the dispatch office. Tomorrow was pay day, when he would have to prepare all the wages for the non-combatant army staff employed in various jobs around Brisbane. It would make a change and required some skill but was far from satisfying. All he could see from his ground floor window was a dirty factory wall with one window high above his own. He didn't know if the factory was working as the front was hidden from his view. By the time he returned to Spring Hill each day the workers would have gone in any case. He picked up the scratched, Army issue plate from which he had just eaten a greasy meat pie and lumpy mashed potato and walked over to the stained sink in the corner. He threw the plate into it with such force that it ricocheted around the bowl several times.

He pulled the letter he had received from Tom out of his pocket. Not that there was ever much detail in his letters but Henry had been cadging what information he could about his old unit from anyone who crossed his path. A company was still in the thick of it in New Guinea. He longed to be back with his mates in battle. Just the same it was good of Tom to write to him. *Keeping his spirits up Tom called it.* Now Henry was no longer in his intelligence job he received very little information about their movements but Tom had managed to sneak a bit of a run down on their movements through the censors by using a sort of code.

*"After the fracas at the river camp we moved on to the next holiday destination, some  60 miles to the north. Another nice little seaside resort. Lots of red tinted birds waiting to be named.  Sharing with some of our neighbours from across the ocean who weren't too happy when we arrived after lights out. We took them to task about the dark welcome as we were told our way would be well lit. We were berated for not paying attention to the overhead lighting from the opposing holiday camp."*

Tom's letter gave Henry his first good laugh in months. His old mate had managed to tell him how they had moved from Finschhafen to Scarlett Beach and still had less than cordial relations with their Yank allies after they ignored enemy aircraft and landed without lights to guide them.

Henry's despondency was only relieved for a short time. He still needed a stick to get around. He had been assessed as B grade which meant he would never be assigned to active duty again. He hadn't been able to bring himself to contact Connie. He didn't want her to see him in his crippled state. He was sure she would be sympathetic but he didn't want her pity, he wanted her love! He felt that as a cripple he had nothing to offer a woman and certainly wasn't in a position to support a family. He slumped down on his narrow bed and lay there staring at the peeling ceiling and the cracked walls.

"God, why have you done this to me? Have I been such a poor servant that you felt the need to punish me in this way?"

⚜

Henry was working his way through the pile of wage slips when a name caught his eye. It was Fernando Cesaro, an ambulance driver. Henry's heart leapt – maybe he was related to Romano. Henry's guilt at leaving Romano in the desert to die made his hand shake. Memories of that horrible time came flooding back. *I should contact this Fernando and perhaps be able to communicate to Romano's family what a brave person he was.* Henry went out to the next office to talk to his supervising officer. "Tell me Captain, is it permissible for me to contact any of these people on the payroll?"

"Why do you want to do that?"

"There's a name here of someone who may be related to a young man I served with in the Middle East. He didn't make it back. I would like to contact his family."

"Who is it?"

"Fernando Cesaro."

"Oh him. He usually calls in here to collect his pay on his way back to his lodgings. He's on release from Cowra you know. A POW."

"Oh my God," said Henry incredulously.

"There's no need to be alarmed. They are all harmless. It's ridiculous the way they have locked them up. They are very hard-working citizens."

Henry was still in a state of shock and struggled to find the right words to answer the Captain, "Hell no, I'm not frightened. I think he may be my friend's father."

"Couldn't be that. His son has just returned from overseas. Was missing in action for some months apparently." Henry stood fixed to the spot. His heart was in his mouth. *Romano's alive, I just don't believe it!*

"Hey, what's up Henry?" Captain Wilson asked. "You look like you have seen a ghost."

"It has been a bit of a shock to me. It seems like my mate is still alive. I had given him up for dead."

"Look, when Fernando comes in tomorrow for his pay I'll send him in to see you."

"Yes, please do, please do," said Henry as he walked back to his office in a state of disbelief. He sat down at his chair, put his head in his hands and started to cry.

Henry opened the door of the cab and stood looking at the old farm house. He had thought a lot about it on the train on the way to Innisfail, but now that the moment had arrived he was quite nervous about it.

"Do you want me to wait for you?" the cabbie asked.

"No, I think I may be here for some time." He handed the driver a 10 pound note.

"Keep the change."

"Gee thanks mate. Sure you don't want me to wait?"

"No, I'll be fine." He walked slowly towards the run-down house. Sure could do with some tender loving care, thought Henry as he looked at the shabby paint and the rusted iron roof. As he walked up onto the front verandah, he heard the murmur of voices from the back of the house. Rather than knock he followed the verandah around to where the voices were coming from. Seated under a large fig tree in a faded canvas deck chair was Romano. He was thinner than Henry remembered but there was no mistaking the piercing brown eyes as they turned in his direction. Henry tried not to look at the tell-tale folded up trouser leg.

"Henry, it's great to see you." Henry stood there for moment unsure whether he was going to get a welcome or not but he couldn't contain himself and he rushed over. He bent down next to Romano and gave him a good old fashioned bear-hug. Tears were streaming down Henry's face as he squeezed the life out of his former partner.

"Geez Henry, you'll finish me off for good if you keep that up."

"Sorry mate, I just didn't think I was going to ever see you again."

Henry turned to look at the older woman who had just come out of the back door of the house carrying a jug of iced lemon juice. She was dressed in black from head to toe and had the same sharp-sighted look as her son.

"Well, who do we have here, Romano? An old friend?"

"Mama, I'd like you to meet Henry Thompson, my partner in crime in the desert."

The dark eyes narrowed. "The one who leave you to die?"

"Mama I thought I had explained it to you. He had no choice; we had important information to get back."

Henry walked slowly towards Romano's mother and held out his hand. "I am very pleased to meet you Mrs Cesaro. You should be very proud of your son. He is a very brave man."

"He need to be with friend like you." She refused to take the proffered hand.

"Mama, will you please stop it. Come sit down Henry and tell me what on earth happened to you?"

Romano's mother grudgingly placed a chair next to Romano's deck chair, strode back inside and slammed the door.

"Don't take any notice of Mama; she's still coming to terms with my condition. I tell her she should be glad I am back at all. I certainly am."

"I wish I could feel like you. I blame this cursed war and everyone to do with it for my injury."

"Come on Henry, we knew what we were getting into. Are you going to tell me what happened?"

"My own fault I guess. Had a bit of a mishap with a machete in the New Guinea jungle. I owe my life to my off-sider. More than I did for you."

"Look Henry, I feel no malice towards you. We both did what we had to. It was our duty."

"Yes, but I seem to have always been the one to leave my comrades in the lurch."

"What you did helped to turn the tide of the war in the Middle East and I don't doubt that New Guinea was much the same."

"How did you manage to get out? I really thought I had left you to die. It has played on my mind ever since."

"I don't remember much but apparently I was found by a nomad Kunta tribe who nursed me back to health. My first memory is waking up and looking into the face of a big black man with a thatch of fuzzy hair and thinking I had gone to hell!"

"I don't have such memories. I recall every agonising moment. I'm destined to be a cripple for the rest of my life."

"Hey, don't feel like that. We can still be productive members of society you know. Think of all that experience we have to pass on to others. I'm starting an administrative job in intelligence as soon as I have regained my strength."

"I'm destined to be stuck in some mundane job I'm afraid."

"Why don't you get in touch with Colonel Coulthard? He's the one who helped me."

"He transferred me to Brisbane. I don't think I'm going to be much use to anyone."

"Henry Thompson. This is not the man who taught me all I know about desert warfare. Please tell me you are not going to give up like this."

"You put me to shame Romano, but I just can't see it going any other way." Henry hung his head in shame at the way he was talking. It was his darkest moment.

***

Henry alighted from the bus and looked up and down Main St. It was midday on a sultry Friday in Murwillumbah. Storm clouds were rolling in and people were hurrying in all directions, trying to get their weekly shopping done and get home before the weather turned nasty.

*Forgot how ferocious these storms can be at this time of the year.* It had been nearly two years since he had been home. Nothing had changed really. Bryant's Hotel was still there in all its classical glory. He toyed with the idea of calling in to see if Shirley was on duty but he knew his mother would never forgive him for that so he turned on his heel and walked the short distance to the taxi rank. He would not be able to negotiate the steep climb to Peter St in his current disabled state. *What a homecoming, not the triumphant war hero, just a broken down shell of a man with fewer prospects than when he left.*

As the cab pulled up in front of his family home his mother rushed out the front door and down the steps. Before Henry had left the cab she threw her arms around him and hugged him so forcefully that he almost lost his balance.

"Hang on Mum, let me get out. It takes me a bit longer to get up and about these days." He turned to the cab driver to offer payment but he was waved away.

"No charge to you son. We look after our returned soldiers around here." Henry straightened up and turned back to his mother to face the moment he had been dreading.

"Oh, my poor boy! I thought you had recovered from your injury."

"I'll never be recovered, I'm going to be a cripple for life so you had better get used to it."

"Come on, let's not get morbid about it. Come upstairs, everyone is waiting for you."

It was several hours before Henry could excuse himself from the family and well-wishers his mother had gathered together to welcome him home. The arrival of the afternoon storm had sent them scurrying for their homes. Not too soon for Henry. He walked out to the back landing and looked out over the valley just as the rain began to fall. It was still a majestic site even in this light. His father came up behind him and put his arm around his shoulders.

"It's good to have you home Henry. I've missed you." Henry felt a dull ache swell in the pit of his stomach.

"It's good to be here Dad. I wish I had done more to make you proud of me."

"From all reports you did do us proud, my boy. The Army kept us informed of your whereabouts. Well, as much as they were able anyway. I understand your efforts in the Middle East and New Guinea were vital to the allied successes. "

"And what have I got to show for it. A B grade broken down body and no prospects for the future."

"I'm sure the Army will take care of you son. They will need men like you after this is all over. There is going to be one hell of a mess to clean up."

"And plenty of fractured friendships to be mended. That's worse than the material and physical damage. There are a lot of broken minds out there as well as bodies."

"You have that lovely little lady of yours to go back to."

"I don't think so, Dad. I think she has given up on me. Besides, I have nothing to offer her now."

"That wasn't the impression she gave us."

"What do you mean? Did she write to you too? She seems to have been in contact with everyone else but me!" There was a note of despair in his voice.

"Well, she did come to see us. All the way up here on the train. She's one very brave lady."

"What on earth did she do that for? Why didn't she write to me? I have had no contact with her since I left Sydney last May."

"She told us you had a bit of a spat before you left. She still cares for you Henry. I think you should at least make the effort to go and see her."

Henry squared up his shoulders and stuck out his stubborn chin. "There's no way I'll do that until I have something to offer her for the future."

"Don't leave it too long or you may miss out on something you will never be able to recover." With these cryptic words his father turned and strode back inside.

Henry walked slowly up the stairs of Army Headquarters in Sydney. He could get around without his stick now but it was still a slow process. He was still waiting to procure specially made shoes but the war effort came first and he'd been told he may have quite a long wait.

The train trip had been long and uncomfortable, and sleepless. Henry was having second thoughts about even being here. When he'd returned from visiting Romano he was so impressed with the way that he was handling his disability that he contacted Colonel Coulthard to discuss his own situation. So here he was, about to be interviewed about the possibility of a full-time job in intelligence. He paused at the top of the stairs, turned and looked back down Pitt St. The throng of people who bustled their way around seemed almost oblivious to their surroundings and the other people around them. It seemed to Henry to be more like a movie than real life. Would he be able to live in the city permanently? Was this his idea of a place to raise a family? He was still a country boy at heart. He sighed and turned to enter the building.

He was shown into the office of Brigadier Barton. A small man with round horn-rimmed glasses was seated behind a desk so large that it dwarfed him. He looked intently at Henry who looked nervously around the room. The furnishings were lavish and the memorabilia on the walls told him that this was a person of importance. The Brigadier stood up and walked around the large desk to where Henry waited apprehensively. Henry could see that even though he was of thin build, he was really quite tall. He held out his hand to Henry and the grip that he applied to Henry's gingerly outstretched hand was not that of a weak man. It made Henry flinch.

"Pleased to meet you, Thompson. Sit down and make yourself comfortable." He gestured at the plush velvet covered arm chair nearby.

"Pleased to meet you too," said Henry and then he belatedly added "sir".

The Brigadier eased himself up against Henry's side of the desk and rubbed the point of his chin between his thumb and forefinger while looking directly at him. This was a gesture Henry had seen often in the top brass. He couldn't help thinking that it must be taught to them at Officer's training. "So you want to join our Intelligence Corp?"

"Well I would like to find out more about it." Henry shifted nervously on his chair.

"It's a big commitment, you realise. Your whole life would revolve around your work."

"I have been doing field work in my own unit for the last three years."

"I'm well aware of that. You wouldn't be here now if you hadn't acquitted yourself so well in those duties. I have had nothing but good reports about you."

"I did my best, sir."

"You will sometimes need more than your best if you take on this job."

"I was hoping I could be given some sort of desk job."

"Everyone wants those." He replied with a chuckle. "There are not quite enough to go around."

"I have a disability you know."

"I know everything there is to know about you. Sometimes having a small affliction like you have, and I am assured that is all it is, is an asset in the intelligence game. It can act as a camouflage for your real purpose."

"I would have thought it would hamper me in some situations."

"Obviously we would take that into account before you were assigned to anything."

"I wouldn't be away all the time would I?"

"A fair bit of the time I am afraid. It would take a very understanding family to co-exist with a field officer in our service."

"You realise I am married sir."

"But I understood you are separated. I know everything, remember."

"I am hoping to reconcile with my wife very soon. I just need to have some sort of job prospect before I contact her. I am not much of a proposition otherwise."

"I will be prepared to accept an application from you but you will have to talk it over carefully with your family before you apply. It is a very difficult life for a family man."

The Brigadier reached over his desk and handed Henry a bundle of papers. Henry stood there for some time holding them before he held his hand out. "Thank you for giving me the opportunity, sir. I will try not to let you down."

CHAPTER 62

# RECONCILIATION

Henry walked slowly up the street towards his sister-in-law's house. The street looked shabbier than he remembered. He stood at the gate and gathered his thoughts. He didn't really know what sort of reception he would receive. Would Connie even to be here? In a way he thought it might be better if she wasn't, then he would be able to find out from her sister how things were with her.

As he was contemplating whether to go in, the front door flew open and out came his nephew Jerry. *My goodness, have I been gone that long, he must be a foot taller.* Jerry stopped dead in his tracks when he saw the figure outside the gate. It took him a moment to recognise his favourite uncle. He rushed straight to the gate and grabbed Henry by the hand.

"Come on Uncle Henry. Come in, Mummy is out in the garden."

"And your Aunt Connie?"

"She's not here; she's gone back to Cowra. She's been sick. She's living in Gran's house. Gran died you know." *Something else no-one saw fit to tell me. And Connie's not well either. I'd better try to fit a trip to Cowra in before I have to report back.*

Henry let Jerry pull him through the gate and around the back of the house. "Slow down there my boy. I can't go as fast as I used to." His young nephew dragged on his arm.

"Mummy said you had a sore foot. Did those damn Nips shoot you?"

"No, they didn't do it. I did it to myself when I was in the New Guinea jungle."

370

"Jerry, where are you?" A familiar voice called from the back of the house. "Jerry, how many times have I ...." She stopped mid-sentence when she saw Henry.

"Well, well, well if it isn't the returned soldier himself. Wondered if you were ever going to get around to visiting us."

"The same old loving sister-in-law. I'm stationed in Brisbane now. If I'd known you were going to give me such a loving welcome I would have flown straight here from New Guinea and skipped the six weeks I had in hospital."

"Don't you get smart with me Henry Thompson. You know what I mean. We didn't know what to think when you didn't get in touch. We knew all about your injury."

"Didn't think you would want to hear from me now that Connie has given me the flick."

"Are you sure of that?"

"It's pretty obvious isn't it? She hasn't written to me since I left for New Guinea last year."

"Have you written to her?"

"Thought about it but when I started to see those letters from her to Reg Wentworth, I decided there was no future in it."

"You two! You are the stubbornest pair of people I know."

"Jerry tells me she's gone back to Cowra."

"Oh yes, and what else did this loose-tongued son of mine tell you?"

Jerry pulled at his mother's dress. "I didn't tell him anything else, honest Mum."

"Just as well for you. Now go inside and see what your sister is up to. I want to talk to Henry."

"What was that all about? Is there something I should know?"

"W...w...well Connie hasn't been all that well lately," stammered Dottie. "I really think you should go and see her for yourself so you two can get things sorted out once and for all."

Henry looked her straight in the eye and said in a shaky voice, bordering on tears. "I think I will do just that. There are some things I need to know."

"You may be more surprised than you think." She took Henry's hand and led him inside.

"Let's go and have a nice cup of tea and we can work out how to get you to Cowra as soon as possible."

***

Henry stood at the corner of the street leading to Connie's grandmother's house. The last time he walked down here the autumn leaves were falling. Now it was spring and instead of the leaves floating down to the ground to form a multi-coloured carpet, bright green buds were opening as if signifying a new beginning. Henry stopped under one of the largest trees, closed his eyes and offered a silent prayer to the skies. *Please God let this be my new beginning too.*

He hesitated at the front gate before moving slowly around to the back of the house. The uneven ground of the yard made it hard to walk without his stick but he was determined that when Connie saw him for the first time after so long he was not going to look like a cripple. He limped around the corner and there she was, hanging washing on the line. He stood still taking in the vision that he had dreamed about so often. She had her back to him and she appeared much thinner than he remembered.

"Hello Connie." There was a tremor in his voice. She didn't appear to hear him but he realised she had. Her hand had stopped mid-air as she was reached down to the old cane clothes basket in its rusty frame. After what seemed to Henry an extraordinarily long time, she turned slowly around to face him. Her face was very pale and she had dark circles under her eyes.

"Henry, what are you doing here?" Her voice was very quiet. A lump formed in Henry's throat as he took in the emaciated figure in front of him. He limped across the few yards left between them, at one point almost losing his balance. He took her by the shoulders and saw the pain etched deeply in her eyes.

"Connie, what on earth have you been doing to yourself? I have never seen you look so ill."

A flash of her former spirit lit up in her eyes. "You don't look a picture of health yourself."

"Come on let's go inside. We have a lot to talk about." He took her hand and led her up the steps at the back of the house.

"I still can't get used to Gran not being around but at least we can go into the parlour now." Connie pulled her hand away and sat in the single armchair in the corner so Henry had no choice but sit on the long sofa on his own. They sat in silence for a while, as if each was waiting for the other to speak. Henry finally turned towards her and looked deep into those beautiful eyes he remembered so well.

"Please Connie. Tell me what is wrong. I know you haven't been well."

"It hasn't concerned you for months, why would it concern you now?"

"I thought you had given up on me and when I saw those letters from you to Reg, I was even more convinced."

"How did you know I had written to him? Did he show them to you?"

"No, I was still in charge of the mail in and out. I recognised your writing."

"I thought you had wiped me out of your life but I still had to know what was happening to you."

"Reg told me that when we were holed up in the jungle of New Guinea. I didn't know whether to believe him or not. I thought he might have been trying to keep me going. I owe my life to him you know."

"He always was a good friend. But that's all he was, a friend." Henry could see tears welling. He rose quickly and covered the short distance between them. Just as he took hold of her hands to pull her to her feet, a noise from the next room stopped him in his tracks. A baby was crying loudly. Connie jumped up, pulled away from Henry and ran from the room.

Henry stood fixed to the spot. *Has Connie taken to child–minding to raise some extra money? No wonder she was so run-down. She always was the first one to volunteer when ever looking after babies was on offer.* He knew how much she adored children. He hadn't moved when Connie re-entered the room juggling a chubby wide-eyed baby on her hip. Henry saw his first glimpse of the woman he remembered as she gazed adoringly at the child in her arms.

"Evan," she said in a soothing motherly voice, "meet your father."

The colour drained from Henry's face. Of all the things that had been running through his mind to explain Connie's apparent state of exhaustion, this was not one of them. "Y...y...y you mean – he's ours? Yours and mine? Are you sure?"

Connie's face broke into a broad smile. "Of course I'm sure. Can't you see the family resemblance? Your mother says he is the image of you as a baby."

"My mother has seen him?"

"I took him up to visit them."

"Why didn't someone tell me?" The penny had just started to drop about the veiled references from his father and then Dottie about the urgency of him coming to see Connie.

"I asked them not to."

"Why would you have not wanted me to know? You knew I was as keen to start a family as you."

"I thought you may have changed your mind about that. I didn't want you coming back to me just because you had a son." Henry moved quickly over to his wife and child and enveloped them both into his arms. The tears were now streaming down his face. He felt elated.

"Oh my darling Brownie. I can't tell you how much this means to me. I have dreamed about this day since the moment I met you. I love you both more than I thought I could ever love anything."

Evan squirmed in his father's tight embrace and managed to get a plump little arm free and took a healthy handful of Henry's hair, giving it a good tug. Connie laughed, pulled herself away and held the wriggling child out to Henry.

"You will have to get used to that. He is a curious little devil – needs to grab everything in his sight."

Henry gingerly took his son in his arms and realised how solid he was. "Well, it looks like I have found my match already. Bet he'll make a great wicket-keeper!"

———————

Henry walked up the stairs at Army headquarters in Sydney for the second time in as many months. He had reluctantly returned to Brisbane when his leave ended. The two weeks he spent in Cowra with Connie and Evan had been the happiest of his life. He decided he would try to get his discharge from the Army as soon as possible. He had been offered a permanent job in intelligence and had been recalled to Sydney to see Brigadier Barton. He had spring in his step and there was a new confidence in the way he moved these days. He felt no apprehension this time as he strode into the Brigadier's office and held out his hand returning the firm pressure of the high ranking officer's grasp with some of his own.

"You are looking well my boy. Nearly recovered from that injury now?"

"Still a bit of bother at times sir, but I can live with it."

"Good for you. You know what we have called you here for?"

"Yes sir, and I am very honoured to be here but I would like to know a bit more about the position I am being offered."

"That is one of the reasons we called you in. I would like to acquaint you with what some of your duties will be if you accept the job."

"That's exactly what I want to know, sir."

"You realise there is going to be quite a bit of overseas travel? Sometimes you will be "undercover" so to speak and won't be able to tell your family where you are?"

"I guess you know that I have reconciled with my wife and have a son."

"Yes, of course we know. That is why you have to carefully consider our proposition."

"So there's no possibility I could be given a job closer to home?"

"I'm afraid there's nothing at the moment Henry."

"When do I have to give you an answer?"

"Well, we would like it as soon as possible but I have organised a week's leave for you so you can go back to Cowra and discuss things with that lovely wife of yours."

"You know her?"

"I have seen photos of her and read her file. Remember we have to be absolutely sure of things before we offer these jobs. From all accounts she would be one of the few wives who would be up to the pressure of having her husband in such a position. She's one very special lady."

"You have done your homework haven't you? I'm not sure she would appreciate knowing there is a file on her but I know she would accept whatever choice I make. I am not sure I want to be away from her for long periods again. We have had very little time together in the three and a half years we have been married."

"That is why we want you to be sure it is what you want before you accept."

"I appreciate being given the time to consider it."

"You better be off now. I expect you will want to catch the night train to Cowra."

Henry stood up, hurriedly saluted this likeable man and tried not to seem to be in too much in a hurry as he rushed out the door. The way he was feeling, he could run to the station. Perhaps things were starting to fall into place in his life after all.

Henry was seated on the love seat at the back of Connie's home jiggling Evan on his knee. The vista hadn't changed much since he looked out over this scene the day before he left for Darwin but so much else had happened in that time that he could hardly focus on his surroundings. The sky was still clear and blue and the trees were now fully covered with their summer foliage. The gardens were in need of attention but that was understandable as Connie had much less spare time since Evan came on the scene.

"Henry, darling could you come here for a moment? There are some things around the home that a woman in my condition should not be doing," Connie's voice came from the kitchen.

Henry rushed inside. "What do you mean? Your condition? Are you still unwell? I thought you said the doctor was pleased that you were finally recovering."

"You are a bit slow aren't you?  The only thing the doctor is not so pleased about is that I would get into this condition again so soon after Evan's birth."

"You're pregnant again?" said Henry incredulously.

Connie gave the little throaty chuckle that Henry found so endearing. "It seems like I am one of those lucky (or maybe not so lucky, you may think) women who is so fertile that I only have to look at a man to get that way. Thank goodness you are here this time. Are you pleased?"

"Of course I am, sweetheart."

"You have seemed preoccupied since you arrived. Is there something you are not telling me?"

"I think you should sit down and listen carefully to what I am going to tell you. We have a very important decision to make."

"If you are going to tell me that you are going back into action, I don't want to hear about it."

"But Connie – this is a decision we must make together."

"When have you ever brought me into the equation before? I won't wait again. It took all I had to get through the three and a half years that have just gone, seeing you for less than two months in all that time. I can't do it again!"

"Don't you even want to hear about it? I thought you would be proud of me and happy that I have been offered such an important job."

Connie stormed out of the kitchen and slammed the door. Evan started to squirm in his father's arms as if to confirm his mother's reaction. Henry stepped back outside and looked wistfully out over the peaceful backyard and wondered why this setting was never helpful as he tried to resolve the conflicts in his life.

<hr>

Henry sat on the back verandah. The sun was starting to sink behind the distant reddish-tinged hills that Henry always associated with Cowra. Connie was inside putting Evan to bed. It had been a long day. Henry had been thrown off balance by Connie's reaction to the news about the offer of the intelligence job. She had always insisted in the past that they should each do whatever made them happy. Being married to another person did not mean that you owned their soul, she had said. Now she wasn't even prepared to discuss it with him. He knew that her being pregnant again made a big difference but he still had to find a way to support his growing family.

How things had changed, thought Henry. But he had seen how war did funny things to people. He only had to think about his relationship with Reg to reflect on that. Here was a man he despised for so long, who ended up saving his life. Now he found it hard to think ill of him in any way even though he had caused Henry so much pain in the past.

Connie slipped silently down beside him before Henry realised she was there. He tenderly placed his arm around her shoulder and pulled her closer. She stiffened and sat up straighter at his touch. "Connie, can't we at least talk about it."

"I just can't face the thought of having you away for long periods again so soon after getting you back."

"You had a rough time with Evan. I now realise that and I will never forgive myself for not being there for you when you needed me. But now we are a family we need to be able to talk about things."

"I'm sorry Henry," she said turning to him with tears in her eyes. "It's just that I am still getting used to the idea of that, and now I am pregnant again it is all a bit much for me."

Henry pulled her closer and she relaxed a bit in his arms with the tears now freely flowing down her face. He took his handkerchief from his pocket and gently dried her face.

"My darling Brownie, I love you more than I imagined I would ever love anyone. I will never hurt you or let you down in any way."

"Oh Henry, why do we do this to each other? I'm sorry and I do know how much this intelligence job means to you. Tell me about it."

"Not if it is going to cause you so much grief. I applied for it when I thought it was all over between you and me. It doesn't seem so important anymore. You and Evan and the new baby are my whole life now."

"But what are you going to do when you get out of the Army?"

"Let's cross that bridge when we come to it. I am going to phone Headquarters tomorrow and tell them I am not taking up the job offer."

"Maybe you shouldn't be so hasty. Perhaps they can work something out that won't take you away so often."

"I have already spoken to them about that. There is nothing available at the moment."

"Maybe it could come up later on if you take the job now."

"No, there is no way I am going to leave you at all if I can help it, especially not with another baby on the way. I have to be back in Brisbane by the end of the week and I am going to put in my request for a medical or compassionate discharge as soon as I get there." Henry felt Connie relax completely in his arms and she turned her adoring face to him. Henry's heart swelled so much he thought it was going to burst right through his chest wall. A lusty cry from Evan sent Connie scurrying back inside.

Henry again looked out over the back yard. The once lovingly manicured lawns were now brown and dry with spindly seed heads waving in the light breeze. Weeds in the garden seemed to overshadow what was left of the beautiful roses, chrysanthemums and daisies that Grandma Starr had taken such pride in tending. The old gum tree in the corner had several hanging limbs holding precariously to their lofty positions. *Must do something about that before Evan starts playing out here.* The seat creaked as Henry slowly swayed back and forth. *Must fix this seat too. Maybe I should get rid of it altogether. Doesn't bring back good memories for me.*

He cast his mind back to the first time he and Connie were seated here. They'd had their first real argument. He recalled the day when he, flushed with excitement about being posted to Darwin, came across Connie and Reg engrossed in each other. Now his life was at last falling into place. When he left home to join the Army he was full of high ideals and ambitions about how he was going to make his mark in the world. He was going to make a name for himself by trying to sort out the differences between people of different races and backgrounds. War had seemed to him to be the worst possible way to do this. Taking another man's life in the name of peace seemed to Henry to be in contradiction to the law of God. He was going to change all that. He was going to rise to a high enough rank in the Army to be in a position to influence the course of the whole of mankind. His parents were going to be so proud of him.

His war service had made this conviction even stronger. His experiences  in the desert with Romano and Heinrich and then with Reg in New Guinea had made him feel that while war brought people closer, it didn't solve the problems that caused the war in the first place. Ordinary people the world over seemed to have the same aspirations and plans for their own lives irrespective of the colour of their skin, where they lived or what religion they were brought up under. All of this lofty ambition had almost cost him the two things in his life that now seemed worthwhile, Connie and Evan. Of course he had the war to thank for meeting her. *But really, two people so meant for each other would have had to meet somewhere, sometime, no matter what. It would have been destined by God.*

Now that all those ambitions had dissipated, he knew his best contribution to the world would be to be the best husband and father he could possibly be. He would bring up his children to be tolerant of all their fellow men and respect the right for them to think and act differently. They could worship a different God and still be worthwhile members of the human race. He now realised that being well-known or revered would not necessarily make one scrap of difference to the peace or otherwise of the world. Small contributions, like his, were necessary from large numbers of people, not big contributions from a few all-powerful individuals.

Henry sighed contentedly, leant back and closed his eyes and started to turn his mind to the enquiries he would be making tomorrow. He had learnt so much, but now, at last, he was going to see if there wasn't a way to go back and finish his education.

# EPILOGUE

Ten years ago when my mother died, my sister and I were packing up her things when we came across a bag of letters. They were over 60 years old – written by our father to our mother during the Second World War. We had been unaware of their existence until that moment. Our parents had met while my father was in basic training in Cowra, where my mother had lived all her life. Their courtship, which was conducted almost exclusively by mail and their subsequent marriage three days before my father embarked for the Middle East, was laid out before us like the pages of a book.

How powerful is the written word. How sad it would have been if we had not found those letters, we almost threw them out as rubbish! It was a whole chapter in our heritage. It also made me think about the number of times that this story had been played out in other families and other wars, on both sides of these conflicts. Ever since that day I had a strong conviction that someone had to tell their story, not only to future generations of our family but to the world at large.

It was only after my circumstances changed several years ago that I started to feel that I could be that person. Not for fame or fortune but to leave a legacy to my family and its future generations, and to history. I want them and anyone else who chooses to read what I finally came up with to realise the powerful part that the written word can play in their lives.

The idea of writing it as a work of fiction, based on their characters, formed after years of research and the realisation that as powerful as those letters were, they didn't depict the whole story. Censorship and lack of records would have made it almost impossible to write an accurate account as a family history, so I decided to use the information in the letters and official records of my father's unit (the 2/3rd Pioneers, AIF), as the background for a novel with, I hope, historical significance. The war photos used on the cover were taken by my father during his tour of duty in the Middle East. I have supplied details of them on my website. I have also included many other photos and family history details. The maps I have included in my book and on my website highlight the actual places my father's unit was stationed.

My parents both survived the perils of war and went on to successfully raise six healthy and successful children, staying happily married until my father's death in 1988. Their life after war was not without hardship and they made many sacrifices raising their children, instilling in them the values and convictions espoused by the characters in my book. I am eternally grateful for their love and devotion to each other, as well as to myself and my brothers and sisters.

I would also like to acknowledge by writing this story, the many men and women of all nations who have put their lives and relationships on hold to fight for their country during wartime.

I hope I have done them justice.

Gloria Swan.
www.gloriaeswan.com

# ACKNOWLEDGEMENTS

The publisher wishes to acknowledge the following sources of the historical background information used in this work of fiction.

Every reasonable effort has been made to attribute correct copyright ownership where possible. Should any attribution be in error, the copyright holder of any material wrongly attributed should contact the author or publisher and every effort will be made to correct this information for any future reprints.

The Churchill Centre: BBC Archives.
BBC Archives: World War 11. www.bbc.co.uk.
En.wikipedia.org : The Fuhrer Directives.
En.wikipedia.org : Fireside Chats.
En.wikipedia.org : 101st Airborne Division.
www.Hitler.org/speeches.
johncurtin.edu.au.
www.defence.gov.au.
www.awm.gov.au.
The Cowra Guardian.
The Palestine POST.
World WAR 11: H.P. Willmott, Robin Cross, Charles Messenger.
Mud and Sand: 2/3 Pioneer Battalion at War: J.A. Anderson & G Jackett.
"Holed up in the Desert" The Desert Campaigns 1940-1943. Ray Hayward.
Jungle Warfare: Australian War Memorial 1944.